07 04

STRAND PRICE
$1⁰⁰

CONSIDER THE LILY

CONSIDER THE LILY

ELIZABETH BUCHAN

Crown Publishers, Inc.
New York

Published by Crown Publishers, Inc. 201 East 50th Street,
New York, New York, 10022. Member of the Crown
Publishing Group.

Originally published in the United Kingdom by
MACMILLAN LONDON LIMITED a division of Pan
Macmillan Publishers Limited. Cavaye Place London
SWIO 9PG and Basingstoke

Random House, Inc. New York, Toronto, London,
Sydney, Auckland

CROWN is a trademark of Crown Publishers, Inc.

Manufactured in the United States of America

LIBRARY OF CONGRESS CATALOGING-IN-PUBLICATION DATA

Buchan, Elizabeth.
Consider the lily / Elizabeth Buchan

p. cm.
1. Man-woman relationships—England—Fiction. 2.
Country life—England—Fiction. 3. Gardening—England—
Fiction. I. Title.
PR6052.U2,14C65 1993

823'.914—dc20   93-14735 CIP

ISBN 0-517-59565-6

10 9 8 7 6 5 4 3 2 1

First American Edition

FOR ELEANOR ROSE, MY PARTICULAR FLOWER

ACKNOWLEDGEMENTS

Although some readers will recognize the topography and description of Nether Hinton, I would like to assure them that both Hinton Dysart and its garden are imaginary. So, too, is the loop of the river which I have boldly relocated. Similarly, none of the characters in the book are based on living persons.

Several people were instrumental in the writing. Ursula Buchan who took time off from her own book and hectic schedule to help, advise and redirect me where I went wrong. I am greatly indebted and grateful. Fred Stevens without whom this book could not have been written. His generosity in giving me his time and allowing me to plunder his book, *Crondall Then* (available in the village stores) is boundless. So, too, is his gardening skill. Kate Chevenix Trench and Sarah Bailey for their sensitive input. Jane Wood, Suzanne Baboneau, Hazel Orme and Caroline Sheldon for their faith, expertise and hard work.

I would also like to thank David Austin for sending me information and photographs about his English Roses. Any mistake is mine. Also my sisters, Alison Souter and Rosie Hobhouse. Not only are they loyal supporters cheering on from the line, but also my chief critics. I have not forgotten the lunch club.

I read, enjoyed and mined for information hundreds of books. Chief among them: *An Anthology of Garden Writing. The Lives and Works of Five Great Gardeners*, Ursula Buchan (Croom Helm, 1986), *Flowers and their Histories*, Alice M. Coats (Hulton Press, 1956), *A War Imagined: The First World War and English Culture*, Samuel Hynes (Bodley Head, 1990), *1939, The Last Season of Peace*, Angela Lambert (Weidenfeld and Nicolson, 1980), *The Private Life of a Country House (1912–1939)*, Lesley Lewis (David and Charles, 1980), *1914* (Michael Joseph, 1987) and *Somme* (Michael Joseph, 1983), two unforgettable books by Lynn Macdonald from which I took incidents and verbatim reports, *Medieval English Gardens*, Teresa McLean (Barrie and Jenkins, 1989), *The Countryside Remembered*, Sadie War (Century, 1991).

The number of gardening books on the market are legion but I would like to mention two in particular: *Making a White Garden*, Joan Clifton (Weidenfeld and Nicolson, 1990), and *The Flowering Year*, Anna Pavord (Chatto and Windus, 1991). Again I took many ideas and made use of the expertise in the books and would like to acknowledge the fact.

Lastly, yet again my family have had to put up with a great deal. To my parents, my husband, Benjamin, and my children, Adam and Eleanor, thank you.

In the garden, more grows than
a gardener sows

Spanish proverb

PART ONE

DAISY

1929–30

CHAPTER ONE

IT BEGAN with a wedding in June 1929.

Matilda Verral – who hated waste and anything to do with horses and who was always known as Matty – stepped from the path across the ironwork bridge over the river and into the south garden of Hinton Dysart. Behind her lay the grassy hump that hid the remains of an earlier Tudor building, a cluster of oak and beech trees and the pink-red wall that the original Sir Harry Dysart had ordered built around the house and garden to enclose it. In front of Matty was the new house, although that was a comparative term, surrounded by a wilderness of tangled and rampant plant life which threw itself against the house's beautiful walls, and sucked life from the wood and stone. Couch grass, nettles and creeping convolvulus embroidered the terrace under the south-facing windows and the parterre below, in which a few woody-looking roses struggled for survival. On its east wall a *Clematis montana* throttled a 'Bobby James' rambling rose. Lush and clover-filled, the grass swished up against the trees and through the once perfect yew circle that sealed off the top lawn from the lower.

It was an Eden, an English Eden, from which the magic had been leeched through neglect. A spoilt Paradise from which hope had trickled away.

Matty stood drinking in the scene, a small, well-dressed, nervous figure, chilled by the sight, but not sure why. Perhaps it was the waste. Perhaps there was something in the atmosphere. Or perhaps it was the cool, weed-filled river which reflected the trees in a dappled spectrum which made her shiver.

She jumped as a couple of guests, stiff and hot-looking in their outfits, walked over the bridge and stopped beside her.

'Just follow the path,' said one of the men to Matty, assuming she was lost.

'Thank you.' Matty shook herself into attention and, treading carefully in her high heels through the blighted garden, did as they suggested.

Only two hours earlier the cousins had been dressing in the spare bedroom of their hosts who lived just outside the village of Nether Hinton. Neither Matty nor Daisy had brought a maid down from London and the Lockhart-Fifes had none to spare – so shocking, said Daisy who loved to tease, how one has to make do in the country.

One leg crossed over the other, she sat in the puffed chintz bedroom chair and buffed her nails while Ivy Prosser, a village girl with ambitions to better herself, coped with the challenge of dealing with Londoners.

'Matty. Those earrings don't suit the dress, nor do they suit you.' In general, Daisy said what she thought, but since she was rarely malicious and because she talked good sense, she was often consulted and always forgiven. It was part of her charm. 'Lend them to me instead, Matty. Do.'

Her cousin looked up from the jewellery case on the dressing table littered with silver-topped pots, brushes and a powder bowl. The mirror reflected a comfortable, but Englishly shabby, bedroom, the sash window wedged open with newspaper and two beds covered in unfortunate pink cretonne. Ivy was brushing Matty's fine, foxy-coloured hair with hands that were not quite steady. The triangle of face beneath an unflattering bob did not register anything, but inside her Matty felt her black demon stir. Picking up the earrings from the box, she screwed them into her ears where they hung, opulent and too large.

'I want to wear them,' she said with the nervous shake of her head which always made Daisy's teeth grit.

A tension in the room deepened. Daisy looked at her cousin – at the bird bones of her wrists and ankles, at the pale face with its prominent *café-au-lait*-coloured eyes that were so frequently scared and troubled, at the surprisingly full lower lip – and shrugged. Ivy helped Matty out of her dressing gown to reveal a

4

crêpe-de-Chine, lace-edged corset which made absolutely no impression on Matty's sparse figure. With a swish of silk, Daisy, who had been endowed with long limbs, slenderness and a full, firm bosom, got up, took Matty's place on the stool and began to spread Elizabeth Arden's Ultra Amoretta foundation over her cheekbones.

'Is marriage an outdated institution?' she asked her reflection in the mirror. 'The Archbishop of Canterbury puts the question to Douglas Fairbanks Junior, nineteen, and Joan Crawford, twenty-three, film star and cigarette card pin-up. Neither party will comment but get married all the same.' She pulled a face.

Despite herself, Matty smiled. Daisy so often put her finger on the funny or irreverent side of things, on the slant that Matty often considered but never had the courage to express. The unexpected, provoking gibe or *aperçu* that made people laugh and contributed to Daisy's mystique.

'After all, we don't know the Dysarts.' Daisy turned her attention to her neck. 'So why are we here? Getting married should be an intimate business. I don't want strangers staring at me when I give away my life.'

Matty raised her eyebrows. 'I thought you wanted a big wedding.'

'Yes. And then again no.' Daisy, who certainly planned on a substantial affair, took off the lid of the powder jar and shook out the swansdown puff. The sweetish odour in the bedroom intensified. As she powdered her nose, Daisy shot her cousin a look.

'Anyway, we do know the Dysarts,' Matty plodded on. 'We met Polly and her father at the ball last year, and the Lockhart-Fifes can't *not* go as they are such close neighbours and made such a fuss about bringing us.'

'We could stay behind.'

Ivy moved away, picked up Matty's discarded dressing gown, smoothed it with reverent fingers and hung it up.

Unintentionally, the cousins' eyes collided in the mirror. A childhood of misunderstanding was contained in the exchange, an accumulation of irritation and impatience – exasperation on

Daisy's side, stubbornness born of desperation on Matty's. The moment passed: Daisy lowered her lids, applied Vaseline liberally and questioned, not for the first time, the Almighty's wisdom in so arranging it that one could never choose one's relations. Matty lowered her hat onto her head, speared it with a hat pin and picked up her handbag and gloves. It was too late to remove the earrings which did, indeed, look wrong. As she let herself out of the room, Matty acknowledged that, once again, she had been manoeuvred into taking the wrong decision. It would have been so easy to agree with Daisy, even to have lent her the earrings. Instead, she had taken refuge in a pride that had never served her well.

Assorted prints of horses and birds lined the staircase, interspersed with photographs of hearty Lockhart-Fifes in cricketing gear or colonial uniforms. Matty pulled on her gloves as she went down, reflecting that it was so much easier not to have to deal with people, how much better the world would be if she were the only person in it, and shuddered at the prospect of a whole afternoon trying to keep conversationally afloat.

Upstairs, left to the undivided attentions of Ivy, Daisy sprayed herself liberally with Matty's L'Origan scent and directed the girl to sprinkle some onto her handkerchief.

HARRY

Consider the lily, my mother said.

It is one of the most famous and celebrated of flowers. Sometimes confused with other plants that steal from its lustre – like the Guernsey lily – it is, to be strictly precise, a bulbous, herbaceous perennial whose genus is closely related to the amaryllids, irises, orchids and, surprisingly, not so far removed from grasses and sedges.

And yet . . . and yet, it is a flower that keeps its secrets.

Swaddled by three outer sepals, the bud conceals three inner petals, and on each is traced a nectary furrow leading to the heart of the bloom. There, attached to a trilobed stigma (I like using the proper names: they pin down the chaos of things) . . . is the ovary surrounded by three filaments. At the tip of the filaments are the anthers. Weighed down by their sticky pollen these swing freely and shower golden rain.

And the flower itself releases an erotic, haunting scent that drifts, half remembered in dreams, half captured in the olfactory memory – but never quite. That, of course, is its power.

Long ago the lily was used as a fertility symbol. Later, it was stolen by the Christians and used in their worship of Mary, the Mother of Jesus: and the lily, both fertile and pure, became the perfect symbol for the Annunciation. One of the many lily legends runs thus: when the Virgin Mary died and ascended into heaven lilies were found massed in her tomb.

St Catherine's vision of Paradise was characterized by angels wearing lily wreaths and when she died her blood was said to have flowed as white as the lily. Lilies were grown in monastery gardens and, in a suitably English variation, in rectory gardens, used by the clergy for Lady altar and Lady chapel decorations.

But I think the lily is too strong and too flamboyant for chastity.

You see, it is not a flower to grow in woods alongside the violets and drifts of bluebells. The lily belongs in a garden where it can be seen: elegant, intoxicating and airily poised. For the sweet short summer season before oblivion.

Consider the rose.

Found wild over the northern hemisphere, it is a flower more than usually susceptible to domestication and ripe for use in literature and painting. Obedient, voluptuously varied, beautiful.

It was said that the red rose was the emblem of the Goddess of Love, a symbol of the blood of the martyr and also the 'flower of God' — the five petals representing Christ's bleeding wounds and its thorns, his crown. To the medieval mind, the rose embodied many things. A wreath woven from the mystical rose represented the closed circle: the inviolate womb of Mary into which only God could penetrate. Roses were used as tokens of love and grief, and monastic burial grounds were planted as rose gardens. Rose legends reached their peak in the twelfth century, and were woven into the medieval preoccupation with the Virgin and her rose-dowered sanctity.

The Romans brought roses to Britain to soften this outer reach of the Empire. The Crusaders captured the damask rose as a trophy of war from which sprang the perfume industry (a rose in your garden with damascene ancestry will always be sweet-smelling), and later the formidable women of Elizabethan and Jacobean manor houses pounded rose petals with precious gums, barks and balsams to make pomanders, toilet waters and pot-pourri powders.

During the thirteenth century *Rosa gallica*, the apothecary's rose, flourished in Europe. From it were devised the things that soothe and comfort: sweet puddings, melrosette, rose-petal water ices, rose cake, rose-scented liquors and, for the ladies, Oyntment of Roses. *Rosa x centifolia* (the original cabbage rose) first appeared in Dutch flower paintings in the early seventeenth century. The Empress Josephine helped to whip up the fashion for roses and when the repeating chinas and teas were introduced into Europe, rose breeding reached fever pitch. In 1867, the first hybrid tea, 'La France', made its début.

See how much there is to know. How it takes a lifetime to find out. It never finishes, my mother said.

Rose names read like images from a poem, don't you think? Gallicas, albas, mosses, Portlands, robust Bourbons, noisettes, climbers, ramblers, rugosas, polyanthas, floribundas, and, my latest passion, the English rose . . . So, too, do I love the shape and texture of the rose. From the scrambling wild varieties, to the blowsy dames of the deep cupped hybrid musks.

And the rose twines its way into old tapestries, paintings, poems and myth. Simple and yet complicated, a gardener's necessity and yet resonant with symbolism, beautiful but touched with danger, drawn from many sources, but English, English, to the last thorn.

All my life, and I am now over sixty, I have studied the lily and the rose. Their contrasts never fail to fascinate a tidy mind such as mine – but with a temperament which also craves the colour and mysticism.

As the visitors to the nursery come and go, I think about these things: echoes and illusions that have a bearing on the story. They don't suspect that I know this place better than anyone for I was brought up here. It is – it was – my childhood domain. No, the visitors see a shortish, middle-aged man with a moustache, a little faded, a little stooped, but healthy-looking and anxious to help. Sometimes I serve at the counter, and they queue up, clutching their roses, and ask questions which I answer as best I can. Then they leave, their cars and coaches rolling out of the lower field, and silence descends over a place whose past is slipping further and further away.

In my dreams, I return to the house and the garden as they were in the good years. Night after night, I walk across the circular lawn surrounded by its guardian wall of yew, and up the grey stone steps to the house whose windows shine pink in the

9

dawn and purple and sheet gold in the evening, hoping to find the life that was once there.

You can't ever go back, I know that. But I have learnt it is hard to be the last.

Because I am dreaming I hover as a winged presence above it: I can see everything ... the pleached lime walk, the parkland beyond, the stone statue in my mother's garden. On my right is the river, fringed by ash and willow and its border of anemones and fritillaries in the spring. I can see, too, the wild area, fretworked by poppies, and the kitchen garden, colonized by vegetables and blue starbursts of borage. I stop by the house and look over to the walled rose garden where the alba and Bourbon roses mass over a bed of old-fashioned pinks and penstemons. In my dream it must be June, for I am rolling a petal from the 'Fantin-Latour' between my fingers. It leaves a faint, clammy smear on my skin.

Time becomes jumbled. Sometimes I am young, sometimes the stooping figure I have become. But I know each plant here, as I know the smell of wet earth after the rain has swept in from the west, the dry, dust-laden smell of summer and the smell of frost-nipped rotting fruit in autumn – and my heart somersaults in pain because it no longer belongs to me.

Then I wake in the cottage in Dippenhall Street. In the next room Thomas is sleeping quietly, quite different from the mercurial person of the day, and I am alone.

Soon there will be a small army descending on the house to polish, mend and scour. Custodians in blazers will stand in doorways and direct the visitors. 'How nice it smells,' the visitors say, invariably, for Mother's pot-pourri is famous, and walk around the Aubusson carpets in rubber-soled shoes and peardrop-coloured tracksuits.

Then I dream again.

Sun-filled and polish-scented, the house enfolds me, its silence broken only by the chime of the Tompian by the front door. Ageless, I run down the wide staircase into the hall, peer into the drawing room and turn left into the dining room. The table is laid for a ghostly gathering of twenty, monogrammed linen napkins standing to attention on the plates. At one end of the room, my mother's portrait reminds me that I have lost her – and I don't wish to be reminded. I turn away. At the opposite end of the room hangs the portrait of my father. Painted when he was in his fifties, his hair is still fair; the artist was kind and only suggested the age lines. He is dressed in riding clothes, one leg bent in front of the other, the impeccable cut of his jacket obvious even to those untutored in Savile Row. Only his hooded eyes, with their slightly troubled, distant expression, suggest that he was anything but an English country gentleman and respected member of Parliament perfectly content with his life.

Gripped by the memories, mine and others, I stare at him and my dream changes into the old nightmare.

Again I ask myself: who am I? Where do I belong in all this?

CHAPTER TWO

POLLY DYSART entered the church of All Saints, Nether Hinton, on the arm of Sir Rupert, her father, to the expectant hush that normally greets the arrival of a bride. Unlike her more fortunate younger sister Flora, she was not a good-looking girl, merely passable in a healthy, rather jolly manner. Yet today her looks had risen to the occasion. Granted Polly was a shade too broad for her grandmother's remodelled satin dress and, being tall and large-hipped, of a different shape from the corseted waist and bosom for which it had been made, but it sat well enough and the Honiton lace veil (washed carefully in tea by Robbie) billowed around a face rendered soft and pink from emotion.

The Reverend Mr Pengeally made his opening remarks and Flora allowed relief that Polly had made it to the altar to wash over her. Her father had been against the marriage, for no better reason than that James Sinclair, stockbroker, was, in Sir Rupert's opinion, nowhere near good enough for a Dysart, even if he was ambitious. James's family did not matter a twopenny toss to her, Polly had sobbed into Flora's shoulder after a tense encounter between her fiancé and father – she was desperate not to lose the one man who was likely to marry her. Flora, who knew Polly and her permanent grudge against life better than any, had remained silent.

She stole a look at her bridegroom's unremarkable profile. The situation had been delicate. James was ambitious, but also sensitive, and not unnaturally he had taken offence at the implication that he was lacking in both social and financial credibility – particularly as the Dysarts were known to be as poor as church mice. But they possessed something very desirable: breeding, stretching way back through a history of leet courts, manor houses, knighthoods, internecine wars, and the armorial bearings reposing in the College of Heralds.

'Do you take this man . . .?' asked Mr Pengeally, levelling his short-sighted gaze onto Polly's face beneath the veil.

She does, yes, she does, thought her sister. Half choked by the smell of lilies, Flora grasped her bouquet tightly in her gloved hands, and the nightmare receded of processing with Polly into the church from which the bridegroom had bolted.

'I do,' said Polly loudly, and Flora made a mental note to search out the charity for distressed stockbrokers and make a large donation.

Too provincial, considered Susan Chudleigh from her vantage point at the end of the pew. (Susan possessed only one yardstick with which to measure things: an inflated notion that anything outside London was not worth considering.) This wedding is too provincial for words. She turned her head forty-five degrees in order to target the guests on the right-hand side of the church, and saw no one that she recognized or who looked worth pursuing. At least, Susan thought complacently, assessing Polly's clumsy hips and half-grown shingle under the veil, my children are good-looking. Her face hardened, however, when her gaze encountered a diminutive figure standing beside Marcus. Try as she might, and God knew she had tried for twenty years, Susan could not bring herself to love her niece, Matty.

Because the pew was full, Daisy was pressed up against her mother. Susan's surreptitious sweeps over the guests and a certain rigidity of her lips gave her away and Daisy had a shrewd notion of what Susan was thinking. Even at a wedding – no, especially at a wedding – Susan concentrated on the business of social analysis and it never failed to amuse her daughter.

Religion held little appeal for Daisy, or, more precisely, the Church of England variety rendered her angry and frustrated. It preached nothing to her except *Do* and *Don't* and, in the end, when she tried to dissect the meat from the bone, its certainties slithered away. Thus Daisy occupied herself during the theological bits of the Reverend Mr Pengeally's address by counting the number of polka-dot frocks in the congregation. There were five:

black on beige, black on white, two whites on black and daring red on black. Daisy tugged at the skirt of her own geometrically patterned frock with its fashionably longer hemline so that it appeared even more so.

Five pews ahead, on the opposite side of the aisle, sat the bridegroom's family. From the back, they presented an unbroken line of stiff collars and regimented haircuts, interspersed with rather dull dresses and trimmed straw hats. Directly across from them sat the Dysarts and Daisy applied herself to working out who was who. She fixed on a figure in a grey morning suit with fair hair slicked well back and concluded that that was Polly's brother, Kit. At the other end of the pew sat Sir Rupert, a bull-necked, broad-shouldered man who, judging from the angle of his head, was gazing not at his daughter but at a point above the altar. Behind him was a woman in a navy blue coat and a hat that could only be described as lacking, who appeared to be staring at something on Sir Rupert's shoulder.

The previous evening the Lockhart-Fifes had let drop at dinner that Sir Rupert had fought in the Great War and had suffered from it, although they had been vague about how. The information had been delivered in a hushed tone and Daisy had understood: the Chudleighs also had friends who had survived, some burnt, some missing limbs or coughing phlegm, and it had often struck her that a component of their spirit had also been blown to bits in the stink and carnage over a decade before. They frightened Daisy, these survivors; today's men who, by some trick of history, had become yesterday's.

'Love is a bottomless well . . .' said Mr Pengeally, nearing his conclusion.

Is it? If this was true, Daisy had not observed her parents drawing upon it, more like a teacup, and she considered nudging Marcus to share the joke but thought better of it.

Beside Daisy, Matty's small gloved hands tapped her prayer book – 'claws', Marcus called them in his kindly but patronizing way. She looked down at her lap: it was true. The leather concealed their dry, papery skin. She smoothed out the wrinkles in the glove and tried to ignore her hands.

At the altar, Polly climbed to her feet and allowed James to lead her into the vestry. Seven minutes later, exactly as Rupert had allotted on the timetable, they walked back down the aisle.

Outside, a mild June sun poked at intervals through billowy clouds and sent shafts of light through the avenue of limes that led up to the church door. It had rained earlier that morning, and the hoofprints left by the horses on the mud road were filled with water. The guests chatted in groups about scandals, hunting and farming practices, leavened with gossip, and Polly would have been hurt and offended had she known how little her wedding featured compared to these important topics. Nevertheless, the villagers, many of whom had abandoned their Saturday tasks to walk up to the church gate, took in every detail.

Mrs Dawes, the Dysarts' cook and housekeeper, scraped a slick of mud off her boot and watched the bride and groom pose for the photographer in front of the double doors. 'Not bad,' she commented. Mrs Dawes had no particular affection for Polly.

Ellen Sheppey clutched at her handbag and scrutinized Polly. 'Yes,' she agreed. 'But not as pretty as my Betty, is she, Ned?'

A little washy from two pints in the Plume of Feathers, her husband, who worked in the kitchen garden at the big house, could not be bothered to answer.

'Well, I admit, your Betty does have an edge.' Mrs Dawes sounded a shade waspish. A widow of many years, she had never managed to produce any children before Albert was taken from her. She lapsed into silence at the might-have-been and then said, 'It's not like the old days, is it, Ellen? When Sir Rupert got married, me mam took me to look at the huge tent on the lawn and the wedding breakfast laid for five hundred.'

'No.' Ellen raised herself on tiptoe. 'It was different then.' She turned to Ned and said crossly, 'Cat got your tongue, Ned?'

The photographer issued a request and Dysarts and Sinclairs clustered around the couple. The Sinclairs were of middle height and inclined to plumpness and the Dysarts towered beside them. Inch for inch Polly matched James; Flora, overdressed in her bridesmaid's silk georgette, was taller even than her sister, and Sir

Rupert, chest braced in military fashion, seemed huge. An example of the rumpled good looks in which Saxon men specialize, Kit dominated the group. Sunburnt from a recent trip to Turkey and Albania, he kept himself a little apart from the others, and gazed over the fields as if he wished he was somewhere quite different. Long-nosed with blue eyes under heavy lids, Kit's was almost a lazy face. But not quite. It had charm, yes, a hint of an unsettled depth, kept private – the face of someone, perhaps, who was a loner.

At last Polly and James broke free from the photographer and made for the waiting car, leaving the guests to pick their way down the path fringed by drenched shrubs to Hinton Dysart. Over the centuries obstinate Dysarts had refused to take the longer way round to the church and slashed their way with small swords and canes through the scrub until the path had become part of the local topography.

Her hat pulled down over her eyes as usual, Matty lagged behind because, she told herself, she wanted to look around. Having lived in London for most of her life, interspersed with quick dashes for the country Fridays to Mondays, her experience was urban and the smell of the churchyard whirling with blown lime blossom was pleasant. In the end, she could not put off the difficult part of the proceedings any longer and tagged on with the last of the guests.

She crossed the bridge, stopped and looked through the fringe of trees. Further up, there was a tiny boathouse and a landing stage made from a couple of planks. Even from that distance it was obvious the landing stage was rotting and the river in need of dredging. Several centuries ago it had cut a loop around the piece of land on which the house was built, before slicing through a mixture of clay and chalk towards Bentley. Matty watched the weed flap to and fro and tried to assess how deep the water was.

Then she turned her face towards the flat-fronted house – a dreaming house – whose windows reached almost to the lawn, surrounded by the tangle of vegetation and moss-encrusted statuary. It must have been beautiful once, she thought, mentally realigning a stone urn and clearing a path. It still was, in its run-down way.

A flotilla of cars was parked on the gravel in the drive and chauffeurs talked and smoked. Polly was posed on the steps up to the main door and her veil lifted and flurried in the breeze.

'Hold it,' ordered the photographer, and a puff of light exploded in the guests' faces and made them blink. The group fractured and, with a nervous laugh, the bride picked up her dress and ran inside.

A scent of damp grass and of heavy, loamy soil filtered up to Matty. Starlings chattered under the huge plane tree by the river and a string of raindrops slid down the balustrade of the stone stairs. Slowly, Matty climbed the steps.

She placed her high-heeled shoe over the threshold of the hall and again she stopped. For as sure as she knew anything, she knew that turbulence and old grief were trapped within the walls of the house, imprisoned and unexorcised. As much in surprise as in dismay, for these feelings were quite new, she drew in a sharp breath. Then, as quickly as they had come, the dissonance faded. Only an echo remained. Head down, she passed quickly on to the dining room.

Whereas Daisy, ushered into the hall by several interested male guests, gave an exclamation of pleasure. She saw a square, beautifully proportioned room, with a plaster ceiling worked into flowers and pineapples, shabby Persian runners on a stone-flagged floor, an Adam fireplace, family portraits and a sofa, upholstered in faded brocade, set against the fireplace.

'How . . . how complete,' she said.

'Good,' said a voice behind her, and Daisy turned round.

'I'm glad you like it,' said Kit Dysart.

'I do, very much.'

Kit found himself the focus of a pair of blue eyes so dark that the iris melted into the pupils. They were offset by lashes which were thick and glossy but not *nearly* long enough, according to their owner, good cheekbones, a wide mouth and a long neck. It was a fresh, vivid face, flushed with health, and rendered a little mysterious by the angle of the tilted hat. But it was not so much the arrangement of features that made Daisy, rather a fusion of spirit and body that lit her from inside.

She was used to scrutiny and she waited for a second or two before asking Kit, 'Has your family always lived here?'

'Yes. Originally there was a Tudor house which a great-great-great grandfather, Sir Harry, demolished. He had made a pile in India and came home to build a house in the latest fashion.'

'Slaves?'

'Good heavens, no. Sir Harry made his fortune trading in spices. Besides, slaves came from Africa.'

Daisy laughed and Kit thought he detected genuine relief in the sound. 'Well, that's all right, then. You're quite respectable.'

'We haven't been introduced.'

'Daisy Chudleigh, and who cares too much about intro-ductions?'

'Hallo, Daisy Chudleigh.' Her smile hit Kit in the region of his stomach. Glowing, set off by her pink dress and hat, seemingly unconscious of the effect she was making, Daisy was not at all ordinary.

He stared at the carmined mouth as he said, 'Of course, this kind of house is no longer fashionable.'

'That's what I like.'

At that Kit smiled back: the house was important to him, so much so that if he was asked to describe how important, he would have retreated in monosyllables. Pressed, he would have said it was part of his blood and bone.

'Will you take me into the wedding breakfast?' she was asking. 'Providing you don't have to field a great-aunt or something.'

'My relations are dispensable,' he said. 'And Great-aunt Hetta has just lost her escort.' He offered his arm to Daisy.

'Won't she be mortally offended and rewrite the will?' Daisy laid a finger on his arm.

'That is a gamble I'm going to take.'

For a second, Kit and Daisy looked at each other, and then he led her into the dining room.

Uncharacteristically, Polly had set her heart on a large

wedding, but her wish had not been granted. Rupert was too stretched financially and it was not, he informed his daughter, as if she was marrying a duke's son. At this reproof, Polly burst into tears, a habit she had acquired during her engagement, and Rupert, gazing down at her shingled neck where the hairs were just beginning to grow, gave himself up to irritation.

'Of course,' he said in his cold way, which actually concealed powerful emotions, 'it might have been different if you were marrying Bowcaster's son.'

In the end, Rupert sold a pair of candlesticks, and, in return for their outlay of silver card cases, leather blotters, fitted luncheon baskets and toast racks laid out in ranks in the library, the guests were served *consommé Madrilene*, *filets de sole Bercy* and *selle d'agneau bouquetière* (or, as Rupert put it, French muck), washed down with a Château Haut-Brion 1913 and Château Yquem. The less-favoured guests were placed at tables in the library and drawing room. The more fortunate were in the dining room, one of Hinton Dysart's most remarkable features as each of the four walls were covered by oil frescoes, so fashionable in the 1760s. They had been painted, went family lore, by an Italian artist who inadvisedly fell in love with Sir Harry's youngest daughter and hanged himself in the cellar when Sir Harry banished him from the house. The frescoes were still lustrous and dominating, deflecting attention from the smoke marks on the ceiling, the flakes of paint scattered under the windows, and the lacework of mould on the wooden shutters.

Matty noticed these details. Those were precisely the sort of things that caught her eye, and as the conversation and bursts of laughter (mainly from Daisy's end of the table) rose and fell, she built up a mental picture of the house. Clearly it required attention, from the grimy plasterwork, to the linen tablecloths whose hems had unravelled. Instinctively, she understood that this was a house whose bones were beautiful, would always be so, but which, like age spots, imperfections were beginning to mar. She directed her gaze through the window to the garden and found herself wishing she was out there, walking through the damp grass over the shadowed lawn.

'Miss Verral?' Her neighbour touched her on the elbow. 'You'll have the hot news from London. Is it true the Prince of Wales is selling up his steeplechasers because the King requested it?'

The two subjects, Aunt Susan had taught Matty, that will *always* get you through sticky conversational patches are the Royal Family and ghosts. Falling at the first hurdle, Matty was regretful. 'I'm afraid I don't know.'

'Oh.' Her neighbour, a young man with a crop of freckles and greased-back hair, was disappointed.

I must try, thought Matty frantically. 'I did hear someone say—' she began, but was interrupted by an elderly gentleman who exclaimed, 'Socialism?' Then again on a higher note. '*Socialism? The devil!*'

'Mr Beaufort.' An earnest woman with plaits coiled like earphones tried to argue. 'It is a fact of life. Socialism has arrived, and we have to live with it. Now we have a Labour government again.'

'And a woman in the cabinet,' said Matty who made a point of reading newspapers.

'Good God,' said Mr Beaufort and turned away. Over the bowls of fruit, Matty's eyes met the woman's and they exchanged a smile. Matty felt better.

An hour later, Polly stood in her bedroom in her petticoat. Her abandoned wedding dress lay on the floor beside her. Flora knelt to pick it up.

'You next,' said Polly brightly, to mask the nerves that had begun to jangle at the prospect of being alone with James – and the other business. Flora brushed at the creases in the dress and draped it over Polly's single bed.

'I should jolly well hope so,' she said.

The bride sat down on the bed with a thump and kicked off her satin shoes. 'Did my dressing case get packed . . . and my night things?' Her wedding ring was very obvious on her left hand. 'Flora . . .' She looked up at her sister. 'You will come and visit us? Often, I mean. For a decent stay.'

Flora squeezed Polly's hand. 'Course, silly.'

Polly fingered the bedspread. 'I've always hated this colour,' she said in a tone that indicated she was making discoveries. 'But now I don't want to leave it.'

'Get dressed, Polly.' Flora held up Polly's chiffon going-away dress.

Polly shivered. 'I'm a bit nervous.'

Flora fastened the tiny buttons up the back and began on the sleeves. 'Everyone seems to survive it,' she said carefully, drawing on a knowledge of married life that was vague in the extreme.

Flora watched Polly do a passable imitation of floating down the main staircase, at the bottom of which the guests had bunched, and felt guilty. She did not like James and disliked even more the rented house on the outer fringes of Kensington.

The guests pressed forward to say their goodbyes. Polly extended a hand, glove voguishly wrinkled at the wrist, and muttered her goodbyes to the cheeks pressed against hers.

'Good luck, Polly.'

'Good luck, Mrs Sinclair.'

She touched her cheek to Flora who kissed her sister extra hard to make up for her disloyalty before Polly disappeared through a snowstorm of confetti into the waiting car.

'Thank God,' said Flora to Kit as they watched it disappear in a shower of gravel. Her shoes pinched and there were damp patches under her arms. 'Now perhaps everyone will go.' Kit gave her a nudge and Flora looked to her right.

'Oh, Lord,' she said. Matty, who stood beside her, had, quite obviously, overheard. 'Sorry, but it has been a long day.' Keen to make up for her rudeness, she continued, 'I gather you and the Lockhart-Fifes are coming over for a game of tennis tomorrow afternoon.'

'Yes,' said Matty. 'We are.'

The aftermath of any big event leaves a backwash and it was evident in the unnatural languor of the Dysarts the following day. After ordering the young to shake up their livers with a good game, Rupert took the adults off to the drawing room where he bored Susan Chudleigh with family history over anchovy toast and strong Indian tea.

Kit had hauled his old flannels out of the drawer, and Flora had located a dismal pair of shorts from Polly's room. They faced an immaculately turned-out pair of Chudleighs who, after the first exploratory balls, proved excellent players. Dysart solidarity was called on. Kit, disregarding aching legs and the heavy feeling around his eyes, began the attack. Marcus riposted with punishing shots and Daisy proved equally fiendish. Although not as powerful a player as her brother, she was fast and accurate. The game swung this way and that. Flora hugged the back line, Kit guarded the net, the Chudleighs beat a path back and forth across the turf and shouted encouragement to each other and insults to the opposition.

'Come on, Kit,' said Daisy at one point. 'You're a walkover.'

Roused, challenged – and disturbed by the white figure – Kit shot a return over the net. Marcus lobbed the ball to the back of the court. Flora swooped low and sent it back.

'Got you,' Kit called.

Daisy laughed. 'By no means.' And so it went on. Back and forth went the ball and so did the challenges and Matty, who never played games because her heart had been weakened by rheumatic fever, watched at the side and gained the curious impression that Kit and Daisy were holding some kind of private conversation.

She sat on the bench and sipped at the lemonade issued by an alarming woman whom the family called 'Robbie' and fell into her habit of negative reflection. Why am I not like Daisy, fast and free? Why do I lack that connection (Matty thought of it in terms of an electric plug) that would link me into life? That would make me like they are.

None of these questions produced sensible answers, and she thought of the mother she had never really known and wondered for the ten-thousandth time if Jocasta would have been the sort of person to help her daughter.

It was hot. Matty pushed the rug off her knees and fiddled

with the glass. Her eyes with their slightly startled expression assessed the world over its rim. I'm rich, she told herself, I'm twenty-three, my health is, at last, under control, and I *must* stop seeing things so blackly.

'Got you,' shouted Daisy. 'It's all over, bar the shouting.'

The figure of Robbie carrying lemonade reinforcements emerged through the lime trees that edged the tennis court. A large woman who walked with a confident sway of her hips, with dark, wavy hair plaited and coiled on the top of her head, Robbie was not so much fat as well made and well covered.

'I should imagine you're enjoying yourself, Miss Verral?' Robbie made it sound like an order. She put down the jug and dabbed at the sweat on her upper lip.

'Thank you, yes.'

Robbie had already formed her opinion of Miss Verral: a poor thing if ever she saw one. She replenished Matty's glass and then, on closer inspection, changed her mind. Miss Verral's chin had an obstinate look so the girl couldn't be all pap.

'Have you lived with the family long . . . Miss . . . er?'

'Call me Robbie, Miss Verral. Everyone does.' Robbie tucked the rug back around Matty's knees. 'I've been with the family over twenty years and looked after all three. They've become mine really, though they don't like me to say it.' She straightened up. 'Instead of my own, I suppose. My fiancé was killed in Belgium, you see. And after him I didn't fancy marriage much. Besides there weren't many to choose from the ones left. There.'

No, I don't suppose there were many tough enough, thought Matty, as Robbie attacked the cushions behind her back. Retrieved from their winter dormancy in the shed, they released clouds of dust. 'Of course,' said Robbie, banging a cushion in emphasis, her body shaking with the movement, 'things are quite different here now.' She banged a second. 'Money,' she added cryptically.

Matty was not sure that she had heard correctly and if she had she did not want to discuss it. She deflected the subject.

'Lady Dysart,' she asked, 'when did she die?'

'When the children were small,' replied Robbie. 'She was

American, you know. *She* had money, but of course that's all gone.'

'Thank you, Robbie,' said Matty. 'The cushions are very comfortable now.' On occasions Matty could sound adamant and, once again, Robbie's gaze flicked to the obstinately cast chin. The two women measured each other up – one small and nervous and on the brink of discoveries, the other used to running things to her satisfaction.

'Leave some lemonade for us,' shouted Flora from the court. 'It's blistering.'

Matty leant back against the bench. The sun was gathering strength by the minute, and the figures of the tennis players were outlined sharp and clear against the startling green of the limes. The ping of the ball on gut, the flurry of pigeons and, above all, a sense of encroaching summer laid a gentle compress on Matty.

After tea, Kit offered to show the Chudleigh party around the garden. 'The house is being cleared up after yesterday and we would only get in the way.'

He led them down the pleached lime avenue at the back of the house towards the ha-ha, which was the only barrier between the garden and the fields where cattle grazed. Then on to the old boathouse and the river glinting in the afternoon sun.

'I'm afraid it isn't what it was,' said Kit, pointing at the garden. 'But one day . . .'

Matty could tell that 'one day' mattered to Kit very much. Daisy blew out a stream of cigarette smoke and said nothing.

'Oh, never mind, Kit,' said Flora, 'I like it as it is, all wild and how it wants to be.'

'I agree,' said Marcus, who didn't but who was rather taken with Flora.

They made their way down to the river and walked along the fisherman's path past the plane tree. 'Look,' said Kit at one point. 'The view.' Obediently they scanned the horizon which was marked by a low ridge that sloped towards Alton. The landscape was not luxuriant or deeply wooded, except for dark patches of green here and there indicating a pocket of clay. Otherwise the chalk ridges ran alongside fields already jade with corn.

'Nice, isn't it?' said Kit abruptly to hide his feelings.

Daisy stamped out her cigarette. 'You have deep roots here, Kit.'

He flashed her a look which said, Yes, I do. They retraced their steps around the back of the house towards the walled kitchen garden on the west side of the house. 'There's Sheppey, the gardener, over by the raspberries.'

At their approach Ned put down his secateurs and pulled off his hat. He was a thin man, weatherbeaten and horny-nailed.

'I hope you don't mind us interrupting you, Sheppey?'

'Oh no, Mr Kit.' Ned did not smile, but he looked gratified. 'I was just securing the raspberry canes. We shall have a good crop this year.'

'Good,' said Kit. 'I'm sorry about the nectarine.' He gestured towards the south wall where hundreds of nail holes pitted the bricks.

'Yes, sir. That dratted bug got it.'

Daisy looked at her watch. Suddenly she felt out of place and thought longingly of London and of the Hansons' houseparty she was due to join later in the week. She moved back a step and her foot crunched on splintered glass from an abandoned cold frame.

They left the walled garden and went to look at the grassy hump where the earlier Tudor house had stood. Matty was beginning to feel tired, and depression was drifting over her. Earlier Dysarts had worked on this garden. One of them had planted the roses, another the irises. Still another had put in the yew-encircled lawn and clipped it into conformity, while someone else had planted the pleached limes. Now the spirit of their efforts had slipped away and vanished.

At the south end of the lawn, the path petered out into dense bramble mixed into overgrown laurel. Daisy waved a finger in its direction. 'Is there anything behind that?'

His eyes hooded, Kit said flatly, 'Only another bit of over-grown garden.'

Puzzled by the note in his voice, Matty looked at the scrub

26

and her attention was caught by a movement in the thicket — a flash of blue among the green. She peered harder and, without warning, abject misery streamed through her body. An anguish and desolation that she recognized from her own loss so long ago. Then it vanished, leaving Matty white and breathless.

'Are you all right, Matty?' Daisy asked, and then explained to Kit and Flora that Matty sometimes had 'turns'. Matty went as red as, a moment before, she had been white.

'I am perfectly fine, thank you,' she said.

All the same, she allowed Marcus to slip his hand under her elbow. They returned to the house in silence, Matty holding tightly onto Marcus's linen-sleeved arm, which felt so reassuringly normal, telling herself she had imagined the whole episode.

CHAPTER THREE

THE HISTORY of Nether Hinton contained a blueprint which, if you cared to explore it, matched many such communities in the south of England. Bypassed by great events, including the railway line, rocked now and again by small changes, self-sufficient, self-absorbed, myopic in the best sense, it was a community as bound by its own laws as if they had been enforced by Parliament.

Originally the parish had extended over some 28,000 acres (including areas of nearby Farnham, Aldershot and Fleet) and the hundred of Nether Hinton is recorded in the Domesday Book, bequeathed to the Bishop of Winchester for the support of the monks at that holy centre. Since then, fate had treated the village with a reasonable hand. On the dissolution of the monasteries, Nether Hinton was seized by the Crown and, after the intercession of a politically adept Dysart, handed back to the Dean and Chapter. Over the years bits and pieces were hived off from the parish, leaving a tangle of tithing boundaries and long-established loyalties.

Much of Nether Hinton's surrounding country formed part of an ancient forest, celebrated in the pub names, the Horns, the Old Horns and the North Horns. South of the village at Barley Pound traces of Roman and Norman occupation still linger. Close to that rises a grass mound over which are scattered traces of mortar and masonry and the experts will have it that it hides one of William the Conqueror's castles. To the south runs the Harroway, along which trudged Saxon traders towards a southern port.

Nether Hinton is not without its own riches — the buried mosaic pavement and a Merovingian hoard of gold coins found on a partridge shoot, for instance, and who knows what more lies undiscovered? In the copses, marshes, streams, park, fields and uplands is a rich, diverse plant life, including bee orchids. Otherwise, there is an unusual mixture of London clay running alongside chalk (in Heath Lane there were both brickyards and tileries). Many natural springs continue to run water – even during the legendary drought of 1921.

After the excitement of the Civil War, in which actions of some importance were fought in the village, Nether Hinton settled down to the proper business of life and, variously at one time, there were a silk factory, watercress beds, a blacksmith, a hop kiln, a brewery, a grocery business, a basket factory – plus two pairs of stocks, both operational.

Besides Hinton Dysart, Nether Hinton boasted several big houses run along traditional lines, of which one was said to be haunted by a squire murdered by his servant. Ghostly carriage wheels were said to be heard in the drive from time to time.

Hinton Dysart was situated at the west end of the village on Well Road. Snaking between the fields bisected by hedgerows and in summer bright with poppies, corncockle, charlock and mayweed, the road was still paved in places so that occasional cars lifted blankets of dust. It led directly into the Borough at the centre of the village and out again, via Pankridge Street, towards Turnpike Road which, like many turnpikes, had a path beaten around the back by toll evaders.

At ploughing time, the rooks rose above windswept plough teams dancing on the turn of the land at the top of the ridges, and the dusk settled over horses plodding home to the rattle of chain and harness. In twilit winter days, the ground rang to the sounds of hoofs and the swish of the muck spreader, to the cries of workers harvesting 'January King' cabbages while lines of sugar beet and potatoes under straw and earth clamps shone in the frost. In summer flies rose in clouds over swaying crops, stooked cornfields and herb-rich meadows. The sweet smell of greenish flower-strewn hay and drying hops tickled the nose. Pigs rooted on the grasslands, poultry foraged under the sodden grass and fruit bushes, and the streams feeding the watercress beds ran clear and cold.

On a windy day, like this June afternoon, it was possible to hear the corn soughing, the crack of elm and oak branches over by the hopfields and the rusted tin-can caw of the rooks. And from Well Road, sheep and cattle dotted the horizon like the colourful, quirkily drawn images from a medieval book of hours. It was plain, unadorned southern England, content to be so.

The bakery at the top end of the village (known as 'Top Taylor's' in contrast to 'Bottom Taylor's' at the other) was over-warm, and flour dust hung in the air. The shelves were stacked from the morning's bake, and Jacko was loading up the oak wheelbarrow for the deliveries. In the back room, Mr Taylor was plastering strips of dough around the oven door to keep the heat in for the Coburg bake.

Mrs Taylor was coughing when Ellen Sheppey ushered Simon Prosser inside. She and Ellen exchanged a look over Simon's head.

'Slice of your rice pudding, please, Mrs Taylor,' said Ellen and mouthed over the boy's head, 'Hungry again.' She looked for her purse in her bag. Simon was half blind, had one foot turned inwards from a birth defect and a mother who did not care very much.

Mrs Taylor stopped coughing and reached under the counter for the circular baking tray in which she baked the rice pudding which had saved some of the villagers from absolute hunger in bad times. 'I'll give you an extra wedge to take home, Simon,' she said, sweat glistening on her scraggy wrists. 'But mind you eat it all. Don't give it away.'

Simon took the pudding, pulled back the waxed paper, sank his teeth into the slab – and vanished. Wrung by the pity which always made her feel useless and disturbed, Ellen watched his progress along the street and longed to take him in her arms, absorb him into her sagging, generous body.

'Those kids were having a fair old go at him,' she said. 'I gave 'em what for.'

'Thank you is a foreign word in some places,' said Mrs Taylor, replacing the baking tin. 'Mind you, I wouldn't expect anything else.'

Ellen laughed and the two women spent fifteen minutes or so

gossiping: a minute analysis of the Dysart wedding and the forthcoming jam-making session at the bakehouse.

'I'll be seeing you, then,' said Ellen. 'But I'll take one of your best lardy busters for the old man.' Mrs Taylor put her hand over her mouth and coughed, creating another haze of flour dust. 'Take care of that cough, then.'

Run these days by his middle-aged, and less popular, grandson, Mr Barnard's brewery lay adjacent to the blacksmith's yard, housed in a one-time corn-drying shed, a section of which had been set aside for making ginger beer and lemonade. The women, dressed in identical overalls and buttoned shoes, were already at work — a multiplicity of curves cancelling any pretence at uniformity. They talked quietly among themselves with an occasional rise in volume whenever someone made a joke. Clean cod bottles and their marble stoppers were stacked ready beside them.

Fastidious at all times, Ellen tied a calico square around her head and pulled the knot tight: it made her feel queasy to think of anything joining the ingredients in the vats. Kat Harris chose that moment to shake with laughter and the marcelled ridges on her head bobbed up and down like wood shavings in water. Ellen frowned and looked away.

She scoured out a red earthenware pan ready for mixing up the big order for ginger beer that had come in from Farnham. Into it she measured root ginger, cream of tartar, yeast and essences, added the correct quantity of spring water and covered it with one of the thick, clean cloths stacked on the bench. Then she turned her attention to the contents of the pans she had made up two days previously. The liquid in them seethed and churned, and bubbles fizzing to the surface broke into the hush that had fallen over the shed. As Ellen skimmed, Simon Prosser's blank-looking eyes haunted her, reminding her of dark things she did not understand and tried not to think about.

'Hey,' said Madge Eager, her friend, 'did I tell you about Alf's—'

Holding a full pan of ginger beer, Ellen turned and caught her foot on the iron bar that anchored the table to the wall. She staggered and overbalanced. With a whoosh the liquid cascaded onto the floor. The pan dropped from her hands and fell heavily on her knee.

'Hey . . .' Madge repeated.

Ellen sat in a mess of sodden cotton and sticky ginger beer. Pain thrummed behind her kneecap and sprouted up and down her leg. 'Sweet Fanny Adams,' she said, and bit her lip.

'Here.' Madge threw down her spoon and helped Ellen to the bench. 'Clumsy coot.'

'It's my knee.' Ellen leant against the wall, dislodging a spray of whitewash over her head, temporarily deprived of speech.

Madge yanked up the wet overall and placed a hand on Ellen's already swelling knee. In an effort to gain control, Ellen rocked and clamped her mouth shut. She wanted to cry in great, noisy bursts, as much for the pain as for the dangerous feelings at the back of her mind, for the pity of all who were lost and hurt, and for the things that she was powerless to do or undo.

Madge wrung out a cloth in cold water and wrapped it round the injured leg. 'It's the best I can do, Ellen love,' she said. 'It'll help the swelling.'

Ellen extracted a handkerchief from her pocket and blew her nose. 'That was bloody cack-handed,' she said. 'I wasn't concentrating.'

'Never mind.' Madge brushed at Ellen's headsquare and wiped away the moisture under her friend's eyes with the flat of her thumb.

By the end of the afternoon, the pain had receded into an ache, but the knee was difficult to bend. Ellen moved warily and did less work than normal.

'Ladies, please.'

She was knotting a fresh compress when Mr Barnard junior entered and gave his customary bleat for attention, an anxious-looking man who conveyed the impression that his business was an insupportable burden. Perhaps it was. The brewery was one of the chief employers for the village and its produce, which included the ginger beer, lemonade and a little cherry cider, was well known in the area. Indeed, Mr Barnard was fond of boasting that their fame had reached Winchester, but Ellen never believed him.

Over the years, he had developed tricks to counterbalance his lack of natural authority, and he climbed on a chair to address the workers. His starched collar required attention and he seemed washed-out by the June warmth. One hand, with bitten finger-nails, pulled at the pinchbeck watchchain draped across his waistcoat to check the time – a gesture designed to avoid having to look at the audience.

'Listen, please, ladies,' he addressed the upturned faces, 'listen', and the power he held over them gave him the spur he needed. 'Things are not going so well at the moment, and it is necessary to lay off some . . . a few . . . of you.'

There was a profound silence in the shed, and several minds looped the loop for reasons why it should not be them. Barnard had been clever, of course: survival came before unity.

'In the circumstances, it can't be helped.' Disconcerted by the hush that had fallen, stony and hostile, over the floor, Barnard trailed to a finish, ashamed of his poor performance.

'That's what the bloke said when he couldn't bleedin' get it up,' Madge muttered to Ellen.

Ellen did not manage a smile.

'It's the times,' Barnard said. 'Things aren't going well.'

His listeners knew he was speaking the truth. Last week, Dr Lofts had relayed the news that a blanket factory in Winchester had let go forty men, and Bob Prosser came back from visiting his brother in Southampton with news of worsening hardship in the docks. You couldn't dispute facts. You could only hope that with Ramsay MacDonald back in government he would do what he said and reduce unemployment.

'I only need four of you to go for the present.' Barnard shifted from foot to foot on his perch. 'You can't say I'm not being fair if I say I'm going to choose four whose men are still in work.'

The joke of it, thought Ellen, was that Barnard's suggestion *was* fair. You had to hand it to him. What was not so funny-ha-ha was that she was in the firing line. Beside her, Madge stared down at the floor and refused to look at her friend. Alf, the daft bugger, had been gassed on the Somme and hadn't done a day's work since he was carried, wheezing and bubbling, back home. Out of sight, Madge's fingernails dug into the fluff that lined her pockets.

Ellen flexed her leg: the kneecap felt like a badly fitting lid. 'Well, that's me gone,' she said quietly.

Madge did not look up but said, 'It could be worse, love.'

After she had collected her wages, Ellen began a painful progress home. Every so often she was forced to stop and rest. She had been paid off, all right. Barnard had even pressed an extra ten shillings into her hand, which, after two seconds' reflection, she had accepted on the principle that if Barnard wanted to buy himself a washed-clean conscience she was not going to quibble. Outside Pilgrim's Cottage she stopped to take a look at the knee and what she saw frightened her a little. The skin had puffed up into a flecked purple ruff like a plum tart at harvest. Ah well, she thought, at fifty-four nobody cared about her knees any more. She let the skirt of her frock drop.

At the end of Croft Lane she stopped and looked up towards the ridge where the Roman villa was said to have been. The sky was lashed with azure and cream, and Hinton Dysart gleamed in the sun.

June was a funny month: full of milestones and pointers. Her mother had died in June – just given up, Ellen always considered, tired of hard work. That was before the Great War. She and Ned had married in June and produced Betty who had been coaxed into the world just before midnight on the 30th. Exactly seventeen years later Betty left to marry Sam Ellis who ran a grocer's shop in Winchester, leaving behind a space; an uncomfortable space, that neither she nor Ned referred to much.

Clifton Cottage stood by itself in the field to the south of Hinton Dysart. Up on the ridge behind it was the old Harroway where Ellen and Ned had often walked when he was trying to make up his mind whether to marry her or not, to touch her or not.

He was a careful man, her husband.

34

Caution routed by need, Ned *had* eventually pulled Ellen to him. She had pressed her face into his shirt which smelled of soil and strawberries, and allowed him to kiss her hand and then her mouth.

Ellen was in the outhouse, pushing the washing through the mangle when she heard Ned walk up the garden path. Glad of the excuse to stop, she stacked the clothes into the basket and went through to the kitchen.

'Ellen.' Ned sat down in the chair by the fireplace to unpick his laces. 'Where are you, girl? I'm hungry.' A boot fell to the floor, and he kicked it into the niche beside the range. Ellen watched him from the doorway.

'You get more like your father every day,' she said rather sharply. 'Worse.'

Ned gave his wife one of his slow stares. 'And you,' he said, 'are a terrible woman.'

'Do you want me to light the copper for a bath?'

'No need.' Ned watched Ellen limp across the room. 'What on earth have you done?'

Her reply was muffled by the oven door, and Ellen explained as she was dishing up. 'It was carelessness,' she said and, as so often happens when recollecting an injury, wished she could have a good cry. Instead, she spread dripping on a piece of bread.

'Bad luck.' Ned bit into the pie and soaked a piece of bread in the gravy. Unwilling to spoil his meal, she waited until he had finished before telling him her news. He took it well, only tamping down the tobacco in his pipe with extra emphasis. She poured two mugs of tea out of the brown pot with Littlehampton-on-Sea written on it and shoved one across to him.

Ned's fingers, thickened now with work and incipient arthritis, curled around the mug and steam wisped upwards. 'Don't worry,' he said. 'We'll manage.' In that moment, Ellen knew that Ned had never really liked her working. The discovery was surprising — one of the small but significant milestones that flashed into her married life and required thinking over. Ellen sat down in her chair and pulled her workbasket towards her. She waited to see if Ned was going to make any further comment about the money.

'I've tied in the raspberries.'

'You'll be pleased, then.'

'Not as pleased as I might be if I'd more help.'

'So you've said many times.'

Ellen undid the slide that kept her hair in place, refastened it and peered at the needle and thread that had failed to connect. 'At least they have you.'

Ned drew in a lungful of after-supper smoke and observed the Rhymer apple tree through the window. 'It's a darn pity,' he said with the I-can't-do-anything-about-it look that irritated Ellen.

She had heard it many times and she smiled tartly as she pulled the needle through the shirt. Money, its availability or, more, its lack, pulled them together in a curious kinship: her and Ned, careful with every last blessed brass farthing, and the Dysarts, who could not afford to paint their house, nor to employ enough gardeners.

'You must have been hot,' she said. 'I've brought you back some lemonade for tomorrow.'

Later, before they went to bed, Ellen and Ned walked round the garden which was not very big, for Ned did not have much spare time, but extremely productive. Its disorder bothered Ellen sometimes – she wanted to look at rows of obedient chrysanthemums or begonias – but Ned insisted that it stayed as it was, a cheerful mixture of flowers and vegetables that perked him up, he said.

As they moved from plant to plant, the dusk deepened over the fields. Every now and again, Ned snipped at some particularly exuberant growth. Ellen pointed to the butterfly shape of a white iris and Ned bent down to examine it. The pricks and rubs of the day faded, and she felt at peace.

Ned took her arm and Ellen, bothered by her knee, leant against her husband. If there were any confidences to be made between the two, it tended to be now.

'Never mind, girl,' said Ned. 'We'll ask at the house if they have work. You did your best.'

36

He squeezed her arm, and Ellen knew it was as much as she was going to get of comfort. But it was all she needed.

'Do you know, Ned, the old goat bought me off with ten shillings . . .'

Dr Robin Lofts was not tall, in fact far from it, but he was still too tall to stand upright in many of the cottages he found himself visiting at all hours of the day and night. The patients who had accepted the new doctor teased him about it.

'Part of the job, Doctor. Stiff neck an' all.'

'Goes with your stiff upper lip, does it?' Rolly Harris, Robin's brother-in-law of six months, was a joker, whose currency occasionally wore thin. This gibe, with the implication that Robin was scrabbling faster than was decent up the social ladder, had been done to death but since Rolly appeared, God knew how, to infuse Ada, his sister, with a radiance that was positively blinding, Robin forgave him.

Rolly's blacksmithing business was situated in the Borough between Top Taylor's and the stores. Well trodden, well frequented, piled with bits of harness, scarred leather and old horseshoes, Rolly's yard was, as usual, full of people who had stopped to talk. School had just finished and some of the boys were passing the time before their tea.

'Take her over there.' Working on a carriage horse, Rolly straightened up from a hind leg, and shouted at an Eastbridge House groom leading in a chestnut first-timer. 'Tie her to the post.'

Confused and disorientated, her sides rippling with fussy, panting breaths, the filly shook her tail and sent a whinny over the yard.

'Pass us that file,' Rolly asked Robin, who obliged. Rolly tossed the carriage horse's shoe onto the heap for scrap iron, and pared the exposed hoof. A chunk of horn dropped and bounced off Rolly's pitted leather apron.

'Give us some help,' he asked, measuring the hoof for the new shoe. 'The filly hasn't been shod before and will take a bit of coaxing.'

Robin was tired, but Rolly did not often ask favours, only gave them. That was why, until he organized his house and surgery, Robin was living rent-free with Rolly who already housed two other brothers and a sister.

'All right.' Robin took off his jacket and rolled up his sleeves.

Rolly whipped the tongs out of the forge, tapped the glowing shoe with a hammer and plunged it into the water tank. Then he fitted the shoe. A smell of singeing hoof joined the horse smells, rotting rubber and dust. 'You can paint the hoofs, when I've finished,' he said.

Robin did as he was told. The horse's flanks shuddered with heat, the flies circled and dived, sweat filmed his hand, and the horn disappeared under a black slick. 'There you are,' he muttered. 'Smart as paint.'

Rolly walked across the yard. 'I hear Jack Batts got to hospital all right,' he said, inspecting Robin's handiwork.

'Yes. I was pleased about that, but the Huggins family wouldn't let me over the doorstep. Said they wanted the old doctor back and they didn't think a stranger should poke his nose into their affairs.'

'Aye, I see their point.'

Rolly let the hoof drop and Robin added, 'I wouldn't mind so much if it was true. When I pointed out to Granny Huggins that I'd been here for six months and my sister was married to you she said she didn't care who was married to whom, she still didn't want strange buggers ferreting around in her chest.'

Rolly laughed. 'Go carefully with that Vera Huggins. She's daft and she's mean.'

Rolly went round to the horse's head and ran his finger down the black nose. 'Not long, lad,' he said gently. He waited until the horse stood quite still, and then gripped the bridle and coaxed him with little whispered sounds back into the shafts of the trap.

Neither of the men noticed Flora Dysart dismount by the gate. Not that Flora wished anyone to take any notice of her: still suffering from post-wedding lassitude, she had nothing particular to do and she was happy to stand and watch. She stripped off her gloves, stuffed them into her pockets and pulled Guinevere's reins over her head.

Johnny Daniel and Sammy Prosser stood over by the gate and Sammy whipped off his cap. 'Can I lead her through?' he asked.

She smiled at his eagerness and handed over the reins. 'How's Simon, Sammy? I haven't seen him for some time.'

'He's all right,' said Sammy, busy with Guinevere and intent on demonstrating to Johnny how skilful he was with the bridle. Amused, Flora followed the horse's rolling backside into the yard where the last buckle was being tightened on the carriage horse's harness.

'Miss Flora.' Rolly wiped his hands on his apron and stepped back, obviously pleased. 'Are you in trouble?'

'Guinevere's dropped a nail or two up at Caesar's Camp. Have you got time to deal with her, Rolly? Will it take long? Not that it matters, of course.' Flora had a tendency to rush at her words, and often muddled them. 'I don't want to keep Ada waiting. What I mean is, I'm sure she's cooked your dinner and you've got lots of people waiting, I can see.'

'For you, Miss Flora . . .'

Rolly glanced at the forge, which still had plenty of life, and nodded. Flora ran a finger down the black carriage horse's nose. 'What do all you horses do with your shoes?'

'Eat 'em, Miss Flora.'

Flora stroked and patted and Robin could tell she knew exactly the spot to place a soothing finger. So this was one of the Dysarts. He allowed himself a prolonged scrutiny from his vantage point by the shafts and saw a tall, well-built girl dressed in jodhpurs with a short-sleeved linen shirt and a plait hanging down her back. She seemed pleasant, open and harmless.

'Over here then, Sammy,' Rolly ordered. Reluctantly, Sammy yielded up Guinevere, twisted the peak of his cap to the back and returned to his post by the gate, where he lolled importantly.

'Isn't it your tea-time, you two?' Flora looked at her watch. 'Your mothers will be waiting.'

. With a clatter of hobnails on the yard surface, the boys took

39

themselves off. Flora relaxed against a pile of wheels and watched Rolly. A fly buzzed peaceably by her head, the men talked quietly to each other, Guinevere tossed her nose skywards as Rolly hooked up her back leg and there was the familiar, soothing smell of warm horseflesh. Content, Flora closed her eyes and rested her head against a wooden strut. Then she opened them again and squinted through the sun. 'You must be Ada's brother,' she said to Robin. 'The new doctor.'

'Yes, I am,' he said in a voice which retained a trace of the Hampshire burr.

'And you were brought up in Alton—' Flora came to an abrupt stop. She *was* going to say 'and you are living with Rolly until your house is repaired, which, considering you have just had to buy into the practice, must be very expensive for you,' but realized it would be rude.

Robin understood the hesitation. It amused him that his precise social status had been raked over and assessed by the family. He realized he presented a problem to the social experts – not quite villager, but not gentry. He knew perfectly well that an event as important as his arrival would have been chewed over in every pub and over every gate for weeks. What he had not been prepared for was quite the detail with which it had been broadcast.

'I'm not really a stranger, Miss Dysart. My parents used to live up towards Clare Park but they moved to Alton before the war.'

'But you've been studying in London. You must understand,' said Flora, explaining to the outsider, 'that now you are Tainted with Sodom and Gomorrah.'

'I do see.' Robin stuffed paint-splotched hands into his pockets. 'Do I not score a point if my sister is married to the blacksmith?'

'Of course.'

'Then I should set about marrying one of the local girls at once.'

Flora considered him. Robin was slight, almost delicate, a

little undersized, even. He had white freckled skin which, when he was exhausted, took on a grey tinge. It looked a little grey today. He seemed older than she had imagined from the gossip, although he wasn't, only tired from years of hard study in bad light, of working during his free time and too many hasty meals. The mixture of youth and age in his features made him enormously attractive – particularly with a large fleck of paint beneath his right eye.

'Marry a local girl?' Flora replied, her whip swishing to and fro, and again forgot to choose her words carefully. 'If you like. It would prove that you mean business.'

He raised an eyebrow as much as to say, Why should I not?

Flora knew at once that in suggesting that he was playing at being doctor, she had put her great big size seven foot in it. 'What's wrong with Maidy?' she asked after an awkward second's silence, and pointed towards the back door where Rolly's youngest sister was standing, crying.

'Maidy's just passed the labour exam, and she'll be going into service in Farnham.'

'I see. Oh, poor Maidy. She won't want to leave home.'

'No, Miss Dysart. I don't think she does.'

Robin and Flora regarded each other across the social divide – on one side those who serve, on the other those who are served. Flora felt uncomfortable.

'Do you know if Maidy asked Mrs Dawes up at the house if there was work?'

Robin did not take pity, nor did he wish to spare her feelings. 'You earn better wages in Farnham,' he said.

Sweat sprang across Flora's upper lip. She pulled her yellow string gloves out of her pocket and attempted to wriggle her fingers into them, but had trouble doing so with Robin watching. He turned away. She was big, young, unwittingly arrogant and vulnerable, but her flesh was a healthy buttermilk, slicked with summer dampness that unaccountably quickened his responses.

'Rolly will get your horse.'

He made no effort to help her onto Guinevere's back, but

once up Flora was on surer ground. The mare snickered affectionately and sent her tail dancing. Flora gathered up the reins. 'I did not mean to offend you, Dr Lofts. Did I do so?'

He knew he should not mind that she was up there on the horse at an advantage, and normally he would not. He shrugged and stepped back. 'No, of course not.'

Flora turned Guinevere round in a tight circle. 'Bye, Rolly. Good luck, Maidy,' she called out. 'I'll see you soon.'

Robin never knew why he said what he did say, for he never admired people who laboured a point. 'I don't think so, Miss Dysart,' he cut through the goodbyes. 'Maidy doesn't get a day off until Christmas.'

Half-way along Well Road, the bone cart bound for the flock and glue factory passed Flora. For a couple of seconds, she and the driver were neck and neck. The cart bounced along beside her, before it pulled away, spraying maggots shaken loose from the bones onto the road.

The smell made Flora retch and she squeezed Guinevere's sides and urged her into a trot.

HARRY

I forgot to say: lilies are greedy feeders. Ask any gardener. They drive down roots which, like hidden drones, suck goodness out of the earth in the service of the flaring trumpet flowers glittering in the sun, awaiting violation by the bees.

Of course, lilies have their enemies. I watched Mother battle for years against slugs. In the end, she decided coarse sand heaped around the bulb when it was planted was the only answer. I often think of those mortally wounded molluscs crawling away to die of a thousand cuts.

Ironically, Mother never liked lilies, but my father did. 'The queen of flowers, darling,' he would say. To please him, my mother planted them all over the garden, which had become famous by then. There they are still. The lovely Madonna, *Lilium candidum*, the Regale, *Lilium regale*, 'Achilles' and the exotic, knowing 'Black Magic'.

No, Mother preferred roses. She understood them, loved them, even the diseases and pests. 'The froghopper is at it again,' she would say, cheerfully, or the greenfly or the sawfly. I think she liked the rose's conviviality: the way it forms a natural complement to other plants. She admired its fertility – its generous, remontant, fat-budded fertility and easy propagation.

Neither she nor my father would like the motorway that now runs near Odiham, nor the housing developments built in unsuitable brick that infill the village, nor the neon glow over Farnham at night, nor the forest of television aerials where beeches once rustled.

No matter. Nothing can, or should, remain still. Not even

families. They change, break up, knit closer, fall apart – or draw to a faltering conclusion.

Like ours.

When you first take up gardening, or rather *it* takes you up, blooms are all important. I used to tease Mother about that and tell her she had never got past the hors d'oeuvres. Later, the architecture of the garden becomes more important: the bones which support flesh, if you like – the contrast in foliage and structure, the shape of one leaf against another. Think of a hosta's ebullient shape or *Alchemilla mollis* (Lady's mantle) whose acid yellow blooms and scalloped leaves foam along a border. Think of the allium with its spherical head of star-shaped purple flowers (which, like us, go stiff and dry in death). Or the Falstaffian cardamom swaggering and bullying its way into life. Contrast those perpetual qualities with the acrylic colours of the modern dahlia or the kiss-me-quick qualities of the annual bedding plant. Do you see what I mean about progression?

For the novice, the first steps in gardening are the most difficult. There is much to learn, wrote a great gardener, Miss Gertrude Jekyll. But, unlike the lessons in love or hate, even the lessons in money, they are pleasant, oh, so pleasant, and the fallings by the wayside do not wound, only teach. The beginner, said Miss Jekyll, should be both bewildered and puzzled, for that is part of the pre-ordained way; the road to perfection. Each step becomes lighter, less mud-clogged, until, little by little, the postulant becomes the novice, the novice the fully professed. Oh, yes, Miss Jekyll, you were so right. A garden is a grand primer. 'It teaches patience and careful watchfulness: it teaches industry and thrift: above all, it teaches entire trust.'

44

CHAPTER FOUR

POLLY HAD bequeathed several daughter-of-the-house duties to her reluctant sister and when the telephone rang a week after the wedding, Flora looked up from the hash she was making of a flower arrangement in the hall. Since Ellen was balanced on top of a stepladder wielding a feather duster, Flora dropped two long-stemmed sweet peas back into the pile of cut flowers and lifted the receiver.

'Hinton Dysart.'

'Hallo. Hallo? Oh, you are there. This is Susan Chudleigh. Could I speak to Miss Dysart?'

'This is she.' With a smothered sigh, Flora hooked a leg around a chair leg, pulled it towards her and manoeuvred her bottom onto the seat. She was planning to ride up to Roke Farm and check out their foal, Myfanwy, and round by Wheeler's Dell and Itchel Manor, with a last call to Danny, and she had a feeling that Mrs Chudleigh was about to insert a spoke in the wheel.

'How nice to hear you, Miss Dysart, and thank you again for allowing perfect strangers to your sister's wedding.' Susan Chudleigh did not exactly gush – she was too clever for that – but almost.

'Do call me Flora, please, Mrs Chudleigh.' Flora dangled the scissors over her knee and pressed the open points gently into the flesh so generously parcelling her thigh and wished she could cut it off. Snip, snip.

'Flora, then. I won't keep you, but I have a little proposition.'

Flora raised her eyes to the ceiling in need of repainting: 'little propositions' had a way of taking up all day.

'Mr Chudleigh and I have decided to be daring this year, and we have taken a villa near Antibes for August and September. We wondered if you and your brother would care to join the houseparty? You would be very welcome ...' You mean Kit

45

would be very welcome, Flora thought. 'Very informal. Nothing smart.'

Flora was acquiring a useful mental dictionary of social euphemisms and concluded at once that 'nothing smart' meant precisely the opposite: dismal shorts and made-over silk georgette would definitely not do. She injected what she prayed was enthusiasm into her voice. 'What a ripping' (Susan Chudleigh was the sort of person who made you say ripping) 'idea, Mrs Chudleigh. I'm sure Kit and I would adore to come.'

'Well, it's not Biarritz, of course, but lots of people prefer this area. We're bound to bump into friends.' Flora was not to know the hidden text to Susan's last comments read that, since Matty had offered to foot the bill, Ambrose Chudleigh had insisted they kept the holiday as cheap as possible and Biarritz was not on.

Flora glanced at the clock, and the scissors disappeared down the side of the chair. 'How *lovely*. And how kind of you to think about us.'

'Well, I don't mind telling you that both Marcus . . .' Mrs Chudleigh paused for a second 'and Daisy were very taken with you two. We talked it over and this seemed an excellent way of getting to know you better. Next year you will be so busy with the Season, of course.' She assumed an intimacy with Flora's coming-out plans that made the latter wince. Her voice sharpened. 'Can I take it you will say yes, Flora?'

Flora made an effort and unclamped her lips. 'Mrs Chudleigh. It's a perfectly lovely invitation and I know we will both want to come, but I must speak to my father first. May I ring you back?'

'Ye gods!' she said, putting the telephone back on the table, and left Ellen to stare after her retreating back.

Kit and her father were closeted in the 'Exchequer'. Flora's riding boots clattered on the stone flags as she ran down the kitchen corridor (originally white, now dingy cream) past the general dump for outdoor things – mackintoshes, coats sprouting trailing threads along their seams, torn hacking jackets and a collection of unclaimed hats – and past the gun room with its almost empty cabinets.

46

The Exchequer had been so dubbed because it housed title deeds, letters, the family Bible, a framed genealogical tree written in Gothic script, and a less romantic accumulation of bills and business papers. Wreathed in pipe smoke, Rupert was standing looking out of the window, and from the set of his shoulders it was obvious that things were not progressing smoothly. Seated at the table stacked with papers, Kit rolled a pencil between his fingers. It was the monthly accounts meeting that all parties dreaded – and since Rupert was not gifted with financial acumen, nor able to allow Kit, who was, to take decisions, the results were predictable: Rupert turned sarcastic and Kit simply withdrew.

Kit asked himself often if his father's attitude stemmed from mere bloody-mindedness or whether he disliked his children so much that he was not prepared to yield them any autonomy. If asked, Rupert might have told his son that nothing was more certain to needle middle age into bloody-mindedness than keen, competent youth, and that Kit could wait his turn.

'Can I interrupt?' Flora was a little breathless.

'If you must, Flora.' Reluctantly, Rupert acknowledged his daughter's presence. I wish, thought Flora not for the first time, that money had never been invented. 'Is it urgent?' he asked, resuming his contemplation of the kitchen courtyard through the window. Caught at certain angles, his daughter's face rang a peal of distress and guilt in Rupert's memory, so he tended to avoid looking at it.

'Kit. Father. Mrs Chudleigh has asked us to join a houseparty near Antibes for the summer. What do you think?'

Kit leant back against the chair struts with just a hint of triumph. 'I thought she might.'

'*Kit!*'

He rolled the pencil across a bill. 'It doesn't take much to work out Mrs Chudleigh.'

'Awful woman, fit only for neutering,' commented his father from his position at the window. Rupert was sometimes surprisingly coarse. 'I suppose you want to go?'

47

Kit's expression became quite still. Watchful, even.

'If you don't want us to, Father,' said Flora quickly, 'we won't.'

'Well, *I* would like to go.' Kit mouthed 'Shut up' to Flora, and addressed his father's turned back, a stonewalling tactic of Rupert's that he and Flora knew well.

'Sir,' said Kit. 'Why don't you nip up to Ardtornish for some stalking? The change will do you good.'

It was at this point that Flora realized how important the outcome was for her brother. Troubled and a little apprehensive, she looked at her watch. 'I must go. I have masses to do.'

'You have a standing invitation, sir,' Kit pressed on. 'You told me that yourself.'

Kit had calculated correctly: the idea of damp, peaty Highlands, sweeping palls of rain, sodden ferns and mosses and the rusty, almost blood-coloured water of the Morven peninsula diverted Rupert. 'I might do that,' he said. 'I could take Danny.'

He and Flora had won, but it was prudent not to linger on the subject. Kit pulled the account book towards him and resumed their previous conversation. 'Shall we sell the Lady Meadow then, sir?'

'No.' Lighter than his son's, Rupert's blue eyes assumed a belligerent expression. 'Never sell your land. You must cling on to it, even if the ship is sinking. Do you understand?'

Rupert was about to climb on his hobby horse, and to forestall this Flora intervened. 'If we're short of money why don't we ask Cousin Andrew in Boston to help us? We all know he has pots.'

As soon as she had spoken, Flora knew the extent of her stupidity. Cousin Andrew was second cousin to their dead mother, rich, condescending, and as unlikely to dispense charity as Rupert wished to receive it.

'I don't think that's such a good idea,' said Kit, shooting a look at his sister which asked, Why undo my good work?

'No,' said Flora.

Rupert whipped round and wrenched the pipe out of his mouth. Flora felt her stomach dive at the prospect of a confron-

48

tation. But all Rupert said was, 'That's enough, Flora. As usual you speak out of turn.'

'Sorry,' she said, and again looked at her watch without seeing it. 'I didn't think. I mean, it was just Cousin Andrew—'

'Cousin Andrew has nothing to do with us,' said her father, in the way he had of dismissing something of no account, and Flora felt even more miserable. She looked at Kit for help but he jerked his head towards the door. The message was unmistakable: Leave Father to me.

'Go away,' said Rupert. 'We are busy.'

Nothing was ever said, but it was there, always there: the tissue of misunderstanding, of habit hardened into the immutable, of repression and unshriven grief. Plait unravelling, hands bunched inside her cardigan pockets, Flora hovered on one foot then another. Too young at eighteen, too inexperienced and lacking in knowledge to untie the threads that tangled her family, she grasped at the only available straw.

'Well, France will be lovely,' she said brightly.

At Eton Kit had been solitary but not in the sense that he had no friends. A cricketer, regular overspender in 'sock', prize winner for the English essay, and witty in a dry, subversive manner, he attracted the attention of other boys. Onlookers never knew what to expect. Sometimes, Kit was a ringleader in the thick of it, sometimes so cool and distant that he barely spoke. Other times, at crucial points, he hesitated, felled by an inner crisis, and if he got away with this failure of nerve with the boys, it infuriated the masters who expected better of a boy so promising.

He left Eton unscathed by the attitude of his friends, some brilliant, who regarded the College and Oxbridge afterwards as the glittering prize in life. For that instinctive recoil, Kit was grateful. He looked forward, not back. He did not like to look back. Ever.

Chimeras, however, have many forms, and Kit's visited him in the summer of 1926. Riding with Max Longborough from

49

Constantinople to the Yemen over fever-ridden plains, through mountain defiles, past starvation and poverty, and places where flowers grew through eyesockets in skulls by the wayside, he had fallen in love with the Middle East and, above all, with the desert. Max and he had been hungry, dry-lipped, sand-blind and thirsty, but the desert's harshness and its demands had slipped into Kit's bloodstream and flowed alongside his rootedness in Hinton Dysart. Should he, could he, settle there instead? Kit wrestled often with the idea – but to abandon his home *would* be to cut out his bone.

Provence in August reminded Kit of the Middle East – almost. There was the same clear, intense air coruscating a terrain that had not seen rain for months, and the same heartless expanse of enamel sky with scrub etched below, blanching to white in the dawn. There the similarities ended. Provence was languorous with scent: resin, crushed thyme, garlic and new bread, hot stone and hot earth. At night cicadas played until the sun slid round the corner of the Villa Lafayette and laid a finger of light on the turquoise swimming pool and the carved stone pot planted with geraniums.

From his bedroom window, Kit stood naked and watched the sun and smoked his first cigarette of the day. It was five thirty in the morning and it had been too hot to sleep much that night. He stretched until his bones cracked, reached for his bathing costume and, towel over his shoulder, walked barefoot along the 'boys' wing' and let himself out of the house.

He padded along the terrace and looked up at Daisy's window. Villa Lafayette was a two-storeyed house with shuttered windows which had been left to weather in peace for generations until the South of France began to be fashionable. Luckily, the original tiles and the archways had survived the frantic installation of new bathrooms, a billiard room, and the all-white décor so fashionable just now.

There was a trace, the merest hint, of chill as Kit slid into the pool and struck out for the far end. Bubbles of light broke across his vision, and the water parted with a slap. At the end, he turned and began the second lap. When he surfaced Daisy was waiting.

She had on a bathing robe of cornflower blue that exaggerated the colour of her eyes and emphasized her chestnut hair. 'Shush.' She placed a finger on her lips and then pointed at the house.

He trod water and looked up. During a wakeful night he had visualized Daisy's slender but full-bosomed body in detail, and wondered if anyone else found the combination of its voluptuousness and the suggestion of boyishness in her forthright manner as fascinating as he did. He hauled himself over the edge, sat down beside her, scraped back his hair and pinched his nose.

'Isn't this fun?' Daisy leant back on her hands and let her feet dangle in the water.

Kit smoothed the hairs on her goosefleshed forearm with a finger. 'What are you doing up so early? I imagined you treasured the beauty sleep.'

'I was waiting for you.'

'Good.'

'It's going to be hot again.'

'Whenever is it not?'

Daisy lifted her cooled feet onto the stone, and clasped her knees. 'I love the heat. I love the smells. I love being here.'

'*Nothing* to complain of?' Kit observed the bit of Daisy's neck which ran up into her bobbed hair.

'Why should there be?' Daisy hesitated while she decided whether to be frank or not. 'Except for the bad stomach when I arrived.'

'I suffered in Constantinople, and there were no bathrooms to speak of.'

She smiled uncertainly at the intimacy of the subject. 'Will you go back?'

'I'm tempted to spend my time travelling. But there is the house to think of.'

Daisy surprised Kit with her next comment. 'You need an anchor, Kit Dysart. Otherwise you are the sort that drifts for ever.'

He sat up, intrigued by the novelty of her viewpoint, and considered it rather profound. 'What do you mean?'

'Am I right?'

'I don't know, Daisy.'

'I am right,' she said simply. Daisy was on territory that she understood. It was not a knack she was particularly proud of because it was no effort: the instinct to form these conclusions was something she happened to possess.

'Perhaps,' he said.

The sun whitened the stone coping bordering the pool, and spread across their backs. A hush had fallen, the anticipatory moment before the sun gripped the day. Already brown, Kit's skin was silky and warm-looking and Daisy wanted to touch it. She turned her head to look at him.

'An anchor?' he said, and Daisy suddenly shivered.

'Shush,' she said again, and glanced at the house. 'They might hear us.'

Matty looked out from the bedroom she shared with Daisy. Woken by the echo of voices over the water, she got up to investigate and regretted it. As she watched, Kit leapt up and pulled Daisy to her feet. She gazed at him with the look that, Matty knew, drew the recipient into an intimacy impossible to resist. Daisy struggled for balance on the stone and her robe fell open to reveal a well-worn bathing costume – but it never mattered what Daisy wore, for she wore anything well. Kit tugged at the robe, Daisy resisted, then pulled it off and dropped it into the pool. She stood, laughing at Kit, her hair a bright splash of colour, before slipping into the water. Kit followed and pulled her, a wet, chestnut Nereid, towards him, and the space between their faces narrowed and blotted out. Like a huge flower, the robe billowed and sank.

Matty allowed the muslin curtain to drop back into place and sat down on her bed. The sheets were damp and crumpled from the night, most of which she had spent sweating and staring into the darkness. The heat made her breathless and dark circles had formed under her eyes within days of their arrival. She noticed with distaste the beginnings of a pink heat rash on her arms.

She went into the bathroom, ran the cold tap and threw her nightdress onto the floor. The bath was far too big, and she was forced to stretch out her foot, ballerina fashion, to steady herself, but the water was life-savingly cool. Taking a deep breath, she slid under the surface and stayed there as long as she could.

The old dream of her parents had returned during the night, of the last time she ever saw them when Matty was five. Mounted on their Arab mares which they had bred at the family home in Damascus, their well-bred faces matched their tailored khaki desert suits. Her mother carried her notebook filled with jottings on flora and fauna – Matty still had it – and her father's saddlebag bulged with empty specimen jars. In her dream, she watched them ride the horses up the sand dune and pick their way along the crest and knew, from her dream vantage point, that they had forgotten all about their daughter.

Matty surveyed her outstretched foot. She was not sure if she could ever forgive Stephen and Jocasta Verral for making it obvious to her at that moment that she was not important to them – nor had Matty's need for them struck them either. Particularly when they lay dying, in a stuffy tent, of typhoid picked up by drinking bad water at the Sann'aa oasis.

Matty sat up straight in the bath and addressed her parents' bodies laid out on Army and Navy camp beds as she had last seen them. 'I never knew you were so small, Mother, but I expect that is the effect of death. We all shrink in death, I suppose. I just want to say that, somehow, I will be a credit. I'm making a muck of it at the present, I know, but I've just got to grow older. I'm trying. It's partly the result of missing you, partly because I don't think either of you gave me your best gifts, just a mixture of the bad.' She paused and then added, 'You have no idea what it is like to be left alone.'

The bath towel, huge and white, enveloped Matty. It ruffled along the ground as she waddled into the bedroom. The day ahead seemed a long one, full of noise. Flora's jolliness. Marcus's practical jokes. Her aunt's ever-present cool contempt. Kit and Daisy. The towel drifted to the floor and Matty allowed herself to look out through the window.

The pool was empty with only the scarlet comma of a stray geranium petal to break its glassiness.

*

53

With her pleated cotton skirts and geometrically patterned tops, her cheap straw hats which she turned into the impossibly chic, and her trick of making people want to look at her, Daisy dominated the holiday. They were young and, Matty excepted, full of energy, and Daisy led them, with Kit a close collaborator, on swimming parties, picnics and evening expeditions up scree-peppered paths and over aromatic scrub where they walked for miles along the cliffs, watching the sun slide under a darkening sea.

It was too hot one evening to go far and they sat down to rest. Thyme and sage scented the air and in the water below fish pushed in and out of the rocks. Marcus sat on a rock by the cliff edge and tossed stones into the water below. Flora passed him ammunition and rubbed a twig of thyme between her fingers. Even at six o'clock the sun was still fierce and she pulled her hat down over her face. It allowed her to watch Marcus who was beginning to intrigue her, and she wondered what went on behind his clean, English complexion and impeccably trimmed moustache.

Daisy flicked her scarf across her shoulders.

'Are you burnt?' Kit edged closer so that his thigh almost touched hers.

'To the bone,' she replied. 'Sun, sea and the prospect of a garlicky dinner tonight. Perfect.'

Kit marched his fingers up and down the flat rock. 'No one will kiss you,' he said under his breath.

'Won't they?' Daisy teased and dared him, and Kit's fingers came to an abrupt halt. What are you doing to me? he asked Daisy silently, his wanting of her mixed with an elixir of sun, wine and liberation from confining clothes.

'Your cousin,' Flora was asking Marcus. 'Will she be coming this evening?'

'I expect so,' said Marcus.

'Is she enjoying herself?' Flora was curious. 'She seems . . . she seems, well, not to very much.'

'Matty,' said Daisy, 'always feels left out. It's her life's burden and there's nothing we can do to help.' She got to her feet, brushing dust and pebbles from her skirt. 'Come on. Why don't we go to the port to dine tonight instead of staying at the villa?'

It did not take much to persuade Susan Chudleigh to abandon the role of chaperone for an evening. The business of nannying the youth was tedious and tiring. She imposed one condition. 'Matty goes with you,' she said, thinking that she could not bear to spend an evening alone with her niece. 'She needs bringing out of herself.'

Marcus and Kit handed the girls into Ambrose Chudleigh's black saloon and negotiated the coast road with more dash than skill. Marcus drove and Kit hung out of the passenger window to give warning of rocky outcrops over the road. Their destination was the Café de la Marine in the port – 'So authentic, so *nostalgie de la boue*,' remarked Daisy. After that, they planned to go in search of a casino.

They dined outside in the airless dark, overlooking the fishing boats and the harbour wall. The tables were occupied by regulars, a few tourists and a swelling contingent of English exiles – artists affecting short-sleeved cotton shirts, their women striped fishermen's jersey's, writers and journalists who declared their creative engines rusted up in stifling England. Kit placed himself next to Matty at the table: Daisy's earlier remarks about her cousin had made him curious.

'I haven't had a chance to ask you if you are enjoying yourself. You look as though you are feeling the heat.'

Matty's hair hung lankly over her face, and her face powder clung to a rime of sweat. She pushed away the china bowl containing *loup de mer*, and crumbled bread between her fingers. 'Yes,' she said in a low voice. 'I am finding the heat difficult.'

'It's a matter of will power,' Kit told her. 'Tell yourself not to mind.'

It was a novel approach for Matty and she floundered for something interesting with which to respond. 'I see.' Bread crumbled furiously onto the tablecloth.

'Do you?' Kit gave one of his lazy smiles. Only one corner of his mouth went up when he did that: amused and hinting at irony.

55

The smile was part of his charm, and at that moment the unused bits and pieces of Matty's heart went click, and she fell in love. Candle-light patched their faces and with a new greed Matty fastened her gaze on him. Kit drank some wine and tried again. 'Tell me what Daisy was like as a little girl,' he said in a low voice.

His question was transparent, and burrowing among the tangle of new feelings inside Matty's breast, she was conscious of despair.

'*Did* you get on as children?'

'No,' she said with the characteristic shake of her head. 'We didn't. We are too different. I'm very quiet.'

'Are you?' said Kit thoughtlessly.

'Daisy had the friends. I didn't so much because . . . well, I was ill a lot when I was a child.'

Kit pushed Matty's wine glass towards her. 'Have some,' he said. 'It's rough but invigorating.' He watched as she obeyed. 'Why were you ill?'

'I don't know. Ever since I was a small child in Damascus—'

'Damascus! What were you doing there?'

'I lived there,' she said. 'My parents bred Arab horses, and grew roses in a small way until . . .'

Kit put down his glass. 'Until what?'

The chatter of the other diners seemed very loud. 'Until they died, of typhoid. When I was five.'

'I'm sorry.' Kit sounded very distant and Matty was quite sure she had said something wrong. As if he did not *want* to accept what she had said. The moment passed, and he resumed. 'Roses, you say?'

Matty smiled and the candle-flame lit up her face. 'Autumn damasks. They have a very rich scent.'

'Yes, I know.' For a moment, Kit was back in a courtyard in Bokhara where he sat drinking tea, a mass of roses spread under the olives, and an old restlessness stirred. Daisy's laugh brought him back.

'Don't be absurd, Marcus.' She addressed her brother across the table. 'We will never have another war. It was all decided in a railway carriage.'

56

Marcus lit a cigarette. 'My sister's ignorance is profound so don't take any notice of her.'

'I, dear brother, am entitled to hold an opinion. Whether or not it is a good one is another matter.'

'*Touché.*' Kit raised his glass to Daisy, who was as pink and flushed as the roses he had been remembering. 'If I were you, Marcus, I wouldn't be so rude to your sister. They have a way of exacting revenge.'

'My saviour.' Daisy kissed the tip of one fingertip and blew it across the table to Kit.

With an effort, he turned back to Matty. 'You know about roses?'

'Only a little,' she replied seriously. 'I've kept my parents' notebooks and records, but I've never actually grown them.'

'It sounds as though you should try.'

And it sounds as though you are bored, thought Matty, and drank as much of the wine as she could manage.

Kit looked out at the forest of masts, and the lights flaring at the end of the harbour. A fishing boat was coming in and the crew's conversation sounded clearly over the water. Fuelled by the wine, Matty grabbed her chance.

'You know the East?'

Kit swivelled back to her. 'Quite well. It gets to you the East, doesn't it? Especially the desert. Clean and unforgiving. I've stayed in Damascus twice. You must remember what it is like?'

'Oh, yes.' At least, thought Matty, I share this in common with him. It was followed by a less worthy thought: Daisy did not. 'Did you know that martial law has been declared in Jerusalem and that the Arabs are crossing the Syrian border?'

'Really!' Kit looked at her with sharpened interest. 'Are you sure?'

'Gambling, I think, *mes amis.*' Daisy scraped back her chair and stood, her arms spread as if to embrace the world. '*Allons.*'

Kit laughed at her impersonation of the *patron*, got to his feet immediately and Matty lost him. She took another gulp from her glass and felt it trickle down her throat. She had always known there was a dark edge to her spirit: a place where anger and jealousy met and cohabited. She had so little, so very little, attention or affection, and Daisy who basked in these things was given them just like that. Anger stirred in Matty and, appalled by its intensity, she remained seated.

Holding out a hand to Kit who captured it, Daisy waltzed along the waterfront. 'Angel, angel boy,' she sang. 'I think I'm squiffy.' Behind her, Flora smiled into the darkness and allowed Marcus to tuck his hand under her elbow.

'So you're squiffy,' said Kit, pulling Daisy to him. 'But I like it.' His hands slid up her wrists. The sea went slap, slap on the waterfront and around the harbour it was lit with reflections from the lights. Beyond that was darkness. Daisy drew in her breath.

'It's too, too lovely,' she whispered to the head close to hers.

If Susan Chudleigh had not allowed the sun to dull her wits, she might have had second thoughts and nipped the affair in the bud. After all, Daisy was practically engaged to Tim Coats. But she did not. After an exhausting year of social rounds, charity work and organizing unsatisfactory domestics, she was content to let her guard slip and complacency take over. What did it matter that Kit and Daisy were obviously head over heels? He was a good catch. Socially he was very desirable, far more so than Tim Coats – Susan visualized how Lady Dysart would look on the envelopes. Hinton Dysart was a landmark, a little dilapidated perhaps, but everything had disadvantages. Where Kit did not score was in the matter of finance for, courtesy of his father who had made money manufacturing carpets, Tim was rich. Nevertheless, Kit and Daisy made a visually exciting pair, and, despite her worldliness, Susan was affected, as they all were in the Villa Lafayette, by the erotic charge between them.

Ambrose Chudleigh was clearer-sighted, but even more fatigued. He was seriously worried about the state of the world's economy – the Americans had called back all their loans in Europe and demand was slackening in the States itself. What, he asked his wife, did this forebode? Don't ask me, Susan replied. That's your problem. So concerned was Ambrose that he made arrangements to cut short his holiday and to depart at the end of August back to London on a salvage operation. He did not feel disposed to interfere with his daughter's love affair.

'But,' said his wife, as they lay in their twin beds and listened to the diners threading their way through the garden, 'if the markets are going to crash, we must get Daisy married off to one or other of them.' She reran calculations in her head and wondered if she had made a mistake in favouring Kit.

There was silence, broken only by a smothered giggle from Flora under the window.

'What are *her* investments in?' she asked.

'Matilda's?' Ambrose sighed. 'Don't be obvious, Susan. You know I can't give you that sort of information, and, anyway, who knows what is going to happen?'

'I just wondered.'

'Well, don't.'

'Will we be all right, Ambrose?'

Ambrose's answer was accompanied by the rustle of starched sheets. 'We don't have anything much to lose. You know that.'

Silence.

'Nothing's the same,' said Susan into the dark.

'What do you mean?'

'Since the war. It broke things up.'

Realizing he was not going to get much sleep, Ambrose switched on the light and reached for his sleeping pills and the glass of water. The water made his moustache gleam. 'Since you mention it,' he said, 'I must check Matty's portfolio. We have a duty to safeguard it.'

'She *would*,' said his wife bitterly for the thousandth time, reflecting on the skin-of-the-teeth operation that kept the family swimming in the kind of society to which Susan aspired. 'She just would have the money and not you.'

This was not fair. It was not Ambrose's fault that his sister Jocasta had married a rich man. (What is more, Jocasta had been

59

generous to her brother, to the extent of bequeathing him the leasehold of Number 5 Upper Brook Street.) Not fair at all. Ambrose crunched the pill between his teeth, winced at its aloe taste and then lay back to deal with the hot night.

CHAPTER FIVE

THE *BOUILLABAISSE* contained mullet and langoustines, and the sauce was very thick and red. At an adjacent table a sailor with a disfigured mouth scooped up the fish with a spoon and dunked his bread in the liquid. The misshapen lips stretched over the metal and each time the sailor swallowed he grimaced. The restaurant, a crowded, dimly lit *boîte* on the quay at the Cap, was that sort of place, thought Daisy: as fascinating to observe as it provoked easy conversation.

'Delicious,' she said, intrigued by the informality of the candle and paper tablecloth. It fitted in with the picture of France that had evolved in her mind: colour, heat, freedom and lack of constraint. 'It's just right.'

In order to have some time alone with Daisy, Kit had bribed Marcus to take Flora and Matty to the restaurant further along the quay. I'll behave, he promised, and he was sure Mrs Chudleigh would not object. Marcus was no slouch. On condition, he bargained, that he get some time with Flora. Done, Kit had said. A gentlemen's agreement. It was nothing of the sort, said Marcus who, from time to time, displayed flashes of humour.

One of the waiters wound up the gramophone which sat on the zinc bar, and the record scratched out a song about love spoilt and betrayed. Its despair affected Daisy and she put down her spoon. 'It's so sad, it bothers me.'

The door opened and the draught blew out the candle on their table. Kit relit it with his cigarette lighter. The shadows thrown by its flare did a St Vitus' dance across the white paper. 'I don't like to think of you being sad. Especially now,' he said, snapping the lighter shut.

Daisy watched him drop it onto the table. 'One must be

sometimes,' she said. 'Afterwards there is the luxury of being happy.'

'I know that,' said Kit. 'But I have a request. You are not to be sad this evening.'

'Have you got something to write with?'

He tossed her a pencil from his jacket pocket and she drew a face on the paper, a round with two big eyes.

'A question, Kit. Which is more foolish? Being too sad or too happy? Is someone born with a tendency to unhappiness or is it something they acquire, like teeth?'

With a stroke, Daisy added a mournful downturned mouth to her creation.

She had a way of asking provoking questions, things which were near the bone, and he threw this one back at her. 'Can you be too happy?' he asked, knowing that he was overwhelmingly so, sitting in the babble and darkness with Daisy, tempting the mothy old goddesses who sat on Olympus and controlled human fates.

She pulled a piece of wax off the candle. 'It's probably unwise to be too happy but that is not to say that one should not be. I don't think you can avoid discomfort or pain.'

'*Daisy!* Will you stop it?' Kit tugged the pencil away from her, and slashed a grin across the face on the paper. 'There. Here I am, having carried you off by stealth, and you talk of pain and misery.'

She wrinkled her nose at him. 'But, Kit, you have to think about these things sometimes.'

'Not tonight,' said Kit, who did think of these things.

The door swung open and shut like a metronome until the barman propped it open and the flat, shiny sea was framed like a picture. The *boîte* was packed and smoky. At the bar fishermen with weatherbeaten arms and blue trousers were drinking *marc*. At the tables older men in linen suits dined young men in tight trousers and skimpy sailor shirts.

'Teri! *Encore.*'

'Coming, Monsieur.'

'Teri, poppet. Where are you?' said a plaintive voice. 'You're keeping me waiting.'

Voices gave counterpoint to the music and the popular Teri was kept busy. Every so often he addressed a remark to a woman, dressed in a striped sailor's top and blue trousers, who sat at one end of the bar drinking anis. Cradling a glass smeared at the rim in one hand, she peered through the smoke from under a hennaed fringe, and the scarlet fingernails on her other hand went tap, tap, on the bar's surface. A cigarette burned in the ashtray beside her, and the diamanté clip on her clutchbag caught and fractured the light. She seemed entirely at ease in familiar surroundings.

'I wonder who she is.' Daisy was intrigued.

'Perhaps she's one of the local—' Kit checked himself in time.

Daisy leant back in her chair and eyed Kit. 'I know what you mean. You can say it, you know.' She examined the woman with redoubled interest. 'I wonder what her story is.' Daisy reached for Kit's cigarettes. 'I do wish my French was better.'

'Perhaps she was taken in adultery and cast forth into the world by an irate husband.' Kit grabbed Daisy's hand and she dropped the cigarette packet. 'So be warned.'

'Is that what you would do?' Daisy sounded thoughtful. 'No forgiveness? For a little matter of the flesh?'

'You can't mend a smashed vase.' Kit was serious.

'Only if you consider it has been smashed.'

Her answer unsettled Kit for he imagined it indicated she had gone beyond him on the subject of infidelity. He imagined, too, finding Daisy in someone else's bed and felt the outrage of the betrayed.

'If I ever—' he began, but she anticipated what he was going to say and interrupted.

'Now you *are* being absurd.'

True, he was. Nothing was settled between them. Kit dipped his bread into the *bouillabaisse*. Daisy was unlike any other woman he had met. Light years away from the awkward, rather jolly girls whose eyes begged him to single them out at dinners and dances. In the past, Kit had felt sorry for them: their freedom was limited, their ambitions for marriage of necessity predictable. No wonder, as they sat garnished with their mother's pearls in chaperoned chastity, that they appeared powerless – and he quite forgot that if one of them had attracted him the power would have shifted.

Daisy *was* different, and he marvelled at how much so and why. Like her chestnut hair, she was filled with springing life. There was an element of attack about her. A readiness to lock horns. He knew without asking that Daisy would pack her bags and follow him into the noise, clutter, hard journeying and lotus-tinged luxury of the East. As Kit ate, he pictured the two of them riding in the desert, a hot wind tugging at their clothes.

'Daisy,' he said. 'Can you drag your attention away from Fifi or whatever her name is? I want to talk about you.'

Eyes glittering with enjoyment, Daisy pushed the candle in the bottle aside to see him better. 'Good, I love talking about me. I'm such a fascinating subject.'

There was silence.

After a second, the teasing died from her face. Daisy reached over the table and cupped Kit's cheek in her hand. 'Darling Kit,' she said softly, and with a queer, muted sound Kit reached up to imprison her hand.

'What have you done to me, Daisy? I came to the Villa Lafayette a free man.'

'You were never free. No one is.'

'Are we prisoners, then?'

'Absolutely.'

'Of whom?'

'Of what, rather, in your case. Your home, stupid.'

He reflected. 'I expect you're right, but I hope you aren't.'

Daisy made to take away her hand. 'Leave it there,' he said. 'Don't take it away.'

'Kit, darling, I'm getting cramp.'

Reluctantly he allowed her to drop her hand back into her lap. 'What do you want from me?' she asked, at last. 'An anchor?'

Kit was not given to dramatic statements, or to quick decisions, but now he said, without a moment's pause, 'You. For ever.'

Pupils dilated in the gloom, she tried to fathom what lay behind the uneven smile. 'Did anyone ever tell you, Kit, you should be a film star? Your floppy hair and brooding eyes would be perfect.'

'Daisy.' Simultaneously exasperated, maddened and intoxicated by her, Kit felt he was running down several roads all at once. 'Will you talk sense.'

She turned her attention to the question. 'For ever,' she repeated.

'That's what I said.'

'I don't have a penny to my name, you should know that. Yes, I know Mother and Father put on a reasonable show. Just. Matty's helps, you know. But there is nothing for me when I marry.'

Kit refilled their glasses from the carafe. 'Why mention money? I haven't said anything about it.'

'Oh, yes, you have, without realizing it, of course. Besides, money is important.'

'Not that important.' As he spoke, Kit knew that Daisy had put a finger on the only issue that did have a bearing on his decisions.

'You're wrong, Kit. I didn't go to Eton but I know money is significant even if it isn't everything.'

'Thank God you weren't a boy, and Eton isn't all it's cracked up to be.'

Daisy shrugged. 'Matty and I shared a governess whose ignorance was only matched by an ability to suck up to Mother. As a result, my mind is a ragbag.' She stuck out the tip of her tongue at Kit and grinned. 'But, then, girls are not supposed to have brains, are they?'

She was teasing him again and Kit said nothing; for it was precisely the sentiment that had been expressed often enough in Eton's changing rooms and freezing studies.

'Don't be so touchy,' he said.

'Don't be so stuffy.'

The conversation was veering from the path Kit wished it to take. 'Enough,' he said, retrieving the initiative. 'Let's dance.'

He pulled Daisy close. She smiled, sank against his shoulder and fitted her cheek against his. Her hair smelt of rosemary and verbena and her skin sweet and musky. Under her dress, her breasts pressed into him and he felt his body tighten in response. Slowly, they circled the dance area. Plagued by their own memories, the older men at the bar watched them.

'*Êtes-vous anglais?*' called out the woman at the bar as they circled past her.

'*Oui,*' Kit replied. '*Oui. C'est ça.*'

'Come and talk to me, then, English. I need a dose of the old Alma Mater.'

Kit and Daisy looked at each other and Daisy whispered, 'It would be fun.' Reluctantly, Kit removed his hand from Daisy's bare, warm back and ushered her to the bar. The woman shoved two bar stools towards them with a cork-sandalled foot.

'I'm Bill,' she said.

'Daisy Chudleigh and Kit Dysart.' Daisy held out her hand and the red talons touched it briefly.

Bill leant over the bar and tugged at the minuscule apron tied around the waist of the waiter. 'You drink anis?' she asked and, without waiting for an answer, said, 'One each for my guests and a double for me, Teri sweetie, there's a love.' She smiled, revealing perfect white teeth. 'You don't mind talking to a has-been, I hope. I won't keep you long and you can tuck it away under the section labelled "good deeds in a naughty world".'

Kit balanced his drink on his knee. 'I can see you live here.'

'Oh, yes, sweeties. This is my home now.' Bill poured water into her glass and Daisy watched the spirit transmogrify from crystal to cloud. She sipped at her own and swallowed experimentally. Bill clinked her glass on Daisy's.

'Cheers.'

'Why did you leave England?' Daisy wasn't sure about the anis and wrinkled her nose at the taste. Bill looked at her sharply.

'Dear me,' she said. 'I thought it was obvious, but I forget that the dear old Alma M. likes to keep its virgins in complete ignorance.' She sucked at her drink. 'Because, my dear child, it suits me here. But I would like to know how England is.'

Kit looked up from his drink. 'Not good. We have a Labour

66

government but rising unemployment. Not to mention income tax.'

'I know, I know,' said Bill. 'Picture it: socialists on every street corner.'

'No,' said Kit. 'Unemployed on street corners.'

'That's bad,' said Bill. Daisy did not think she sounded as though she meant it. A silk pouch embroidered with Chinese symbols lay beside Bill's glass. Daisy watched as she picked it up, extracted a pinch of a dark powdery substance and tapped it into a cigarette paper with some tobacco. 'Forget it, I say.' Her fingers worked at the paper and its contents. 'Life is cheaper over here, better, too, and nobody expects anything from you. That makes it easy.' Under her fringe Bill was frowning a little. 'On the other hand, it can be curiously disappointing.'

She poked the end of the cigarette paper into place with her nail and licked it. Beside Daisy, Kit went very still. Bill flicked at her hair and appraised them both. 'You look nice, the pair of you,' she informed them. 'Young, unbothered. Still children, really.'

'Twenty-five,' said Kit protesting.

'Twenty-two,' echoed Daisy, and added a shade defensively, 'only just, though.'

'Take it from me, you're at a good moment in your lives . . . before you have found out too much about yourselves.'

'Is that a bad thing?' Daisy wet her fingertip, leant forward and placed it on a speck of the substance left on the bar top. She examined it with interest. 'Finding out about yourself.'

'Depends what you find out, sweeties.' Bill lit the cigarette and inhaled. Smoke wreathed out between her glistening lips and curled over Kit and Daisy. 'Here,' she said, holding out the cigarette now bordered in scarlet. 'Help yourself. It's on me.'

'Thank you.' Daisy reached over.

'No,' said Kit at precisely the same moment. 'No, thank you.' And he pushed aside Daisy's outstretched hand.

Bill closed her eyes. 'Up to you,' she said, both sharp and dreamy-sounding at the same time. 'It's up to you.'

'Kit.' Daisy was annoyed by his interference. 'Do you mind?'

67

He hesitated, cupped Daisy's chin with his hand and said, 'Yes, I do. Very much. This stuff is dangerous.'

Bill reopened her eyes. Her pupils had grown large and black. 'Do I look dangerous?'

'It's not your business, Kit.' Daisy pulled away from him. 'You mustn't tell me what to do.'

Kit took her hand. 'Come with me,' he said.

'No.' She shook her head.

'Don't let's quarrel.'

'You are not quarrelling,' said Bill, taking another lingering drag. 'It's sex talking.'

Kit threw back his head and laughed. 'Wonderful,' he said. 'But enough.' He slapped some francs down onto the bar and, without further warning, grabbed Daisy and hustled her through the door.

She was furious with him. 'What do you think you're doing?'

'Sex,' called Bill after them. 'See if I'm right.' Daisy felt a giveaway flush sweep over her cheeks.

Outside, she fought free of Kit and moved away into the shadows beside the harbour wall. 'You shouldn't have done that,' she said at last. 'I was enjoying talking to her and I have a right to do as I please.'

Kit took his time lighting a cigarette which he passed over to Daisy. Then he lit one for himself. 'Sorry,' he said. 'But that stuff is dangerous, Daisy. I've seen a lot of it out East. Believe me.'

'What *did* you see out East?' Daisy leant against the warm stone.

'People who lived for it and not much else. Their families suffered, and if it really got to them, they died very nastily.'

'Why?'

'Opium's addictive.' Kit paused. 'The need for it can outweigh everything.' He paused again and the wine he had drunk came to his aid. 'Because the dreams it brings are wild and paradise-filled.'

'Hmm.' Daisy raised a finger and pointed at Kit. 'You tried it.'

Kit blew out a stream of smoke. 'Yes.'

'And?'

He shifted back through the memories. Lured by its promise

and blurring of senses, he had gone willingly with the drug. Offers had been made by his attentive host and Kit – young, curious, away from home – accepted.

Of course, the drug had led to other things.

Sent in with instructions to please, the boy's limbs were pale coffee against the sheets, and heat bathed both of them in sweat. The touch of skin against skin had been unforgettable; so had the sensation that began in the groin and bloomed all over his body. In the darkness, gender had been left behind, and there was only the business of satiation and its aftermath.

'And?'

'That's why I know how dangerous it is.'

Daisy gazed at the sea beneath the quay and digested the implications. Every so often a bubble of light broke the surface of the water as a fish moved about in the shallows. A salty tang merged with the acrid-sweet smell of sewage. Behind the quay the black shapes of olive trees on the slope above the village straggled up to the crest, and there were flat slabs of shadow where terraces had been cut from the hillside.

'I have to see things for myself,' she said. 'Like you have.'

'You also have to be careful.' Kit moved closer to Daisy and his hands again snaked up her wrists. Then he pulled her towards him and she went quiet while he held her so tight that she almost cried out.

'Tell me,' she said at last. 'Tell me about it.'

Trust did not come easily to Kit but this was one occasion when he had to make a leap. Hesitant and with none of his usual irony, he told Daisy about the coffee limbs and his drug-disordered defloration.

'A boy?' was all she said, both appalled and stimulated and, like many lovers, jealous more of a past in which she had not figured than of the thing itself. But she was also affected powerfully at the sharing of Kit's secret. After a minute, she buried her head in his shoulder, thought about Tim Coats waiting in England, and then forgot about him.

'I think I understand, Kit.' And then a bit later. 'Kiss me.'

Kit's lips were hot and dry on Daisy's. They brushed her

cheek, and travelled down the length of her tantalizing neck to the hollow at the base. She tasted of salt, damp face powder and scent. He muttered something which she did not hear and she placed a hand on either side of his face and tugged at it. He raised his head. A lock of hair fell over his forehead, and from under it he gazed at Daisy with unconcealed want.

'Oh, Kit,' she said. 'Am I boyish enough for you?'

At that he kissed her hard on the mouth, before wrenching her shoulder strap down and kissing the exposed breast underneath. Helpless, she let him.

Along with the desire coursing through their flesh was the knowledge that they belonged together, that their bodies fitted, and the leaping burn of delight in meeting a mate. For Kit was sure that here was the woman who would heal whatever lay, dark and unfinished, in his mind. And Daisy knew that Kit accepted her as she was.

By the time they pulled apart, Daisy's lips were bruised and swollen and Kit's upper lip was beaded with sweat. With a groan, he let her go. She swayed slightly and pulled her shoulder strap back into place.

It was her turn to be daring. 'Is that all?' she asked.

He shoved his hands into his pockets and forced himself to think of multiplication tables and unpaid bills. 'You know it is.'

'No coffee legs tangled in sheets?'

The idea of unpaid bills had no effect on Kit. Shuddering a little with frustration, he circled her face with his hands, tilting it up so that moonlight played on the bruised mouth and managed to say, 'No.'

She was half sorry, half relieved, for sometimes Daisy's impatience to live life and her curiosity frightened even her. 'All right, Kit darling. I'll learn patience, but kiss me again.'

Kit obliged. As his mouth hovered above hers, pulled into its uneven smile, he said, 'I don't mind waiting,' and Daisy tightened her hold on the tall figure bending over her while the cicadas beat out their rhythm.

*

70

Dysarts never liked to lie in bed: it was a family trait. Although the party had returned well after four o'clock in the morning, both Kit and Flora were up at seven thirty and on the terrace. They sat side by side at the breakfast table and watched the gardener's laborious trips with the watering can to and from the lead tank at the bottom of the slope.

Flora inspected the sunburn on her arms and held out a leg for inspection. 'Hmm,' she said. 'I need watering.'

'Cold cream,' advised Kit and pushed away the croissants.

Flora scratched at a patch of peeling skin. 'I've applied tons and tons.' She held a strip up to the light. 'It's fascinating, Kit. You can see its structure.'

'If you have a shred of pity left in you, Flora, spare me.' Kit poured hot milk into the coffee bowl and took a mouthful, glancing up at the cousins' bedroom as he did so. Flora directed a look at her brother. She had witnessed him in the throes of calf love before, but it was with an odd, apprehensive feeling that she now realized she had never seen him with *that* look on his face. Flora was also quick enough to know that whatever *she* might feel about this — envy that Daisy might have her brother, jealousy that she had to share him — she must keep it to herself.

'You're very smitten, aren't you, Kit?'

'Beyond reason,' said Kit, in an attempt to fob her off. Then he relaxed and was truthful. 'Very.'

Flora could not resist one jab. 'I expect you're not the only one. Daisy gets about. You know she has a boyfriend back in London. Matty told me.'

She regretted it, for the shut look snapped down over Kit's face and the conversation terminated. Both Flora and Polly wore the same expression in difficult situations, but Flora knew that Kit retreated faster and more thoroughly than any of them.

'Belt up, old girl, and eat your breakfast,' he said.

Removing the black cherry jam from his reach, she helped herself. Kit proffered the croissants. 'Take two and you'll be even fatter.' She made a face at him while he drank his coffee. Smarting from the gibe, Flora buttered her croissant then changed her mind, scraped it off and wondered if she dared return it to the butter

71

dish. Really, it was too bad because she wanted to talk to Kit. She needed his advice and now he was in one of his don't-approach-me moods. Then she thought: How ridiculous. One does not ask advice about love affairs of one's brother.

Was it a love affair, the sticky encounter that she and Marcus had had last night?

She tried other words to describe it and, because she was honest, 'burlesque' was one of them.

Clearly Marcus was no strategist in sex and had chosen his moment badly to press himself on Flora, who was ignorant and required care. This was hardly surprising for Marcus's strongest recollected emotion was his hysterical fear when, aged seven, he had been dispatched to prep school by his mother. Since then he had neither trusted nor understood women. Yet Flora attracted him in a basic way and, like his sister, he was curious. Without preliminaries, Marcus had grabbed Flora under the olive tree and kissed her. His moustache felt like a . . . like a rodent rooting round her mouth and he smelt of wine and brandy, and every instinct in Flora told her that this was a sham. Nauseated, she pushed him away and begged him not to. After that, they had said goodnight to each other very politely.

Immaculate in black with white fluttering streamers, Adèle, the maid, stepped through the french windows onto the terrace and handed Kit a telegram.

Kit picked up the paper knife. 'Hope it's nothing serious,' he said, and slit the envelope.

'Another hot day, Adèle.' Flora ground out her nursery French.

Adèle's olive-skinned features remained expressionless. '*Oui, Mademoiselle.*'

'Is it always as hot at this time of the year?'

'Not always, Mademoiselle. It is the year of *la grande chaleur.*'

Unequal to further conversation, Flora gave up and contemplated the steaming garden. The sun was already strident. She sighed and scuffed her shoes on a rogue patch of thyme that had worked its way between the terrace stones. Only then did she register the baffled, frozen look on Kit's face. Oh, God, she thought. Father's done something.

'What is it?'

He tossed her the telegram and she read: FINANCIAL CRISIS STOP COME HOME STOP NEEDS SORTING OUT STOP RUPERT STOP PS WARNING STOP CHUDLEIGHS DON'T HAVE A BLOODY PENNY STOP

'Don't pay any attention,' said Flora urgently. 'Don't. Don't!'

'Have you been telling tales, Flora?'

'Of course not.'

'Sorry.' Kit pushed back his chair and got to his feet. 'So where did Father get the idea that I am the sacrificial lamb?'

'Mrs Chudleigh would have told him about you and Daisy. Quick as say knife.'

'Of course.' Kit hovered by the stone balustrade and ran his fingers up and down the coping. 'Now where does that leave Daisy and me in Father's plans? That I mustn't get involved because he wants me to marry money, I suppose.'

Flora couldn't bear that. 'If you love Daisy, marry her. It's very simple.'

'It's not simple.' Kit faced his sister. 'I don't know what Father has gone and done, but he's right in one aspect. We have to maintain Hinton Dysart.'

Flora wiped cherry jam off her mouth. 'Does it matter if the house falls down? Does it, Kit? A bit of brick and stone and some documents with "Dysart" written on them. Anyway, what does Father mean? Has he lost all our money, or just a bit? Hadn't you better find out?'

In the heat, the butter had turned muddy gold and crusted rims had formed around their coffee bowls. So brilliant and exotic a few moments ago, the colours in the garden had become hard and indifferent.

Oh, Kit, said Flora, silently addressing her brother's retreating back. I see trouble and if I could be the one to marry someone rich and stop all this silly nonsense, then I would.

*

73

'Hallo.'

'Hallo, Father, can you hear me?'

'Can I what?'

'HEAR ME.'

'No need to shout.'

'What's happened? Why do I have to come home?'

'I've lost a great deal of money on the stock exchange, if you must know.'

Kit digested this. 'How much, sir?'

'A lot. Well, almost all our capital. Something's going wrong with the market. It's panicking and I didn't trust Hepworth to deal with it.'

Kit began to understand. His father had been given a tip over sherry by a neighbour or some such person and as a result had told Hepworth, their money man, to go to hell after disregarding his advice. 'How serious is this, sir? I need to know.'

'Very,' said Rupert heavily. 'Very serious indeed, and I gather the market is not going to get any better.'

Static on the telephone line cracked across their conversation which both swelled and faded in volume. Kit pressed his father. 'There is no chance of recouping?'

Kit could hear Rupert blowing out pipe smoke and thought how much he would like to wrench the pipe out of his mouth.

'Yes. I am afraid that is so,' said Rupert, at his most clipped. Kit drove his hand into his trouser pocket. 'I want you to come home. I gather you're thick as thieves with the Chudleigh girl and I want you to stop all that. This is no time to get yourself entangled.'

There was no hint of regret or apology in his tone, nor had Kit expected there to be.

Susan Chudleigh reacted acidly to the news that Kit was returning to England on business matters. 'Oh, yes,' she said, drawling the words, a technique which imperfectly hid her rage. 'I am sure your dear father would only request you back if something serious had happened.' She understood the implications of Rupert's directives, and ran over in her mind the chatty letter she had written to Rupert to see where she had gone wrong. 'I

74

will excuse you both, of course. I am sure Flora would not wish to stay on any longer without you.'

'I'm sure she wouldn't mind.'

'Of course she would mind.' Susan was not going to dispense hospitality to an undeserving cause. She had different plans for Marcus – who could flirt as much as he liked, of course – and, now that Kit was removing from the scene, Flora was not included in them. Kit stared at his hostess hoping that not one feature in the hard face would ever echo in Daisy's. Of course, he had met Susan's type many times, but it had never before struck him that she was a creature that at all times should remain under a stone.

'You have been very kind,' he managed to say. 'Thank you.'

He left Susan, who went to seek out her daughter. She found her lying in a bath with a mud pack on her face.

'Sit up,' she said to Daisy. 'I want to know what's happened.'

Daisy obeyed in a wash of scented water. Her eyes were pools in the mudflat of her face which cracked as she replied. 'What are you talking about?'

'Think,' said her mother. 'Where did you go wrong last night? Did you throw yourself at Kit Dysart?'

'What are you talking about?'

'You know,' said her mother. 'You know as well as I do that you were hoping to hook him. Well, you've botched it. He's off back home.'

'Don't be silly, Mother, he's staying for September.'

Susan watched mud rivulets run down her daughter's shoulders, and said, 'No, you little fool. He's going tomorrow . . . on the night train.' She watched Daisy subside into the bath and added, 'Well, what do you have to say?'

Daisy lay quite still in the clouded water. 'I have nothing to say, Mother. It's probably a problem at home. I'll see him in London.'

'Oh, I don't think so, Daisy. I think he is clearing out. He's been warned off. Finish.' Susan pulled the handle of the bath plug. It made a hollow sound.

'No.'

'You're more of a fool than I thought. Kit Dysart would have made a good husband if you'd got in quick.' Susan folded her arms and thought for a moment. 'But I suppose he had his disadvantages. Now you're left with Tim, and you'd better pull yourself together because you're no spring chicken any longer. I hope Tim doesn't hear about this episode.'

Daisy's confidence faltered. Had something happened to Kit in the night? Had he been seized by fear of being trapped, by the memory of the boy? Daisy's thoughts swirled like the draining bathwater. And why, most hurtfully why, had he not come to tell her first?

'Is that all you care about, Mother?' Daisy wanted to be very quiet and to concentrate on trusting Kit, but Susan was not going to go away. 'Really, if marriage is all that is required to rescue the budgets, I'll get the next man I meet to propose.'

Her mother sat down suddenly and extracted her cigarette case from the pocket of her slub linen dress. 'No, Daisy, it isn't all.' Her face with its armour plating of make-up softened a trifle. 'I want you to be happy.' She inhaled. 'But we have to be sensible and practical. Not any man will do, and Kit was suitable . . . and titled.'

'Oh, yes, titled,' said Daisy.

'If only—'

Susan's familiar litany was starting. Daisy broke in, 'If only we had Matty's money. Yes, I know. Well, we haven't. Now, listen. I did not, as you put it, get in quick and get him to propose, but it was understood. So, if Kit is leaving . . .' She covered her eyes abruptly with her hand. 'I don't believe it,' she said, more to herself than to Susan.

'If he *is* going,' she continued, 'you must make nothing of it. Not until I have sorted it out.'

Susan looked curiously at her daughter, as if she had made a discovery. 'You really do care for him?'

Cigarette ash dropped in a soft arc to the floor.

'Go away, please,' Daisy begged.

Susan got up, straightened the pleats of her dress (a Patou copy run up in a basement) and walked over to the door, leaving behind a trail of smoke and Chanel No. 5.

'The Dysarts will take Matilda back with them as the wretched girl can't seem to stand the heat. You and Marcus will stay here as we planned and I've rung Annabel and asked her to come and join us. That will cheer you up.' Susan pushed the door open. 'At least we won't have Matilda moping about.' The door swung on its hinge and she was gone.

Dressed in a blue cotton frock and matching shoes, Matty walked down the passage and witnessed a strange sight: Daisy sitting up in an empty bath with a mud-streaked face crying into her flannel.

HARRY

Late summer is the time for a little dead-heading and snoozing in a deck-chair over Pimm's — and at my age I should be doing precisely that but I don't. (Have you noticed how people like the old to act their age, particularly the young?) Non-gardeners ('Are there any?' asks Thomas in a resigned tone) might imagine that the gardener relaxes in high summer and enjoys the fruit of his brooding, whittling and labours instead of dreaming of autumn and the whiff of bonfire. Something urges me on: the knowledge that I do not have much time left and a reluctance to waste it.

I look at my arms with their slackening flesh and I cannot imagine that it was these, brown and muscled in those days, that clutched the handlebars of the Harley-Davidson as I roared up the drive of Hinton Dysart, dressed head to foot in leather, to tell my parents that I had been suspended from Oxford for climbing into college after hours once too often.

(That, my friends, was a long time ago, and a long journey ago and I don't feel the experience was wasted. I went off to France instead and learnt about life.)

There is an old Chinese curse: may your dreams come true. In their way mine have, but I don't feel cursed. I feel complete, absorbed in the work I like best.

For example, I have conducted a little survey of the most popular plants in the nursery and the results are interesting. Top — of course — is lavender, and why not? Second is *Euonymus*, 'Emerald 'n Gold', perfect ground cover, weed-smothering and eye catching. Third is the choisya 'Sundance' with its bright yellow leaves and scented blossoms. Fourth is *Potentilla* 'Red Ace'. Fifth *Spirea* 'Goldflame'. Sixth is a newcomer. *Lavatera* 'Barnsley'.

Beautiful, heat-loving candy pink flowers designed by nature to sway in the summer breeze . . .

Talking of summer, I have been delighted by the results of my latest experiment. Last year I pirated a dry, south-facing bed outside the walled garden and set about re-creating the *maquis* in Hinton Dysart. It is an awkward, dry, scrubby place and I don't think the guardians minded too much. I planted lavenders and Jerusalem sage, the autumn flowering snowdrop, *Galanthus corcyrensis* which likes to bake in the summer, drought-loving irises and my much loved grey and white *Convolvulus cneorum*. A word of warning, *maquis* plants grow leggy in a soft, damp climate and require hard pruning in the spring, but that is small outlay of effort for such rewards.

On warm evenings I wander up to inspect the bed and smell the thyme – and I am reminded of my youth, of my time in Provence and, of course, Thomas, who I met there.

A last thought. Gardeners are a strange breed – and there are a lot of them – garrulous, obsessive, as competitive as industrial warlords and always have been. Like the gardener in Shakespeare's *Richard II*, they perceive the world in terms of the garden. The Alpha and the Omega. I know I do. So did my mother. Here we are – young, middle-aged, plump, bony, badly dressed, overdressed, rich and poor, clever or not – circled together in the communality of a shared passion which excludes others.

From my position at the till, I watch visitors walk the grounds: through the wisteria tunnel, across the circular lawn down to the special garden where they linger, only to be drawn back to the walled rose garden. Quivering with delight, snoopy, inquisitive, acquisitive, eager to learn, some with concealed plastic bags. Only this morning I watched an old lady in a Burberry mackintosh and green wellingtons help herself to a cutting from the *Ceanothus* 'Trewithen Blue'. Yet another with diamond rings flashing on her fingers pulled up a shoot from the herbaceous border. Later I went to inspect the wound: Diamond Rings had plundered the

Tradescantia virginiana, the spiderwort or Trinity flower —
Mother taught me all the names. Or, she said as she showed me
the components of the plant and parted its angled leaves, Moses-
in-the-Bulrushes. See, my darling, where they hid the baby until
he was found.

CHAPTER SIX

B Y LATE afternoon of that same day the arrangements had been made. The Dysarts and Matty were scheduled to leave for Nice after lunch the following day and to catch the night train to Paris, a journey of a day and a half.

The telephone was kept occupied and so was Kit, dashing in and out of Antibes. There was a fuss at the lack of first-class sleeping compartments, relief when the railway officials were made to appreciate the unthinkableness of second class. Train timetables were consulted, dinner arrangements debated, the hapless Adèle was ordered to count and recount the luggage – trunks, hat boxes, crocodile dressing cases, golf bags and tennis rackets heaped in triplicate. All day the business of departure raged in the Villa Lafayette, masking the other drama.

As a rule, when plans went wrong Susan took out her irritation on Matty, and now she launched a full-scale campaign. 'It will be a relief not to have you moping around the place,' she informed her over afternoon tea. 'You look dreadful, too. All . . . all blotchy.'

Matty bit her full lower lip. 'I'm sorry, Aunt Susan.'

'As usual you're perfectly dreary company. Have you no conversation at all, Matilda? I can never understand how so much money can be spent on you to so little effect.'

Matty knew better than to defend herself and thus she endured the lecture which mixed accusations of not appreciating French governesses, trips to Mainbocher's salon, silk underwear and the best medical care (which neither of her cousins were privileged to enjoy) *and* the good home in which Matty had been the interloper for twenty years. For her part, Matty thought that Marcus could not have cared less about any of the above and, far from watching from the sidelines, Daisy had always shared in the benefits of

Matty's French governesses and silk underwear. In fact, Daisy spoke French far better than any of them.

Smoking furiously, Susan paced up and down the white drawing room like a gilded reptile, giving vent. Matty listened to her with one ear, and with the other to a voice in her head which adjured her to take no notice: Susan could not really hurt her.

Untrue. Her aunt did hurt, frequently. And, in one important respect, she was right. Matty was an interloper – an orphaned ugly duckling dropped into a nest already occupied by a bird of paradise.

Matty could think of nothing to say, so she held up an arm to inspect a mosquito bite on her wrist. It looked pink and spongy, but was hard and hot to touch.

'And another thing, Matilda, please stop scratching those awful bites. They are quite disgusting.'

'Leave her alone, Mother.' Daisy, who had come in from a solitary walk on the beach, sat down on the sofa and lit a cigarette which she smoked in jerks. 'Don't pick on her.'

Matty was not sure she liked Daisy's kindness any better than her impatience. Still, being kicked in the shins was marginally preferable to being kicked in the stomach. She stole a look at her cousin and, because her own feelings for Kit had sensitized her, found herself in the novel position of feeling sorry for Daisy. Daisy was skilled at looking as if she did not have a care in the world but today a tell-tale whiteness at the corners of her mouth told Matty a lot about Daisy's private turmoil. She tried to make light of the situation. 'I'm sure Aunt Susan didn't mean it.'

Daisy shrugged a bare shoulder and changed the subject. 'The weather's changing. A wind's blowing up.'

It was true. The sky was light violet, and the leaves fluttered in the trees.

'Goodness me, it's getting late.' Matty stood up. 'I will come and say goodbye later. Unless you would like me to say goodbye now.'

'You won't be a nuisance to the Dysarts, will you, Matilda? No sponging on their good will.' Susan was not sure why she was bothering to issue the edict as she did not care much what happened to any of them. Habit, she supposed.

'No, Aunt Susan.' Eyes fixed on the rug, Matty shook her head. 'I'll see you in London. Is there anything you want me to do before you get back?'

Daisy finally snapped. 'Oh, go away, Matty,' she said. 'Hurry up and go.'

'Now who's being unkind?' said Susan as the door closed behind Matty.

'I am,' her daughter replied as she let herself out through the french windows into the garden.

Kit discovered her sitting on the stone bench by the swimming pool. The *mistral* was gathering force and she was watching the branches of the fig tree dance to its tune.

He stood in front of her and looked down at her huddled figure.

'Hallo, Daisy.'

She clenched her hands in her lap. 'Hallo, Kit.'

'I've been trying to speak to you all day, but I had to go into Antibes to make arrangements.'

Daisy examined her fingers and noted that the knuckles showed white through the tan. 'I was here.'

'My father has asked for me to go home. As soon as possible.'

'I would be both blind and deaf not to realize that.' Daisy managed a smile. 'Adèle is hysterical.'

He dropped onto the bench beside her. 'Daisy, we talked about money the other night, do you remember?' She nodded. 'My father has a financial crisis on his hands and my presence is required.' He reached over and pried open the knot made by her hands and twined his fingers into hers. 'Daisy, this is important. I can't make any decisions at the moment. About us, I mean.'

'I wish I'd never brought up the subject of money.' Daisy had been so sure that Kit would brush aside her objections voiced in the *boîte*, and a greater part of the day had been spent convincing herself that he would take no notice of a financial crisis, and that her mother would be proved wrong. Surely Kit would see the *necessity* of committing himself to her there and then, of seeking her out and saying – metaphorically, of course – come with me, the rest doesn't matter.

Kit had not sought her out, and her vision of a knight on a white charger (or in Kit's case a camel) faded. In its place stood Susan, a told-you-so smile curving her hard mouth, and Kit busying himself with *Bradshaw's* and luggage labels.

'I thought it wouldn't—' Impatient with herself for being impatient, and hurt that he did not share her feelings, Daisy pulled her hands away. 'It's funny, Kit. I thought we knew each other better than we do.'

Perhaps Kit did not love her? Really love her. Otherwise he would wish to settle things. Wouldn't he? Daisy had been so sure. The doubt planted when Kit confessed about the boy which she had thought did not matter, now began to, and Daisy found she was more shocked and frightened by the episode than she had supposed. Kit was staring at her, desirous and tender, but he also wore an air of distraction. Hair ruffled in the wind, his finger tapping at the passport in his jacket pocket, Kit, Daisy divined with a chill, had already moved on.

Idylls were temporary by their nature – and the one at the Villa Lafayette had dissolved at the ring of a telephone. Kit was called back and, it seemed to Daisy, was returning willingly into the world of telegrams and anger. Under the beat of Daisy's yearning, pulsed a disappointment that he was both safer and more conventional than she had imagined.

No. Daisy checked herself. Perhaps she was wrong and it was nothing to do with safety. Was her disappointment, asked the honest bit of her, owing to Kit not having put her first?

The *mistral* blew coldly between them. She dropped her head into her hands. 'Have you got something to read on the journey?'

'Yes.'

'If Matty gets breathless, her drops are in her crocodile travelling case.' She got to her feet and dusted down her skirt. 'I thought I'd better warn you.'

'Daisy, don't go like this.'

'I thought I would make it easy. You're saying that, after all,

84

you don't wish to marry me. You're saying we had a nice time, but it's over.'

Kit was so taken aback that he laughed. 'Daisy. No. That's not what I mean,' he protested.

WARNING STOP CHUDLEIGHS DON'T HAVE A BLOODY
PENNY STOP RUPERT

Across his mind flashed an image of Hinton Dysart on a spring morning, set in tangled green and serenaded by ring doves. It was followed by the darker image that always made him want to run away . . . as far and as fast as he could. He hovered on the edge of anger. 'Be patient, Daisy.'

He's been warned off. As sharp as a razor, Susan's words cut into Daisy.

'Daisy.' Kit slid his arms around her and held her tight. Dust blew in from the road and the wind whipped around them. Daisy shivered inside the prison made by his body.

'Luggage labels, Kit, and telephone calls. That's what it boils down to. I think we should end this conversation. There isn't any point in it.'

Kit took Daisy by the shoulders and forced her to face him. 'But you do understand?'

Wild with hurt, and with despair because it had all gone wrong, she lost her temper. 'What is there to understand?' she blazed.

In the fading stormy light, her face turned pale, foxlike and unreadable. Her eyes narrowed in rage, and her hair lost its brightness. For a moment, her beauty and sureness were gone, and she seemed out of her depth.

As quickly as it had erupted, Daisy's anger died. 'Kit, I'm sorry. That was unforgivable.'

'I have to go home to Hinton Dysart,' he repeated, teaching her the fact as if to a child. 'I cannot abandon it or my father, and I have nothing to offer a wife at the moment except a mountain of debt.'

It was on the tip of her tongue to ask, 'Since when did a huge house and garden constitute nothing?' Instead she said, 'And I have nothing to offer you?'

'Please. Don't.'

She stood by the carved stone pot and deadheaded the geraniums. As she watched the faded petals yield to the *mistral*, she contemplated the wounds of a love affair – its humiliations, its quicksands, and spoilt promise. 'I thought it would be different, Kit,' she said miserably. 'I thought we would make it.'

Her mother was right. Kit had been warned off.

'Daisy!' All rivers, however clear, flow over mud, and mixed into Kit's passion for Daisy was a sediment – and a wariness – that stemmed from a long time back. 'I wish I could make you understand, my darling Daisy. Everything's all right. Truly.'

'Oh, Kit.' With one of her graceful, unpredictable gestures, Daisy turned to Kit, and her arms snaked up his chest and around his neck. 'Are you sure?' She pressed her body into his and willed him to say: Come with me.

Tempted to say 'to hell with it', aching from the contact, Kit hesitated – and thirty seconds passed that were to colour the rest of his life.

With a waft of bruised geranium, Daisy released him, turned and made her way across the lawn to the terrace. 'I'll see you in London,' she called.

'Daisy.' In panic at the peremptory leavetaking, Kit moved too fast, slipped and fell onto a knee. Wincing, he scrambled to his feet while Daisy's diminishing figure slid in and out of the shadows, insubstantial and unearthly. Then he limped after her, caught up and grabbed one of the straps of her pink dress. 'Don't say it like that.'

Daisy waited for Kit to drop his hand. 'I understand, Kit, really I do. Look, I've been meaning to tell you. There's someone else . . . someone who wants to marry me.' Her beauty had returned and in the stormy afternoon, she seemed lit up by the drama of the moment and by an emotion he did not recognize. 'His name is Tim, and I'm probably going to say yes.'

Kit's grip on her shoulder was savage and she cried out.

'You're making it up.'

86

'No.'

'I can't believe it.'

With a shrug Daisy moved away. 'It was fun, wasn't it, Kit? I enjoyed our time together.'

'Fun . . .' The word hung in the dusk. Kit stood motionless as she walked towards the house. 'Yes, it was,' she called over her shoulder. 'I shall think of it when I'm back in London.'

'Daisy. Listen to me . . .' Kit was planted into the stone.

'It didn't take much, did it?' A thin, disembodied voice floated back to him.

'To do what?' he called out, forgetting there were other people in the villa. 'To do what, Daisy?' he bellowed in bewilderment.

'To be put off.'

Daisy vanished through the curtains at the french windows.

No sponging on their good will. No sponging on their good will.

The overnight train from Nice to Paris clacked out the message and Matty, a book unread in her lap, listened to it. Sometimes it sounded as hard and metallic as Aunt Susan, and at others it whispered as the train glided over points and down gradients.

Perhaps she was a little light-headed with fever from the infected bites, for strange thoughts filtered in and out of her brain. They drifted, tantalizing and out of reach, and she tried to catch them – rebellious, daringly coloured butterflies in the bell-jar of her mind.

The mirror in the compartment swung to the rhythm of the train, and her reflection became a many-angled composition. There was her blotched face, so different from Daisy's beauty, which Matty would never have. The demon of jealousy stirred. So unlovable compared to Daisy, it whispered, so uninteresting, so unformed.

No sponging on their good will.

Outside the window, France slid past, the lights of towns and villages beaded along the track. Already it was cooler, and when they nosed between foothills of the Alpes-Maritimes a scent of pine overlaid the smoke.

Matty poured water into the basin and began to wash for dinner. Two years ago, she had been browsing through a selection of American periodicals and had come across an article by the American feminist, Emma Goldman, which she had never forgotten. Emma had said: 'True emancipation begins neither in the polls, nor in the courts. It begins in a woman's soul.'

Matty well remembered her shock when she read the words – a sense that she had encountered something daring and grand in scope. Of course, she did not consider they applied to her – Emma was much too heroic for the soul that huddled inside Matty's delicate frame, the stepping stones to Emma's bold state of mind too far apart.

And yet. And yet.

No sponging on their good will.

She thought back to the Villa Lafayette, criss-crossed with vivid sensation – sun, sea, the intensities of falling in love, jealousy. Marcus and Flora. Daisy and Kit. Mosquito bites. Sweat-bathed nights. Unfamiliar longings.

He wouldn't want me, Matty told herself, hugging a mental picture of a remote figure who made conversation about Damascus and roses. Never. But then, she added, that was not surprising. She wouldn't have wanted herself.

She began to dress.

With a shriek the train steamed into the station in Paris and came to a halt. For a moment there was peace, and then porters began to move down the platform to the sleeping compartments. Steam spread in layers under the roof, windows released from leather straps and doors swung open. A trickle of passengers descended from the train.

Matty paused before negotiating the drop to the platform in her high-heeled shoes, and a porter came to her aid. Despite no sleep, for she had sat up thinking all night, she was stylishly dressed in a grey georgette suit and a head-hugging hat. A green silk scarf fluttered from her neck, and emerald earrings glinted in the early light. She was followed by Flora, feeling unwieldy and all elbows in a silk coat and matching dress.

A porter ordered their taxi, stowed luggage and installed them inside. Hung-over from the brandy he had consumed after dinner and exhausted after a sleepless night, Kit gave an over-large tip and climbed in after the girls.

It was still early, but the gas-lights in the city had already been extinguished. A night-army was in the process of dispersing – cess-pool cleaners and street-car track repairers whose acetylene torches spluttered violet sparks which turned yellow in the dawn – but for this half-hour or so, the city hovered, half nocturnal, half diurnal, in the pearled light.

A horse-drawn cart had misjudged its path and was slewed across the street outside the station, so the driver chose an alternative route, which took them through back streets and shabby, peeling *quartiers*. Kit caught the scuttle of a prostitute and her pimp, and the opium stagger of a woman emerging from a *fumerie* in the Avenue Bosquet. The beauty in the sinister caught his attention, not for the first time. The Parisian underworld, for instance: secret, violent, full of mysterious *oubliettes* and paradisical dreams, erotic, drug-filled and often fatal. He wished that he, too, was staggering into the dawn.

The car pushed across the Quai de la Mégisserie where the *clochards* were stirring, and roosters in the seed stores crowed. The sun was rising behind Notre Dame and the smell of bread and ground coffee perfumed the air.

The beauty of the buildings and the Seine caught at Kit. His limbs and head hurt from the brandy, and the aftermath of alcohol and weariness was indistinguishable from the ache for and loss of Daisy.

'Oh, look,' said Flora, bunched into her corner of the car. 'Flowers. Masses of them.' Kit peered obediently through his window into the sun. But all he could see were the slippery lines of a distorted face. His own.

*

On deck the breeze sharpened as the ferry drew out beyond the confines of Calais harbour. A skein of gulls followed the wake, chorusing to each other. Every so often they dived for fish and scraps, and rose gleaming into the sky.

Because he was tired, Kit felt the change in temperature more acutely. He turned up the collar of his mackintosh and pulled his trilby low over his eyes. Below the ferry, the water churned ice-green, flecked with rubbish and orange peel. The coast of France was fading out of sight. Drinks were being served in the first-class bar and lunch in the restaurant. Kit wanted neither and, unless his hangover wore off, the odds were that he would never eat or drink again.

He slumped on the rail, and allowed the spray to spatter him. A gull rose, with a piece of melon rind in its beak, and it was now that Kit realized he was deeply and bitterly angry.

Kit darling, dearest. Don't pester me. I can't . . . I can't take it. Why don't you run along and play with your sisters? Leave me alone, dearest, there's a good boy.

The echo of an old memory, its lies and betrayals mixed with the new ones, fermented in Kit's mind. With it was the knowledge that he should have said something to Daisy but had failed to do so. It was too late.

Tim Coats. Well, Flora had warned him.

A heave from the ship brought him up sharply against the rail. He retched. Acid burned in his stomach, as corrosive as the mental picture of taking Tim Coats by the throat and of squeezing until the skin flowered bruises and Tim was broken. Whoever he was, of course.

Concerned for him, Flora watched Kit out of the restaurant window. Matty and she were eating lunch, which was good. Especially the salted English butter and mint sauce. Flora fell on them as eagerly as on long-lost friends, ate lashings and enjoyed every mouthful. After she had finished she left Matty to a second cup of coffee, went on deck and sat down out of the wind where she could keep an eye on her brother.

Kit was bent over the rail, and Flora's feeling of well-being was eclipsed. God knew what he was thinking, and where he had left it with Daisy, but she suspected it was at a point satisfactory to neither. The breeze had swelled into a wind, and she pulled her hat down firmly onto her head and drove the pin into the thickest part of her coiled plait to anchor it. She was glad to be going home. Villa Lafayette had been fun, but it was an odd place. She had glimpsed adult feelings and their consequences – which had made her uneasy. At this point, a less than pleasing recollection of Marcus's moustache tickling her upper lip intruded on her thoughts. Under the protection of her hat, Flora turned red.

Flora yawned and leant back. One of the first things she would do on her return was to check on Danny and the hounds, and take a look at Myfanwy, the foal. With luck, the blackberries would be at their peak and she planned an expedition up Itchel Lane. How soothing, she thought, and how English I am. The mellowness lasted precisely a minute and a half. Flora had forgotten they were returning to a financial crisis, to Rupert and the manoeuvres that would have to be made to resolve their problems. What manoeuvres? she asked herself, failing, yet again, to come up with a solution.

'Don't even think of it,' Kit had warned Flora at dinner on the train the previous evening when she suggested she went out to work, and he frowned at her for discussing family matters in front of Matty. 'Women and work do not go together in Father's reckoning.'

'But it would make sense.' Flora was aware that she was not very persuasive, but she persisted. 'And lots of women are beginning to work these days.'

'What would you do?'

'Couldn't she learn to type?' interjected Matty unexpectedly.

She could, Kit replied, having considered the suggestion. But it probably would not get Flora very far.

'Listen, old girl.' Kit had flicked a finger against the wine glass so that it rang – a warning note. 'You won't get out of the front door. Father would chain you up like Bluebeard rather than have a daughter who worked.'

Muddle. Flora squinted through her half-closed lids. I muddle through. We muddle through. Typing? The notion of an office did

91

not appeal. Medicine? She permitted herself a vision of driving around Nether Hinton in the pony trap with a black doctor's bag beside her. But medicine involved rather more than cutting a dash around a village. Examinations for one thing. Father? Kit was right. He would chain her up – or the modern equivalent.

What it boiled down to was that Flora had neither the worldliness, the knowledge, nor the habit of taking charge of herself to make dramatic changes. Sobering but true.

She picked up her copy of Michael Arlen's *The Green Hat* and smoothed the pages. Daisy had recommended it and she now knew why: its heroine was very like Daisy.

Her thoughts flitted this way and that and, after a while, Flora fell asleep.

Three other women were eating breakfast in the restaurant. One was young and expensively dowdy. The second, decked in unnecessary furs and made up with scarlet lipstick and Vaselined lids, looked no better than she should be – but since she was undoubtedly beautiful and exuded inviting sexuality, men hovered at her table. At a table opposite, an older woman in a grey felt hat and a sensible Harris tweed suit hugged a glass of brandy and soda as if her life depended on it.

To give herself courage Matty also ordered a brandy and soda. When the steward brought it the restaurant heaved with a clatter of china, and she braced her feet on the carpet. Her hand shook only a little when she raised the glass to her lips, and Matty was encouraged. Freed from the heat of Villa Lafayette, she felt better. Stronger. More determined. More like the women she wished to be like. She gulped down another mouthful.

If Matty was going to do what she planned, it had to be now while her courage was high and her inhibitions were down. The moment was right – a powerful instinct told her so – but her terror was such that she thought she was going to faint. Two minutes later, half the brandy and soda had disappeared, and fanned, warm and supportive, through her. Dear Emma, Matty headed her prayer, whoever you are, I want you to know you have a lot to answer for and I, for one, hope that you are right.

She got up, permitted the waiter to pull back her chair and to escort her out of the restaurant. Outside, the wind immediately attacked her hat and roared past her ears, and waves threw drifts of spume over her face. Kit was still standing at the rail, gazing back towards the vanished French coastline. Stepping carefully over the deck in her inappropriately high heels, Matty approached him.

'Excuse me,' she said softly.

Evidently Kit did not hear her for he said nothing.

'Excuse me,' she repeated, and touched his forearm. Puzzled by the interruption, Kit turned his head and looked down at his travelling companion. Later, he remembered thinking how badly she carried fatigue. She looked ill, frightened and very small. The wind whipped a strand of hair across her cheek and she pushed it back with a hand that trembled visibly.

'I hope you don't mind me interrupting you,' she said.

Normally polite, Kit's expression was not inviting and she shrank inside. 'No,' he said, barely concealing his reluctance. 'Of course not. Do you need help?'

Matty lost her nerve and floundered. 'I was just wondering what time we will dock.'

Kit pushed aside thoughts of the weary business of settling debts and making decisions about what to sell, what to keep, how to stay solvent, and consulted his watch. 'Another hour,' he replied. 'Are you feeling all right?'

'Perfectly, thank you.'

There was silence.

'Could I get you something to drink?' he asked over the noise of the wind.

'No. No, thank you. I've had a very good lunch.'

After that exchange Kit appeared to forget she was there, and gazed out over a sea heaving with white crests. Matty looked down at the deck, at her feet braced against the swell. Someone had dropped a raisin scone, and it lay squashed into a heap of black and white crumbs. Anger at Kit's indifference stirred life into Matty, and her skinny demon knocked in her chest. She tugged at Kit's sleeve.

'There is something I would like to ask you,' she blurted out, but half her words were lost. Kit cupped a hand to his ear. 'Something I would like to ask you,' she shouted into the wind.

'Yes,' he said, tight-lipped.

Matty was almost deterred by his stony expression, but her anger was growing. Go on, it urged.

Propelled by its force, Matty began again. 'I wondered . . .' The spectre of Emma Goldman filled her vision with a grand and daring dream. Matty ground out between set teeth: 'I think you should marry me.'

CHAPTER SEVEN

THE ENSUING furore was astonished, furious, bitchy and sometimes deeply critical.

Flora took one disbelieving look at her brother as they drove from Farnham station to Nether Hinton and burst into tears. 'But Matty hates horses, Kit. Can't bear them. She told me. They give her nightmares. You can't marry her.'

'Flora!' In the half limbo that overtakes someone who has leapt over the edge, Kit was irritated by Flora's distress. 'That's the least of my worries.'

'Kit . . . why on earth?' Flora blew her nose hard and tried to concentrate on something neutral. The car drove on through fields with crops stooked in matronly rows, and the countryside displayed itself in a palette of English colours, grey-blue, green and post-harvest gold. Flora delved into her scanty resources for the right comparison. 'It's the money, isn't it, Kit? Matty's like those poor women in Africa being sold off for their nose rings or neck shackles. The house *isn't* worth that.' She pulled hard on the hanging strap and looked straight ahead. 'Not for someone like her.'

'Why not for Matty?'

'She's — she's not your type, Kit. Anyway, everyone knows you love Daisy and you don't love Matty, and you should love the person you marry.'

Quite right, thought Kit. Experience had taught him otherwise and he was touched by his sister's defence of romantic love. 'Even so, I can't go back on my word now,' he said.

'Of course you can. It's not too late yet.' She blew her nose again and stuffed the handkerchief into her handbag. 'Why on earth did you suggest it in the first place?'

95

Kit considered telling the truth – that Matty had caught him when alcohol, remorse, anger and jealousy had reduced him to the lowest point, when one course of action seemed as good as another and, for once, he had acted without thinking. Then, there was the truth (admittedly crude) that Matty had money, which she was offering him in bucketloads – and the whole bloody mess was about money. A business deal, if you like, she had pointed out, pale under the mosquito ravages. You need money, I have it.

What do *you* want? he had asked. And she had told him. I want a home. A place where I can be myself. You have that.

She had stepped back, rocking with the swell on her absurd high heels, and named the sum that she was worth. It was, she added, perfectly possible to live in mutual harmony if both parties agreed to be honest. Kit thought he caught a flicker of anger in the brown eyes, and missed the desperation.

'Yes,' he said, his hangover obscuring the sensible answer, 'yes. I accept.'

How straightforward it had been, he thought from his limbo. How uncomplicated and undeceitful. No disappointments, no betrayals. Simply a market transaction struck over Deck 4. The wind blew Matty's hair into chaos and she gave up trying to keep her hat anchored onto her head. Otherwise, braced against the ship's roll, mouth clamped shut, she remained quite still until he was forced to ask her if she would mind leaving him alone.

'*Why* did you do it, Kit?' Flora was hurt and puzzled.

Whatever the nature of the bargain, Kit knew one thing: since he had chosen to say yes Matty was owed loyalty. 'Matty is all right,' he said. 'Don't worry.' He tucked his arm into Flora's. 'I rely on your support, Flora.' Flora refused to look at him.

'Promise me,' he said. 'No scenes. No regrets. Just your backing.'

'I suppose everything must change.' Flora hated change and distrusted it.

Perhaps she and Matty would be friends, share confidences and trust each other. Perhaps not. In her heart Flora considered Matty feeble.

Tyson slowed the car, turned into Croft Lane and drove past

the church. Flora looked out of the window towards Dick's Wood: Rob Frost's team had been at work and now they were resting in their shaft harness and harrumphing into nosebags. Rob and his horses were rarely apart, and he sat smoking on a sack a few feet away, dressed, as always, in his father's working suit and puttees, from the war, which he could not be persuaded to abandon.

They were home. Kit's drawn, troubled face made Flora feel guilty and she pulled herself together. 'I promise, Kit, no scenes.'

The house was as they had left it, only the impressions were sharper for having been away – woodsmoke, polish and damp. After the brilliance of France, it was familiar yet different: dark, muted, composed of greys, dull whites, deep greens, browns. Flora sniffed and smiled.

'Hallo, Robbie,' she said to the figure waiting at the bottom of the steps.

Tanned from a fortnight in Brighton and even heavier around the waist from stout and fish and chip suppers on the seafront, Robbie had been idle quite long enough in her opinion. She surged forward, large and snapping with energy.

'How's my special girl?' Flora managed a smile and Robbie did not notice how fixed it was. 'Well, I must say I don't think the postman had much to do while you were away. Only two postcards from France.' Flora persevered with her smile. 'But, then, I'm sure there was far too much to do to think about me, and here I was worrying that you were well and looking after yourselves.' Robbie patted the silk on Flora's shoulders. 'Very nice, dear, but rather Frenchy for home. I think abroad has suited you, although you're a bit peaky.' To Kit she said, 'Looks a bit as if *you* have been overdoing it, Mr Kit.'

Planted in front of the empty fireplace, Rupert waited for his children in the drawing room and smoked a pipe. Last time he had been in France . . .

. . . *August 1914.*

It was chaos. The Central Co-ordinating Committee's *War Book* in Whitehall ran to several million words and covered every move, problem, question, and library book borrowed by a would-be soldier. In the first two weeks of the war those regulations had called for 120,000 horses: trams yielded up their heavy chargers, farmers their work-horses, gentlemen their thoroughbreds, and a kicking, shuddering force was urged up the gangways into waiting ships.

With them went 80,000 men, 80,000 rifles, bandoliers and iron rations. Stores, forage, field-guns, shells and munitions. 80,000 hearts beating with a mixture of apprehension, jingoism, a let's-get-at-'em and an idea that the war ahead would act like Condy's fluid on latrines – disinfectant to wash away the indulgences of Edwardian England.

How the horses screamed when the cranes grappled the slings around their bodies, how they died of terror and vertigo in the holds, how they quivered on the cobbled quayside at Boulogne. How their grooms sweated and vomited down in the rolling holds. One of them, Eric Danfer, was past it by the time they got to Boulogne, the first casualty of the war.

'Sir,' asked a new recruit, Danny Ovens by name, 'what do I do with Danfer?'

Rupert cast his eyes over the bodies hanging out of windows, up lamp-posts, crowding the hill behind the town and saw, pinpointed among the tricolours, two plain black habits.

'Give him to the nuns,' he said, in the clipped manner that hid his nerves.

The camp was four miles away from the town. The march took them through choked streets and up a steep hill to the heights overlooking the sea. It would be some time before the officers' horses were unloaded – though the transport officer was doing his best – and Major Sir Rupert Dysart tramped with his men over cobblestones in the blazing heat.

When darkness fell over the untidy canvas village and the paymaster had refused to exchange any more pennies for francs, a smell of blancoed webbing, hot men and beer assaulted the nose. Civilians from the town walked up to the encampment to watch. Since many of them were women, the sounds of laughter and flesh-on-flesh came from the shadows and the few private corners.

One of the ladies, with large eyes and frizzed hair, accosted Rupert as he strolled along the cliff top. She was older than her sisters, but fresh, appealing, willing. She had light brown hair between her legs and under her arms, strong thighs and a handsome bosom under her cotton basque. Afterwards, Rupert lay beside her, grateful and satiated, for it had been two years since Hesther had permitted him her bed.

Rupert stayed with her for a long time that evening, concentrating on being alive, on breathing, on feeling army serge rub against his skin, her flesh under his lips. He forgot that he, too, was older than most of his brother officers and that he had left behind a house, children and a wife who did not love him and whom he had grown to dislike . . .

'Here are our travellers,' said Robbie, advancing through the door and manoeuvring herself directly into Rupert's line of vision. 'All travel-stained, so mind you don't keep them too long, sir. They need to wash.'

Autumn sun slanted in through windows and exposed bare patches on the carpet, but the room seemed chilly and Flora shivered.

'Sherry?' Rupert asked, as if neither had been away. Without waiting for an answer he poured a glass and held it out to Flora. 'Why are you shivering? Go and put some clothes on if you're cold.'

When Flora returned in her less sophisticated but more serviceable dinner frock, Rupert and Kit were talking hard. There was more grey in Rupert's hair than Flora remembered but, then, she never dared look too hard at him. Rupert's gaze quizzed her. 'Kit's told me his news. He doesn't waste time,' he said. His tone indicated approval.

In truth Rupert had been taken aback by his son's announcement but he was not going to waste breath on what, after all, was welcome news. He balanced his whisky glass on his knee and said, 'I'll contact my agent and the solicitor at once.'

This was the territory on which Rupert operated. There was

no question of asking if Kit was happy, if he loved the girl he was going to marry.

Dinner was conducted in comparative amity and, after Flora had left the men to the port, Rupert shifted his bulk into a comfortable position and lit a cigar.

'Good foaler, do you think?' he asked his son, tapping his silver cigarette case.

'Good Lord, sir. How would I know?'

'The hips, my boy. Look at them. What do you think you do with horses? You don't want a pig in the poke. You want value for money. And an heir.'

Kit did not wish to think about Matty's body. With an effort he recollected her non-existent hips and dismissed their implications. 'May I remind you, sir, that it's Matty who has the money. Perhaps she should look carefully at me.'

'She did, my boy. And she liked what she saw. A house. A title. A good-looking chap with no obvious vices.'

'Tell me, sir, were you always so cynical?'

The thick fingers clenched for a second and left prints on the polished table. 'Are you being rude, my boy? Or have you come back Frenchified?' Rupert's gaze slid past Kit and rested on a portrait of a long-dead Dysart.

Kit wadded up his napkin and tossed it onto the table. 'Will you excuse me?' he said. 'I've got things to do.'

'Kit!'

Kit paused in the doorway. 'Yes?'

'It's been done before, you know.'

'Selling oneself for a mess of pottage?'

Rupert gave one of his rare laughs and stubbed out the cigar. 'Well, I wouldn't call a quarter of a million pounds that exactly, but, yes, if you like.'

Sleep did not come easily to Kit that night and he drifted in a half world, rocked by boats and trains. A pinpoint of light danced before him, widened, expanded and burst into dazzling circles. Then he was riding in the sun's clean glare towards the white-out of the horizon. Sweat trickled down his shoulders and under his arms; camel dung tanged in his nostrils and the eyes of Arab boys were dirt-ringed and limpid. Kit rode on, shamefully aroused, pursued by a sense of terrible loss.

You can change your mind before it is too late, Flora had said. But a pebble rolling downhill has a habit of gathering speed. From Kit's thirty seconds of hesitation in the garden of Villa Lafayette and from an ill-timed hangover, the stone skimmed and bounced along the slope, faster and more purposeful by the moment. Rupert was quick to inform the editor of the social page in *The Times*, where the announcement was read and debated. To withdraw then was to humiliate Matty, and Kit shrank from that. A date was settled, caterers alerted, dressmakers put on overtime. Matty was deluged with congratulations, some genuine, others not.

Oh, yes, it was far too late for Kit to change his mind and, with preparations so far advanced, no honourable man would consider doing so.

'Good Lord,' said Polly in her most irritating manner from the depths of an old-fashioned sofa in the morning room of her house at Askew Road, 'selling yourself to the devil, aren't you, Kit?'

Polly was pregnant and it made her lethargic. She was unfortunate in that it made her look awful as well, with dispirited ribbons of hair slinking round her head. 'Well, at least you'll have money.'

'For Christ's sake,' Kit was driven to snapping, 'nobody talks about anything else.'

'But that's what it's about?' Polly peered at her brother and life came into her face. 'Isn't it, Kit? Isn't that why you've done it – because the family is in such a mess?'

Kit silently acknowledged the hit and realized he had yet another problem: defending Matty from gossip. She may have offered herself as a gilt-edged commodity but that did not mean that every matron from Mayfair to Knightsbridge should have a field day over the exact nature of the engaged couple's relationship.

He set about spreading the information, discreetly, that his forthcoming marriage was the result of a bolt of lightning which had struck them both on holiday.

'You realize this is suicide?' Max Longborough telephoned from the Old Cataract Hotel in Assuan. 'Who is the girl? Have you gone mad?'

'No,' said Kit, feeling that was precisely what had happened. 'Back me up, old boy. Please.'

'I'll do one better and take you away. Come with me on the Petra trip. If the girl loves you she'll wait.'

'It's arranged, I'm afraid, Max. I can't back out. Nor should I.'

'Chivalry died with King Arthur, my boy, and there is absolutely no need to martyr yourself for outdated notions of being a gentleman.'

'No,' said Kit.

'You're talking shackles for life, old son. Wouldn't you prefer what I'm offering?'

'I would, but it's not possible.'

Max cursed all women in his tatterdemalion Arabic, and then asked, 'Do you love her. *Bouleversé?*'

'Yes, of course I do,' lied Kit.

'Bollocks,' said Max, and Kit imagined him at the other end of the line, smoking furiously and shrieking into the telephone. 'You do nothing of the sort. I can tell.'

MONTE CARLO
DEAREST KIT STOP I AM SORRY I AM SORRY STOP I
MADE YOU DO THIS STOP WILL YOU FORGIVE ME
FOR BEING SO STUPID STOP I DO UNDERSTAND
ABOUT LUGGAGE LABELS AND TELEPHONE CALLS
STOP REALLY I DO STOP I WAS BEING STUPID AND

SELFISH STOP IF YOU PERSIST IN MARRYING
SOMEONE ELSE PLEASE NOT MATTY STOP SHE DOES
NOT LOVE YOU STOP PLEASE NOT ANYONE BUT ME
STOP DAISY

I CANNOT BACK OUT NOW STOP KIT

DON'T UNDERSTAND STOP WILL TRY STOP HAVE
YOU FORGIVEN ME STOP CANNOT BEAR IT
OTHERWISE STOP DAISY

'*Nice* work,' said Susan Chudleigh icily when she arrived at Upper
Brook Street. 'Very smart girl.'

Dressed in blue silk with a scale pattern superimposed on it,
she rested a hand on a hip.

'Did Daisy come back with you?' asked Matty.

'I've sent her to Monte with Annabel for a little while. They
can stay with the Beauchamps. Your telegram came as a great
shock and she needed to get away. You will appreciate that, of
course.' The lid of the pink glass cigarette box rattled as Susan
rooted around with a fingernail. 'You *do* appreciate that, don't
you, Matilda?'

'Of course.'

Susan's gaze lingered on Matty's Molyneux crêpe evening
gown and her pencilled eyebrows crawled up her forehead. 'Did
you sleep with him, Matilda? Is that it? Surely it can't just be the
money.' When Matty did not answer, Susan gave a supercilious
smile. 'Aha, so that's it. Well, I never thought you capable of
jumping over traces. I must say, I think it's rather daring of you.'

'Aunt Susan, it's *nothing* like that. I couldn't possibly do such
a thing.'

'No, well. Perhaps not.' The suggestion that Susan approved
faded from her voice. 'I don't suppose you would.'

That left her to cast around, and fail, to find the explanation
as to why Kit Dysart – who could have had any heiress he chose
– should plump for the plucked chicken that was her niece. Oh,
well, she concluded, I suppose one heiress is much like another,

certainly after twenty or so years of marriage, and perhaps Kit is not choosy.

Matty nerved herself to ask, 'How is Daisy?'

Susan fiddled with the cocktail shaker on the drinks table. 'In a dangerous mood, I would say.' Ice clinked in the cocktail glass. 'However, *I* will have to deal with that. More worry.' She jabbed the cocktail stick into a maraschino cherry. 'I think Daisy doesn't feel you behaved well.' Susan's façade slipped. 'Nor do I.'

'No, I don't suppose I did,' agreed Matty, the exchange slashing the razor-thin reserves of her confidence into ribbons.

Clink, went the ice in Susan's glass. She turned to face Matty. 'Why the hell, Matilda, did you have to go and do this to us? Why Kit Dysart – of all the men in London you could have bribed into marrying you? Is that your way of thanking us after all we have done? I think you are wicked, I really do.'

See, Matty addressed her dead parents, Emma having temporarily deserted her. If you hadn't died, none of this would be happening.

Marcus was the only member of the Chudleigh family to express concern for Matty. 'What about you?' he asked. 'Are you quite sure this is what you want?'

Used to hostility or indifference, Matty was taken aback.

'After all,' said Marcus, eyeing the whisky decanter, 'you're in for a life sentence, and I don't think you're really cut out for the lady-of-the-manor bit. They're a rum lot, too. The old man's a touch potty, I think. Lost it in the war, they say.'

Images crystallized of dispensing tea and cakes at the annual fête, of hosting dinner parties and hunting teas. Of being looked at. Oh my God, thought Matty. What have I done?

Once launched, Marcus persisted. 'Kit will want a good show, he's that sort of fellow. I mean, we do know you better than most and speaking honestly . . .'

Something stirred in Matty which, because it was unfamiliar, she did not at first recognize as protest. 'Oh, no, you don't,' she said.

'Don't what?'

'You don't know me at all, Marcus. You have no idea of what I'm like.'

Marcus gave in to the decanter and poured himself two fingers of malt. Over the glass he assessed his cousin. 'I'm beginning to think that we don't,' he replied, his tone conveying several nuances, none of them flattering. Clearly, he felt that the conversation was swimming into deep emotional waters so he paddled for the shore. 'Anyway, I should tell you I don't approve. I think it a mad idea and,' he got to his feet to emphasize the point, 'very disloyal to Daisy. As her brother, I hold that against you.'

Later, spooning up consommé at a silent dinner table, Matty had a good idea of how Don Quixote must have felt when he tilted at his windmill.

At the end of October, Daisy returned from Monte Carlo, French-hatted, tanned, unapproachably dazzling. Almost immediately she went away again, to stay with Annabel in Yorkshire, and did not return until the week of the wedding. She said nothing to Matty at all.

Three-quarters of an hour before her wedding, Matty, acutely conscious of the marinade of expensive materials sheathing her body, descended the stairs at Number 5 Upper Brook Street. She was met by Daisy at the bottom, and it took considerable self-restraint not to turn on her heel and go straight back up.

The hall and drawing room were filled with floral arrangements by Constance Spry who, as a special favour to Susan, had arrived in person prior to the party the previous evening to tuck what looked suspiciously like a cabbage into an architecturally principled arrangement of white flowers. The effect was very chic. Beside it lay Matty's bouquet, a stark, Japanese-inspired spiral of hot-house lilies.

Daisy's glass was angled precariously and champagne puddled on the skirt of her tiered crêpe dress. Above it, her cleverly made-up face was beautiful, implacable – and drunk. 'Congratulations, Matty. You've done it.'

Matty's heart, already pounding, beat a tattoo of panic that the scene which, so far, had been avoided, was brewing. 'I don't know what you mean,' she lied.

'Spare me, Matty. We all know what this pantomime is about.' Daisy grabbed the newel post for support. 'You've won,' she announced to her cousin, and up-ended the remains of the champagne into her mouth. 'Put it this way . . . and I'm sorry to be crude. We both wanted the same man. My mistake was that I didn't realize you were prowling around the same territory.'

'Daisy. Don't! Please.'

'I'm told that surprise is the essence of attack, and I see now it is. Perhaps you should join the army, Matty?' Daisy seemed struck by the idea and looked thoughtfully at her cousin. 'Of course, I would be the first to admit that all is fair in love and war.'

'You're drunk.' Matty picked up her train and prepared to edge around Daisy, who frowned and dropped her glass onto the parquet floor.

'Hold on, Matty,' she said, and her voice slid into an unnervingly sober cadence. 'No insults. That's my side of things.'

Matty tried again. 'Daisy, why don't you go and get some coffee? There isn't long before the car arrives.'

'So what if I'm tight? It's not my wedding.' She brushed at the champagne stain, and repeating slowly and with precision, 'It's not my wedding, is it?' Then she snapped her fingers. 'Don't worry, no one will know. Except you.'

'*Please, Daisy.*'

'"Please, Daisy." Did you say please when you asked Kit to marry you? It's a well-brought-up thing to do, you know. Saying "please" when you propose.' Taking Matty off guard, Daisy leant forward and cupped her cousin's chin. 'Please, Matty, I'm going to say – *please* listen to me, I have something I wish to say to you, and I want to say it to your face.'

Thud, thud went a machine in Matty's chest. It shook into life her nerve endings and sent messages to her brain: take flight; endure pain; taste joy; face whatever is coming.

106

Matty steadied. She put her hands behind her back and said quietly, 'Do you want to say it in the hall where someone might overhear?'

'I don't mind in the least where I say it.' Daisy gripped Matty's chin until her eyes watered. 'I want you to remember your wedding day as the day we were honest with each other.'

In Honiton lace and the Verral tiara, her mother's earrings flashing, Matty's face turned whiter than the creamy antique veil. She forced herself to return Daisy's stare. Daisy looked searchingly at her, and then, abruptly, dropped her hand and stepped back. With a flash of guilt, Matty saw a kohl-tinted tear trail down Daisy's face.

'Champagne tears,' said Daisy, wiping her nose with the back of her hand – even then managing to remain graceful and exciting. 'Too stupid.'

Matty began to shake in earnest at the enormity of what she had brought about. At her instigation, three hundred starched and chiffoned guests sat waiting in St Margaret's, Westminster. At the reception, enough food to service the Sun King's court was beginning to curl at the edges. Florists had been plundered, seamstresses had sat up all night. Two families had been turned upside down.

Unexpectedly, Matty had played a *grande finesse*. As a result, a man who had no feeling for her was waiting to marry her and take her away through a pea-souper fog to a strange life, and her cousin's exquisite face had turned into a *museau* of grief.

Heedless of creases, Matty clutched her arms around her chest and hugged herself so tightly it almost hurt. The slippery material of her dress folded over her fingers and she rubbed it with her thumbs. Fright was making her breathless.

Daisy surveyed the half-crouching figure, and a gleam of sense penetrated her. 'Here,' she said impatiently. 'I shouldn't have said anything.' She pulled Matty's arms down. 'Stop it, Matty, and I'll stop it too. Otherwise you'll never get through.'

Matty tugged at her imprisoned hands. 'Say it, Daisy. Whatever it was you were going to say.'

Daisy's heels screeched faintly along the parquet floor as she steadied herself. 'It's not important any more.'

'Say it, Daisy.'

The command brought Daisy up short. Suddenly she pressed a hand to her mouth while she fought to bring herself under control. Her dress was wet from spilt champagne, and her mouth was dry. 'I was going to say this in spite and anger, but now I just say it out of grief, Matty, and hope you remember it.'

'What, Daisy? For God's sake, tell me.'

Spreading out her fingers in a gesture of hopelessness, Daisy bent her head and said, 'When he comes to you tonight, he will be thinking of me.'

There was a long, long pause.

'Of course he will,' said Matty. 'Who else?' Shocked into silence, Daisy lifted her head and stared at the diamond-frosted, satin-encased bride. 'You don't imagine,' said Matty, 'I would think anything else. I'm not stupid. But I think *you* should remember that Kit was in trouble.'

'It was my temper, that hateful telegram, his father . . . all sorts of things.' Daisy's fist pummelled her anguish onto the newel post. 'Why you, Matty? Couldn't you have left it alone, however much you disliked me?'

The intimacies of hatred are as powerful and revealing as those of love. The cousins looked at each other and made their discoveries.

They could hear the family preparing to leave the drawing room. Matty lifted her veil and pulled it down over her face. Under its silken confines she paled into ghostliness. 'Don't you see?' she said. 'I was the only one who could help.'

'My God,' said Daisy, 'I didn't know you were so hard.'

Daisy finished vomiting. The bout had been prolonged and noisy, but it catapulted her into sobriety. The final glass of champagne had sunk into her cramping stomach, which signalled its rebellion. Daisy knew she had made a major mistake and fled upstairs.

There, she had stuck her finger down her throat to speed up the process.

Black letters spelt out ROYAL DOULTON from the depths of the lavatory bowl. Daisy stared so hard at them that they wavered in front of her watering eyes. After a bit, she hauled herself onto her elbows and rested her head between her hands while she waited for the world to stabilize.

'You overdid it, my girl,' she said aloud.

Being sick twenty-five minutes before Matty's wedding was not the simple, cleansing action Daisy would have liked: it had not purged draggled pride, or exasperation at her own behaviour, or the hurt.

But, then, loss was a long business — a bereavement of expectation and hope, a ratification of loneliness. Loss meant that something unique had been given marching orders . . . for first, between her and Kit, there would have been passion, and then the strands of trust and affection to bind them together through the years.

Requiem for something that did not survive. She pictured a tombstone set in the bloody wreckage of her heart. With an effort, she dragged herself to her feet, sat on the edge of the bath and permitted herself to cry.

'I love you,' Kit had said in the gardens of the Villa Lafayette, inhaling the scent of her hair.

'How much?' challenged Daisy, who had not read *King Lear*. 'Tell me.'

'Let me see.' Kit dropped a kiss onto one eyelid and kept it pinned shut with his lips. Then he pinioned the second.

Daisy got in first. 'You could ask properly to marry me.'

Kit gave up on her eyelids and concentrated on exploring Daisy's fascinating neck. 'Not yet,' he said, and half closed his eyes. 'You must wait until I'm ready.'

The sun slid down into the sea, and in the misty violet evening Kit had kissed her over and over again until she felt the sweetness of abandonment.

He never did ask her properly.

There was a hammering at the bedroom door.

'Hurry up, Daisy,' Marcus said. 'The parents are agitating. Are you all right?'

'Fine,' she lied.

Daisy pulled up her skirt, extracted her handkerchief from her stocking top and stood up. 'You're not used to being thwarted, are you?' she asked her reflection in the mirror. 'You don't like it.'

She pulled open the drawer and rummaged among the gloves and belts. At the back, concealed by a rose-coloured scarf, lay a photograph. Taken in France, it caught Kit standing at the water's edge, shirt sleeves rolled as high as they could go, trousers held up by a fisherman's leather belt. He had not known he was being photographed, and the print captured a young man's dreaming face and sun-bleached hair. She sat on the dressing stool and said goodbye.

'I hope you think all the suffering is worth it, you stubborn fool,' she murmured and stroked the printed mouth. Her finger slid to the eyes, hovered, and then she took her hand away. For a few more seconds she concentrated on assembling fragments of memory. They would have to last a long time.

A minute later, she was sitting at her dressing table, redoing her face. Damp chestnut hair lay on her forehead and stuck to the sides of her cheeks and she rubbed it between her fingers. Her lipstick went on unevenly and she smoothed it impatiently over her lips. Framed by still matted lashes, her eyes looked out from under her hat with a new expression.

Tucking her handkerchief back into her stocking, Daisy pulled her suspenders into line, dropped her skirt, picked up her corsage of white rosebuds and maidenhair fern. A rose petal shed on the crêpe and she brushed it away.

Something had finished that could never be repeated.

CHAPTER EIGHT

17 January 1930

It was TERRIBLE WEATHER on the day [wrote Susan
Chudleigh to her cousin languishing in the Argyll
wilderness], one of London's best pea-soupers. Matilda
wanted to get married in St James's, but I put my foot
down for St Margaret's. Would you believe it, the
wretched girl nearly collapsed with nerves, but we
brought it off in the end. Still, the Verral diamonds
looked impressive and the champagne was the best
Ambrose could procure. (I must say, Maud, I am hugely
relieved she is off my hands.)

Daisy was ravishing in dark green, and very well
behaved. Portlington's son took a shine, I believe, and
Tim Coats (very, very rich) is as keen as mustard. The
bridegroom gave an excellent speech, and I wore mauve
and white.

Whatever my feelings about Matilda, I have to tell you
I managed a very smart wedding, despite Ambrose's dire
warnings about the need for economy, etc., etc., and the
state of the stock market. During the reception a big
crowd gathered outside No. 5 Stanhope Gate (where the
reception was) but I gave orders not to turn them away.
Why not let them enjoy the sight? Look out for the
Tatler. They have gone to Devon for a few days. After
that they are going East for several months while repairs
are made to Hinton Dysart.

Yes, Ambrose is worried about the financial situation,
thank you for asking. Why America let itself get into such

111

a state, I don't know. It was very irresponsible and now everyone is suffering . . .

Susan stared at the muffled, gritty light filtering through the window, a *moue* of discontent and ill-temper pursing her mouth. Then she rang for the parlourmaid, pointed to the fire and watched in silence while the girl built the coals into a pyramid.

The fire hissed, smoke eddied up the chimney in puffs and Susan opened her account book, which she consulted every Monday morning. The 'outgoings' column now recorded a considerable sum. It was extraordinary how little things – flowers, stockings, confetti, teas at the Ritz – managed to add up to so much. Against the 'incoming' column there now existed an ominous blank. Matty would no longer be paying her aunt a contribution for her upkeep.

Susan very much regretted its absence.

SEFTON HOTEL,
DAWLISH
9 January 1930

Dear Aunt Susan,
I am sorry not to have written sooner, but the journey here was *exhausting* and I have been in bed for the last two days recovering. But I wanted to thank you, first, for arranging the wedding. Second, for looking after me all these years. I also wanted to say I am sorry it was a duty for you rather than a pleasure.

There, she thought, I've said it.

The hotel is comfortable and well run by Mrs Peters. She is a rather lovely woman, with fair curls and an interesting aquiline profile. It is a great relief to be in a place which feels like a home and where we need not dress up. The view from our suite is enchanting, even at this time of year, and there are lots of birds. Kit goes out walking a lot and we meet for dinner . . .

The portable writing desk weighed heavily on Matty's knees. She adjusted it and wriggled into a more comfortable position. It was tempting to write the truth, if only to unburden herself. Tempting but unwise.

The silences between Kit and her were sometimes so oppressive that several times Matty had been on the point of ordering her bags packed and returning to London. Then she became breathless and the world was reduced to concentration on releasing the band twisting around her chest. It was not that Kit was inattentive, far from it, but it was the attention and politeness of a stranger. Which he was, of course. Matty wondered what happened to famous people after they had brought off spectacular coups. Did a new prime minister wake up the morning after the election with a dragging feeling of 'What now?' as she did? Did Rembrandt apply the last brushstroke to Saskia and feel there was nothing more to do after the magnificence of his creation?

Matty picked up her pen. 'The fish is excellent,' she wrote and then inspected her nib. Nothing wrong with that piece of information. The trouble was there was nothing more she wished to say to her aunt.

Fish.

'Your aunt is a piranha,' Kit had informed her over sole coated in prawn sauce.

'What's that?'

'A flesh-eating fish.'

At that they had looked at each other across the table and laughed – for the first time – over the shared joke, which got them over the raw patch after Matty had inadvertently mentioned Daisy and Kit had gone silent.

Fish, Matty thought, and picked up her pen.

A cliff top
11 January

Darling, beloved Daisy,
I am writing this overlooking the sea in the only patch out of the wind that I can find. Forgive the scrawl. The sea is furious, the sky leaden and the rain of the most

penetrating kind, but I want you to know that you looked more beautiful than I have ever seen you at the wedding, and it nearly killed me. I have never loved you so much. I will never feel for anyone like this again.

This is the last time I will ever tell you that, and the last time I can or will write to you. Kit.

Shivering and coughing, Kit eased himself to his feet. Rain was sweeping in from the sea and hit him squarely in the face. Then came the punch of the wind. He stuffed the letter into his mackintosh pocket, turned up his collar and began to pick his way along the sodden turf and patches of scree. The gulls screamed over the wind and, despite his collar, the rain seeped down his back. Again Kit coughed, felt the spider's legs of fever run down his arms and legs, up into his head, and surrendered to them.

UPPER BROOK STREET
14 February

Dear Kit,
Thank you for your letter. Don't worry, you don't have to say anything more. Daisy.

The envelope was addressed to c/o Max Longborough, The Old Cataract Hotel, Assuan, in savage black letters. Daisy laid it on the salver in the hall, ready for the evening post, and picked up the corsage that had just been delivered. 'With the compliments of Mr Turner', read the legend on the card, and underneath, scrawled in black ink, 'Dearest Girl, Do make a chap happy and come to dinner.'

A second, more elaborate, arrangement of orchids lay beside it. That card read: 'Portlington'. Neither of the cards interested Daisy, but the corsages were exquisite and she studied them. Both would add a certain something to her well-aired evening gown, which required an extra touch here or there – else it and she would die of boredom. Perhaps Portlington's orchids at her waist? On the other hand, Turner's gardenia would lie just so on her shoulder and its scent was delicious. Daisy was *not* going to allow herself to think it did not matter one twopenny farthing what she wore to where.

She picked up the gardenia, smelt it, and her newly grown hair fell in a bright screen over her face. Breathing in the scent, she concentrated on assembling her scrambled will-power. Corsages and suchlike had to matter. She would make them matter. They were the pegs on which her future hung. Hats, dresses, fork teas, *thés dansants* ... After all, if you considered something important, then so it was, and never mind that the wounds from her love affair were seeping blood.

Eeny, meeny, miny, mo. Daisy picked up Portlington's orchids.

'All right, old girl?' called Marcus, from the safety of a whisky glass in the drawing room.

'Yes, of course,' she said.

'It does no good to brood moodily over a mirror, you know. It induces instant panic and a highly expensive dash to Elizabeth Arden.'

Daisy laughed. 'Marcus, you are a fool.'

THE OLD CATARACT HOTEL,
ASSUAN
21 April 1930

Dear Flora,

Here we are back in Assuan after an exhausting trip. In fact, it was a bit too much so Kit left me behind in base camp while Max and he rode on into the desert, playing at being Bedouins or something. (Please don't tell him I said that.) I was hoping to write to you with a piece of good news but it has come to nothing. Perhaps next time I write . . .

But I am enjoying myself very much, far more than I imagined I would, and I remember so much more than I thought from my childhood. Anyway, we are going to spend a few days here, sightseeing, and then take a boat down the Nile and begin the leisurely journey back home via Damascus (because I want to see my old house) then on to the great theatre in Ephesus and motor up through Italy. We should miss the hottest weather.

Kit is well, very sunburnt, and excited. He and Max talk for hours and I'm often asleep by the time he comes to bed.

Assuan itself is fascinating. It was once one of the most important towns in Egypt because it lay on Nubia's northern border and, apparently, there was once a brisk trade in gold, ivory, slaves and spices. I've been busy buying jewellery and one or two good paintings which I am looking forward to showing you. With all good wishes, Matty.

PS   I do hope the builders are getting on as fast as possible and it is not too dreadful. Kit wishes to know if they have started on the roof and if they received his instructions?

HINTON DYSART
30 June 1930

Dearest Brother,
In plain words, this is torture. There is dust in monster heaps and no roof over the attics. Father is foaming at the mouth at the inconvenience and has retired to his room and won't come out. Robbie is in the vilest of tempers with me, but is resolutely jolly with Father which he hates. I'm terrified by the pair of them and the staff are threatening to rebel. Meanwhile, I picture you and Matty tucked up in first class enjoying wonderful expeditions and I think *it really is too bad*. However, this *is* the fate of the Single Woman. Miss Glossop did warn me of its perils. Therefore, on Polly's suggestion, I am sending Robbie to her on holiday (question: can looking after our screaming nephew be a holiday?), and I am dragging Father off to Ardtornish. By this stage of the letter, I hope you are feeling guilty.

I can't bear to see the house like this and it is certainly not fit for pigs and Mrs Dawes practically fainted into

Ellen's arms yesterday because she saw two rats! The Chief Builder with whom I have developed a Deep Friendship promises me that it will all be over by Christmas. Where have I heard that phrase before?

Exasperatedly,
Flora

PS   The new doctor is really rather nice. It's funny — although he comes from quite a poor family and his parents used to live up by Clare Park, you wouldn't know that when you meet him as he is terrifically well presented and forward looking.
PPS   I feel as though my whole world is being pulled apart and nobody cares.

Before the builders wrought more devastation, Flora and Mrs Dawes had agreed to clear out the old nursery rooms at the top of the house. Flora stood in the doorway of the schoolroom, where shadowy hands reached out and plucked her back into the small, often secret, world of childhood. The nursery floor had been the sisters' domain, in which Kit, set apart by the superiority of boarding school, did not figure, and those silent, sometimes tedious, hours spent up there were imprinted like an X-ray onto Flora.

Nine a.m., lessons. Eleven a.m., milk and biscuits. Twelve o'clock sharp, a brisk walk. Luncheon at one o'clock, followed by half an hour lying flat on the floor, for the sake of their posture, while Miss Hunter/Glossop/whoever read to them, from which vantage point Polly and Flora played Spot-the-Pink-Knickers, and the furniture seemed huge and strangely angled. Three o'clock, lessons again. Five o'clock, tea. Bread and butter on a flowered china plate and *plain* cake.

Miss Glossop, Flora recollected, had not cared for the Hanoverians: history had been weighted in favour of the Plantagenets ('so chivalrous'), the Tudors ('so clever and so right for England'), and the Stuarts ('so romantic and doomed'), and boiled down to a chronicle featuring a surfeit of lampreys, butts of Malmsey and little gentlemen in black velvet. In English lessons Miss Hunter concentrated on parsing, which sounded like a disease, but conferred the ability to single out an adjective from a noun. Geography was confined to twirling a globe.

As an education, it had not left Flora with many reserves. But that narrow, claustrophobic routine had been vital – for it had given her a childhood. It had been safe, and Flora and Polly had needed Miss Glossop, Miss Hunter and the others to get them through.

> HOTEL ROMANA
> ROME
> *5 July 1930*

Dear Flora,
Did anyone ever tell you that patience is a virtue? Remind me to do so when I get back.

Seriously, I am very sorry it has been so difficult for you at home, and I hope the Ardtornish solution worked. Keep Father there as long as possible. As soon as I am back on the 15th I will come and take over.

Would you be very kind and ask Friendly Builder if he has received my letter about (a) replacing the drawing room windows, (b) if it is possible to put in the new kind of radiator? He has not replied on these points.

Matty seems well and is busy sightseeing. She spends most of her time in art galleries while I tramp round ruins. Funnily enough, she seems quite a different person when travelling, almost animated – you remember how down she was in France? She tells me she is looking forward to coming home.

Your loving brother,
Kit

PS   What's this nonsense about being unmarried? What do you think the performance next year is in aid of?

What Kit did not add to his letter was how much easier it was to get through the days when he and Matty made separate plans.

Dear Matty,

Are you feeling any better? I hope so. Dr Lofts promised me he would keep a strict eye on you.

As you see from the above I've left the club and I am now installed in our new London flat. It is reasonably spacious, with a good drawing room for entertaining. Certainly it is big enough for your luncheon parties when we launch Flora next year. I think you will find it comfortable.

I have engaged a cook-housekeeper, but I leave you to choose the maid. Mrs Waters assures me that there is a good registry in the Edgware Road. (I hope you are impressed by this grasp of domestic matters.)

However, for the flat to be properly shipshape we must wait until you are well enough to come up here yourself. It needs your touch.

We were lucky to leave Egypt when we did as a nasty situation appears to be blowing up. There were anti-British riots in Cairo which left six dead. Let's hope that things don't get too inflamed.

Which reminds me, I saw a man walking up and down the street by Marble Arch yesterday and I was very struck by the message on the placard.

I know three trades
I speak three languages
Fought for three years
Have three children
And no work for three months
I only want one job

I watched him for a long time and his predicament made me boil with anger and pity. It can't be right that this is happening.

Yours affectionately,
Kit

PS A piece of gossip that might amuse you. The Prince of Wales has been spotted leaving the building after cocktails. Perhaps he has a friend here?

Mrs Christopher Dysart, Kit wrote, aware that it took a conscious application of will to do so. He had a wife, but although that was undisputable it did not register with him: he was wearing his marriage like a new suit that had not worn in. He placed the envelope on the stack awaiting the post and readdressed himself to an unfinished letter to a Mr Raby, a man of affairs who had been recommended to him and possessed the advantage of being independent of any previous dealings with the Dysarts.

To put you in the picture, the family has recently suffered from the effects of bad investments and this has resulted in serious embarrassment. My wife, however, is anxious to put to use the portion of her capital to which she is entitled by her trust. I would like your ideas as to where it would be both safe and productive.

As to myself, would you consult the Dysart portfolio and assess if anything is salvageable. If it is, I would like it to remain separate from my wife's account. I am interested in the development of the wireless which I am convinced will become a household item, and the recent formation of the British Broadcasting Company bears out this opinion. I would like to invest in a company developing a machine that will plug into the electricity mains and incorporate the loud-speaker into the design . . .

There was comfort to be had in the business of re-orchestrating the family fortunes and Kit was making every effort to keep himself occupied. One year and twenty-three days since he had said goodbye to Daisy, there were now days, welcome days, when he did not think about her at all.

120

WHAT IS ALL THIS ABOUT DAMNFOOL WIRELESSES
STOP CONSULT ME BEFORE TAKING DECISIONS STOP
WHY AREN'T YOU USING OUR MAN STOP REPEAT
YOU MUST CONSULT ME STOP RUPERT STOP PS
COME HOME

NUMBER 5
UPPER BROOK STREET
26 November 1930

Matty,

Goodness! You are brave to invite the Chudleigh family down to Hinton Dysart for Christmas, and I salute your courage, or is it your thick-skinnedness?

You will see it's impossible. Of course we will meet from time to time, and I will be polite, but I don't really want to see you or Kit, still less at Hinton. I have also persuaded Mother not to come either.

Selfish and self-obsessed this might seem to you, but it is what I feel, and I must be honest.

Don't worry, I am joining Tim Coats's skiing party in Bavaria which promises to be huge fun. I am quite looking forward to sniffing out this new Germany that I have been told about.

I could never bring myself to say this before as you never struck me as possessing the gift for happiness, but be happy if you can and take care of him.

Daisy

CLIFTON COTTAGE
NETHER HINTON
5 December 1930

Dear Betty [Ellen licked the tip of the pencil which had worn down to an inch and a half.] I hope you are well and your veins are not hurting too bad. I would like to see you very much and your Dad and I wondered if we could come over on New Year's Day when I will have a day off?

Big things have taken place here. With Master Kit
marrying and all that, and the house being done up.
Quite different it is now, you would not recognize it,
spanking fresh paint, a new roof, new windows. It does
look nice and now she is back from the honeymoon
Mrs Dysart is starting to do the inside up. I can't say
her taste appeals to me though.

Displayed in isolation on the mantelpiece above the range,
Betty's photograph seemed to nod at Ellen. At least, that is what
she imagined, even if Ned did tell her she had lost her marbles.
Ellen always wrote letters to her daughter facing the plump, rather
blurred image. She liked to feel they were in direct contact, as if
those years with the little girl, her two plaits and print pinafore,
were not quite so far behind.

She turned over the paper and described Matty on the verso.
After a paragraph she looked up. 'You know, I don't think it's
right with those two,' she told Ned.

'What's new? The master never had any time for *his* missus.'

'You mean the other way round. She couldn't abide him,
Ned.' Ellen paused while she weighed up the benefits of being
virtuous and remaining silent against the satisfaction of airing
gossip. 'Did I tell you what Madge heard?'

Ned enjoyed chewing the cud as much as Ellen, but he did not
let it worry him. 'Tell me, girl.'

Ellen chose her words. 'Well. Between you and me, Madge
says Lady D. had something going for her brother. Nasty, really,'
she added, in an attempt to clear her conscience.

'And I say don't poke your nose in what ain't your business,
Ellen.'

Your Dad says [Ellen knew Ned was quite right. Again
she licked the pencil and was rewarded by a watery
outline on the page.] I'm poking my nose in but I don't
think Miss Polly or Miss Flora were very pleased when
Mr Kit married Mrs Dysart. Despite the money. And Mr

Kit is a restless one and Mrs Dawes says he wanted to marry someone else. There.

'Isn't it tea-time?' Ned got to his feet. He stood behind his wife and massaged gently at the nape of her neck where he knew it ached.

Ellen dropped the pencil and stared at the photograph. 'I look awful, Ned, nowadays. Don't I?' Her daughter's young face nodded back. 'I'm growing old.'

'So you are,' said Ned, giving his wife's shoulders a quick squeeze.

In panic, Ellen swung round. 'Ned, do you really think so?'

'It's true, my girl.' Face hidden, Ned bent over to stoke up the coal in the range and put the kettle on the hob. 'You'll be knocking at the pearly gates any minute.'

'Get off, Ned.'

'True, girl.'

'Not yet awhile,' said Ellen grimly, and rubbed her still swollen knee. 'You'll have to put up with me for a time yet.'

'Tea?' Ned leant the poker against the stove and peered at the pie inside the top oven. 'Or have you gone on strike?'

The smell of cooked meat and pastry filled the room and the kettle began to do a steam dance.

That reminds me [wrote Ellen to Betty], the recipe for rook pie. Use only skinned breasts, otherwise the pie will be bitter, and layer with the best beef and a bit of fat bacon. Season. Add some liquid. Cover with pastry . . .

HINTON DYSART
NETHER HINTON
HAMPSHIRE
10 December 1930

Dear Mr Hurley,
Your name has been recommended to me by Lady Foxton and Mrs d'Arborfield. I have had one or two

disappointments recently and I wish to consult someone such as yourself as soon as possible in the New Year.

Could your secretary contact me at the above address in order to arrange this? I would like to emphasize again the urgency.

Yours sincerely,

Matilda Dysart

HARRY

Gardens are like families, don't you think? Each time the season repeats itself it draws on the past: each plant tied in to its parent. Every child that is born is determined by what took place before it was conceived, and the cycle goes on renewing itself until it is broken or played out — and the secrets are lost.

Each of us, then, comes with a hallmark, as permanent as the silversmith's stamp. With plants, it is luck that determines whether or not the sun shines and the rain falls at the right time in the right quantities. Luck, and the love of the gardener who watches over them. Certainly, the manner in which we carry the burden of our past is up to us, but we, too, need luck.

Each summer when the garden groans under its own generosity and the visitors clog the pathways of the walled garden, I am reminded of this.

I was lucky.

PART TWO

MATTY

1930−31

CHAPTER ONE

THE SMELL of an English country house is unique: its inmates can sniff an approximation anywhere in the world and say, 'Ah, yes.' In the Malaysian jungles, riding over African landscapes, or dying among Flanders poppies, they dreamed of tea-time in the library and of damp tweed and wet dogs steaming by the fire. Starch, Brasso, human sweat trapped in wardrobes, game hanging in the larders, boiled ham, mould in the cellar and the flat scent of cold earth streaming in through the window on a December morning.

In the weeks before Christmas the smells in the house at Hinton Dysart turned sharp and spicy. Lifted from Lee Wood, a Christmas tree shed its needles onto the hall floor, apple logs released their scent from the fireplaces, orange and tangerine peel perfumed the dining room and Mrs Dawes enveloped the kitchen in cinnamon, cloves, allspice — and brandy. Under these fresh assaults the lingering residue of paint, linseed oil, putty, new wood and freshly made up chintz was routed.

'It's more like home now,' Flora told Matty over afternoon tea by the fire when the builders had finally departed. 'The house doesn't seem so foreign. More like it was. Only nicer, of course,' she added kindly, interpreting Matty's stricken look correctly. She went on to say that Matty should not take her comments as criticism. Matty, who was not at all sure she understood her bewildering in-laws and equally uncertain how to behave with them, spent a sleepness night worrying that she had overdone the improvements.

On the day before the Christmas guests — her first guests — were due, Matty roamed the house with Ivy at her side, checking the toothpowder and bath salts in the bathrooms, the McVitie's biscuits in the tins on bedside tables, that there were enough towels, enough pillows, enough hairpins, enough blotting paper, enough ink . . . and prayed that she would pass the test.

'Kit, can't you do something about Matty?' Flora begged. 'She's fussing about like a headless chicken and it's making Father tetchy.'

Bearing a glass of strengthening gin and tonic, Kit eventually discovered his wife with her head in the linen cupboard. 'I've been sent to tame you. There is a general protest at the high level of activity.' Matty's reply was muffled. 'Please, Matty. Why don't you come and sit down in the drawing room and read the newspaper?' He held out the glass. 'Have a drink at least.'

Matty barely glanced at him. 'Later,' she said. 'I just want to be sure . . .'

She prodded a pile of towels. Kit stared at Matty's excellently tailored but decorous rust and beige tweed suit, over which she had tied one of Mrs Dawes's aprons, and protested, 'Really, Matty, we have the servants to do that sort of thing. There is no need—'

'Will you pass me the list on the table, please, Kit?'

Kit obeyed. He had already learnt that Matty could display a stubborn streak. 'This isn't going to become a habit, is it?'

'I don't think so.' Matty's face peered round the cupboard door, looking flustered. 'You can't expect people to do things for you unless you are willing to show them how.' She grinned unexpectedly. 'Aunt Susan told me.'

He found himself grinning back. 'No. I don't suppose you can.' He was still holding the gin and took a sip. 'Damn,' he said. 'I wasn't supposed to have this. It was for you.'

Matty stretched up to the napkins on the top shelf of the cupboard. She was far too small to reach them easily and a pile fell onto the floor by her feet. She swooped down to pick them up. Kit's amusement vanished and a wave of irritation buffeted his good intentions. Disappointed with himself, ashamed, and guilty because he felt both, Kit put down the glass on the table and walked away.

The guests – Polly, James and young William, Great-aunt Hetta, Lady Foxton, Max Longborough – arrived together on the 3.40 from Waterloo to be collected by Tyson at Farnham station.

Immediately on entering the hall, all of them remarked on Hinton Dysart's renaissance and proceeded to divest themselves of a mountain of coats, gloves, boots and scarves.

Lady Foxton dropped a huge, fabulously expensive and hideous mink coat into Ivy's arms and told her to be very, very careful with it.

Polly ran a critical eye over the waxed floorboards, painstakingly restored banisters and plaster ceiling. 'Gosh, Matty. You have made a difference, hasn't she, Kit?' She pecked Kit on the cheek. 'I mean I wouldn't have recognized the house. So . . . so expensive-looking. I do hope something of the old Hinton Dysart is left.'

Her remarks echoed Flora's, and Matty, who had stepped forward to welcome her, froze and found herself saying, 'How sweet', meaninglessly to the baby.

Very early in their marriage, Kit had asked Matty whether she minded if they kept to separate bedrooms. He spoke as if it was a formality, as if he did not expect anything else. Thus on Christmas Eve she woke alone to the dilute darkness of early morning in Hesther's old bedroom, and smelt winter in the garden outside. For a time she lay warm and untroubled, from habit expecting to hear noise – clattering milk pails, the rasp of a car's gears – only to luxuriate in the silence. She remembered that life had changed.

After a minute or two, Matty opened her eyes and pushed the sheets back from her face. The roses on the chintz curtains swelled and then shrivelled in the draught from the open window. Eddies of freezing air washed over her face.

Perhaps . . . perhaps *this* time. Matty concentrated her forces and hoped that she felt sick. But, hard as she tried, she did not and when she rolled over she understood why. Then she hauled herself upright, switched on the light and examined the stain on her nightdress.

'I won't cry,' she said to her concave stomach and smeared thighs. 'Not this time.'

She had wept twice before, when the red blotch arrived to disfigure her underwear and sheets in Egypt and when the English doctor in Rome had said, 'There, there, patience. With your problems and physique, Mrs Dysart, it doesn't do to count chickens.' Matty did not feel patient or resigned, only frustrated, despairing of her body and ignorant because she did not know enough about it to try to put things right.

Instead she fell into the old habit. 'You can't sparkle, Matty, nor play tennis, nor get your husband to love you. Nor . . .' a deep doubt had rooted, 'nor become pregnant.'

What if . . . what if she could not bear a child?

Matty pulled her nightdress down over her legs. The pleasure and comfort she had experienced on first wakening dissipated into the uncertainties of her new life.

After she had washed, Matty slipped between the curtains and looked out of the window. Slivers of opal light slanted over the garden, smoothed flat by frost and winter. Gooseflesh stippled her arms and marched up her legs.

Last night she had waited a long time, willing Kit to come to her, if only to say goodnight. She heard him walk up the staircase and down the corridor. She knew it was him because she had learnt the sound of his footsteps, and, shuddering a little with nerves and hope, she waited for a knock on the door.

It never came.

Matty put out a finger and drew a heart on the frosted window pane. Its lines did not quite meet and it was misshapen, more like a lump of stone. She stared at it and acknowledged what she had not dared to acknowledge previously – that when she married Kit she had not understood what she was taking on. She had no idea that unhappiness could stretch indefinitely like a piece of knicker elastic.

Daisy's face hovered in the frost-spun patterns on the window. Kit will be thinking of me, she had warned. Oh, yes, Matty had thought in her ignorance. Don't you think I don't know? I've thought it all out, Daisy. But she hadn't: she hadn't known what it would be like to hold the nettle of unreciprocated love day after day, night after night. Or to feel that there was another person in your bed.

*

132

'It's a new one,' Kit had explained to Matty, folding a blue silk Paisley dressing gown over the chair in the bedroom of the Dawlish hotel, and coughed. In contrast, his pyjamas were well worn and washed into softness. For that matter, so was Matty's nightdress, a much-loved Viyella one which buttoned up to the neck. ('For goodness sake, Matilda,' Susan had expostulated. 'You can't take *that* on honeymoon.')

Since it was freezing in the bedroom and a maliciously inclined draught whistled under the door, Matty had buttoned it up to the neck and tucked it over her feet. Kit shivered and kicked off his slippers. Matty took a quick look at his feet and was pleased: as she suspected, Kit had nice ones, bony and strong, with pedicured toenails. She liked that. He coughed again, finishing with a distinct wheeze.

'Do you mind if I turn off the light?' Matty shook her head. Kit flicked the switch and remained for a second or two beside the bed before sliding in beside her.

This is it, she thought, surprised at the ordinariness of the event.

'Kit,' she said, twisting the hem of the top sheet round and round her fingers, 'I know this is not what you wanted.'

He did not move. 'Matty, do you think this is the right time to talk about this?'

'Not if *you* don't want to.'

'Do you want to?'

Matty reconsidered the Pandora's box the conversation would open. 'No,' she said hastily. 'No.'

'Agreed.' Kit unbuttoned his pyjama jacket and pulled it off, so that it lay in a bundle between them. Holding her breath, Matty reached over and touched a smooth shoulder with a fingertip. The blood thudded in her ears. Kit did not move, and she lay petrified at what she had done. Eventually, he rolled towards her and put his arms around her. She was cool to touch but he felt burning hot. His mouth brushed her neck, and Matty inhaled a male scent of cologne and tobacco, and felt the shape of a male body with unfamiliar steppes, terraces and plains. Uncertain whether or not to put her arms around him, she waited.

'Try not to be frightened,' he said, and coughed into her ear. 'I'll take care of you.'

Because Matty loved Kit she had not been able to prevent herself cradling her palm around the back of the fair head above hers and Kit recoiled. Not much, but enough. 'Sorry,' she said, and snatched away her hand.

'Look. Could you take this thing off?' Kit grappled with the buttons of the nightdress. 'I think it would be easier without it.'

She tried to help him, but the material had tangled round her ankles. 'Good God,' he said, 'it's more effective than a chastity belt.'

The final button released, and Matty struggled free. In the dark, she heard Kit draw breath, and he touched her on her breast.

Topped by an almost pre-pubescent nipple the breast beneath his hand felt as flat and cold as a china doll's. She's so small, he thought, like a child. And what desire he had summoned, died. In an effort to rekindle it, he bent over Matty and kissed her, his mouth dry and hard on hers.

'Please,' she whispered, 'please.'

Kit shut his eyes and held tight to the memory of an Arab boy and hot excitement. He thought of Daisy in a shabby bathing costume at the Villa Lafayette, full-breasted and bright-haired. Lit from within. A vice squeezed at his heart. He lay on the china-doll breasts of his wife and groaned – and felt her hand slide down his back.

'Please,' she whispered. 'You will have to help me.'

Shocked by Matty's predicament as well as his own, light-headed with the onset of fever, Kit ran his hand down the bird bones, which barely lifted the skin at the hips, and between her legs. 'It's all right, Matty,' he said hoarsely. 'I'll make it all right.'

Imprisoned by ropes of jealousy, self-pity, illness and a starved heart, Matty made a supreme effort to disentangle herself, and strove to give Kit the gift of her love. And he, in his turn, surprised by the generosity and fervour he unlocked in the small body, was comforted.

Later when they both lay separate and awake he said, 'I think I've got flu.'

He had not hurt her then, or on subsequent occasions, but the flash of intimacy between them had never been repeated. Their couplings were guarded, increasingly skilfully accomplished, but never again with that surrender to emotion. Once or twice when Kit rose above Matty and looked down into her haunted eyes, he caught a certain expression – of hurt and yearning. Then the suspicion that Matty loved him nudged, unwelcome, into his mind and Matty, realizing that this was so, hid her feelings.

RIP. Matty's finger scratched on through the frost patterns and traced the names of her parents, Jocasta and Stephen. Then she drew a baby's cradle. 'Rockaby,' she wrote and then scrubbed it out with her fist.

She was empty, empty, empty.

Ten minutes later, correctly dressed in a tweed costume, hat, gloves and thick stockings, Matty slipped down the back staircase and bumped into Ivy bringing up the first relay of early morning tea.

'Excuse me, ma'am.' Surprised at the sight of her mistress up so early, Ivy flattened herself against the wall.

'That's all right, Ivy. I'm . . . just a breath of fresh air . . .' Matty brushed past and hurried, brogues clicking, down the kitchen passage to the back door.

Once she had left the protection of the house, the cold grew sharper. The air streamed into her lungs and Matty dug her hands into her pockets and walked over the lawn towards the river, feet crunching on the frosted stones. Already she felt better.

She halted by the bridge and gazed upwards through the frozen still-life of the plane tree. Nothing moved in the trees or flowerbeds. No pulsebeat in the tangle of dead things and crusted earth. Only the white frost rime on the grass blades appeared to possess life as light played on the ice crystals. Matty's breath streamed into the air, and the blood flowed out of her onto the rag, which grew wet and heavy.

Her feet were turning numb, and she walked back across the lower lawn and through the yew circle towards the house, leaving a trail of footprints on the white carpet. She stopped by the terrace to take a last look at the slumbering garden – and, suddenly, her hands clenched inside her gloves.

Even in the patchy, uncertain light Matty could see that hers were not the only footprints on the lawn. Beside them was a second pair: small, neat, perfectly matching marks.

I'm mad as well as barren, was Matty's first thought. Her second was more rational: somewhere a child was playing a game. She swivelled at the sound of pebbles clattering down the stone steps behind her and gasped. There on the steps was a child.

She called out, 'Who are you?'

Like a struck tuning fork, the air vibrated in Matty's ear with a high pitch of the F sharp, so high that it hurt. She shook her head to clear it, and the objects surrounding her – steps, yew hedge, lawn – subtly distorted like reflections in an old mirror. Disorientated, she grabbed at the stone balustrade and, although its texture, encrusted with moss-like growths, made an impression through her glove, she also knew without question that her hand was resting on air. Her fingers and toes turned icy cold.

The child turned and fixed on Matty a pair of disturbingly familiar light blue eyes. She was dressed in a good coat with a velvet collar, gaiters and bonnet. Strands of flaxen hair escaped under its rim, and her chin was chapped from the cold. As far as Matty, who had no experience of children, could assess, she was about five years old, and possessed the seriousness of a child concentrating on something important to it. After scrutinizing Matty, she continued up the steps.

'Wait,' called Matty. 'Who are you? What's your name?'

The child paid no attention and scrambled up to the top where she stopped, held out her coat skirts and performed a little skipping step by one of the stone vases. She appeared absorbed and contained; but every so often the blue eyes flicked in the direction of Matty.

'Please wait.' Matty ran up the unreal-feeling steps and her hat went flying onto the grass. She left it there. 'Where do you come from?' she asked.

The child smiled, and Matty found herself rooted to the flagstone. The F sharp was now so high and so painful that she pressed her hands hard against her ears, struggling with a force that appeared to be sucking and emptying her body. In the Matty shell that was left behind was immeasurable misery.

But it's not my pain.

On her knees, Matty squeezed her head so hard that everything went black. When she opened her eyes the child had vanished. She scrambled to her feet to look across the lawn, but she was too late: the footprints were dissolving.

In the background, remained an echo suggesting all manner of unease. Then it stopped.

Knees smarting, Matty sat on the steps and found herself sobbing: from fright, for the child that was not in her body, for her longing to have something, someone, who needed her — because she was obviously going mad — for her bitter grief when, as a five-year-old child, she had found herself alone. For the rag-bag of her life.

'Are you all right, madam?'

Matty was crying so hard that she failed to register the creak of a wheelbarrow, or the figure of Ned Sheppey, muffled up against the cold in a corduroy jacket and scarf.

Ned picked up Matty's abandoned hat and repeated his question and she flushed at being caught with tears freezing on her face by the gardener, and of what he might say to Ellen and Mrs Dawes. 'Thank you, Mr Sheppey,' she said. 'I was just going inside. I like an early-morning walk.'

'Shall I call someone, Mrs Kit?'

He seemed both incurious and kind. Common sense came to Matty's aid and told her that it did not matter what Ned had seen or not seen.

'Thank you.' Matty accepted the hat, jammed it onto her head and asked, 'Mr Sheppey, do you have any grandchildren?'

He did not appear to think her question odd and answered at once. 'Yes, ma'am, but not living here.'

'Does Ivy have a little girl that she brings to play round here, or Mrs Dawes a granddaughter?'

With her tearstains and disarranged hair, Matty reminded Ned strongly of his own daughter. 'No, Mrs Kit.'

'Then . . .'

'Yes, Mrs Kit?'

Whatever it had been – vision, possession, breakdown – it was too complicated to discuss with Mr Sheppey. Matty pushed her aching body upright, rubbed her eyes with the handkerchief and said the first thing that came into her head, 'What are you doing with the wheelbarrow, Mr Sheppey?'

'Taking the lily-of-the-valley to the shed to pot them up in the good china. That way I bring them on early, for the house. I always do at this time of year. It's a tradition, like. They smell nice inside.' He picked up a plant and held it out as if it was the most natural thing in the world to do, and Matty left the step to inspect the bundle that said nothing much to her.

'Very nice, Mr Sheppey.'

Mr Sheppey was wearing string mittens and his cracked fingers and black-rimmed fingernails stuck out from them. The manner in which his hand curved around the plant caught Matty's interest. It was a gardener's hold, an easy one, born of long acquaintanceship.

'Your hands must hurt in this cold.' Matty pointed to a cut on his right forefinger which was clotted with a mixture of dried blood and earth. 'You must take care of that, Mr Sheppey. It might go septic.'

'You gets used to it, Mrs Kit. My father used to say, you can't garden if you don't dirty your hands. He was head gardener here for upwards of thirty years. Thank you all the same.' Ned replaced the lily-of-the-valley in the wheelbarrow. He seemed perfectly happy to stand in the cold and to talk, but Matty was aware that she was being minutely observed. 'Do you like gardening, Mrs Kit?'

'Me?' Matty spread her hands and inspected the fingers sheathed in their expensive gloves. 'I haven't really thought about it . . . but—'

'Lady Dysart did. She had plenty of ideas, but it's different now. There's too much to do here without help so I keeps to the kitchen garden, except for a few odd things.'

'Yes,' she said, soothed by the Hampshire burr.

Mr Sheppey seemed to understand that she was troubled and kept talking. 'I do up pots of narcissi for the spring, too, because of the smell. I've got them in the greenhouse. Would you like to choose the pots for the house?'

'I think I would, Mr Sheppey.' A thought struck Matty. 'Perhaps I ought to come and find out what you're doing in the garden, anyway.'

They looked at each other and, for different reasons, liked what they saw.

'Good morning, Mrs Kit, then.' Ned patted a plant into place, touched his cap and hefted up the wheelbarrow handles.

Matty watched him make his way across the lawn, a sane figure in a real world, and set about convincing herself that nothing whatever had happened to her that was out of the ordinary.

'You've had me in a fright.' Robbie accosted Matty on her return to the bedroom. 'Here's me worrying my head off and your breakfast getting cold.'

Matty peeled off her gloves, dropped them onto the bed and kicked off her shoes. Robbie scented another opening. She eyed the shoes with satisfaction.

'You've never been outside? You'll have caught your death. It really is too bad.' Robbie steered Matty towards the armchair and anchored her into it with a tray. 'Eat up, Mrs Kit.'

The Lapsang Souchong had the sweet, smoky taste she adored. Matty fished out a floating leaf with a teaspoon and drank it gratefully. Then she reached for a triangle of toast and the butter.

'That's right, Mrs Kit.' Robbie attacked the bed and clicked her tongue at the stain on the sheet. 'Have you been taking the tonic I told you about?'

Matty closed her eyes for a second. 'Yes, Miss Robson.'

'Well, never mind, then. There's always another month. Mind

you . . .' Robbie stripped off the sheet oblivious that every fibre in Matty's body protested against her nosiness and the assumption that Matty was now her property. 'You'll have to try harder. There are things you can do to stop the monthly visitor.'

'Really, Miss Robson!' The idea of Robbie lecturing her on her fertility floored Matty but, while appalled, she was fascinated.

'Well, Mrs Kit.' Robbie drew out the words as if she was back in the nursery, the Little-Miss-Manners-School-of-Life tone which Matty had rapidly grown to dislike.

She forestalled the lesson. 'Miss Robson, this is a private subject, not for discussion.'

But Robbie was not easily beaten and over the years she had fought and won many Waterloos in the pursuit of her duty. 'There's no need to get on your high horse,' she said, whisking sheets here and there. Matty chewed some toast and watched her: Miss Robson pulsed with energy and she suspected there were hidden forces suppressed beneath the blue serge. Robbie turned her attention to Matty's clothes for the day. 'You can't have an heir quick enough, you know. That's your duty. That's what you're here for.'

Matty's chin came into play. 'Miss Robson. That is enough.'

Robbie shook out a pair of silk stockings. 'You just concentrate on yourself, never mind anything or anyone else. There's time enough afterwards. Lady Dysart produced Mr Kit nine months to the day. Mind you,' Robbie paused for effect, 'I think I shall speak to him. He really shouldn't go away to London so much.'

Matty's tolerance vanished. 'Miss Robson,' she said, 'you will do no such thing.'

'Don't take on, Mrs Kit,' said Robbie in a kindly tone, and rolled up a stocking. 'Mr Kit and I are just like that.' She crossed two forefingers. 'And Flora. There's no secrets between us.' She attacked the second stocking. 'He needed me, you know. They all did, and I saved them. So you just leave him to me. If you will excuse me saying so, I know how to handle Mr Kit.'

Do you? reflected Matty grimly. 'But, Miss Robson—'

'No buts, if you please, Mrs Kit.' Robbie laid the second

stocking down beside the first and they sat, two beige ring doughnuts, beside Matty's suspender belt. 'I'm here to help you. I'll be back to run your bath in ten minutes.'

Matty was finishing her breakfast when Kit knocked at the door. 'Sorry to interrupt. I'm on my way to a disgracefully late breakfast. Everyone else is late too.' He smiled down at his wife.

Matty flushed soft pink. 'You're not interrupting.'

'What are you going to do today?'

'Goodness,' she said, pushing her teacup aside. 'I must get a move on. Lady Foxton will be wanting breakfast in her room.'

Kit dug his hands into his pockets. 'Stop flapping, Matty. Your rage for perfection has resulted in a perfectly ordered household.'

She had succeeded in irritating him, and Matty knew it. She was also aware that if Kit had made a similar remark to Daisy she would have batted it back: *But, darling, that is what makes me so fascinating.*

Eventually Kit asked, 'Are you feeling all right?'

Matty was startled. 'Yes, of course. Why?'

'I met Robbie in the passage.'

'Ah.' Matty wanted to cry out at him, 'What *are* you doing talking to Robbie about something so private? It isn't any of her business. This is between us.'

Kit shrugged. 'Better luck another time, Matty.'

Do couples who do not understand one another ever succeed in having children? Matty supposed that they must, but she also wondered if the fact that Kit did not love her had something to do with her failure each month. Corn seed would not settle on parched ground and there was nothing moist or nourishing in Matty.

Kit made an effort to soften the atmosphere. 'I must say, you have made it nice in here, Matty. You have a real gift for that sort of thing.'

Matty tensed, for she had been nervous of changing too many of Hesther's things. 'I took out some of the furniture as it was a little cluttered. I hope you don't mind.'

'Yes, I suppose it was. I seem to remember my mother liked

141

things all jumbled up.' Kit had little interest in and none of Matty's flair for details. He was aware only that, under her short reign, Hinton Dysart had become comfortable and homelike. He had given Matty licence to do what she wished, but requested she take into account both Rupert's and Flora's wishes. It's difficult for them to adjust, he had said looking at her seriously, so you will be careful?

Matty had been clever. One of her first acts was to sit regularly with Rupert and to listen to him. Then she considered the occupants of the house, and the house itself. As a result, nothing was too smart and jarring, but everything was clean, polished and fresh. Meals appeared on time. There were flowers everywhere, and bowls of pot-pourri scented the living rooms. Somehow the unmanageable areas became livable-in, dark corners light and yielding, and the interior balance of the house shifted.

'Are you going to be able to cope over Christmas with all the comings and goings? Especially with Great-aunt Hetta and Lady F?' Kit was asking.

Apparently Great-aunt Hetta required the undeviating attention of a companion, and a constant supply of bile beans for a costive digestion.

Matty grimaced. 'At three shillings a box for bile beans, we're in danger of going bankrupt.'

Kit made for the door. 'Don't let Lady F. bully you.'

Matty reached for her notebook. Today, Christmas Eve, there was a lunchtime sherry party for the village and Christmas dinner for thirty-four to which Mr Pengeally and his spouse, who had designs on Matty's time, were bidden. The seating plan ensured that Mr Pengeally sat next to Matty and, since hair grew out of his ears, a stigmata that repelled her, Matty did not relish the prospect. The Boxing Day meet was scheduled to take place in the drive . . . stirrup cups . . . picnic lunches, cold collations for those remaining at home and, of course, tea for the hunters on their return.

'*Look* at me, Matty,' ordered Kit from the doorway. 'Can you cope? Just say the word and I'll put a stop to it all.'

Her expression was calm. 'Even to Great-aunt Hetta and the bile beans?'

Kit was never sure when Matty made a joke. He smiled politely. 'Even Great-aunt Hetta.'

'Well.' Matty stood up in her stockinged feet. 'It's fine and everything is planned.' She crossed over to the door and placed a tentative hand on his arm. 'I *can* cope, you know.'

There it was again, the tiny, but definite, recoil. In an attempt to disguise it, Kit reached for the door handle. I wish Daisy was dead, thought Matty, and her demon hammered under her ribs.

'Good girl.' Kit rallied. 'It's nice to think that the old traditions will keep going at Christmas. See you later, Matty.'

In that moment Matty almost hated him.

Mrs Dawes was feeling belligerent, brought about by panic, unfamiliarity with her new mistress and more than a touch of what she termed 'tincture' for her back. Realizing this, Matty negotiated her way around the rocks while details for lunch and dinner were finalized between them. Then she made her mistake.

'The hunting tea in the drawing room, please, Mrs Dawes. Crumpets, muffins, sandwiches, fruit cake and ginger snaps.'

Mrs Dawes said a rude word in her head. Aloud she said: 'You mean the library, ma'am. It's always in the library.'

'I think the drawing room will be more comfortable.'

'Miss Flora won't like it.' Mrs Dawes considered the extra tablecloths she would need and had not prepared. A mutinous look descended over her features. 'They won't like it, ma'am, and I don't think I can do it, ma'am, at such short notice.'

'Mrs Dawes,' Matty tried. 'I think—'

'Can't do it, madam.'

What would Jocasta do? What would Emma Goldman do? More to the point, what would Aunt Susan do? The answer was quite plain. Matty ignored Mrs Dawes's last remark and asked, 'Do you have the anchovy paste we ordered from Farnham? It's my husband's favourite.'

'Three pots, ma'am.'

'Good. We've done everything, then, haven't we?' Matty

smiled to show goodwill and indicated that Mrs Dawes could go. 'Have the family finished breakfast yet?'

With difficulty Mrs Dawes shook her aching head. 'No, ma'am.'

'I'll go and see what is happening.' Matty got up from the desk in the morning room. 'Thank you very much for all your hard work.' Mrs Dawes practically tottered to the door. 'And, Mrs Dawes, it is tea in the drawing room. Is that quite clear?'

Mrs Dawes did not reply.

Cheered by her small but significant victory, Matty went to the dining room. Greenery filled the hall and the holly looked cheerful beside the Christmas tree. She put her head around the door. The sideboard was cluttered with silver chafing dishes, containing kidneys, bacon, and scrambled egg, and two teapots. At the table the family were eating and talking. Kit waved a fork on which was speared a kidney. 'Do you remember the time when he took us back through Caesar's Camp and Paradise and—'

'Oh, yes,' Polly cut in. 'You came a cropper that day.'

'And I still bear the scars.' Kit stuck out a leg. 'Trust you to remember, Polly.'

Flora giggled and got up to refill her cup. She was dressed in her riding habit and her big frame looked its best under the nipped-in waist and severe lines. Her hair was braided into a loop, and her skin was shiny with health and innocent of powder. 'Pride before a fall,' she said in a wiseacre voice.

Rupert held out his cup. 'Give me one, too, Flora.'

It was the first time Matty had seen her father-in-law so relaxed with his children. 'Let's hope the weather holds,' he said, looking out of the window. 'It's just right.'

'Tally-ho!' shrieked Polly and banged her knife down on the table.

None of them noticed Matty standing by the door. Alone, stomach aching, she observed them for a moment longer and then closed the door.

CHAPTER TWO

TRUE TO form Flora woke at dawn on Boxing Day, and stumbled round her bedroom in the dark in a frowst of hair and iced breath. She had been too tired the night before to wash properly: her eyes were sticky and there was a disgraceful piece of orange peel under one thumbnail.

'Pig,' she muttered to the mirror and, in the spirit of truth, added, 'Fat pig.' As a penance she washed from head to toe which left her gasping.

Dressed in a pair of Kit's trousers and a jersey, she let herself out of the sleeping house, and headed over the field towards the cottages at Jonathan's Kilns, drawing in lungfuls of freezing air.

It was quiet and still out in the fields. She sped between the hedgerows – timeless, almost untouched – over leaf mould crisped on the top, damp and tender underneath, and through grass frozen into still life, materializing from out of the mist by the cottage. To someone watching she might have been a flaxen-haired emissary from a time when the land was river and forest.

Brazen, the retriever bitch, whimpered in her pen at the end of Danny's garden and Flora stopped to whisper, 'Good girl', and to remove a burr from the tangle of cinnamon hair at her neck. Brazen nudged her shoulder in response, pushed a wet nose into her neck and Flora smiled.

Danny had been up for an hour or so, seeing to what he called his family. The local hunt was a rich one and Danny had been employed as kennelman since Rupert had transplanted him from London to the village. Rupert had provided the tied cottage and, in return, Danny helped out with the Dysarts' horses. (Occasionally, he stood in for Tyson as chauffeur but passengers had to be sure he had not been at the whisky.) Since both hounds and horses were Danny's meat and drink it was a lazy-daisy job, as he said in his broad Cockney.

Danny had been waiting for Flora, who always came to see him before a meet, and in the cottage the kettle was on the hob. He was pouring warm milk into buckets for the pregnant bitches which were staying behind when she arrived and nodded in greeting. In the other pen was a whirlpool of dangling tongues and flailing tails, and the noise was deafening. Stirred by it, Flora laughed because the day was beginning, because she was cold and it was fun to be cold sometimes – because it was all such fun.

'How many couples running?' she shouted above the din, and picked up a bucket of milk. 'Ow.' She winced at the warmth stinging her fingers. 'That's hot.'

'Fifteen.' Terse to the point of silence at the best of times, Danny never bothered to say good morning. Flora turned her back on him because she knew he did not approve of anyone spoiling his hounds, put down the bucket, stuck her milky fingers through the netting and let Bouncer lick them.

'There, boysie. Nice, isn't it?'

'Stop it, Miss Flora.'

Danny never bothered with good form, nor with being polite to his superiors, for Danny was a free spirit who had alighted on their hearth. With the exception of Rupert, no one really *knew* Danny, only that he had limped into Hinton Dysart from a trench on the Somme, a stranger with trench-foot and a mashed-up leg, an unshakeable attachment to Rupert, a taste for sentimental poetry, solitude and drink. All of which Rupert (uncharacteristically) supplied and told the family to bugger off if they raised the subject.

Danny unlocked the first pen and beckoned to Flora. She picked up the bucket, pushed her way through the palpitating flanks and wet muzzles and poured the contents into a trough. The noise level fell dramatically.

'There, my lovelies.' Danny wiped his nose with the back of his hand, and ran it down the flank of the bitch huddled at his feet. 'Not so good, Lady, luv? What's the matter?'

Lady whimpered and Flora hunkered down beside Danny on

the concrete. 'Is she ill?' Danny gently shoved Lady over so he could examine the opposite flank.

'Maidy-Lady,' Flora stroked her, 'we can't have the best nose in the pack out of action.'

Lady buried her head in Danny's breeches and with the tenderness of a lover, he spread his fingers over her chest and listened.

'Danny, look.' Flora pointed at a red patch between the toes of one of Lady's front paws. 'She's lame.'

Danny never addressed a human if he could address an animal. 'How did you get that?' Danny took Lady's muzzle in his hand and said, 'You stupid bitch. Why didn't you tell me before?'

In the old days, Danny's uncanny gift would have landed him at the stake and, awed as ever, Flora watched as man and animal exchanged information and concluded how much easier it would be if she concentrated on animals and gave up the struggle to understand her family. Or herself, come to that. Lady dropped her nose, and her tail went slack. Danny pushed her aside and got up.

'Knacker's yard for clapped-out bitches.'

Flora sniffed at the air, and looked up. 'Should be a screaming scent,' she said. 'Just right.'

'Depends,' said Danny, and she knew he had gone silent on her. She scrunched her fingers under her armpits and waited for him to collect the pans and lock up the pen.

Danny stopped to stick a Blue Prior cigarette, made from local tobacco, in his mouth and smoked it as they walked through the yard, scattering hens. By this point, he had unbent enough to tell Flora the latest gossip.

'The new farmer over at 'Amptons' 'as put three of the fields to plough. It'll foul the scent.' He picked tobacco off his lip. 'Probably doesn't 'old with 'unting.'

'Mr Terence keeps poultry,' Flora pointed out. 'Of course he'll be sympathetic.'

'Bloody right.' Danny pushed open the door and they went inside to the immaculately kept cottage that was Danny's home.

Sloshing with tea, Flora made her way back to Hinton Dysart to a cacophony of renewed baying. Danny's strangeness and his silences never bothered her as they had Polly, who considered Danny an intruder, and frightening. 'He and Father always act so oddly together,' Polly complained. 'I don't understand it. Danny seems more family to him than we do.'

Flora had to agree, and since she was at that age when her own feelings muddled her, she had no answer. What she did know was that Rupert, bottle in pocket, marched down the road like the soldier he had been, twice, even three or four times a week, to Danny's cottage and had done so since she could remember. Later, flushed, sometimes belligerent, sometimes maudlin, the pair emerged. Occasionally, they went on a spree over by Odiham, and Flora sometimes saw them come home with exaggerated care in the twilight. The sight made her feel funny: awkward, embarrassed and, curiously, let down.

Once she had seen Danny naked, washing by the fire in his kitchen, a thin, white-skinned figure with a dusting of sandy hair on his chest and a scar on his thigh. Transfixed by the shapes swinging between his legs, and by the way he cupped them in his hands as he washed, Flora stared, only ducking away when he reached for a towel. She ran home, and never made the connection between the sight and the sensations in her own body. Even so, she hadn't told Polly.

Well Road was slippery and she was forced to hug the centre. A car breasted the rise, drove towards her, weaving over the frozen puddles, and slowed down.

'Morning.' Robin Lofts wound down the window of a Ford which had seen better days. The handle gave an unoiled shriek.

'Morning.' Flora stopped. 'Did you have a good Christmas?'

'Christmas? What's that? Never heard of it.' Robin folded his arms across the steering wheel and smiled, and Flora knew that she was not meant to feel sorry for him. Under his hat, his face was grey with exhaustion. 'I'm so tired, I can barely speak.'

'Oh, I *am* sorry,' said Flora. 'Then you won't be coming out today?'

Robin bent over so his forehead touched his hands and then

looked up. 'Good Lord, no,' he said. 'I never hunt.' He added matter-of-factly, 'I don't like the killing.'

'I see.'

'No, you don't,' he said in the same tone that intrigued, and piqued, Flora, 'but it's quite all right.' Clearly, Dr Lofts held strong views. Flora was aware that she was under scrutiny — a bug under a microscope? or an interesting arrangement of muscles? — and the knowledge that her hair was falling out of its plait gave Dr Lofts an advantage.

Their frozen breath met and swirled.

'The way I feel,' he was saying, 'I shall go to bed for a week and never stir. It was a long night.'

He did not add: a panic-stricken episode filled with the cries of a labouring mother and the spectre of a nearly botched delivery because he, the doctor, had been too tired to notice that the baby's heartbeat was dropping.

'Nothing bad, I hope,' she said, brushing away a wisp of hair trapped between her lips.

'Only birth.' Robin found himself wondering what it would feel like to plait Flora's hair back into place. 'A tricky breech.'

Flora hoped she was not blushing. After all, birth was *perfectly* natural. Nevertheless, her eyes slithered away from his gaze and fixed on the Gladstone bag on the passenger seat. 'Will somebody give you breakfast, Dr Lofts?' she asked, imagining she was on safe ground, and then realizing, with something approaching desperation, that he might think she was prying into his private life. 'I mean . . .' Now she did go bright red. 'I'm sorry . . . but you might be called out again.'

Robin groaned theatrically, and covered his ears. 'I instructed my sister, Ada, to keep bacon and eggs on the go and if anybody, anything, gets in the way of this man and his bacon . . .'

The idea of food made him feel more energetic. He sat up in the car seat and some of the exhaustion left his face. Flora noted that where his neck met his collar the colour of the skin was lighter and a scar puckered the tip of his chin. Now that made him interesting. Moreover, she approved of the way his eyebrows were unusually dark for his colouring. Back in the nursery,

Flora's book of jungle animals still sat on the bookshelf. Dr Lofts reminded her of a mongoose. A beautiful brown animal with telling eyes, which, with a flick of its head, could sink its teeth into the enemy and never let go.

'Are you enjoying your work in Nether Hinton?'

'Was it you,' Robin's interesting eyebrows questioned Flora, 'who warned me I would have to live here for fifteen years before I would be accepted?'

A little piqued he hadn't remembered she had told him that in Rolly Harris's yard, Flora smiled nevertheless. 'Goodness,' she said. 'It's that bad?'

He was silent, tapping his finger on the steering wheel. 'Yes,' he said, and a hint of uncertainty in his voice made Flora's heart quicken in sympathy.

By now she was sure she was frozen to the last toenail. 'I really must go. I am sorry you won't be following the hunt, it's the tradition round here on Boxing Day, but I understand. I do hope you get some rest, Dr Lofts.'

Robin depressed the accelerator, and sent a cloud of black exhaust into the sparkling verge. 'Thank you. I will.' He shoved at the gear stick.

'Dr Lofts, do you need any help at the surgery at all?' Flora spoke off the top of her head. 'I mean, if I helped at the surgery then people would—' She came to a halt.

They looked at each other, and Flora imagined she detected a flash of impatience and offence, and thought: He is rather frightening. Then Robin's face cleared and he smiled, and she saw beyond to a sweetness and gentleness she did not normally associate with men.

'Thank you,' said Robin. 'I'll certainly think about that.'

'Goodbye, then,' she said.

He watched her tall figure with its attractive, pear-shaped bottom walk away, and concluded that she had not meant to be patronizing. Rather, in keeping with her generous body Miss Flora Dysart possessed a generous spirit.

*

By ten thirty the drive was seething: sightseers, grooms, horses shifted and stamped over the gravel and left hoof indentations on the edge of the lawn.

'Flora! Hallo, there. Is Polly here?' Cecil Chanctonbury urged his mount through the crush alongside Guinevere.

'Hallo, Cecil.' Cecil always pronounced his name *Ceecil*, but Flora could never bring herself to do the same because it made her laugh. 'Happy Christmas, Cecil. Polly's over there.' She pointed her whip in the direction of her sister. 'Groaning, no doubt, at how stiff she'll feel after today.'

'Flora. There you are.' Harry Goddard cut Cecil off and edged his horse neatly in between the two. 'How are you?'

'Excuse me,' protested Cecil.

'Bad luck, old boy,' said Harry, and waved him away. 'The spoils to the strongest and all that.'

Flora tried not to giggle. 'Harry!' she said reprovingly. Her habit caught on the end of Harry's spur and she wrestled to free it. 'I wish,' she said for the hundredth time, 'that I could always ride astride.'

Harry helped to rescue the black worsted. 'I think you should know that when George Sand appeared on the hunting field in breeches, *tout* Paris observed she had the biggest bottom in France.'

'Harry!'

'Wish I could see yours, old girl. Would make my day.' Harry touched his heels to his mount's sides and it shimmied forward. Guinevere picked her hoofs up over the iced gravel and followed.

'Where's Father?' Flora asked Danny, who was handing round the mulled wine.

Danny jerked a finger in the direction of the stables just as Rupert, whip held high, clattered into view on his raw-boned bay beast. Challenged by the noise and colour, the bay responded and backed up against the wall with an explosion of frozen gravel. 'Keep still, damn you.' Rupert slapped his horse's neck.

The huntsman had driven the hounds into an untidy bunch by the corner of the house. The whipper-in cursed, and wielded his whip at the rogues who were determined to break ranks. Their baying took on a higher, more frantic, note.

'Don't bloody do that,' shouted Danny above the noise, when the whip was used too enthusiastically on Jupiter.

'Shush, Danny.' Not wishing for a scene, Flora touched his shoulder. Frowning, he glanced up at her.

'They're *my* 'ounds, Miss Flora.'

She stared down at him, struck by the contrast between this taut, anguished Danny and the softened, naked man on whom she had once spied.

Danny handed Flora a glass of wine. It trickled down her throat, sweet, almost cloying, releasing its afterburn. Her senses flared in response, and when she looked up, her vision alcohol-edged, the world was twice as bright.

As if piped onto the trees and bushes by a master confectioner, the frost glittered silver white. Behind them, lit from cellar to attic, the house reposed on a carpet of ice, its paintwork gleaming. In front of it swirled the kaleidoscope of the hunt: scarlet and black coats, dripping noses, breeches strained over thighs, top hats, encrusted here and there with green. Warring with the scent of frost, was the odour of fresh horse droppings and the yeasty tonic note of horse and sweat. Voices, hounds, horses and movement counter-pointed against each other – so familiar and so much part of Flora.

The sun was beginning to patch the carpet of ice. Her muscles tightened in anticipation. She told herself to be careful: a lot of ground was sheltered, north-facing and treacherous. Guinevere arched her neck and jumped back on stiff legs. Drops of her drink splattered down Flora's habit and she handed back the glass to Danny.

There's nothing like it, she thought, dabbing at the spots of liquid. Nothing.

Matty had retreated to the steps out of the way of the horses and Kit edged alongside her on Vindictive to say goodbye.

'Good luck,' said the small figure huddled in a musquash coat.

'You will take care?' A matching hat was pulled down over her face so that only her mouth was visible.

'Don't worry.'

Matty handed up a packet wrapped in waxed paper. 'Anchovy paste sandwiches,' she said. 'I know you get hungry mid-morning.'

'Terrific,' said Kit and stowed them in his coat tail. 'I've never had that sort of treatment before.' He grabbed Matty's leather-clad hand and kissed it with affection. Flora, who had just ridden up, was taken in – she had no idea how much easier it was for Kit to demonstrate affection for his wife in public.

'How kind you are to me,' Kit said to Matty, whose mouth unclamped in a smile of relief.

Robbie waved from her position at the top of the steps. 'Think of us back here, won't you?'

Danny told the whipper-in to bugger off and went to fetch the gun which always came with him out hunting. Just in case.

With a cracking of whips, flushed from drink and cold, they moved off into the rising sun.

Kit and Flora rode up in the front, Kit, from long habit, settled into Vindictive's rolling stride, confident that his horse liked nothing better than an obstacle-strewn gallop. As he and Flora turned left out of the drive, he looked back to the foreshortened figure of his wife on the steps watching them. Brother and sister raised their whips in farewell.

Hunting fraternities are the same everywhere and were repli-cated in hunting country all over England that Boxing Day, as recognizable as a Surtees print. So, too, were the rituals, and topics of conversation: gossip about bloodstock and breeding, familiar jokes – and the secret quasi-sexual thrill that pulsed under the hunting coats.

The horses could not be persuaded to walk, and the riders jogged past Jonathan's Kilns, filed through the narrow hunt gate and then let their horses rip over the turf towards the straggle of beeches at Long Copse.

As always, Guinevere did her convincing imitation of a crab at the sight of an open gate. She sidled up to the opening, pranced as Flora scolded her, and then barged through knocking Flora's leg on the post as she did so. Then they were away over the mud-freckled turf with the wind cutting across Flora's cheeks.

The hounds drew at Long Copse. The field watched, tense and expectant, the horses pricked their ears and shuddered in a cloud of vaporized breath.

Then it began. The lead hound had worked his way to the far corner of the copse and sounded. Another took it up, and in a split second the music of a pack in full cry reverberated through the chilled air.

A bowler-hatted farmer in ratcatcher on a roan lifted his whip and pointed to the west. 'Charlie's gone over to Horsedown,' he said to Flora. 'They'll be crossing the hedges.'

Flora shivered pleasurably in anticipation.

A surge of horses, a cry from the riders, and the line broke. Everyone went for it together across the field, through the gate and up into Swanthorpe's territory. Too busy holding in Guinevere to think, Flora guided her over the hedge, then a post and rails.

A delicious, tingling feeling exploded in her chest. *This is what I love.* The sound of hoofs over turf drummed in her ears, the muscles in her legs clenched and rose with the horse, the bruise on her shin ached and swelled. The roan thundered past, bearing the farmer.

'Charlie's going to double back,' he shouted. 'Stick with me, Miss Flora.'

Panting hard, Flora reined in Guinevere, and together she and her companion picked their way up the grassy rise above the valley floor. Down below, they saw the hounds check and, for a few minutes the pack milled, noses hard to the ground. Again a hound sounded and the pack raced back down the valley.

'There's Charlie.' The farmer jerked his whip, and Flora saw quite clearly the fox climbing up into a ploughed field, its coat almost the same colour as the russet soil.

'My God,' said the farmer. 'He'll take them over the hedges.'

Flora strained to get a better view. 'Hurrah,' she said.

154

The hedges were a series of blackthorn barriers as high as a horse's withers. They guarded gaping ditches and were talked about with respect as the biggest in North Hampshire. They took nerve and a steady hand.

The field was now moving up the plough where, a few seconds ago, Flora had seen the fox. The horses floundered – and then they were out, bearing left across the grass that led to the first of the hedges. Itching to follow, Flora watched the scarlet arc of the Master's coat as he soared over the first obstacle. A grey followed, ridden side-saddle and, after that, the whole field made a gigantic charge.

After the first hedge, two horses galloped on riderless and after the third there was another. Flora breathed in sharply. 'Ye ancient gods, go on, Kit. Go on, Father. DO IT.'

'I've got to go,' she said to the farmer. Away she went down the slope in a hail of mud.

Rising and falling like a wave over the hedges, Rupert's bay pounded over the ground in between. The hounds bayed, high and excited. Then, as the stallion rose for what must have been the seventh or eighth time, he appeared to stop in mid-air, a powerful, scarlet-topped icon, before crashing down. Spinning in a lazy parabola over his horse came Rupert.

Splayed over the hedge, the horse lay quiet for a terrible moment, then struggled frantically before crashing with a scream onto its rider below.

Matty fought the desire to retreat to her bedroom and remain there for the rest of the day. But it was Boxing Day, the house was full of guests and Mrs Dawes was treating her to sighs and long silences. In addition, Polly's nanny was apparently being sick in the servants' cloakroom ('A little bit sinister, don't you think, Mrs Kit?' commented Robbie), and the baby appeared to have taken against Robbie. Babies had more sense than she had supposed, concluded Matty. The day stretched out, milestoned by domestic crises.

'I had no idea,' Matty confided to Mrs Pengeally over coffee, 'that running a house was so full of problems. Everywhere I turn I trip over someone's hurt feelings.'

This was quite a speech for Matty, and a measure of her irritation. Mrs Pengeally looked magisterial – something she was not often able to do as the vicarage was small and, worse, understaffed. 'Dear Mrs Dysart, if I can be of any help do let me know.'

'For instance,' Matty fiddled in her cuff for her handkerchief, 'Mrs Dawes does not wish to serve tea in the drawing room for no other reason than that it has always been served in the library.'

Mrs Pengeally's mouth had sprouted a coffee fringe and she scrubbed at it with her serviceable handkerchief. 'Ask her advice first,' she said. 'I always think that works.'

'Does it?' Matty retrieved hers, delicate, lace-edged, from her sleeve, unaware of the glances Mrs Pengeally was directing at it. 'Mrs Pengeally, I'm sorry to be bothering you with all this.'

'Nothing to it, my dear.' Mrs Pengeally helped herself generously to the sugar. 'Take it from an old hand.' And over a second cup, Mrs Pengeally proceeded to demonstrate just how old a hand she was. So grateful was Matty that she offered to take her out to see how the hunt was going.

It was midday by the time the pony trap was ready. After the log fire in the drawing room, the cold was vicious and, despite lap rugs, both women shivered as Jem, the stable boy, urged Billy into a fast trot.

'There they are.' Matty pointed up the road where a glimmer of scarlet was visible making its way towards the hedges. The horn sounded; unmistakable and provoking.

'Off they go,' said Mrs Pengeally through her handkerchief, and the colour whipped into Matty's face. Forgetting her fear of horses, she half rose in her seat.

'Take care, Mrs Dysart. You'll upset the cart.'

'Can you see my husband, Mrs Pengeally?'

'I think he's there, up at the head of the field.'

Matty leant foward and tapped Jem on the shoulder. 'Drive up the road, please, Jem.'

The thin, sharp air was alive with baying, pounding and whinnying, shot through with the rounder note of the horn which made Matty shiver inside.

'Go on, Jem,' she urged, and Mrs Pengeally clutched at her hat.

At the crest of the slope, the road veered round to the right and, as they went round at a smart clip, they heard the scream from the direction of the hedges. High and full of agony.

'Oh, no,' Matty gasped. 'Oh, no.' The pony jerked up his head and skidded round the corner.

'Don't look.' Idiotically, Mrs Pengeally tried to cover Matty's face with her hands, and as Matty struggled free, she knocked Jem and Billy missed his footing. The trap slewed to a halt, one wheel spinning on the verge, the other rammed into the ditch.

'Let go, Mrs Pengeally. Let me . . . go.' Matty fought free of the other woman, fell down from the trap and ran towards the gate into the field.

The gate catch was frozen but Matty pulled at it with a strength she was not aware she possessed until it yielded. Then, forgetting she had not run properly for years, she tore full tilt over the uneven ground towards the untidy knot of people by the hedges.

It was over when Matty arrived. The bay was already down, the broken bone in its hind leg protruding through the skin. Beside him lay Rupert, arms and legs assembled in strange positions, blood rushing with horrifying speed from a cut on his face.

Matty pushed her way through the ring of people, knelt down and took Rupert's hand. It was a useless thing to do, but the voice in her head dealing with the emergency said it was important, and she cradled it, cold and limp, in her own as if her life depended on it. She shifted closer to the object lying on the turf that was her father-in-law, and mud smeared over her frock.

The stallion screamed again, and feet ran to and fro. Matty continued to stare at Rupert, focusing on the blood-embroidered face and listening to the snoring breaths. More hoofs pounded across the field and Kit, hatless and mud-covered, shouted, 'Where's the gun?'

Danny came running from the direction of the gate with the rifle. He split it, loaded and handed it over to Kit who knelt beside the horse.

'Easy, boy.' Matty knew with dreadful clarity that Kit was almost crying. 'I'm coming. I'm coming.' He piloted the gun to the horse's head and fought to keep it on target as the stallion reared his head. 'Help me, Danny,' he said.

'Get back,' shouted someone else.

'Help me,' said Kit.

And Matty continued to cradle Rupert's hand and to gaze into his face until the gun went off and the screaming ceased.

It required four men to carry Rupert across the field.

One of the spectator's cars raced back into the village to warn the doctor, and Robin Lofts was waiting at the house when the procession arrived. He took Rupert's pulse and ran a professional eye over the angle of his legs. He noted the pallor, the breathing, the wet patch where urine had leaked, and asked to be shown the telephone.

Rupert's children waited as Robin worked. The odours of horse, mud, and disinfectant from his bag filled the library where Rupert had been taken, and the lamp threw a dim, sinister light over the form on the sofa.

'What do you think, Dr Lofts?' Flora grabbed Robin.

'It's serious,' he said, 'and he must get to hospital as soon as possible. The ambulance is on its way from Fleet.'

Kit moved towards the sofa and looked down at his father. Wanting something to do, he bent over to wipe the saliva off Rupert's chin.

Barrenness and death, thought Matty.

An extra loud breath from the injured man brought Robin back to the bedside. Breath soughed in and out of Rupert's nostrils, and a fresh clot of blood appeared in one.

'Quick,' said Polly in a high, panicked voice. 'Quick. He's dying. Do something!'

HARRY

The traditional gardener is at pains to make his garden neat and tidy before winter is set in – but if he wishes to maintain a habitat for wildlife, habits must change.

I sympathize. Controlled neglect is difficult to learn after a lifetime of being tidy, but it is worth it. At least, I think so. A heap of leaves left *in situ* provides a winter base for hedgehogs, and food for birds. Dead stalks provide homes for insects, damp corners a refuge for frogs, toads and newts – and they pay for their keep by banqueting on your slugs and aphids. If you spread the winter digging over the season, hungry birds can feast on the exposed cut worms, or pests.

It is symbiosis between garden, animal and human – a back-scratching arrangement which is easy to effect, offers constant theatre and gives me rare pleasure.

Thomas and I make a point of taking winter walks, and we look out for the fieldfares and redwings who work in gangs on hawthorn berries in hedgerows, what remains of them. Did you know that long-tailed tits are easier to see in winter than at any other time, especially in birch woods? The trackmarks left by animals in the frost and snow remind us of the secret life that continues out of our sight.

Winter has its compensations.

Very often our walks take us past the church. When I was little I often scrabbled around in the graveyard and poked around the building. I don't know what I was searching for. Perhaps it was clues to the past. Looking back, it provided a crucible for my tastes – fusty, a touch lugubrious, and very English.

The village is proud of its church whose original was mentioned in the Domesday Book. Subsequently, it featured a vaulted chancel and a stone tower that was so heavy the walls buckled outwards. In 1846 it was restored. Apart from a new bell frame and altar rails, nothing much has changed since then – an odd repair here and a patching up of the fabric there. The older limes in the avenue were planted in 1759, the younger ones by the Burial Board in 1879 and, until comparatively recently, it was the custom to sing carols from the top of the tower on Christmas morning.

Over the centuries inscriptions have come and gone, some defaced by Parliamentarians who threw entrenchments round the church. A handsome brass under the east window commemorates the lords of the manors of Itchel and Eweshot. As soon as I could read, I traced the names. Giffords, Lefroys, Eggars, Knights, Smitherses, Kings, Snuggses and Varndells – the roster of an English village, yeoman and squire.

If you search on the wall dividing the school from the churchyard you will find a small plaque. It says: IN MEMORY OF HESTHER DYSART, NÉE KENNEDY. Poor, troubled Hesther, who came all the way from America to better her social standing. She, too, is part of the history that makes up this place.

In winter, the garden is like the churchyard, stripped to its skeleton, buff, flat brown, a wasteland, a place of death – and also of rebirth.

CHAPTER THREE

RUPERT DID not die that night, nor during the ensuing weeks when nurses at the hospital kept a twenty-four-hour watch, and the doctor left instructions that he was to be fetched at any hour of day or night if necessary.

A hush fell over the house. The Christmas guests were dispatched home, telephone calls were conducted in crisis-ridden tones, and meals snatched in spare moments. The Christmas tree remained in the hall long after Twelfth Night had come and gone, and Mrs Dawes was forced to give away dozens of mince pies.

'It is likely your father will never walk again,' Robin told Kit in a tense interview. 'His back is broken and he will require intensive nursing care for the rest of his life.'

'Are you sure?'

'Quite sure. What you must decide is if you are willing to have him at home with you, or if you wish to place him in an institution which specializes in this kind of patient. Great advances have been made in this area, and we could find one that is absolutely up to date.'

Kit was exhausted. As often happens to those closest to the victim, the accident had both galvanized and depleted him: he was motoring twice a day to the hospital, and wrestling with the business affairs of the house. He pushed his hair back from his forehead and took Robin's measure.

'There is no question of what we should do,' he said, grimly.

Robin approved the decision. 'I will arrange for your father to come home as soon as possible. You accept that you must engage a nurse?'

Shock had rendered his emotions precarious and unpredictable and Kit felt angry about the accident; delighted — and guilty at feeling so — that, at last, he was in charge; worried by the consequences; haunted by an extraordinary idea that his mother had taken revenge from the grave.

Perhaps if Kit had felt able to talk to Matty, he would have found the solace of thrashing things out, a catharsis from confession. But he did not. Neither did Matty have the courage, nor the wisdom, to take matters into her own hands. Into the vacuum between them slipped Daisy — a memory as powerful and seductive as the lost Grail. Because Kit meant to be honourable, he tried to censor his thoughts — but discovered that no one can guard the unguardable.

Nevertheless, it was Matty who waited up for him to return home, whatever the hour, with a Thermos of soup and sandwiches, Matty who ensured that the fire was kept burning, that the whisky decanter was full and who invited him into her bed when he needed release. Matty dealt with telephone calls, letters of condolence, reorganized meals, took Flora's coming-out at the forthcoming Season into her own hands, gave Kit her capital and urged him to settle business matters as he wished.

Kit should have been grateful. In one sense he was, deeply so. But charity is hard to accept, and Matty was doling it out. Sometimes he looked up at his wife opposite him at the table, or in her chair by the fire, at the pale face, incongruous lower lip and vulnerable eyes, at the *smallness* of her, and was shaken not by affection but by irritation, and wondered how he was going to get through this marriage.

Guiltily, he set out to treat her with scrupulous politeness and consideration.

'What did she say?' Ellen was filling in a coupon and gave Ned only half her concentration.

'She asked me how I made the plants grow. How did I look after them? How did I make a garden? I said it was a lifetime's work. Then she said a very strange thing. "Good," she said. "It might last me." Then she said I wasn't to pay any attention to anything she said.'

'How odd, Ned. The garden's your job.'

'I said my knowledge had taken me a long time to get, not wishing to be rude, like, but I didn't want to waste it.'

'I know *that*.' Ellen spoke from over thirty years of marriage.

The stove at Clifton Cottage was giving off a satisfactory heat and Ned pulled his chair closer. As usual, he sat with legs akimbo, exposing the patch where his thighs had rubbed the corduroy bare, nursing his beer. He looked as though he was thinking hard. Suddenly alert, Ellen abandoned the coupon. It was an expression she recognized, a compound of obstinacy and suppressed excitement. Once upon a time – when they used to walk up towards Barley Pound between the billows of dog rose and honeysuckle – that look had been directed at her. These days, it was reserved for the dratted garden. Sometimes Ellen minded, like she minded about the creases folded into Ned's skin, the slackening under his chin, and his hair, once so thick and tawny. Sometimes she didn't.

She returned to *Good Housekeeping* – lent by Mrs Dawes who, in turn, had been given it with a great deal of graciousness by Mrs Pengeally. 'The fashionable hostess knows that by offering her guests Shelley china she is offering the best . . .' she read. Casting a critical eye over the china, Ellen was thankful she was not a fashionable hostess.

'Are you listening, Ellen?'

Good Housekeeping would have to wait, and Ellen stacked it away. Then she noticed a puddle of beer on the table top and went to fetch a cloth. Ned drank his beer and watched his wife scrub the patch.

'Stop fussing, girl,' he said. 'You're always fussing and worrying.'

'Get on with your beer, Ned.' Ellen pursed her lips, then remembered it accentuated the furrows between her nose and chin and *Good Housekeeping* had said you should not do that. 'I like to keep things clean, particularly if I'm out all day.'

It was an ancient battle between them – Ellen's cleaning and Ned's untidiness – and he did not reply. Instead he said, 'I was finishing the compost when she steals up on me, as quiet as a little bird.' Ned poured a second mug of beer from the stone bottle. 'Do you know what I think, girl?'

'What?' Ellen wrung out the cloth over the sink and folded it before sitting down opposite her husband.

Gently she smiled at him, her touchiness forgotten. Ned was cold and pinched from a day spent outside, and his fingers even more swollen. Ellen's hands clenched in sudden fright. They *were* growing older, the pair of them, and she wanted to protect Ned from what was going to happen, for Ellen found it easier to bear suffering herself than to witness it in others.

She helped herself to the beer. 'I know one thing for sure. You're going to tell me. What *do* you think, then?'

'I think she'd been crying again. Like the other time I found her.'

'Poor lass.' Ellen took a sustaining mouthful. Her tone combined genuine regret and just a touch of smugness at the idea that the gentry had problems as well as ordinary folk. 'I heard that Robbie woman talking to Mrs Dawes. I don't think she or Mrs Dawes likes her. I don't understand it. I think she's a sweet thing, and quite nice-looking sometimes.'

'He'll get used to her. Especially the money.'

'Ned!'

'It's true, girl.'

'It's a shame. Mr Kit is never at home. Still, they have had a bit of trouble. She must know we talk about her.' The beer was relaxing, and Ellen finished hers. She was about to help herself to more when she saw Ned eyeing the bottle, and instead pushed it in his direction.

'I feel sorry for her,' she said. 'She seems such a child among those great lummoxes. So what was going on, then, about the garden?'

Ned shrugged.

He had been working in the kitchen garden, digging over a pile of compost rotting down nicely in the bins, when Matty said from behind him, 'Mr Sheppey?'

Panting slightly, Ned turned. Matty hovered on the path, pale and red-eyed, and when Ned came closer he observed that her eyelashes had clumped into points, giving her a young, uncertain look which made him want to put his arm around her.

Ned Sheppey, they clap people like you in jail, he thought to himself.

'Mr Sheppey. I wanted to thank you for that time when . . . you will remember. I am sorry it's taken so long to say something, but you know about Sir Rupert. You were very kind to me.'

He watched as her fingers pleated and unpleated her coat belt. 'Is Sir Rupert doing well, Mrs Kit, now he's back home?'

'Oh, yes. He's sitting up in bed and asking for proper meals. We were terribly pleased when he wanted a steak and kidney pie.'

It was one of those deceptive afternoons when the sun, shaking loose from the clouds, felt warm and springlike. Matty untied her headscarf and ran her fingers through her hair. The gesture was familiar and Ned searched in his mind for the reference. It came to him. His daughter Betty had always done that – taken off her hat in front of the mirror and combed her fingers through the hair by her ears. Sometimes, she had pressed her face close up to the mirror and sighed at the reflection.

Ned turned his attention back to the compost and spotted some dead couch grass caught in the prunings. He bent down to extract it.

Matty watched. 'Why do you do that?'

'Couch grass is a devil for compost, and I'm going to put these prunings into the bin when I've cut 'em up small, like.' Ned began to shovel crumbly, pleasant-smelling material into the right-hand bin and tossed in an extra forkful of horse manure.

'Beautiful,' he said to himself.

'You make it sound very interesting,' commented Matty from the path. 'I've lived in London for most of my life, so I don't know anything about gardening. Apart from the things in my mother's notebooks. She was a botanist, you see.'

Ned drove the spade into the earth. 'Takes a long time, Mrs Kit. Time and care. This garden has been let go for many years.'

'I suppose the family couldn't keep it up.'

'Yes, ma'am.'

'I'd like to know for sure. I must ask my husband.' She

laughed to hide her embarrassment. 'I haven't discussed this with him, but I am sure the garden is something we will wish to do something about.'

She *was* like Betty, Ned decided. Betty had worn that same expression when she wanted to know something: eager and bright-eyed. *I want to know, Dad. Tell me.*

'Could you take me round the garden, Mr Sheppey, please, and tell me about it and what makes it productive?'

Remembering Betty made Ned feel both prickly and yearning at the same time. He rubbed his arthritic finger. 'Bend down, Mrs Kit,' he said after a moment.

Matty hesitated, and the suspicion crossed her mind that Mr Sheppey might be a little eccentric.

'Bend down,' Ned insisted, forgetting who Matty was. 'Take a handful of the soil.' Still Matty hesitated. 'Go on, Mrs Kit, it won't hurt you.'

Matty did as she was told, scraped her fingers along the earth, feeling it cake under her nails, and brought up some soil. She proffered her palm to Ned. 'What do I do now?'

'What does it feel like?'

Matty gave it an experimental poke with her finger. 'Wet.'

'If you rub some between your finger and thumb what happens?'

'It rolls into a ball.'

'That's good soil, then, Mrs Kit.'

Matty stared at the lump in her hand which did not tell her very much, but she had no reason to suppose that he was wrong.

'That's where you have to start, Mrs Kit. If you take away from the soil, even the good soil you have there, you must give it something back.' Matty found herself nodding as if she had known these facts all her life. 'Every garden needs good compost, otherwise it won't give of its best.'

Matty dropped the ball of earth, and rubbed her hands with a handkerchief. 'I think I understand. I hope you don't mind me asking all these questions?'

Ned mixed a spadeful of grass cuttings into the compost to stop it turning slimy, and forked the mixture back into a compact heap to prevent too much air getting in. He seemed a little flummoxed by Matty's enquiry.

'It's not my business to mind, Mrs Kit.' Then he realized he might have overstepped the mark and said, 'You must ask me what you like.'

Matty stowed her handkerchief in her pocket. 'Mr Sheppey . . .' She groped for what she wanted to say. 'I would *like* it if you explained things to me.'

That was a new one on Ned: it tended to be the other way round with employers and it crossed *his* mind that the new mistress was soft in the head.

'Do you see, Mr Sheppey?'

Do I? Ned asked himself as he dug. Down, swing, up; in the rhythm his father had taught him and his father before that. In the pause in their conversation, broken only by the thud of the spade, Matty and Ned absorbed each other. An interrogatory silence, which, if they had known, put down a milestone in a partnership.

Years ago, Betty had watched Ned fork compost, swinging her legs, tapping a twig against the wheelbarrow, impatient, runny-nosed, eyes screwed up against the sun. 'Dad, come on. Mum's waiting.'

Children were like strawberry plants. You wrapped them in straw and kept the frost off. Then they put down runners and moved on.

'Ask me anything you like, then, Mrs Kit.'

There was relief on her face when she said, 'Thank you, Mr Sheppey. You see, what with one thing and another, I haven't really had time to look at the garden properly.' Then after a moment, she added, 'Show me where you work, please.'

Enclosed by walls, the kitchen garden was peaceful, a private place set apart from the public vistas seen from the house.

Matty remembered from her first visit the nail holes studding the walls where fruit had once been trained. In the sun the brick was a pleasing flowery pink but it was obvious that only half the area was in use. Ned's carefully hoed rows of vegetables were already spiked with green, and the apple trees were in bud. Glass cold frames, some with the panes lifted to let in the warmth, were clumped in miniature villages over tender plants. In the smaller greenhouse Ned had planted out seedlings in discarded Tate and Lyle boxes. Hands in her pockets, Matty stood and observed, and felt herself relax.

She seemed weary as Ned conducted her down the path that bisected the walled garden and into the area that had been allowed to fall fallow – and he had a curious impression that he was leading her by the hand. Even stranger, that she wished him to.

'That was the old dairy,' he said, pointing it out. 'My grandmother used to give me glasses of buttermilk when she made the cheeses. But, you can see, we don't use this bit of the garden any more. It's too much for one person to manage.' His finger moved on. 'That was the rose house, that the peach house and that the vinery. In the old days, you understand . . .'

Once upon time, the glasshouses had been handsome buildings – arcs of shining glass and white ironwork. But now, with their smashed windows, they looked like buildings that had gone blind.

'When did it all start running down?' Matty was profoundly affected by the desolation.

'After the soldiers left. That must have been 1916, in the winter after Lady Hesther died. Sir Rupert decided to keep on only one gardener, that was me. The garden wasn't the same after the war.'

'What soldiers, Mr Sheppey?'

'The ones that had been wounded. The house was used as a convalescent home for officers. Lady Dysart wanted to help out while Sir Rupert was at the front.'

Matty digested this in silence. 'So you don't grow special fruit any longer?' she said. 'What happened to the vine?'

'It was dug up after Lady Dysart died.' Ned appeared to think that this explanation was sufficient, and Matty did not probe.

The inspection continued. Ned was not talkative, but what he said was to the point. He took Matty inside the vinery and the peach house, and then towards a row of sheds built onto the north wall.

Matty poked her nose into the first one, and the chill lapped her face. The shed was jammed with cobwebby bits of wood and wicker baskets with rotting straps.

'What are all these?'

Ned stood behind her. 'We used those hampers to send the fruit and vegetables up to the town house every week. But Sir Rupert sold it when things got bad.'

Mould coated the majority of the baskets. Matty ran her hand over one and it left a green-blue residue on her skin.

When she emerged from the shed, the daylight was bright and she put up a hand to shade her eyes.

'This one was the mushroom house, that the potting shed, and that one the carpenter's shed. That one, there, was the forcing house and this one . . .' Ned showed her through a green wooden door, 'is my office.'

Inside it was very cold, because the room faced north, and the brick floor added to the chill. Matty felt guilty and asked Ned if he spent much time in here. When he said he did, she resolved to procure him somewhere warmer.

There was just space enough for two people to lean against the counter top, which was so fixed that it caught the maximum light from the window. Stacked on a shelf were Ned's account books, their marbled backs powdery with age. On each of the spines was inscribed the name of the house and the date. 'Nineteen fifteen,' Matty read. 'Nineteen eighteen. The war years.' She touched the faded leather cartouche on the spine. 'I was only eight in nineteen fifteen.' A puff of dust rose from the spine and settled. 'A terrible war.' She paused and said, rather self-consciously, 'Sometimes, Mr Sheppey, I think the war will be with us for the rest of our lives. It's always hanging in the background and we can never get rid of it.'

Ned said nothing. He had been too flat-footed and chesty to go.

'Was anybody in the family killed?'

This was safer ground for Ned. 'Lady Dysart's brother, Mr Kennedy. Very fond of him, she was. When the war started, he was over here from America, visiting. Anyway, he wangled his way into the Hampshires with Sir Rupert. You could do that if you talked to the right person. We went to see them off at Farnham station . . .'

The station was choked with reservists making their way to their regiments, and the boys being sent out from the barracks, Ned said. There was a boy trumpeter, too. They blew the orders for the units to go forward with the guns or to cease fire. Only a trumpet can carry over the noise of battle. Anyway, he was there, and a lot of women and children, shrieking and waving banners, some of them crying.

The train at the platform was hung with a rough-and-ready banner made by the village children. In the first-class compartment sat a hamper filled with chicken pies, an Irish ham, hard-boiled eggs and a bottle of port, which Ned's mother had got up for the master.

Anyway, the band did them proud. Lady Dysart pecked Sir Rupert on the cheek and he climbed into the train. He looked fine in his uniform, it suited his kind of looks. Then she and Mr Kennedy talked for a long time – they were very alike to look at. He hugged her and she hugged him, and she pulled down her veil so it hid her face. She was dressed in dark green, Ned remembered, in a material that floated around her feet.

'Mr Kennedy stood on the steps of the train and waved, and that was the last we saw of him. Lady Dysart was not the same after he died.'

'I had no idea,' said Matty sadly.

'I do my seed orders here,' Ned said. Matty took her cue to change the subject.

She gazed at the books, the piles of paper stacked on the bench, Ned's pencil laid to one side and a list of seeds, written in a large hand, tacked up on the wall. She inhaled a mixture of soil and whitewash. There was sanity in the things here, she thought, which must help to douse old griefs. Not even the blood and pain of war could penetrate the heart of a garden.

'Thank you, Mr Sheppey.' She backed out into the sunshine. 'Do you think we could get the garden back to what it was like?'

A variety of expressions crossed Ned's face, all of them unreadable. 'It would take years,' he said.

She pointed to the paths that criss-crossed the walled-in space. 'Isn't it there? The old garden, I mean. Underneath? It's just a question of finding it. And of compost, of course.'

'I felt that mean,' Ned reported later to his wife, 'discouraging her. But she doesn't have an idea how much work there'd be to put the garden to rights.'

It was bath-time in Clifton Cottage, and Ned was in a tin bath in front of the fire. Ellen examined for cleanliness a washcloth, which had once been part of her mother's nightdress, before soaking it in the hot water. She squeezed it over Ned's head.

'You should have been a bit kinder. The poor thing doesn't know what she's doing.'

'It's only a passing fancy.' Ned allowed Ellen to soap between his toes. Hard at the best of times, the water was beige-coloured and scum-flecked. Ellen winced as she knelt on her bad knee to wash Ned's back. It had developed a lump since the accident and was uncomfortable. Ned's skin was dead white across his shoulder blades, and flecked with moles, but where his neck rose out of his shirt collar, the skin was light brown and softly wrinkled. When she had finished, Ellen got up and picked up the towel airing by the stove. 'Up,' she said.

Ned dried himself. A good rub between the legs, over the back and down the arms. He never varied the ritual. Ellen held out his long johns, then his shirt and, hampered by his damp skin, Ned fought to get into his clothing. Ellen went on, 'Mrs Dawes is worried that she's going to poke her nose into everything. I said to her, why shouldn't she? Apparently she wants to have the attics out, and to make a list of everything in the house. If you ask me, Mrs Dawes has a bad conscience because she hasn't kept everything up to scratch. I've seen cupboards of stuff in the old laundry and the attics are a disgrace.'

Ned was not paying attention. 'I suppose it could be done.'

'What?'

'The garden, Ellen. What do you think we've been talking about?'

'Well, I've been talking about something, and you weren't listening.'

Ellen scooped the bucket into the tin bath and brought it up dripping. 'You have to watch it, Ned. That family can be careless. They could be careless with us.'

Ned pulled out his pipe, and knocked burnt tobacco shreds into the stove. 'Been to the cinema lately, girl?' he asked. 'Giving you ideas, is it?'

As soon as Matty felt the moment was right – and she had not quite gauged how to tackle Kit – she asked him if he had plans to overhaul the garden.

Kit was reading a letter from Raby. 'No, I don't,' he said and did not bother to look up. 'Do you think we should put your railway shares into steel?'

'Would you allow me to do so?'

At that Kit gave Matty his full attention. She fiddled with a loose thread on her suit. 'I'm quite keen on the idea and I've been reading about it. Gardening, I mean.'

'Oh.'

'*The Home Gardener's Year* and *Popular Gardening Annual* cost the grand sum of half a crown and there's heaps in them.'

'Good,' said Kit.

'Then there is Miss Jekyll.'

'Yes, I have heard of her.'

'She thinks flowers should be planted in drifts, just like a painting. It's a lovely idea.'

'If you like that sort of thing.'

Matty got up and poured Kit some whisky. 'It's the roses that fascinate me. Listen to this . . . albas, chinas, Bourbons, noisettes . . .'

'Have you gone Pre-Raphaelite or something?' asked Kit, accepting the glass.

'No,' said Matty with a smile. 'Those are the names given to the roses. Bit like poetry, really. So are the colours. Frothing white. Waxy cream. Blush pink.'

Kit put down the letter and spread his arm along the length of the sofa. 'All right,' he said, with his uneven smile. 'You've made your point. What do you want?'

Matty dropped down beside him. 'Let me organize the garden. Please, Kit. It would give me so much pleasure. I wouldn't tamper with it. Only restore it to what it was.'

He stared at her, the remote look, and she realized that she had made a mistake. Kit did not want her in the garden.

He did not want her anywhere.

Kit struggled to be polite. Matty's request touched on complicated feelings, not properly understood nor admitted, dark feelings from which he had distanced himself over many years and which had become a habit.

The house, yes, and Kit was grateful for all Matty had done, truly he was. But the garden belonged to another part of his past, and he did not wish Matty to be involved.

Not yet, anyway.

'Look, Matty,' Kit took both her hands in his and held them tightly — for this problem was not of Matty's making — and gave her the half truth at which he was becoming adept, 'there's too much to do. What with Father and Flora's coming out.'

'Please, Kit.' She looked woebegone and unhappy, and her excitement was visibly draining away. Kit cursed himself.

He took a deep breath and lied. 'I promised the doctor that you wouldn't do too much. He gave me a serious lecture about your health, Matty.'

HARRY

March is a dangerous month: like a sexual tease, it can blow hot and cold, and it is impossible to anticipate which. A gardener *knows* November for what it is, expects nothing of January, but March is different. Seduced by the sun creeping through bare branches and by earth freckling with green, gardeners and, let it be said, plants, enjoy a collective *folie de grandeur*. How many times have hydrangeas, roses and clematis fallen cheerfully to growing, only to be savaged by frost and a north wind?

So, you ask, what can the gardener expect from March? After all, it is named after the god of war. Here I must put in my apologia for forsythia. 'So violent,' says Thomas. 'But brave,' say I. What other plant is generous enough to pour out gold at this time of year? I love it, and look for it each spring.

The forsythia does not sulk, unlike the hellebore. If sited in too heavy a shade, *Helleborus argutifolius*, another favourite of mine, collapses and yields its ghost to the wind. From the safety of the nursery till, I advise its lovers to give it deep rich soil, preferably lime and dappled shade and it will reward you with pale green flowers in March and April. Mix with the *Helleborus orientalis*, throw in a nostrum and good management, and the effect can be startling.

This is not to overlook the primulas or anemones, which do such valiant work under trees. I prefer white anemones, with their plump buds that open into slim white fingers. Once established, you can happily neglect them, a quality to cherish, and they will puff into charming drifts.

Apparently, the numbers visiting Hinton Dysart have doubled in the last five years and a new car park is being constructed in the East Field. 'The roses,' the Trust has concluded in its annual report, 'are the main attraction.'

Yes, that is right, but there are other things about Hinton Dysart. It exudes an indefinable quality, a nostalgia peculiar to England, a sense of order and, lying below the surface, the suggestion that the memory of many lives is folded into its fabric. Traces of old passions and tears, of striving, disappointment and happiness are echoed in the elusive scent of the pot-pourri, in the memorabilia and fading photographs.

Thomas tells me he does not agree. What is remembered by the visitor? he asks. A glimpse of a face in a grainy photograph, or the pink beauty of my mother's favourite 'Queen of Denmark'?

Unlike March, April is a roundabout of sun and rain. A dazzle of warm days and sharp evenings. April means wallflowers in spicy-scented formation, like soldiers deployed on a battlefield. In my grandfather's memory, I plant only tawny crimsons, as dark as the blood on the fields in Flanders.

'Vulcan' is my favourite, and I make sure there are pots of it under the drawing-room window of the cottage, placed in the spot where the sun warms their scent glands – and where Thomas and I will drowse after too good a lunch.

CHAPTER FOUR

IN HEALTH, Rupert was a difficult man and he was even more so in illness. On the afternoon that he returned home from hospital, he demanded whisky and to see Danny. Neither wish was granted then or later – which was just as well as Robbie was waiting, battlelight in her eye, to take on Danny.

In fact, she had been waiting for years, for when Bert Naylor, *Sergeant* Bert Naylor, donned his khaki, pressed the then young Violet Robson to his manly chest in farewell and went off to die of a blown-off head at Ypres, he left behind a woman of passionate emotions. Luckily for Violet, the Dysarts needed her services and, as Violet slipped into 'Robbie' and her life was subsumed by a family that was not her own, so she transferred her energies from the dead Bert to the living Rupert.

'Danny is not to set foot inside this bedroom, Miss Flora,' she said, 'so don't try and persuade him. The doctor said no visitors.' When Flora protested that this was unfair to her father, Robbie silenced her. 'Do you wish me to go against the doctor's orders?'

These days Robbie exuded power, like a cat ready to pounce and what she said held.

Deprived of Rupert, Danny's drinking bouts became more intense and it was seldom that Flora did not find him, either spectacularly drunk or hung-over, hunched on the floor of the pen with his hounds.

'Danny,' she begged, troubled by his decline. 'This isn't doing any good.' She led him back to the cottage, put on the kettle and made him drink tea. Danny settled into a chair with a neatly mended cover – how he managed to keep his house she did not know – and quizzed Flora with a pair of bloodshot eyes.

'What's wrong, Danny?'

'Nothing, Miss Flora. I like whisky, that's all.'

She looked round his home. Nothing much there, but all very clean. On the table lay one of his treasures, *Marching Songs for Soldiers, Set to Well-known Tunes*. Danny saw her looking at it and because he was still drunk, sang,

> 'D'ye ken John Peel, with his khaki suit,
> His belt and his gaiters, and his stout brown boot,
> Along with his guns, and his horse, and his foot,
> On the road to Berlin in the morning.'

'Promise me something,' demanded Rupert when Flora, rendered almost inarticulate by contradictions and hesitations because she was not used to talking to her father, eventually reported this state of affairs to him.

'If I can.'

Angry blue eyes focused on her. 'Damn you, Flora.'

'What is it, Father?'

Rupert turned his head restlessly from side to side. 'Since *I* can't any more, promise me to look after Danny.'

It was on the tip of Flora's tongue to cry out: *But you never looked after us.* Instead she found a lump rising into her throat because Rupert's request was so sad. 'Of course. Danny is quite safe.'

The eyes shifted to the map on the wall. 'I don't expect you to understand.' Cruelly, the pallor of illness had bleached Rupert's florid complexion, and an odour that Flora associated with the elderly emanated from the bedclothes – a smell she had tried to avoid in the past but now could not.

The wall opposite Rupert's bed was sacred to his private gods: no maid was ever allowed to touch the maps and photographs which covered it. The photographs were mostly of scenes taken under fire, or in the awkward intervals between, the sort that was beginning to appear in books about the Great War, and exuded a lost quality. There was one in particular of Grenadier Guards near the Messines Ridge, fighting their way towards an unsteady camera with Croonaert Wood, a burnt-out chapel and a litter of the dead and wounded in the background. Whoever held the camera had been frightened, under fire, or both. Beside it hung a map of the western front in 1914.

Rupert as supplicant presented Flora with a new, and not altogether welcome, side to her father and to her position as a daughter. She stood beside the bed, looked down and said the only thing she could think of. 'I know, Father. I know Danny is your friend. And mine.'

Primed by the drugs, Rupert was drifting into sleep. 'Then take care of him. I am asking you, Flora. Not Kit.'

Why not Kit? she thought, but was pleased that he had asked *her*.

As Rupert drifted into unconsciousness, the Oxfordshire Hussars staggered up towards the cavalry's position, and the London Scottish marched into battle, their pipes a gallant, heart-breaking sound. Rupert was back in the noise, smoke and rings of fire lighting the landscape by the Messines Ridge near Ypres in Flanders. The air vibrated with the staccato of machine guns, and the London Scottish, who had whooped and skirled their way through London and then northern France, played on as they were decimated by German infantry. Until only one pipe rose from the Ridge. Then it, too, was silent.

All day the battle raged and by sunset of what came to be known as Ypres Day brigades had been whittled to battalions, battalions to companies, companies to platoons. The Royal West Kents had four officers left (all subalterns), the 1st Coldstream two, the Scots Guards, Borderers, Gordon Highlanders and Grenadiers five apiece, and Rupert was shaking with exhaustion. Eighty of his company had gone but he was alive and so was Danny Ovens. Both were filthy, hoarse, thirsty.

Neither of them had any idea that the war would last four years – or that they and the remaining troops now burrowing like animals into the earth would end up longing for death.

Rupert sighed in his sleep.

*

Danny's welfare concerned their undemonstrative father far more than the news that the fall from his horse had broken his back, and Kit commented on it more than once. Matty suggested that Rupert was still in a state of shock so he did not understand. Kit rather agreed, but Flora was not so sure.

As for Rupert, he stepped up the calls for whisky and drove the family, and Miss Binns, the hired nurse, almost demented. Strangely enough, Robbie was the only one who could handle him when he got bad.

'No, Sir Rupert,' she said, the energy positively crackling through her blue serge uniform. 'No.'

And Rupert would quieten.

One day Flora's patience gave out and she smuggled in a couple of fingers of Glenmorangie in a glass. Rupert attacked it in two mouthfuls and demanded more. Flora did not give it to him, but later he ran a temperature and she spent most of the evening sponging his face and wrists.

The following morning, penitent, she cornered Robin Lofts outside the sick room and confessed to her crime. She was surprised at how much she minded Robin's look of contempt.

He did not bother to be polite. 'That was a stupid thing to do, Miss Dysart,' he said.

'I'm sorry. Truly sorry, Dr Lofts. But I couldn't bear it any longer. He needed comfort of some sort. Can't you see?'

'Why don't you talk to him instead of giving him whisky? That's what he needs.'

'Talk to Father?' she exclaimed, as if he had suggested learning Hebrew. 'I don't think he'd like that.'

'How do you know, Miss Dysart?'

'Dr Lofts, I know this sounds silly, but I wouldn't know what to say. Father doesn't seem to like us very much.'

Robin absorbed the information and reckoned that he had done enough for the moment by introducing the idea. 'That's up to you, Miss Dysart. But please don't ever give your father alcohol without checking with either me or the nurse.' He became very serious. 'It could have killed him.'

To her surprise, but not to his, Flora gulped and burst into tears. Robin reached into his bag, extracted a clean handkerchief, handed it to her and instructed her to cry as much as she liked. Flora, who would contort herself into knots rather than break down in public, discovered that she did not mind letting down her guard in front of Robin. In bed that night, she went hot at the memory, but while she was snuffling into Dr Lofts's handkerchief, she had had an illusion of being safe. When she offered it back, Robin had said, 'Keep it as long as you want. I have a supply in my bag for anxious relatives and patients.'

Flora resolved to order a dozen from Elphick's in Farnham and donate them to the surgery.

As she drifted towards sleep, it struck her that Robin Lofts was the type of good person against whom one measured oneself – and that was both an exhausting and exhilarating prospect.

These days Robin was even more than usually occupied, both with Rupert himself and with the negotiations required to ensure that matters ran smoothly between Miss Binns, who was used to having things her way, and Robbie, who felt she had high command of the sick room. So far, Robbie had won the skirmishes and Miss Binns had been relegated to night duty.

Even with his additional responsibilities at Hinton Dysart, the surgery and rounds in the village, Robin found time to consider Matty, whom he liked. He also scented a challenge. Matty had not enjoyed good health, and it did not take much for Robin to divine that she was unhappy. Hesitating to draw conclusions, he wondered if what he diagnosed was the understandable, and hopefully temporary, depression of the newly wed discovering that intimacy has its black side as well as pleasures. Or something else?

A couple of weeks later when he bumped into Matty coming down the big staircase, he drew her aside on the landing.

'Dr Lofts,' she said. 'Is Sir Rupert better today?'

'If you mean, is he in any danger, the answer is no. How he progresses is a different matter. Up to a point, he will get as well as he wishes to be.'

Together they went down the stairs and Robin tried to explain himself. 'You see, Mrs Dysart,' he said, 'I am increasingly drawn to the conclusion that patients can take charge of their illnesses and manage them with their minds.'

One hand on the banister, she looked up at him. She seemed to be inviting guidance and he plunged in.

'Mrs Dysart, I wondered, what with one thing and another, if you're getting enough sleep?'

'Oh dear,' she said. 'Is it that obvious?'

By now, they had reached the foot of the staircase where they came to a halt. Matty was growing her hair and it had reached the stage where it was neither one thing nor another and she put up a hand to pat at the wisps. Despite a faint fretwork of lines around her mouth and eyes, she looked child-like and out of her depth.

'Do I look that bad?' she asked.

'Everyone in the family is under strain.'

It was impossible to take offence at Dr Lofts, and Matty did not wish to. He was kind, went out of his way to show he liked her and she felt at ease with him. Perhaps it was because he was not very tall and, therefore, did not dominate her physically as many men did.

Robin had discovered that if you stood perfectly still people did not mind looking at you. He made her look at him. 'May I?' He reached over and checked her pulse against his watch. Lying in his detached, unemotional grasp, her hand shook a little.

Then he examined the tissue-paper skin and checked the open cracks between the fingers. Robin had seen similar conditions on neurotics at the clinic in London where he had worked as a student. 'Is your skin always so dry?'

'It comes and goes.'

Matty allowed her hand to remain where it was, and it crossed her mind that, apart from doctors, not many people had touched her voluntarily. Robin checked the worst areas and, on spreading her fingers, a crack broke open. Matty winced.

'I'm sorry. I'll send up some cream for this.' Robin released Matty's hand. 'I imagine it's difficult for you, Mrs Dysart, marrying into a large family and having to cope with a major crisis?'

Again she brushed at the wayward strands. 'Yes,' she admitted. 'Everyone knows everyone else very well, of course. I am the outsider, if you like, looking in. But I'm used to that.'

So that's it, he thought.

'Well, don't worry, Mrs Dysart,' he said. 'There is a remedy.'

Eagerness replaced the startled look. 'I would be grateful if you would tell me, Dr Lofts.'

Now Robin was sorry he had tackled her, as the answer was not simple. He glanced up at the family portraits ranged on the wall of the staircase, and at the crossed swords just above their heads which had belonged to ancestral Dysarts.

'Time,' he said finally. 'In a few years, no one will remember that you weren't born a Dysart.'

Robin Lofts had not supplied the answer to Matty's predicament because she had not told him the truth – a simple wish to be loved by her husband and to have his baby. During the day there were tricks to keep busy, but at night she had no defences.

In her dreams she circled round the outside of a garden full of flowers and fruit, prevented from entering by a hedge thick with sharp thorns. Inside, Daisy and Kit walked along the paths and sat on a bench in the sun, absorbed by each other. At their feet played the figure of a small, fair-haired girl. In the shadow, and desperate, Matty pushed against the hedge until the thorns pierced her flesh.

Matty sat up in bed, and pushed her hair out of her eyes. It was two o'clock in the morning.

But who will look for my coming?
But who will seek me at nightfall?

Where had she read the poem? She turned on the bedside light and blinked in the dazzle.

But who will give me my children?

182

Not Kit it seemed. Never Kit. Night and the raw defences of sleep blotted out reason. *You never expected him to love you. After all, you bought him.*

For diversion, she shuffled through the books on the bedside table. *Tell England, Rough Justice, The Mysterious Affair at Styles*, her mother's botanical notebook. None appealed, for no book could tell Matty how to cope with a marriage to a man who loved someone else.

But who will seek me at nightfall?

Matty drank a glass of water, turned off the light and lay staring into the darkness. Kit had unlocked many longings, including the sexual one. There, at least, she found it surprisingly easy to give of herself and to respond, however peremptory he was — and she knew that surprised him. It surprised Matty, too, that she found sex easy, enjoyable, not that she had ever discussed it. The problem lay in her craving for intimacy — lacking even when Kit was in her bed.

That — and, of course, her yearning for a baby.

'Matty.'

'Yes, Kit.' Matty was in the morning room and at Kit's entry looked up from the box of photographs on her knee. She pointed at the coffee tray. 'Do you want some?'

He poured himself a cup and stood by the fire. Dressed in an old corduroy suit, Kit, who had been out inspecting a fence by Montgomery's, was flushed from fresh air. He said, 'I wanted to ask if you're quite well. You look a bit off colour.'

On a foray with Mrs Dawes, Matty had discovered the photographs in the north attic and had brought them down to look through them. She waved a photograph at Kit of a dowager who appeared ossified by breeding. 'I wish everybody would stop enquiring after my health. It's kind, but unnecessary.'

More from guilt than anything, Kit pressed on. 'You would tell me, Matty, if you needed to go to London to see someone.'

'Don't worry, Kit. *Please.*'

'I mean . . .' Kit dropped onto the sofa beside his wife and fielded slopped coffee from his saucer into his cup. The newly decorated morning room was now grey with rose silk curtains bordered to match the walls. Dominating it was a flower painting by Gluck in shades of white. Kit found Matty's taste in painting almost disturbing, and he was repelled by this picture's bold, flaring femaleness. He eyed it with dislike and turned back to her. 'I just don't want you overdoing things, that's all.'

Matty said nothing and returned to the contents of the box. She held up a sepia studio portrait of a woman dressed in Edwardian evening dress and a many-stranded pearl choker. The waistline was cruelly laced in, the bosom magnificently pouter, and a pair of sloping shoulders rose from the silk and lace. Yet, despite the jewels and the ostrich feathers, the face seemed unhappy, hinting that its owner found life difficult, even painful. On the back it read, 'Mayfair Portraits. 25 Piccadilly. March 1915'. Matty turned to Kit. 'Who's this?'

He glanced at the photograph and became quite still. 'My mother,' he said at last, and Matty knew that Kit did not wish to talk about her.

She examined Hesther's jaw-line, both delicate and curiously stubborn, high cheekbones, a mass of blonde hair – and felt the jealousy of a newcomer who could not hope to compete with the past.

'She was very good-looking, Kit.'

'Yes.'

'You don't like talking about her?'

Kit rose to his feet. 'No,' he said curtly. 'If you don't mind I'd rather we didn't.'

Matty sneaked another look at the photograph. 'Most people say something about their parents,' she pointed out. 'You have told me nothing about your mother.'

'Please, Matty.' Kit put down his cup and got to his feet. 'Leave it.'

Baffled, Matty scrabbled among the rest of the photographs. Horses, cars, weddings, shooting parties, all with their whiff of ancient history. She pulled out one at random. 'It's of all of you as children,' she said.

Topping them by a head, dressed in a Norfolk jacket and stiff collar, Kit stood behind his two sisters who were dressed in smocked tartan dresses, identical plaits tied with identical ribbon. In the fashion of the time, his hair was meticulously parted and plastered to his head. The camera had caught him grinning: Look at me, he seemed to be saying, isn't life wonderful?

'You must have been nine or ten?' Matty looked up at her husband, tried to puzzle out the adult in the child's image and failed. Then she said, 'The photograph's been torn, it looks as—'

'Drop it, Matty.' Kit had paled and he was breathing quickly.

At first she did not understand what he meant. 'How odd . . .'

Kit removed the photograph from Matty's grasp. 'Please don't,' he said, and threw it back into the box. 'It's none of your business. It's not worth bothering about.'

Matty pushed the box aside. 'Can't I know about your family? You know about mine.'

Kit shook his head. 'Please, Matty. It's not your fault, but it's better left alone.'

Although he pushed them into his pockets, she was sure his hands were shaking and her bewilderment deepened. Matty leant towards him and touched his arm. 'I'm sorry, Kit, if I've upset you. Truly.'

For a moment, she imagined the shutter he had pulled down lifted for a few seconds and she gazed inside. Then it closed, leaving the Kit who hid his secrets well. 'Dear Matty. It's all horribly boring for you.'

'Boring for you' translated for Matty into 'mind your own business'. It was as if he had put out his hands and pushed her away, hard.

Too late, Kit realized what he had done and tried to salvage the situation. 'You silly old thing,' he said in an effort to gloss it over. 'There's nothing for you to worry about.'

He wished that he felt differently, that he was making Matty happy, and put out his arm, drew her towards him and aimed a

185

kiss at the top of her head. 'You will tell me if you need to go to London, won't you?'

'Yes,' she replied in a flat, dispirited way.

Matty should have left the subject of the photograph alone, but she did not. Greatly daring, she returned to the morning room, took out the torn photograph, hid the box and went in search of Flora who was checking tack in the tack room.

'I found this,' she said. 'I wondered who was missing?'

Flora replaced the top on a tin of dubbin. 'Let's see,' she said. 'Some ghastly relation, I expect.'

Matty handed it over. With a smile, Flora took it, examined the image. There was a pause and her smile vanished. 'Oh, yes,' she said, at last. 'I remember it being taken.'

'Who's missing?'

If Matty had expected an answer to the mystery, she was not going to get it.

'No one,' said Flora and she sounded quite savage. 'No one is missing.'

'Are you sure?'

Flora gave back the photograph and swung round so that her back was to Matty. 'I am quite sure.'

Matty re-examined the photograph. It was mounted on thick cardboard and to tear it, someone had needed to apply considerable force. She ran her finger down the jags. What clue was she missing? 'I'll see you later, Flora.'

'Fine,' said Flora, busy with a bridle. But after Matty had left, she dropped down onto the bench. The room was full of comforting things: saddle soap and leather, saddles and bridles used by the family – almost breathing, she always thought. Flora continued to stare at them, her face suffused with an angry red.

Matty went outside. The garden was a mixture of greens and browns and it was cold and damp, but not with the savagery of winter. Over by the tennis court, tits were busy in the cherry blossom, and worms had heaved casts all over the grass. Just for fun, Matty stood on one and surveyed the flattened patch. Her shoes squelched and collected mud. A clump of late aconites was in bloom under the plane tree and she stopped to examine a yellow head – those under the tree were less glossy than the ones growing further out.

Over by the river, the witch-hazel was out and she stared at the spiky-petalled, purple-centred blossom. Its scent drifted through the air towards her and she drew in deep breaths. Crocuses had naturalized by the river bank, and under a clump of leaf mould Matty discovered the mottled leaves and reflexed petals of a dog-toothed violet. She knew that because Jocasta had drawn one in her notebook.

Matty plodded along the river bank until she came to the bridge over which she had first crossed into the garden. Then, as last night's rain splashed on her cheeks from the trees, she turned right and walked beside the trickle, known, for some reason, as Harry's stream. In the wild area at the south end of the garden, the scrub was thickening with spring – an avant-garde sculpture of branches and whippy offshoots. Pinpoints of light darted from the raindrops hanging off branches, and Matty skimmed some off with her finger and sucked, as a child would.

She reached for her handkerchief and encountered the photograph, the junction between image and stiff cardboard. Photographs were not supposed to tell lies, but this one did. It said that here was a happy family. The torn edge caught under her nail, and like, a seismic register, she absorbed old anger and disturbance.

What connection was she failing to make?

A bird in the laurel hedge chattered and she looked up. It was then she realized that the scrub in the south-west corner – where she had seen the flash of blue the day after Polly's wedding – concealed a path. In high summer, leaves blocked it off, but now it was just possible to see it through the bare branches, threading away from the lawn towards the wall skirting the southern perimeter of the garden.

Intrigued, Matty stamped down the worst of the scrub, and pushed herself backwards through the breach she had made. After fifteen yards or so, the scrub thinned and where Matty expected to meet the wall, the path turned a sharp right, through a cluster of silver birches into a clearing.

Surprised, she tried to take her bearings. Instead of running north towards the tennis courts and the walled garden, the perimeter wall curved to create an enclosed and sheltered space. You could not see it from the garden, nor had she noticed it from the road.

She was standing on a rise, and in the dip below rioted ivy, nettles, brambles and elder, at the centre of which was a lump of stone. Puzzled, Matty turned back to reassess the path along which she had come and it occurred to her that the trees fringing it had been planted as a walk.

She swung round and took another look at the sunken area. Something about it suggested that it had not always been lapped by a green shroud. Her thoughts assembled into a conclusion: this had once been a garden.

Without warning, a chill drove deep into Matty's breast, undamming an anguish that forced itself through her body. She wanted to run away, but fear locked her knees. She wanted to scream, but her throat was too dry.

When, at last, she had gained control enough to focus, a child was standing by the stone at the centre of the abandoned garden, solemn and flaxen-haired, dressed in a warm coat with a bonnet and gaiters. Even from that distance, Matty recognized the lost expression in the eyes, and knew the child was in need.

'Wait,' she breathed, and slithered clumsily down the bank. 'Wait for me.' She slipped, swayed and fell backwards. Scrambling to her feet, she held out a hand. 'Wait.'

But the child paid no attention. She backed away from the stone, her feet making no sound.

'Wait!'

The child drew back further. Once again a painfully high note sounded in Matty's ears and she clamped her hands to them. Ivy tangled round her feet, brambles tore at her stockings and her shoes filled with muddy water. Hampered, she slipped again, recovered herself, but when she looked up the child had gone.

With a tremendous effort, Matty reached the stone and fell against it.

'Where are you?'

There was no answer and no noise at all. No birds. No rustling. No high-pitched note in her ears. Nothing, except for her own noisy breathing. It was very still, infectiously so, and Matty, too, quietened.

Gradually, shapes began to make sense. Over by the wall was the still discernible skeleton of a flowerbed. To her right, rusting but upright, stood a couple of wrought-iron arches smothered in greenery. She was standing on what must have been a lawn, metamorphosed by neglect into a wilderness of couch grass, clover and moss. Leaf mould, dank and grey-brown, carpeted the area, giving off its characteristic odour. The stone under Matty's hand was lumpy with lichen. She took off her glove, scratched with a fingernail and a patch of marble appeared, grained with the lightest of dark veins. Matty took a step or two backwards and pulled up some stems of rosebay willowherb at the base. On close inspection, the lump took shape as a statue of a woman carrying a water jug on her shoulder. The figure was gazing down at something by her feet and the artist had caught life in her draperies and in the heaviness of her loose hair. She was smiling: a serene, confident smile. Enchanted, Matty brushed away the layer of leaves caught in the stone folds – and revealed a stone child playing by her feet.

She backed away over the wet grass, turned sharply and went over to inspect the flowerbed by the wall. She did not want to cry. Careless of her coat, she squatted down and stared hard at the earth. Time and neglect, deliberate it seemed, had done damage but not irrevocably so.

Ignorant of many plants though she was, Matty recognized a rose bush and a clematis ballooning up the wall. After a moment, she put up a hand and covered her mouth. She stayed like that for a long time. Somehow she had got to this point in her life, a barren, unloved wife in a family full of secrets. Under that lurked a suspicion that it had happened because she deserved it. Behind the diffidence, the passion for form and design, her vocation for suffering, behind Matty's unused capacity to love, lay the fear that her life had fallen out like this because she was *unlovable*.

A breeze blew over the ridge and ruffled her hair. Her thighs protested from the unaccustomed pose. Somehow, she was going to have to make something of her life – but she did not know how. *She did not know how.*

She allowed her hand to trail along the edge of the flowerbed and encountered a hump. She looked down. Struggling through the leaves and grass was an oval green plant: neat, contained and dotted with yellow shapes. No special skill was required to recognize that it was an ordinary primrose. Bright and full of life – in direct contrast to the sickness in Matty's spirit.

Trembling a little, she brushed the leaves aside, exposing the flowers. 'Oh, yes.' Jocasta's voice floated up from a buried memory. 'Toothed oval leaves, littly darling. Pale flowers with darker eyes and, see, a stem brushed with soft hairs. Write it in your book, Matty . . .'

Very gently, Matty placed a finger under one of the flowers and turned it towards her.

'How did you survive?' she asked it.

The hole left by Matty's forced entry stopped Ned in his tracks. For a moment he stared at the flattened undergrowth and then put down the wheelbarrow and followed suit.

If it was those dratted Prossers playing hookey in the grounds then trouble was coming. Ned itemized in his head the precise form that trouble would take – and halted when he saw Matty's figure crouched over the flowerbed. She looked up at him with a startled expression and time slipped a connection – and it was Betty staring up at her father. He went down the bank towards her. 'Don't take on, Mrs Kit,' he said. 'I don't like to see it, lovey.' He helped her to her feet and brushed leaves from her coat. She smelt of rain and leaf mould, and reminded him of nothing so much as a wren.

Matty gave a choked laugh. 'Oh dear,' she said. Ned produced one of his rare smiles and watched her pull herself together.

After a minute, she asked, 'What is this place, Mr Sheppey? Why is it blocked off?'

'You mustn't worry about that,' he replied.

'Why, Mr Sheppey?'

'I haven't time to bother with it.'

She looked hard at Ned. 'All right,' she said. 'You win for the moment. There is one more thing,' she added. 'Are you quite sure there isn't a little girl who lives round here?'

The clouds shifted and sunlight cut through the trees. In the silence an animal scuffled in the undergrowth. The light spread over the garden turning it from dim green to gold. The rusty scream of a jay broke the peace, followed by a flutter of wood pigeons.

'I'm quite sure, Mrs Kit,' said Ned Sheppey.

CHAPTER FIVE

B Y THE last week in March, Rupert's progress was pronounced steady and both Kit and Matty felt they could leave him to his nurses. Tyson drove Matty, Flora and an excited Ivy up to London where they moved into Bryanston Court in preparation for the luncheons, teas, dinners and balls that would fill the next few months before, exhausted, Society decamped to the country for the summer.

Flora was not happy. 'What do I dratted well want to come out for?' she said from the sofa at Bryanston Court, and added, 'For God's sake!'

'Flora!' Matty was not so much taken aback by the language as by Flora's vehemence. 'But you're going to have such a wonderful time. I wish I'd done it.' Matty wished nothing of the sort, but she had always imagined that it was only she who considered the business an ordeal.

'No, you don't,' said Flora shrewdly. 'You have far too much sense. Own up, Matty.'

'No, I don't,' admitted Matty, who had watched Daisy sail through her Season in a haze of floral tributes and Chanel No. 5 and thanked God the doctor had put his foot down. 'But it's different for you.'

'Sooty boots, Matty.'

'Sooty boots?'

'Miss Glossop said fibbers get struck by lightning.' Flora enjoyed her own joke but then the smile was wiped from her face. 'I'm almost too old. To come out I mean.'

'Nonsense. Nineteen isn't too old.'

'At least you're only being presented as the new Mrs Dysart and don't have any of the anguish of trying to be a success.'

'At least,' agreed Matty drily, for that was bad enough.

She poured out the tea and handed the cup to her sister-in-law. Flora picked up a copy of *The Times* that lay open at the social column. 'Ye gods,' she said. 'Fifteen dances. All that preening, and I don't have nearly enough dresses.'

She could have added that she was terrified — at the prospect of looking lumpy in made-over dresses, of tight white gloves that had to be kept clean, of gilt chairs laid out by the mile, of halting conversations with bored men, of chaperones watching like lynxes from balconies. Of thinking that this expensive and vulgar performance was all nonsense.

Of failing to make a success of it.

Flora was squeezed in a paradox: she despised the business (she said) and yet she wanted desperately not to make a pig's ear of it and to be pointed out as the Girl Who Didn't Take.

'Flora . . .' Matty balanced her saucer on her hand and twiddled the cup around. 'If it's dresses that are the problem, I am sure we can do something.'

Two pairs of eyes met over the gold-rimmed cups. 'Sweet of you,' said Flora. 'But no.'

'I didn't mean—'

'That's all right,' said Flora brightly. 'It's just I don't think you should pay for my dresses.'

'No. No. Of course not.'

There was a small but significant pause.

'Well,' said Matty, extracting her notebook from her handbag, 'we should decide on some details.'

Flora heaved herself to her feet and went over to the window, where she twitched moodily at the chintz. London didn't suit her, she decided. It was for thin, fizzy people who could hold a cigarette at the correct angle and had frightfully amusing things to say. The prospect of the next three tiring and expensive months filled her with bile and gloom — and butterflies in the stomach that woke her with a jolt in the early hours.

'Claridge's?' Matty pressed on. 'Or Stanhope Gate?'

'Aren't we too late to make a booking?' said Flora hopefully. She did not want to hold a cocktail party or a fork luncheon party — or any party, for that matter. But, backed by Robbie, a dangerously agitated Rupert insisted from his sick bed that plans should go forward so she could damn well get married – and to someone suitable.

'I've provisionally booked both,' Matty persisted, who was finding that, as the rich Mrs Dysart, she was able to effect things.

Flora gave in. She dropped the curtain and turned round. 'The trouble with you, Matty, is that you're too efficient. Look at Hinton. The place runs like clockwork now.'

Matty turned pink with pleasure. 'Really?'

Flora recollected the old Hinton Dysart – the dust and dispirited paintwork, lukewarm baths and inefficient lavatories and the cold that, in winter, blew in from Siberia. 'Oh, yes. Really. You've done wonders. You've no idea how dot and carry one we were. Pipes held together by tape and the curtains by pins and that sort of thing.'

'Flora.' Matty busied herself with teacups, milk jug and slop bowl. 'You're not teasing, are you? I haven't upset you with all the changes or made you feel pushed out of your own home?'

'Good Lord, no,' said Flora inspecting a run in one of her stockings. 'I admit I was expecting the worst.' She looked up. 'I wasn't very kind to you, Matty, was I? When you first came. I thought you would take Kit away, or import a form of Susan Chudleighism or . . . I don't know what I thought.'

Matty struggled to reply. 'Flora . . .'

Flora sent her plait flying over her shoulder. 'I am sorry to be rude, but you have to admit your aunt is terrible.'

'She's only an aunt by marriage.' Matty poured the remains of her tea into the slop bowl. 'I'll tell you something, Flora,' she said. 'I hate her.' Long overdue, the confession was liberating, exhilarating even.

Flora drank her tea and returned to the social pages and Matty returned to the agenda.

'Lunch then, at the Honourable Mrs Charles Turner's, Christiana Bellamy's dance, Charlotte Souter's luncheon party . . .'

Swinging kid gloves by the fingers, Kit breezed in and tossed his trilby onto a chair. 'Tea? Good.' He accepted a cup and sat down by Flora. 'Ordeal by cocktail party?'

'Fork luncheon,' she replied gloomily.

Kit peered at his sister. 'Stage fright?'

Flora nudged *The Times*. 'Isn't it all rather stupid? I know everyone is supposed to do it, and Mother wanted—' She stopped abruptly and Matty froze in the act of pouring out milk.

'I wish Mother—' said Flora with an anger that made Matty gasp. 'I wish—' And then, as if frightened by her own outburst, she bent over to attend to the errant stocking.

'All right, sis.' Kit rubbed his hand up and down her back. 'It's all right.'

Flora grabbed his other hand and held it. Her stormy expression cleared. 'Sorry.'

'More tea?' asked Matty.

With an abrupt change of mood Flora said, 'I should warn you, Lady F.'s on the war path.'

'My dear Flora,' said Kit, whose imitation of Lady Foxton was a popular family setpiece, 'can I be hearing this? Not want to do the Season?'

It wasn't that funny, but brother and sister collapsed against the Colefax-and-Fowlered sofa and shook with laughter while Matty smiled politely and poured more tea.

It hadn't been *too* bad, Flora considered three weeks later as she trudged up Upper Street in Islington, map under one arm, a bulky parcel under the other. Yet.

'*Islington!*' cried Matty when Flora informed her of her plan to walk to Miss Glossop's. '*Nobody* walks, not to Islington. It might be dangerous.'

But Flora decided she needed the exercise and would only agree to let Tyson drop her at the Angel. She had promised Robbie to deliver a patchwork quilt to Miss Glossop – 'A token,' said Robbie, making a to-do of brown paper and string, 'of our friendship when she was here.' Flora wondered how Miss Glossop felt about the friendship, but she could not deny that Robbie had taken months to make the quilt.

There was no denying either that it was a relief to escape

overheated rooms and endless plates of salmon and peas. Walking in London was an adventure of a sort and, at the very least, it would provide a topic of conversation at the next function.

Not that Flora's wits had deserted her: she had danced and chatted quite as she had been instructed by Lady F. (and woken up with headaches from too much champagne). She had even attracted one or two titled but, let it be said, spotty men who sent bouquets every other day. Never mind, it confirmed her rating in the Season's hierarchy and sharpened the interest of inquisitorial mothers and their uniformly permed daughters, with whom, she was assured by the former, she would wish to make friends.

Flora swung north up the street. London spread out around her, a territory of secrets and labyrinths, of mysteries and shadows, beauty and squalor.

At the Angel, she passed the pawnbrokers on her left and a little further on the patch of grass known as Islington Green and the old music hall on her right. Had she but known it, Flora was skirting one of Victorian London's most notorious rookeries: a no-go area to police into which fugitives could and did vanish for ever. Traces of that colourful, often violent past, remained and were evident when she turned into St Peter's Street.

Once elegant, the terrace had decayed and on doorsteps sat children who had never tasted salmon and peas in their lives. She passed one house where the windowpanes were all broken. A woman screamed inside and Flora halted. That proved a mistake, for the children immediately made a beeline for her, scenting a victim. They pulled at her clothes, commenting in accents she did not understand. Panicked, Flora pulled away, fumbled in her handbag and found a couple of threepenny bits. She thrust them at the children, and hurried on, hugging her parcel.

Miss Glossop lived in a late Georgian house split into lodgings. There was no running water, and an odoriferous closet on the first floor indicated little in the way of sanitation. Less solid than Flora recollected, Miss Glossop's mouth shaped into an 'o' when she saw her former pupil. She was clearly embarrassed because she had no tea or biscuits to offer. They sat conversing about old times in a room that managed to be both stuffy and cold – and Flora burned at her thoughtlessness in arriving unannounced.

As she performed the rituals of another world, the memory of that episode remained with Flora: the shabby street and silent children, the screaming woman, the bareness of Miss Glossop's room and the manner in which the governess's mittened fingers patted, explored and held tight to the quilt. 'So thick, so warm, so practical. Thank you a thousand times, Flora.'

Nevertheless, Flora was being pressed into a mould. How could she fail to be? Days slid past, skewered together by telephone calls, dress fittings, scrutinies of address books and diaries, exchanges of: 'Is he on *The List*, darling?' 'Is he safe in taxis?', and a couple of lectures from front-line Lady F.

'My dear Flora, you must talk. Talk about anything, it doesn't matter what. Chatter, my girl. Chatter. To be silent at dinner or at dance will be a black mark against you. Don't be clever either. Nobody likes clever women.'

'But I am not clever, Lady F.'

'No, dear, but you sometimes look it.'

'Dear Flora,' said Matty, ticking off a pile of invitations. 'I would never forgive myself if we didn't do this properly. I am sure your mother—'

Flora cut across her. 'Let me tell you this, Matty. My mother didn't care, so please don't worry yourself on that account.' With that revealing snippet, Flora marched straight out to the nearest hairdresser and ordered him to cut off her plait.

On the afternoon of her presentation at Court, she and Matty sat in the car in the Mall, taking pains not to tangle Prince of Wales ostrich feathers and long white trains.

'I feel like a Christmas tree,' said Flora.

It was May and, typically, pouring with rain. Traffic in the Mall was at a standstill and pedestrians peered in at the windows as if Matty and Flora were a pair of waxworks.

'Curtsy to one Majesty,' muttered Flora. 'Sink to your very

ankles, no "bobbity-boo stuff". Madame Vacani was very emphatic about that. Retrieve balance. Get up. Walk one and half steps. Curtsy to the other Majesty. Sink hard. Get up. Pray to the patron of lost causes. Walk backwards out of the room. Kick train as you do so. Do not fall flat.'

'Will you be quiet, Flora.' Matty was trembling inside her oyster satin.

'Photographs at Lafayette's afterwards.' Flora sounded almost demented. 'Why on earth do we do this?'

As nervous as Flora, Matty's palms were wet and the leather stuck to her skin. 'Pinch me, Flora. You are about to come out, and I am about to be presented as the new Mrs Dysart.'

On impulse, they grasped each other's hand hard. The Verral diamonds winked.

'Good luck.'

'Good luck.'

The car eased its way through the gates of Buckingham Palace. Looking back, all Flora remembered was a blur of white walls picked out in gold, a mosaic of medals and dress uniforms, circles of sweat spreading under her arms, rain-distorted faces gawping through the car window and bulging fishy eyes reminiscent of a pair she had once seen in the window of a joke shop.

On the night of Lady Londonderry's ball, Ivy drew the bath and built up the fire in the bedroom. Later, she helped a newly permed Flora into a copy of a Madeleine Vionnet dress which Mrs Snell had run up from a basement in Brown Street, and dusted powder over the broad white shoulders.

Flora stood back and surveyed herself: a pale green satin débutante with Lady F.'s diamond clips and flat shoes. ('Nobody will see them, Flora, and you don't want to be too tall.' 'Are you trying to say I'm a giant, Matty?' 'No, Flora. Not a *giant* exactly.') Released from the plait, Flora's hair had taken on new life and, to her disappointment, the perm had encouraged it in all sorts of liberties. It curled around her head in a flaxen nimbus with a singularity that, admittedly, was not fashionable, but made her both attractive and interesting. Flora did not see it that way, clucked at the mirror, pulling at strands and discarding combs, and made a face at the result. She had wanted to achieve the 'look' for the Season, but had failed – and who would want to dance with a Medusa-headed giantess?

She sat down on the stool and scrutinized her reflection further. Perhaps she had not grown into herself yet? She rather hoped that was the case and that she wasn't stuck in the awkward mould for ever. Nevertheless, her duty was plain: to meet a suitable man, preferably a rich one, and marry him. Since she was used to thinking of herself as a child, the notion felt odd. Common sense also told Flora that she was an acquired taste.

Oh, well, Flora tested her gracious smile in the mirror, and then her gently amused one which she found useful when listening to monologues from crashing bores. It needed only one man to acquire the taste.

At the Beauchamps' dinner party Flora was a model débutante. Helped by sips of wine, she chatted, oh, how she chatted. Matty sat opposite her in a sequined dress and talked to her neighbour, a banker, eating very little. Rakish-looking in his white tie, Kit sat further down the table between two astonishingly beautiful women, every so often looking across and sending her a private signal which made her feel better. Matty pushed pieces of *noisettes d'agneau* under her fork and wondered if she was really feeling as odd as she thought she was.

'Are you up to this?' Kit whispered as he draped a velvet cloak around her shoulders when they left.

'Yes, of course.'

'Not too tired?' He seemed genuinely concerned.

Matty wrapped the velvet around her shoulders and touched him on the arm. 'I'm fine.'

At Londonderry House, the party filed past recumbent stone nymphs and trod up the staircase. Diamonds were in evidence everywhere. They shafted arrows of white to blue light into gilded mirrors and glittered from the tiaras of gimlet-eyed dowagers. Lady Londonderry's diamonds were famous. No matter that the Countess of Airlie's offered a direct challenge, or that huge stones blazed from Lady Spencer's parure, the Londonderry tiara with its matching earrings and outsize diamond brooch riveted her guests as their hostess greeted them.

'Can I have first dance?' Kit asked Flora as they waited outside, and Flora's heart began its now familiar see-saw of dread and excitement.

On Kit's other arm, Matty swallowed, then pressed her arm against her breast, which was very sore. Perhaps this time, she thought, not daring to go further than that.

The ballroom was already full and Kit handed Matty through the press towards the chairs grouped around tables at the end of the room. The noise was ferocious, so much so that the band was having trouble making itself heard. It did not matter: Lady Londonderry's balls were famous as much for themselves as for their mixture of the great and the good – and the not-so-good.

Matty saw Daisy first. She faltered and recovered herself. Misled by the initial seconds when the encounter felt perfectly normal, Kit remained calm. That was before an unseen hand took a knife and peeled away his outer layer of skin. For a second, his fingers dug into his wife's arm and then, with a muttered apology, he released her.

'Hallo, Daisy,' he said.

'Marcus.' Matty did not look at Daisy.

'Hallo, Marcus.' Flora held out a hand.

'Wow,' said Marcus and carried it to his lips. 'Superb.'

Only Kit noticed that Daisy's uncharacteristically red-tipped fingers were shaking.

'Hallo, Kit,' Daisy said, and did not smile.

Daisy's eyes, which Kit remembered as so clear, seemed less readable but she had grown in beauty – or her beauty had taken on another dimension. Experience, or was it suffering? he wondered with a flash of guilt, had tightened the skin over her cheekbones, painted violet under her eyes and added depth to the wide mouth. She was wearing a strappy ballgown of pleated white silk, a spray of egret feathers tilted over one temple and bracelets on her upper arms. She had the 'look' all right, thought Flora staring at her.

Daisy's fringe and scarlet fingernails were new to Kit, and those details threw him for they did not correspond to the image he had carried around. Good manners came to his rescue. 'Why don't you join us at our table for a couple of minutes?' he said.

Marcus had shaved off his moustache and was the better for it. He flashed his sister a glance. 'That's good of you, old chap,' he replied, carefully.

Hours later, but really only five minutes, Kit leant over and removed the dance card from Daisy's fingers. 'Mine,' he said.

'You should be dancing with your party,' Daisy reminded him.

'I'm changing the rules.'

She looked up from her champagne. 'Your wife?'

Matty was being dutifully twirled around the floor by Andy Beauchamp and Nick Reed-Porter had claimed Flora. 'She will understand,' said Kit.

'Of course Matty will understand,' said Daisy, 'but she might not like it.'

She allowed Kit to lead her onto the floor. With a sigh of relief, Kit slid his hand around Daisy's back, searching for the point where her hip swelled and for the bump near her spine which he remembered so well. Daisy's hair drifted across his cheek, and she settled into his arms as if she had never been away.

'How are you?' he asked, because he had to start somewhere.

'Darling Kit,' she said. 'How do I look? Old? Ill? Miserable?' She caught her lip at the last.

'No. None of those things.'

'How is it going? Shoring up the estate, I mean.'

'How is Tim Coats? Did you get engaged? I never heard.'

She nodded in the direction of a noisy group under a gilt mirror. 'He's there. Watching. Yes, we are engaged.'

'Why haven't you married him?'

'Answer my question first. How is the estate?'

She watched a variety of expressions chase across Kit's face, and longed to take his head between her hands and kiss him.

'Don't let's talk about it.'

Daisy laughed. 'But that's why we've risked social ruin to dance. Why you and I sacrificed each other. For Hinton Dysart. We should talk about the house. After all, you do care about it. Greatly.'

'Daisy.' The old questions resurrected. 'I believed you when you said you had someone else. That's why I said yes to Matty. That, and a hangover.'

'Well, at least that's honest.' She sighed. 'I can understand a hangover. Otherwise, I'm tempted to think badly of myself and of you when I consider how I had been passed over for a house.'

'Shut up, darling Daisy. Please shut up.'

'No, darling Kit. I won't.'

Kit bent his head and lightly brushed her cheek with his lips. The music blared. He held her against him and foxtrotted her this way and that. Daisy's breath quickened.

'Hallo,' said someone, Kit did not register whom.

'Hallo.'

'Hallo. Isn't this fun?'

'Darling, what a whiter-than-white nice dress.'

The touch of Kit's lips made Daisy's skin prickle. The fingers of their outstretched hands meshed.

'Wait,' she said at last, 'I can't bear these beastly gloves any longer.' She struggled to remove them and Kit helped her. Daisy glanced up at the area set aside for dowagers. 'I might lose my reputation, of course.'

Kit laughed, and stuffed them in his pocket. 'Who cares? I want to feel your hands in mine.'

Daisy caught her breath. 'Will it always be like this, Kit?' she asked. 'Doesn't it ever stop?'

'You are my Lily of Laguna, my Lily and my Rose,' said the music.

'Dance with me again,' said Kit as the music changed its beat.

'No,' said Daisy. 'Yes.'

At the Dysart table, Matty sat with her back to the dance floor and made wooden conversation to Nick Reed-Porter. A vase of freesias had been placed in the centre of the tablecloth and absent-mindedly Matty touched the petals with her fingertip.

'You will be going to the Chelsea Flower Show, of course.' Stolid, good-hearted Nick ploughed on with the uphill work.

'Oh, yes,' said Matty, feeling sick and shaky.

And Flora, waltzing with Marcus Chudleigh, forgot about Kit and Daisy. Marcus was strong and knew what he was doing. Light from the crystal chandeliers spilt into yellows, oranges and pale blues, while diamonds threw back white fire and the dancers circled. Tangled in the magic, Marcus's strength, her own femaleness, Flora was aware that, after all, life held possibilities.

Marcus kissed her hand and Flora, intoxicated by the way his white tie sat under his jaw, by his sandy lashes and the faint odour of cigar, felt a stirring of sexual desire.

'Oh, Marcus,' she said. 'Isn't this lovely?'

Flora's mood shattered when he handed her back to the table. One glance at Matty's face was enough to bring her to earth. Another look clarified the situation on the dance floor where Kit and Daisy were dancing . . . well, as if no one else was there.

'Ye gods,' she said under her breath and everything was spoilt. She leaned forward and whispered in Matty's ear, 'Do you want me to do anything?'

Matty shook her head. '*No*.'

'Kit should know better,' Flora hissed.

Matty's bird fingers dug into her arm. 'Don't say anything,' she said. 'Then I can bear it.'

Nick Reed-Porter seized his chance. 'Excuse me, but I'm booked for this dance with Venetia Taylor.' He scraped back the chair and waved at a blonde girl in blue taffeta.

Then Matty leant back in her chair. Her complexion was greenish-white. 'Can you get me out of here, do you think?' she begged Flora. 'I need a minute or two.'

'Of course.' Flora's eye fell on the freesias and with a flick of her finger she knocked over the vase. Water dripped onto Matty's dress.

'Excuse me,' said Flora, and marshalled Matty through the guests. 'We need a mop-up operation.'

In the ladies' powder room, Matty sank down among the linen towels and clothes brushes, and dropped her head into her hands. Flora knelt down beside her and put her arms around the shaking figure.

'Don't, Matty,' she said, deeply distressed. 'Don't.'

'People are watching us,' Daisy murmured into Kit's ear.

'Let them.'

'What about Matty?'

Kit missed his step. 'You're right,' he said, and led Daisy back to her table.

She held out her hand. 'Goodbye, Kit, so nice to see you again.'

Somewhere under the new beauty, the red lips, nail varnish and sophisticated fringe, was the memory of a different Daisy who had climbed rock paths and danced in French *boîtes*. 'Goodbye,' said Kit.

She understood what he was thinking and said abruptly, 'Let's not do this again.'

'No.' Kit braced himself. 'When are you getting married? Just so I know.'

'Do you mind about that?' she asked.

It was a relief to feel angry, and Kit flushed. 'Do you think I'm going to run up flags because the woman I love is marrying someone else?'

'Well,' Daisy replied, 'you're speaking to someone who understands perfectly.'

'*Touché*.' Kit gave his uneven smile, and Daisy thought her heart would break in two. 'Daisy, if I were to say I'm sorry would it make any difference?'

'No,' she said, and it was her turn to be angry. 'That's far too simple.'

'Darling Daisy. Darling, darling Daisy.'

'Shush. We have to say goodbye *now*.'

*

At two o'clock in the morning, the Dysart party agreed it was time to leave.

'Please, Kit,' Flora was still angry with her brother for his treatment of Matty, but she wanted to go on with Marcus to a nightclub, 'Robbie isn't here and this is the only time I will have a chance to be *really* wicked. Otherwise, there would be such a fuss.'

Kit looked at Marcus. They made a silent bargain: Kit would leave Daisy alone, and Marcus was on his honour not to get up to mischief with Flora. 'Where are you planning to go?' he asked.

'I thought we'd look in at the Embassy and then on to the 400.'

'Such fun,' said Flora, eyes gleaming. 'Think of all that gloom and vice.'

'Let her go, Kit,' said Matty, holding a fold of her still damp dress in one hand. 'She won't come to any harm. Nick Reed-Porter and Venetia Taylor are going with them.'

'Yes, of course you can go,' said Kit, feeling at least seventy instead of twenty-seven.

'Thank you, darling brother,' said Flora and kissed him. Kit looked over her shoulder and watched Tim Coats put his arm around Daisy and say something into her ear.

The drive back to Bryanston Court was silent. Matty huddled in a corner as far away from Kit as possible.

'Are you all right?' asked Kit.

'Yes.'

Kit felt for his cigarettes, discovered Daisy's gloves and pushed them back into his pocket.

Matty wound down the window with a thump, caught a corner of her velvet cloak on the handle and ripped a piece at the hem. With a sob she jerked it back so savagely that the material ruffled up like a curtain. It was such an uncharacteristic gesture that Kit was dumbfounded.

Despite himself, Kit's mouth twitched because it was funny — the farce that accompanies the drama of painful encounters. 'Did that make you feel better?' he asked, feeling that he liked her the more for it.

She bit her lip and contemplated her cloak. 'Much better, thank you.'

'Matty, I'm sorry. I'm so sorry.'

'It's quite all right,' she said stiffly. 'I don't mind, really.'

Bryanston Court was warm and welcoming. The lights were on in the drawing room and Ivy had left out sandwiches, a Thermos of soup and the drinks tray. Surprisingly, Kit was ravenous.

'My favourite soup,' he said. 'Thank you, Matty.'

Matty held her cup of soup between her fingers to warm them. 'Good,' she said and took a sip.

'You have a talent for organization.'

She smiled. 'Flora said that.'

'She's right. Have a sandwich.'

She shook her head. 'I think I'll go to bed, if you don't mind.'

Kit swallowed a mouthful of soup, got to his feet and escorted his wife down the passage to her bedroom. At the door he stopped. 'Goodnight,' he said.

For a second time that evening, she touched his arm. 'I've something to tell you.'

'Tell me what?'

She kept him waiting just a fraction longer than necessary and unbuttoned her gloves. 'There's a chance,' she said, and stopped, frightened that if she said it the chance would disappear.

'Of what, Matty?'

Matty finished in a rush. 'There's a chance that I might be pregnant.'

HARRY

May is a deceptive month and gardeners should treat it with respect. A cunning month, it endeavours, with longer evenings, stronger sun and newborn foliage, to persuade you it is summer. Sometimes this is true, sometimes not. If it is not the gardener, having given in to euphoria and rushed out geraniums, fuchsias, felicias and salvias, watches helplessly as a frost descends, sword whirling, to slaughter his darlings.

But I love May – the month that ends the winter gestation, the curtain raiser to the seductions of June. In the evenings the light stretches, long, white and tender, across fields stippled by new growth up to Barley Pound and the ancient Harroway. Apple and pear blossom drift in the air.

It is the cue for the clematis to rocket onto centre stage, and I have asked for a white one to be trained across the kitchen garden wall in memory of Ned Sheppey. Strong, tough and reliable, it suits his memory I think. In my cottage garden a blue *macropetala* snakes up into the *Prunus autumnalis*, and the 'Countess of Lovelace', my favourite, is preparing for her double act in powder blue, first in spring as an Edwardian gaiety girl, and then for her return performance in the autumn with a single blossom. Meanwhile, my greedy, scrambling *armandii* caps its evergreen foliage with clusters of creamy, almond-scented flowers.

Every garden should have its aromatic corners and, up at the big house, we have taken trouble to position scented plants for each season. For May, capricious May, I chose the viburnum. Not the most common variety, but the busty *juddii*. The effect is startling *and* it is resistant to greenfly. I sited it by the path so that on their way to the walled garden visitors walk into its sweetness.

Then there is the wisteria walk on the west wall of the new stables. Mother often sat there, and in the evenings Thomas and I wander up from the cottage and walk between the twisted stems. Damp flowers brush at our heads and light filters through like a quattrocento painting. The scent overwhelms us.

Each year I have learnt more: a new fact, some shift in perspective, in design or colour blocking. Never cease learning, Mother told me. Never hesitate to open another door. The garden is deeper, much deeper, than what the eye merely sees, and teaches us truths through the senses. Like water running through time and place, it never changes and yet never ceases to do so.

Truth is buried under many layers and perhaps never can be seen as the whole. But pick up the shards lying in the earth, piece them together and something emerges.

CHAPTER SIX

THE BEDROOM was warm and quiet. Matty remained on the bed where Kit had sat her down. Her Viyella nightdress had been laid out, and there would be a hot-water bottle between the sheets. She looked forward to climbing under the eiderdown and going to sleep. Again, she touched her breast and when it responded with a satisfactory spongy soreness she gave a sigh of relief.

'There's no mistake?' Kit ripped off his tie and draped it round his neck. His hair fell over his forehead and, in his characteristic way, he pushed it back. As always, Matty had no idea what he was feeling but, at least, her news had broken the silence.

'I don't think so.' Being questioned raised doubts in Matty's mind and she sifted rapidly through the facts. Twenty-eight days late. Nausea. Sore breasts. A dislike of perfume . . . A conviction planted in the back of her mind.

'Have you been to the doctor?'

'No. But I'm almost sure.'

'That's very good news, Matty. When?'

She told him and Kit snapped his fingers, one, two; a trick of his. She knew then that he was pleased. Some of the hurt she was feeling relaxed its hold. She smoothed her gloves over her knees and hugged his pleasure to herself. Then she looked up. 'Do you mind?'

'*Mind!*' Troubled by her question, Kit sat down beside Matty and took one of her hands. 'You do ask me funny things sometimes, Matty. And you listen to the answer with those big eyes trained on me as if I was an oracle.'

'I ask because I wish to find out,' said Matty. 'You see, I don't really know you, and you are hard to understand.'

'Oh, Lord,' said Kit, propping himself on his elbows. 'I don't sound very appealing or approachable. I'll have to try, Matty, shan't I?'

She swallowed. 'Only if you want to.'

Her answer appeared to annoy Kit and he got up from the bed and returned to the fireplace. Matty wished she had been as determined as Daisy was. 'Yes, you damn well *should* try,' Daisy would have said. 'I demand it.'

She changed the subject and, with her instinct for rubbing salt into her own wounds, asked, 'How was Daisy?'

Kit looked uncomfortable, miserable and angry all at the same time. 'Daisy is very well,' he replied, choosing the most neutral reply he could think of.

You *can* demand, said Emma Goldman in Matty's head. Go on, Matty.

Fuelled by an unfamiliar mixture of nausea, elation and fatigue, she said, 'Kit I must ask you . . . please . . . in future not to make your feelings so plain. In public at least. It makes it very difficult for me.'

'Matty . . .'

'Everyone noticed.' Matty paused and, thinking that as she had got this far she had better continue, added, 'I minded very much.'

'Yes,' said Kit. 'Of course. I'm sorry.'

Matty pressed on. 'I know what you feel about Daisy. Of course I do, although we haven't discussed it. But please. Not in public.'

The effect was curiously dignified.

'You should get to bed,' Kit said quickly to cover his feelings. 'I shouldn't be keeping you up. Shall I ring for Ivy?'

'No, please don't, it's far too late for her.'

'Are you sure?' Kit paused, and then asked, 'Can I help?'

Matty stood up. 'Could you undo my buttons, please?'

Kit was no good at buttons and it was a minute or two before the dress slid over Matty's shoulders. Pleased by the intimacy, she savoured the touch of Kit's fingers on her back.

'Tired?' she asked, feeling the skin under her own eyes stretch with fatigue.

'Nicely so,' lied Kit, and brushed his finger over the place where Matty's skin thinned over her collarbone. He bent over and kissed her cheek. 'Bed. At once.'

'Kit.'

'Yes,' he said from the doorway.

She turned and with a slight shock he saw that under her silk chemise her breasts looked swollen and her soft, barely pink, nipples were darker and more prominent. Kit swallowed. 'Yes?' he repeated.

'Nothing,' said Matty. She watched the door close behind him and listened as he walked down the corridor. Presently, she heard him moving around the drawing room, and knew he would be pacing up and down between the windows, hands in his pockets.

Soothed by his goodnight kiss, she pulled up the bedclothes and fell asleep thinking that, perhaps, the things she dreaded were not as bad as she thought.

But when she woke next morning Matty was conscious at once that things weren't fine. Something felt wrong: an acid aftertaste, an unease. Back in place was Matty's demon, and she remembered how close Kit and Daisy had danced together and the way her husband's hand had hugged the curve of Daisy's hip.

The pillow had slipped to one side and Matty turned over and tried to doze. An image of the younger Kit as she had seen him in the old photographs – scrubbed and hair slicked back – drifted across her mind. It was followed by a sulky Polly. One by one, they emerged out of the leather box: Flora, in riding habit and top hat standing in front of her pony ... Rupert, in uniform staring into the distance, Sam Browne belt shining in the studio light ... Hesther standing beside her brother, posed by the photographer with a rose in her hand, Edwin in uniform. They were smiling at each other, and it was obvious that they were not interested in the business of being photographed. Matty stared at Hesther. Upswept hair and a square jaw that should have indicated strength and yet Matty knew it did not. The slight downturn of the mouth repeated in Polly, its hint of pain and loss not properly assimilated or mourned. The outlines of the face dissolved, Hesther disappeared and Matty was left feeling cold and sick.

Mother, she wanted to say, searching for Jocasta among the debris thrown up by sleep but, safe on the other side of death, Jocasta eluded her. Then Matty woke up properly and knew with absolute certainty that Hesther's absence was more important than her presence. More important than anything.

She sat up in bed, reached for the telephone, cranked the handle and asked the operator for the Chudleigh residence.

'Why Gunter's?' asked Daisy.

Wearing a pink and white dress from Mainbocher and an Agnès hat, Matty slipped into her chair. 'Why not?'

'It's the sort of place to meet your future mother-in-law.'

'It's lovely,' said Matty, and glanced round. The tables were occupied by bachelor uncles treating their nephews and nieces to the famous ice creams, ladies up for the day from the country and a budding romance or two at corner tables. 'Very elegant.'

'If you like that sort of thing.' Daisy brushed her fringe back under her hat, not a designer creation but worn with chic. Under it her face looked unhappy, tired and, for Daisy, beaten. 'I ordered China tea, scones and cream cakes,' she said.

All morning Matty had told herself to remain calm so she was annoyed to see that her hands were clenched on the tablecloth. A change in a woman's soul, is it not, Emma? she asked her spiritual mentor. And, now, the tiger principle: I have to be the snarling mother tiger who defends her cub with teeth and claws. Matty pictured the dot seeking life in the dark, thudding spaces of her body, and imagined curving her hand around it and protecting it as tenderly as she could.

'You have got to go away,' she told Daisy, transferring her tell-tale hands to her lap. 'Go away somewhere so we don't run into one another or, rather, you don't run into Kit.'

Daisy blew out a plume of smoke and tapped her cigarette case. 'I've said this before,' she said, 'but I had no idea how hard you were.'

'Not hard,' Matty contradicted. 'Never that.'

Tea arrived and it was a minute or two before the frilled

waitress had arranged it to her liking on the table, which gave the
two of them time to think. Daisy continued to smoke furiously.
'If I do go away, Matty? What then?'

'It gives Kit a chance to get over you.' She paused. 'All of us a
chance, actually. You, Kit, me and the baby.' She tried not to let
her elation show too much, but failed.

'Baby!' Daisy poured some tea. 'Well, that gives me no choice.'
She took a mouthful and scalded her lips. 'I hate you, Matty,' she
said, eyes watering, in a light, conversational manner. 'I hate you.'

'Why have you always hated me?'

Daisy searched her memory. 'I haven't *always* hated you. But
you irritated Marcus and me right from the first.'

'But why? I don't think I did anything.'

'That's the point. You never did *any*thing. You were plonked
like a cuckoo into our nest and everything changed because you
were a moulting cuckoo, who was constantly ill. It drove Marcus
and me mad having to tiptoe around. Your money was a problem
too. Have you ever considered what it's like to be on the receiving
end of charity? Marcus and I were grateful for all the nice things
that came our way as a result of the allowance paid by your
trustees, but it also stuck in our throats.' Daisy lit another
cigarette. 'To be fair, Matty, your money wasn't your fault, I
suppose, but you must see that it made it difficult. Perhaps if you
had been a different sort of person then none of the generosity
would have mattered. But you never showed emotion, except
fright, and that egged Marcus and me on. You never stood up to
us.' She paused to tap ash into the cut-glass ashtray, and said,
'You never showed any sign of affection.'

Matty had not seen it in that light before, and she was silent
while she digested the implications along with Gunter's scones.
Inside she cried: You never showed me affection either.

'Then,' said Daisy, and her expression hardened, 'you went
and sold yourself to Kit. At first I wasn't sure if it was to spite me,
or a genuine desire to get him out of a rocky patch.' She gazed
down at her plate. 'I still haven't decided . . .'

'Have a scone,' said Matty.

Daisy peered at her cousin and, to Matty's surprise, gave a

snort of laughter. 'I may hate you, Matty, but you are priceless sometimes. I have to hand it to you.'

Matty passed the plate. 'You must go away for as long as possible,' she reiterated while Daisy crumbled the scone on her plate. 'Otherwise you won't give yourself, or Kit, time to recover, and since we are bound to meet quite often, it would be the best thing.'

'Goodness,' said Daisy. 'I think you're developing a bite at last.'

'Of course, Kit could divorce me and then it would be different.'

'No, he wouldn't do that,' said Daisy, pushing away her plate. 'Dysarts don't get divorced. Anyway, he needs your money.'

'Daisy. Please listen to me.'

'The price?' asked Daisy curiously. 'Are you going to buy me off? You're always buying things, Matty.'

'There is no price,' said Matty. 'You just *have* to go.'

The clear eyes assessed Matty, and Daisy's reddened lips closed tight against feelings that were out of place in Gunter's. Not for anything would she show Matty how much she was hurting.

Light-headed at her daring, Matty drank her tea and waited. Daisy was seldom malicious and Matty was certain that, for all her passions, Daisy would arrive at the right conclusion. Opposite her, Daisy cupped her chin in her hands and gazed at her cigarette case, her hat brim dipping over her face. For the thousandth time, Matty was suborned by Daisy's mysterious beauty and understood why Kit loved her.

'I give you marks for trying, Matty,' Daisy shovelled her things into her handbag and drew on her gloves, 'and I'll think about it.'

'I'll pay for tea,' Matty said.

Daisy frowned and for a second her guard slipped. 'How predictable,' she said, wearily. 'How very bloody like you. Nevertheless, just this once I'm going to pay.' She signalled to the waitress and waited until she was presented with the bill in its leather folder. Matty pulled her gloves over the Dysart engagement ring – pigeon's blood ruby, Burma, of the first water: she

214

had mentally catalogued it when Kit presented it to her – and shrugged her jacket around her shoulders. Daisy retrieved her parcels.

'I shall arrange to go away after Ascot because you have had the courage to ask, and because of the baby,' she said. 'Providing I can handle Mother.'

'Thank you, Daisy.'

Daisy paused before rising from the plush banquette. 'Don't think it will solve anything though, Matty. I am sorry to be blunt and I've said it before. Two thousand miles, three thousand miles, whatever, won't stop me loving Kit nor, necessarily, will it stop Kit loving me.'

She left Matty staring at crumbs, crumpled napkins, lipstick-stained cigarette stubs, not at all sure how the balance now sat.

The afternoon paper reported several items. One: the likelihood that two point six million were now unemployed in Great Britain. Two: following on from its trade and friendship alliance with Poland, the USSR was planning to sign a treaty of neutrality with Afghanistan. Other, less disturbing, items covered the possibilities of the Socialists winning the general election in Spain, and whether or not a new electric tote would be used at Ascot.

The articles on Russia required careful reading, and Matty, fascinated as always by Russia and the East, wondered, as the chauffeur piloted the car into Knightsbridge, whether Russia *was* aiming to dominate the world and make them all Communists.

The first warning – a ripple of discomfort in her groin, light, but determined – came when Matty was being fitted for a skirt with the new longer hemline. She closed her eyes and knew she had tempted fate by allowing herself to browse through the baby department.

She stepped out of the skirt, and a second warning flashed between her legs and up to her stomach. Matty looked up at the assistant and fought an urge to dig her nails into the plump forearms.

'Are you quite well, madam?' enquired a voice.

Deep inside Matty, a seed was pulled up by its bloody roots.

'No,' said Matty. 'No, I don't think I want this skirt.' She handed it back.

'This one, madam?' The girl held out a shorter, cleverly cut skirt on a padded hanger. Her scent was strong, cheap and made Matty nauseous. Because she could not think of anything better to do, she tried on the second skirt. Pat, pat, went the assistant's hands over her bottom and hips. Rip, answered something inside Matty's body, and a cold, hard clod dropped into her groin. She swayed and put out a hand for support.

'Excuse me, madam,' the assistant peered at her white-faced client, 'are you sure you are quite well?'

But Matty was far away, concentrating on the demon that was now ripping the flesh from the walls of her womb. No! She screamed.

No.

After that, Matty could not distinguish much. She heard the terrified assistant say, '*In Harrods!* This is awful. Get a doctor.' There was a blur of light, a prick of a needle in her arm, and the impression of a large hand examining her stomach. The clod grew heavier and more punishing, then nothing.

Some time later, it was night. Matty worked that out because of the electric lamp shining in the corner. Someone sat beside it, and each time they moved, a square of linen danced above a blue uniform. A pad of soft cotton was wadded between Matty's legs, and her arm ached where the needle had gone in. She was thirsty and made an effort to reach for the glass of water by the bed. The nurse, wearing an artificially concerned expression, came over and helped Matty to drink it before tucking her up and telling her to go to sleep.

She awoke properly into daylight. The bedroom at Bryanston Court was filled with late morning sunshine. Matty lay and watched it filter between her eyelashes and observed the colour change as she moved her eyes this way and that. It meant she did not have to think.

'Poor old girl.' Flora stood beside the bed. 'I'm so sorry.'

Matty looked up at her sister-in-law. Flora's nimbus of hair

216

made her seem stronger than usual and she was too weak to fight envy. 'So am I.'

'Kit is beside himself.' Flora dragged up a chair and sank into it. 'Why didn't you say anything? Why didn't you tell us?'

'Kit knew.'

'Oh.' Still not accustomed to the fact that husbands and wives had secrets, Flora looked put out. 'He feels very guilty.'

'He shouldn't. It's not his fault.'

Flora examined the face on the pillow and considered privately that it was Kit's fault. If he had behaved better or, at least, less obviously at Lady Londonderry's ball, then Matty would not have been so upset. Love, Flora concluded after analysis, was complicated and involved odd factors such as timing and luck.

Matty made an effort. 'How was the nightclub?'

'Fun.'

'And Marcus?'

Flora made a face. 'Well,' she confessed uncertainly. 'He wanted to kiss me again.'

The face on the pillow tried to smile. 'Is this becoming a habit, Flora? You know what happens to fast women?'

The remark made Flora laugh, albeit uncertainly, because she was not sure where the dividing line was between fast and acceptable. 'I'll take care, Matty,' she promised. Even so a faint red crept into her cheeks. 'But you don't want to talk about nightclubs,' she said to Matty. 'What can I do to help?'

Matty moved restlessly. 'Will you ask Kit to do something for me?'

'Of course I will.'

'I want to go home. Will you ask him to take me?'

Four days later, Matty woke to a different sunlight and the sound of birdsong. She listened for a moment: the birdsong had sounded different when spring came and now it was changing again for the summer.

Matty pulled herself upright and felt the hammer of headache in her left temple. The clock on the bedside table registered only five thirty. It also ticked comfortlessly at her. Look at you. Tick. Anxious. Tick. Tearful. Tick. Full of dread.

Yes, she told herself, I am all these things. She directed her willpower against the greyness that seeped through her defences.

'Well, Mrs Dysart,' said Dr Hurley, who had descended yesterday from the magnificence of his Harley Street consulting rooms to Bryanston Court before they set off home. 'What have we been doing to ourself?'

'Nothing,' Matty almost snapped.

Dr Hurley stared at his normally timid patient and took out his notebook. 'It's quite natural to be angry, Mrs Dysart.' He took Matty's pulse. 'Now, tell me what happened.'

Reliving details and events did not make them better. Matty explained the missed periods, the sore breasts and the nausea and asked, 'I *was* pregnant, wasn't I, Dr Hurley?'

He put his fountain pen down on the pad. 'To be honest, Mrs Dysart, knowing your history and physiology, I would be surprised.' Matty stared at him, and Dr Hurley made a smooth change of tack. 'But,' he amended, 'strange things do happen, of course.'

She shivered as she engaged his bland look. 'What about next time, Dr Hurley?'

Dr Hurley assumed the expression of professional compassion that got him out of most difficult situations. 'Mrs Dysart, I am almost sure there will not be a next time. Your illnesses, certain irregularities . . . we have discussed them many times and you know my views.'

'Never, Dr Hurley?'

He busied himself with the pen. 'Never is a hard word. But consider, Mrs Dysart, you are luckier than most. You have other things to keep you busy.'

The clock ticked inside its tortoiseshell case. 'Other things?' Hats to tilt over one eye and jewellery to wear and indeed, as Mrs Christopher Dysart, summer fêtes to open. Yes, there was the house to think about: windows to curtain, china to check, meals to plan. Yes. It was good to see the furniture gleaming, to smell pot-pourri in the rooms and to enjoy fresh paintwork on the shutters.

But it was not enough to provision a life, or to please the spirit, or to fill the hole made by her treacherous body.

'Goodbye, Dr Hurley,' she said and he left.

Everything hurt – breathing, talking, dressing, thinking, remembering. Matty examined the rogue crack in the ceiling above the bed, and imagined that it grew wide and enormous, inviting her to climb into the space and lose herself. Below it hung a painting of a woman wearing blue striped trousers by an artist called Suzanne Valadon. ('Good God,' exclaimed Kit on seeing it. 'I can't get over your taste in paintings.') Matty concentrated on the cigarette hanging out of the woman's mouth and felt better.

Inch by inch, she got out of bed. First her feet, second her legs and a great push upright, towards the bathroom. Then her brassière, next her knickers, and a petticoat edged in Nottingham lace. Try to ignore the ache in her abdomen. Concentrate. Stockings. Cotton skirt and blouse. Concentrate. Lace-up shoes. A glance in the mirror. A dab of rose water, a quick pat of the hairbrush. Out of the room, down the stairs and into the sunlight.

It was already warm. Matty took off her cardigan, left it draped over the stone balustrade and made her way down the steps, releasing a waft of thyme. Under the beech tree emerald moss was sharp and jangling in contrast to the brown tree trunk. Matty stopped to look and then, drawn almost against her will, glided on.

At the thicket she hesitated, stepped forward and beat her way along the covered path towards the garden whose hidden life waited for her. At the top of the slope, she halted. Light filtered through a lacework of leaves, a ring dove sounded from the silver birch and its mate answered. Cradled in the undergrowth, the statue stood out, yellow-green with moss, while the choked plants in the flowerbed were drenched in damp. Her eye caught by a blob of pink in the green, Matty edged her way down the slope and knelt down on the wet earth.

Smothered by weeds, leggy and unpruned, a 'Queen of

Denmark' rose flowered in a sugary pink with grey-green foliage. To please itself, thought Matty, liking the idea of its independence, and traced the shape of quartered, cupped petals, dotted with a button eye. Lower down the stem, a fat bud waited to bloom. Matty ran a hand down over her own body: flat breasts, empty stomach, slack thighs. Above everything – above *everything* else – she longed to feel a child's body against her own, and empty, hungry, grieving, she was to be denied it.

What was she to do with her life?

After a few minutes, she brushed the mud away from her knees, rubbed her hands on her handkerchief and looked up at the clematis scrambling over the brick wall. Broken only by the rustle of leaves and the whirr of birds' wings, the silence dared her to move, to break the moment, so she remained quite still. Then, with the lightest and most tender of touches, the sun spread over her tired skin and warmed her tired spirit.

And out of Matty's grief was born a moment of exultation, and the conviction that, at last, she had found her place. She was the garden, the garden was Matty, and they were both living. Somehow, Matty had made her stumbling journey along an unknown road and reached a milestone.

It lasted no more than a few seconds, but it was enough.

Two days later, feeling much stronger, dressed in a linen shirt and trousers, Matty returned to the garden carrying a fork and a trowel. She took off her jacket, draped it over the statue, surveyed the space and began to dig in the flowerbed under the wall.

It required effort to drive the fork into the earth and, to her chagrin, Matty did not possess the strength. After five minutes she was panting. After ten, her back ached and her hands were slippery with sweat – but there was a heap of dug earth. Copying Ned's favourite pose, Matty leant on the fork handle to draw breath. The disturbed earth was alive with worms and indignant insects and she watched them taking cover.

Again she lifted the fork and drove it down, and this time struck a root clump which refused to yield. Matty rocked the fork experimentally, and her foot slipped on the tines. With a thump, the handle whipped back into her stomach.

'Blast it,' she said.

Shocked by the blow and feeling childishly let down by her own weakness, she stopped, unaware that she was experiencing the sort of set-back most first-time gardeners encounter. She dragged her forearm across her sweaty face and suppressed an urge to burst into tears. Not this time, my girl, she told herself. You're only tearful because you're still weak.

Don't be beaten.

You're not going to be beaten.

Beaten, echoed the ring dove.

Matty knelt down on a piece of sacking which she had sensibly brought with her and tackled the mass of roots and grass in the bed. Bothered at first by the feel of earth on her hands, she brushed at them continually, but after a while she gave up, and discovered it did not matter if dirt caked under fingernails. Nor did she mind. Later, Matty grew to like the sensation, as she came to enjoy the smell of wet earth, leaf mould and rotting plants.

Such waste, thought the waste-hating Matty, tossing a slug-ridden bulb onto her refuse pile. Such waste.

Working her way along the bed, she encountered another root which refused to budge. Part of it snapped off, exposing a white circle of inner flesh. Matty pushed her fingers into the earth around it and grasped the fibrous remainder, pulled until her eyes bulged, and fell backwards when it came up. She held it in triumph.

Two hours later, she had managed to clear a patch of three feet square or so and felt like the early colonist in tropical Africa. After its long incarceration, the earth looked lifeless. Not sure if she had been too enthusiastic and unselective in what she had discarded, Matty sorted out suspects from the rubbish to consult Ned as to what they were. He would not approve, but she had an idea she could talk him into co-operating.

That night she slept through until seven o'clock and woke up hungry.

*

The garden was Matty's secret. Like all secrets, it was the better for hoarding and being turned over in the mind, this way and that. For maturing like all good vintages. Matty's plan was simple: to bring this garden back to life. Clear it. Plant it. Watch it grow. Then, only then, would she show it to Kit and, after she had proved to him of what she was capable, ask him again to let her manage the whole garden.

Oh, yes. Years of planning, planting, watching, retrenching lay ahead. Busy years, she thought with relief.

Since the miscarriage, Kit had been punctilious about visiting Matty's bedroom to say goodnight but now he was due to return to London with Flora and to hand over the latter to Lady F. ('Do you always make living sacrifices?' Flora asked bitterly. 'Do you like hearing victims scream?')

'We can't do anything else,' Matty pointed out to Kit. 'Robbie has to look after your father, and Flora must not miss the rest of the Season because of me.'

'No,' said Kit.

'I think you should stay up in London as long as possible to give her support.'

'Well, I will,' said Kit. 'It's nice of you to be so understanding about it.'

Neither of them mentioned Daisy. Kit leant over to give Matty her goodnight kiss on the cheek and on an impulse slid his hand round her shoulders. 'I'm sorry you've been disappointed and miserable, but things will get better.'

After he had gone, Matty did not feel nearly as empty as she often did. Instead she picked up one of Miss Jekyll's gardening books. 'The lesson I have thoroughly learnt, and wish to pass on to others, is to know the enduring happiness that the love of a garden gives.'

Good, thought Matty and marked the place. I could do with some.

Next to Miss Jekyll lay two books by Mr Bowles – *My Garden in Spring* and *My Garden in Summer* – full of humour and artistic arrangements. Beside them were stacked *The English Rock Garden* by Mr Farrer and Mr Robinson's *The English Flower*

Garden, plus an article by the novelist Vita Sackville-West from the *Evening Standard*, which Matty loved for its mixture of the poetic and the practical.

Matty realized that the scope of her ambition needed to be bigger: clearing the earth was fine, but a plan was needed if the work was to mean something. On a piece of paper she drew in the shape of the garden: the south and west sides bounded by the perimeter wall, the east side by the avenue of birches and the north by the scrub.

'Clematis', she wrote and drew an arrow to indicate its position on the west wall. Which clematis? The book said clematises flowered either in early summer or early autumn and were lime-loving. 'Roses'. Matty was keen to have as many as possible. 'Queen of Denmark', of course. The Jacobite rose which she had seen in a painting. 'Maiden's Blush'. The 'Duchess of Montebello'.

Next: '*Salvia patens*' to underplant the roses. Delphiniums and white foxgloves against the wall. Some silver-leaved plants in front of them? Plus a drift (thank you, Miss Jekyll, for the idea) of pink sedum for the autumn. After that, she scrawled '*Trillium grandiflorum* (shady bits)', blissfully unaware of how tricky they were to grow, 'saxifrage?, santolina (must have), *Tradescantia* (blue or white?)'

Circles and arrows sprouted all over the diagram and the list grew.

'Mrs Kit,' said Ned once he had succumbed to a pair of pleading eyes, a request for an extra wheelbarrow, compost, a lesson on planting, an order to buy up stock at the nearest nursery and an injunction for the deepest secrecy. 'Mrs Kit, what are you asking me to do?'

'I'd like you to help me. You know the garden, the bit that no one goes into?'

'Yes, ma'am.' Ned's face wore an expression which she could not place.

'You don't want to be bothering with that, Mrs Kit,' he said after a moment. 'It's not the best place. The soil's tainted.' He added, 'It gets like that sometimes.'

'*Please*, Mr Sheppey.'

She waited. He appeared to be struggling with the wish to speak out, and then the habit of following orders won.

'If that's what you're telling me to do. But I don't like it, Mrs Kit.'

Matty produced her plan. Ned stared at the hieroglyphics and then wiped his mouth with his handkerchief. 'You haven't measured the garden. Nor have you allowed for the plants to grow. You can't start until you've done that.'

Matty sighed. 'Nor I have, Mr Sheppey.'

He smiled, enjoying his little triumph. 'Never mind, Mrs Kit. You can do it again.'

'Will it take long to get the plants, Mr Sheppey? I'd like to come with you.'

'Depends,' said Ned. 'There's only one nursery in the area and they don't keep everything. We'll have to ask around other gardens for seeds and cuttings.'

Every day Matty visited the garden. When she first began work, she found it almost impossible to lift the wheelbarrow. A couple of weeks later she was wheeling it half loaded without losing her breath.

'Mark out the area to dig, Mrs Kit,' said Ned during one of their daily confabulations. So she did.

'Push the spade straight down. Use the shaft to lever the soil, not your back.' So she did.

'Sharpen the blade with a stone. Choose a good day. Dig down one strip to the depth of the spade, Mrs Kit, and make a trench. Jiggle the spade at the bottom to loosen the subsoil.'

The soil peeled back, revealing its secret greys and browns: So shall my life turn over. Matty felt sweat soak into her blouse.

Next, she tackled the second strip, deposited its soil into the first strip and mixed in spadefuls of compost: Go then, and multiply. Scrambled back muscles, jagged fingernails, a smell of turned earth, a gritty feel on her hands: unfamiliar sensations became friendly, part of a repertoire that she hugged to herself.

224

In the end, because it was a huge task, Ned came to help and they cleared and burnt the debris side by side. Matty was impatient for her garden, badgering him for results, and he told her over and over again that it would take time. That the garden required preparation before she could plant it.

'What about the lily bulbs that Mrs Pengeally sent over? Can't we plant those? In a pot, perhaps?'

'You need to know what you're doing with lilies, Mrs Kit.'

'But you know, Mr Sheppey, and you can teach me.'

'Top dressed and staked.'

'Top dressed?' Matty felt much as Echo must have done, dashing about in mythical Greece hearing her words repeated.

'Equal parts manure, lime rubble and loam.'

Next year, thought Matty, the idea giving her extreme pleasure, I will have more roses, more lilies. Hundreds of them.

CHAPTER SEVEN

I'M NOT going to hang around for ever, you know.'
Tim Coats pressed up against Daisy and, since they were
trapped in the crush moving towards the Royal Enclosure, no one
noticed that his hand slid across her bottom. He bent over and
whispered, 'Come on, Daisy. Give a chap a proper answer.'

Daisy smiled. Tim was tall, dark and knowing, and she liked
him. But not enough. He had been surprisingly faithful, in view of
his reputation and the provocation she had given him. 'Down,
Rover,' she said, and brushed his hand away with a finger
sheathed in kid. 'Naughty.'

'Why not, damn it?'

Daisy's eyelashes shielded the expression in her eyes. 'Because.'

Watching her, Tim was conscious of a desire to wring her
neck. Then, perhaps, when the bones cracked satisfactorily, she
would tell him what was going on in that head of hers instead of
holding him – with undeniable skill, but holding him, all the same
– like a bull in a pen.

'It would be fun,' he persisted. 'Think of it, Daise. I want to
settle down. So do you. We like the same things and if you wanted
adventures I wouldn't mind.'

'And if you wanted adventures?'

'The same applies. We understand each other.'

At that, Daisy looked up at Tim – and yet again he examined
the arrangement of features and interplay of colour that made up
the exquisite face. 'How do you know, Tim?' she challenged. 'If
we understand each other, I mean.'

'For God's sake, Daisy. I give up.'

She smiled and turned her head away.

Unusually there had been no rain for the past three weeks
and, in an effort to stem the ravages, millions of gallons of water

226

had been pumped onto the Ascot race course. The result was bright green grass, a ribbon that swirled past the dry, dusty area of the stands. But, in true English fashion, the weather now threatened to make up for the lack of rain. A black cloud sat above the racetrack and the temperature had fallen. Daisy shivered. 'I'm cold.'

For once Tim did not say: Let me warm you.

'Let's hope the weather holds. It would be too ghastly,' said Susan, viper smart in a silk dress, but missing her fur. 'For goodness sake, cheer up, Daisy. You don't look as though you're enjoying yourself one bit.'

'I don't need to cheer up, Mother.' Daisy waved at Francis Beauchamp. 'I am feeling perfectly all right. Would you prefer me to grin like a baboon?'

For once, Susan could not think of a suitable reply. Instead she snapped her bag shut and said, 'This whole outing was arranged for you, though goodness knows why.'

An arched eyebrow greeted this information. 'Don't tell lies, Mother. You enjoy this more than I do.'

Susan shot her daughter a look which did not bode well for the evening. 'Daisy. Please make an effort. All of us feel in the dumps occasionally . . . I do . . . but have you ever seen me give in to them? And in this world, it is no use behaving like a shrinking violet.'

'Mother. Have I ever been a shrinking violet?'

'Well, no.' Even Susan had the grace to agree.

'And what good has it done me?'

Although not by any means a natural mother, Susan was not entirely deficient in maternal feelings, merely a woman who took the world on its own terms, but the bleakness etched onto Daisy's face made her feel guilty for a second or two.

'In my experience,' continued Daisy in the same logical manner, 'shrinking violets do rather well for themselves.'

With a razzle-dazzle of rounded vowels, flapping canvas and the creak of tightening guy ropes, the Royal Enclosure filled up. Outside, the horses being walked up and down played to the house. Bow-legged and prematurely lined from dieting, sweating with nerves and suppressed flatus, their jockeys traced a fretwork of tracks in the paddock. The enclosure was soon littered with horse droppings, saddle-soaped leather straps hung in soft ribbons, bits clinked against horses' teeth, and the jockeys clung to their saddles like exposed limpets at low-tide.

Funny how the men looked like massed penguins, ready to slide into the sea with an escort of floating top hats, thought Daisy. The women in pink reminded her of cough lozenges, those in blue of hyacinths, and the daring ones in white were runaways from a Hollywood film set. She got out her binoculars and swept them over the stands. Then she stopped.

Magnified several times, Kit rose from the subfusc and cohered into the circle defined by the lens. Suddenly Daisy, who had imagined he was miles away, was close enough to make out a blue vein running down the side of his neck. Her grip tightened.

Thirstily, she retraced him. The way his face was put together – ungovernable hair, sun-lines round his eyes, uneven smile. His rumpledness and contradictory elegance. He was talking to Flora – a green leek, thought Daisy hysterically – and his jaw was set in the way it did when he grew passionate about something. Watching, Daisy felt every nerve burn with longing.

Of course, she thought. Of course, I would see him here. For a second or two she reclaimed him for herself. Then the image she held between her gloved hands wavered and broke up.

'Darling, which jockey are you madly fancying?' Annabel Beauchamp teetered up on high heels and slipped her arm through her friend's.

'No one, Annabel, actually. I was looking at the colours. Aquamarine is in.' Daisy lowered the binoculars and eyed the carmine stroked onto Annabel's thin but kindly lips. 'For example, did you raid a paintbox for that red?' The gibe was neutralized by her smile.

'I borrowed it. *Parce que* I was late and had to borrow our supervisor's.'

'Where were you?'

'Marie Stopes Committee.' Annabel gave her charming giggle.

'It's civil war between Marie Stopes and the National Birth Control Association who're accusing each other of stealing their thunder. I made a very good punch bag.'

'Oh, Bel,' cried Daisy passionately. 'You're a good person.'

'Why don't you join me on the committee?' asked her friend. 'I need allies and Marie Stopes needs volunteers.'

'I will, I will,' said Daisy. 'When I come back from America.'

She looked over the Royal Enclosure towards the stand where Kit had disappeared into the shifting colours. 'I love all this, Bel, don't you? Even though I feel guilty about it sometimes.'

Annabel patted Daisy's arm. 'There, there,' she said, quite used to Daisy's occasional flights of guilt. 'We're rich, privileged and pretty. Now what are you going to do? Have a good weep?'

'Rich, privileged and pretty selfish,' supplied Daisy. She turned to Annabel and life had come back into her face. 'And, on a day like this, blissfully gay.' She tucked her hand into Annabel's elbow. 'But I'll join you when I come back.'

Later, Tim Coats picked his way through the hats in the refreshment tent towards Daisy's tilted white affair. 'I trust the champagne has made you see sense,' he said and hooked his finger under her chin.

'If by sense you mean I have to give in to your every wish, then I require some more.' Daisy held out her glass. Tim obliged, and Daisy drank it far too fast.

'I told the Fellowes' to join us tonight.'

'That sounds fine.' Daisy held out her glass for an encore.

'Good God,' said a male voice rising above the hubbub. 'It's Daisy Chudleigh, the flower of them all.'

Tim's expression darkened perceptibly as Daisy greeted a spectacular-looking youth. 'Gordon! Where have *you* been?'

'Searching the world for you, my darling. Now that I've seen you I absolutely know that I must have you by my side for the next race. You don't mind Timmers, old boy, do you?'

'As it happens I do, Latham.'

'Daisy, I implore you.' Gordon wagged a finger at Tim. 'It's a far, far better thing you do, dear boy.'

Daisy looked from one man to the other. This situation was one she understood perfectly. Kit's image faded and with it, for the moment, the trapped, desperate feelings.

All right, she had said later to Tim, when I come back from America I will give you my final answer. Why not now, damn it? he had argued. Because, Tim . . . His knowing hands had circled her neck. Well, hurry up and make yourself ready, Daisy. Get over that stupid man and start to live.

What about love? she had asked.

What about it? Tim had replied. You know I love you.

Yes, what about it? Daisy lay in bed remembering when she and Kit had walked up the path from the Villa Lafayette to the cliff top above, discussing love. Kit had been excited over the idea in Plato's *Symposium* which made a distinction between romantic and sacred love, the latter being the most perfect and refined. Daisy had not agreed. If you love, you love, she argued. It is not more or less. One thing or another. More perfect, less perfect. It is total and there was nothing to be gained by teasing it out.

Kit had gone quiet. He stood, heat beating on his skin, eyes screwed against the glare, tossing stones down onto the rock below.

'I don't think you understand,' he said.

'If you mean I don't understand some bore from Ancient Greece, then perhaps you're right.'

He laughed at that and pulled her close. 'You're perfect,' he said, nuzzling her neck. 'And divine.'

Still, she had been troubled by the distinction, afraid that Kit was ashamed of his passion for her. In the dark, Daisy clenched her fists and felt the nails graze her skin. Where had that left her?

She awoke from a dream, gasping and sobbing. After a while she quietened, and lay crying quietly, her hands still smarting.

Oh, Kit.

CHAPTER EIGHT

ROBBIE RAN her finger along the map frame on the wall which was thick with dust.

'Don't touch it,' said Rupert from the bed.

'You know me better than that, Sir Rupert.' Robbie waited until he had returned to his newspaper before replacing her finger and running it firmly along the wood. She wiped the resulting ball of grey onto her handkerchief. It was always the same: no one was allowed to touch objects hanging on the wall. Robbie did not mind: it was part and parcel of Sir Rupert and she loved every quirk. At night she held those idiosyncrasies suspended in her drowsing mind and turned them round and round – he likes that, not that – until she fell asleep.

She moved on to tackle the paraphernalia of sickness cluttering a room which, until now, had been Spartan. Bottles, glasses, extra blankets. A heap of letters. A pile of bills brought in by Kit and neglected.

She picked up the spoon with which she had administered Rupert's medicine: a distorted face looked back at her from its curved surface and the fancy that her lips were positioned where Rupert's had been sent a *frisson* of excitement through her. Only just in time did Robbie stop herself from putting the spoon in her mouth. Holding it between finger and thumb she placed it on the breakfast tray.

'You haven't eaten your porridge, Sir Rupert.'

Rupert did not bother to reply and Robbie looked concerned. The patient was quiet this morning, too quiet really. Robbie cleared her throat – a preface to one of her let's-make-the-best-of-things-and-ignore-nasty-topics conversations – and Rupert, recognizing the signal, squeezed his eyes shut.

'The village is up in arms over the business of putting in

overhead electricity cables, Sir Rupert,' she said. 'They don't like the notion. What with that and the telephone wires, the village will be a forest of poles.'

'If you want electricity,' said Rupert, wondering how long the circles of rage and frustration floating behind his eyelids would last, 'then you have to put up with it.' The door rattled and in came Flora. Rupert opened his eyes in relief.

'Ah, Flora,' he said, and her heart sank at his tone. 'Finished gallivanting, then? Does the social timetable allow a minute for a knocked-up parent? Is that it?'

'Now, Sir Rupert.' Over by the table, Robbie clinked the medicine bottles together in a sickroom symphony. 'You mustn't be nasty to Flora.'

'Father,' protested Flora. 'It's what you wanted me to do, so you can get me married off.'

For the umpteenth time, Rupert tried to move his legs and failed. 'Where's that Binns woman this morning?' he said. 'Or,' he shot a look of inordinate cunning at Robbie, 'have you routed her?'

'I'm going to ignore that, Sir Rupert.'

Rupert ground his teeth and Flora suppressed a desire to giggle, her habitual response to the awfulness of her father's predicament – a reaction that both shocked and worried her. Over Rupert's head, Robbie wagged a finger at Flora to take care. The patient was touchy today.

Flora sat down in the chair by the bed. 'What would you like me to tell you, Father?'

'Did you behave yourself?'

'Of course.'

'Any suitables?'

Flora suppressed a sigh. 'Only spotty ones and the rest are not exactly queuing up.'

Rupert attempted to reach his cup of tea. Flora leapt up again to help close his fingers around the handle and lift the cup to his mouth. The skin around her father's nails was drying out, and she fought an impulse to drop the cup and run away. He dribbled a little and she wiped him with a square of muslin left for that purpose by the bed. 'So you're back,' he repeated in the confused way of invalids.

'I needed a rest, Father.'

'Just like . . . just like your mother.' The words shot out and took Flora by surprise. Tea slopped over the rim of the cup and down onto Rupert's pyjamas. 'No stamina,' he said, watching the puddle. 'Never did have. No loyalty either. No idea . . . of what she . . .'

'Head up, Sir Rupert. Quick march.' In a miasma of starch and disinfectant, Robbie surged forward, removed the cup and saucer from Flora and deftly fed the rest to Rupert. 'Down the red lane.'

Pinioned and helpless, Rupert gave off world-embracing despair. Robbie patted his hand. 'You'll do, Sir Rupert.' She held his hand a little longer than necessary. 'Now, no more of this talk. It only upsets you.' She went out of the door, a creamily satisfied smile on her lips.

'Flora. Do me a favour. Ask your brother to shoot that woman and stuff her.'

'Father!'

'On second thoughts, forget about the stuffing.'

'Father . . . tell me.' Amazed to be tackling Rupert, adult to adult, she asked, 'Is Robbie driving you loco? I could do something if she is. Pack her off to Polly, maybe.'

Rupert's mood did an abrupt volte-face. 'It doesn't matter any more.'

There were too many years of distance between father and daughter for Flora to ask Rupert what he meant.

Groaning a little, he tried to haul himself further up on the pillows. Flora tugged at him and patted his pillows into shape. She found it an awkward business dealing with the invalid body — all unexpected dead weight and imbalance. Since the accident, Rupert had lost much of his bulk, and now the skin sagged over his cheekbones and jawline in the manner of the chronically tired and ill. White flakes were trapped at the corners of his mouth and in his eyelashes, evidence of his decline which drove a skewer of pity into Flora — and repelled her. But she knew also that she *could* cross the distance and walk towards him. Greatly daring, she took Rupert's brown-blotched hand into her own.

'Don't drool over me,' he said. 'I can't bear it.'

'Since you mention Mother, can we talk about her?' she asked with an obvious effort.

Rupert's fingers pulled free of his daughter's. He did not know why he had referred to Hesther, only that memories choose damnfool moments to resurface. 'Forget what I said.'

'But—'

'I said forget it.'

'Matty will be here soon to read to you,' she said, accepting, yet again, that the questions about her mother which sometimes tormented would remain unanswered. She got up to fetch his library book and gave it to him.

'Danny all right?' Rupert could not prevent himself asking. His voice cut through the silence made by their last exchange.

Flora picked up the book again and traced the sticker on the front. 'Boots Circulating Library,' she murmured. She looked at her father. 'I saw Danny yesterday. He's fine. Lady's whelped with three bitches and a dog. I told him you're allowed visitors. He said he'd think about it.'

'Damned cheek. Give him an inch.' Rupert paused. 'Told him to come and see me, did you?'

'I don't think he likes sick rooms, Father. And Robbie goes on the warpath whenever he's mentioned. Danny's clever, Father. He doesn't want to provoke a major scene.'

'No, I don't expect Danny likes sick rooms, the old bugger.' Rupert went quiet. Just before he fell into an untidy snorting sleep he gave the order. 'Tell him to come all the same.'

Flora watched her diminished father and sighed.

Rupert was back in an old nightmare, inching up a muddied, shell-pocked road on the Somme, nicknamed Pall Mall by one of the wags in the company.

The company, which included Edwin, was back from three days' leave in Amiens. There, the camouflage units worked non-

234

stop; the *estaminets* were open during the day and most of the night, journalists, would-be novelists and anxious relatives swelled the hotel population and, smelling of raffia and glue, girls from the factory offered their services. Clad in hastily acquired khaki – not many remained of the original 80,000 who had fought at Ypres in 1914 – Kitchener's recruits took up the offers. Why not? Chastity was a waste of time.

They drove out from the city in double-decker buses towards the town of Albert and the front line. The road was clogged with motorcycles, messengers and vehicles; in the fields beyond Albert a solitary farmer inspected his crops and ignored the traffic. Outside one of the villages on the route was a first-aid station and someone had raked over a flowerbed and planted it with daisies. As they drew closer to the fighting the noise of the guns swelled from a subdued thud into thunder.

It was July 1916, and at the front a dust-laden, fury-ridden night was falling early, blotting out men, observer planes and barrage balloons. Every so often flares lit the sky above the battle-line, the earth shook and rained dirt, flesh and chalk. Here, the crump of guns pounded iron on bronze into ear-drums and the screams of the wounded were lost.

And yet, between the barrages, doves cooed in barn eaves and larks sang as they wheeled in the clear air above the battle.

The company was detailed to join the Worcesters up by Thiepval Wood. None of the boys commented, but it meant that casualties were bad. After falling-out for cigarettes, Rupert gave the order to begin the slog up to the front line.

At the edge of the wood a humorist had erected a signpost which read: THIEPVAL–BAPAUME–BERLIN. An arrow pointed to the track leading across a marshy valley to the bottom of the ridge only half a mile away, but it took Rupert and his men over an hour to push over the mud-slicked causeways, past the junctions and through a battle haze which masked runners and the stumbling wounded.

'Gas masks,' he ordered, and stepped round the figures huddled on the ground, not knowing whether they slept or were dead. To Paisley Dump, Johnson's Post, Elgin Avenue, said more notices whose humour wasn't so funny any more. At the foot of the ridge, on the west side of the wood, communication trenches spidered towards the front line. It was here that supplies were unloaded, ammunition dumped and, between assaults, men circled in exhaustion.

They waited in the wood. Rupert counted his heartbeats, and thought of Hinton Dysart and of the wife who did not love him. And in the lulls between the screams of the shells filtering through the gas-soaked mist, Rupert was aware of another noise, the sound of fingernails screeching across enormous panes of glass, coming from the no man's land between the lines.

It stretched from the orchards of Gommecourt, through the poppy-dotted fields to Beaumont Hamel, Thiepval and the valley beyond La Boiselle. From it rose the muted screaming, pain-filled sound of wounded Tommy and Hun, welded by blood into uniformity.

What was it Edwin had said to Rupert in the restaurant in rue du Corps Nu Sans Tête over the cognac? Bottles of cognac actually, as much as they could manage. It went something like this . . .

Why should there be this unnatural accumulation of men, animals and food? Why this methodical enterprise to fill mass graves? What has happened to the world? Nothing is in its proper place any more, said Edwin – who had volunteered, remember – neither things, nor ideas, nor human beings.

Then, brandy making his moustache glisten, Edwin had leant across the glasses and overflowing ashtrays. 'If I should die first, Rupert, tell Hesther I loved her best.'

And Rupert replied, 'What do you bloody well mean? She's my wife.'

'And my sister,' Edwin answered in a low voice. 'My sister, before your wife.' And added under his breath, 'I suppose that's not in its proper place either.'

Oh, my brothers, a drunken Edwin addressed the uncomprehending French fields as they bounced back in the London bus to the front. Was it for this, all this blood, all this pain, all these shipwrecked lives, was it for this, O my brothers?

Edwin had been very drunk and that day he had gone out and

died with a hangover near Thiepval Wood, not far from Rupert, as it happened, although it could have been a hundred miles, and Rupert wished it had been a thousand. After Edwin's death, it was finished for Rupert. (And for Hesther, but he did not know that then.)

The shakes, as Rupert called them, came on by degrees and he hid them with drink, although Danny Ovens noticed. It was not just in his fingers, inconveniently failing to meet objects, or muscles twitching in sleep, it went deeper. The shakes went through to his soul, until all of Rupert was shuddering. Little things — a dirty billy can, an undone puttee, officers transferring badges from shoulders to cuffs so they did not present such obvious targets — had become his obsession. You see, explained Rupert in his dream, what was happening to me was so big that it was a relief to go barmy over the small things. Of course, he could not tell Hesther in his letters because he was not in the habit of telling Hesther anything. Especially not after Edwin was dead.

After the first assault when Edwin bought it, the men regrouped in the trenches and waited to go back over the top. Danny Ovens sat and combed his hair. Thick, it was then, and sandy with a tinge of red.

'Give 'em something to look at, sir,' Danny said, pulling his helmet forward. 'When I drive me bayonet through that lot . . .'

Along with Edwin, the company had lost ten men and were feeling battered.

'You bloody fucking fool,' said Rupert, stuffing his treacherous hands behind his back. Danny watched him, one eyebrow cocked.

'So I am, sir, so I am.'

What was it Edwin said? Or was it Danny? Nothing is in its proper place any more.

In the late afternoon, shells bursting like peonies on the horizon, Rupert gave the order once again to go over. As they did so, a man stopped dead in front of him. Rupert cursed and shoved him aside.

'Sorry, sir,' said the man and thrust his face at Rupert's. 'I'm blinded, sir.'

Rupert, taking in the torn-away features, felt the brandy sloshing inside him.

'All right, old chap,' he said.

They pushed on into the fire. Wounded men lay in the shell holes and some of them, mainly Worcesters and Warwicks, cheered as Rupert and his men passed.

'Give 'em hell, sir.'

We're in hell, thought Rupert, wondering if a mind could shatter into pieces, like bone. Or be pulped, like a brain inside a skull pan.

The shelling grew heavier, and the men fanned out in a line, moving like poachers through the trees towards a dug-out held by the Germans up to the west. At the edge of the trees they dropped onto their stomachs and waited for the order while Rupert surveyed the target with his binoculars.

'Grenades,' he said, just able to focus the unsteady lenses, terrified he was going to give himself away. Between them and the dug-out, which might or might not have been abandoned by the enemy, lay twenty yards of churned-up earth.

'Where now, sir?' said Danny.

Rupert was silent.

'We've got to move, sir. Else they'll mark us.'

I don't know. *I don't know*, Rupert wanted to say. I did once know about things, but I don't any longer.

'Where, sir?' Danny's voice nagged at Rupert.

'Take the dug-out. Grenades. From the back.'

'Are you all right, sir?'

'Form the line. Pass the message down.'

Through an evening light that poets might have praised as a delicate gloaming, they slid along the earth, over pulverized wild flowers and past dead and wounded men.

With luck it will be me next, thought Rupert when Tommy Anson dropped his rifle and clutched at his shoulder. A scarlet rose bloomed on his khaki. 'Get back,' he told Anson.

'Break a leg, then, sir,' said Tommy between whitening lips and stumbled off.

Dusk settled over the wood – over the Piccadilly Circuses, the

Pall Malls, the duckboarded Ritzes – much as it was doing in London. A presence whose softened outlines promised peace, comforts, for a few hours at least.

Danny threw himself onto his stomach and wriggled forward. The rest dropped to their knees and gave cover. A second or two later, Bletchford went forward, then Lyall. Danny reached the dug-out, ducked inside, reappeared almost instantly and beckoned. Bent double, Rupert wove towards it and pushed himself in.

Cunningly reinforced with concrete, much of the dug-out had survived the grenades and the previous bombardment, but the stench in it was beyond description.

'Dead Huns, sir,' reported Danny. 'Three.'

Two of the bodies lay in water in which floated excreta and filth. A third had died on a wire bed pushed against the wall. Danny tipped the body off onto the floor, where it subsided with a squelch, and sat down.

'Could be worse, sir.'

Later, when everybody bar Danny had vomited at the stench, two orderlies crawled in through the doorway pulling a stretcher with them. On it lay an officer from the Rifle Brigade.

'Sorry, sir,' said the senior orderly. 'We have to leave him here until daylight. I've given him morphia.'

'All right,' said Rupert. 'I'll take over.' He bent over to loosen the collar of the wounded man and, with a shock, recognized Lucius Brandon from Redfields.

'Rupert, old son!' whispered Lucius. 'I owe you a game of tennis.'

'Where are you hit?'

'In the spine, I think,' said Lucius, and directed enlarged and shocked pupils on Rupert. 'Could you shift the gas helmet from under me, old son? Touch uncomfortable.'

Later Lucius said to Rupert, with tears rolling down his face, 'Jolly good show, isn't it?'

'Yes,' said Rupert.

'The lads?' asked Lucius, and Rupert shook his head. 'The Hamps do all right,' said Lucius, as if he had not noticed.

Later still, Lucius asked for a cigarette, but Rupert's hands were shaking so much that Danny did the honours. Rupert took the lit cigarette from Danny and stuck it between his friend's lips.

'Give me one, too, Danny.' Rupert's voice broke the silence. The others crowded onto the wire bed, or sat slumped in water against the walls. The match flared into the gloom and stench. Rupert bent to take the cigarette from Lucius and saw that he was dead.

The next thing Rupert knew he was outside the dug-out, where he knelt, risking sniper fire, in the gas-streaked air. Shaking, retching, and cursing, while tears poured down his face.

'Sir.'

Rupert never knew how long Danny had watched him before he, too, knelt in the mud and drew the weeping giant into his embrace.

''Old on, sir.'

Danny's arms were hard and wiry, and he smelt of human filth and gunpowder. His skin was rough and unshaven, and bits of tobacco stuck between his front teeth. But his hands felt gentle, oh so gentle, and sure.

''Old on, sir.' Danny patted and held and patted as a mother does a weeping child.

'How can I?' With no defences left, Rupert clutched at Danny. 'I haven't the strength.'

'You 'ave, sir. Just 'old on to me,' went the soft litany.

They remained locked together for a long time while the moon fought free of clouds. The mutter of pain and loneliness rose from shell holes around them, and the occupants waited in the blackness for release. Both men shivered as the temperature dropped and, little by little, the screeching fingernail grew fainter and Danny held onto Rupert, a rough, but unutterably tender saviour.

Robbie came back into the room and Flora pointed silently to Rupert's fingers, marching in his sleep.

'Leave him to me,' commanded Robbie.

Flora fled to the stables. Tyson was out hacking on Vindictive but Jem, the stableboy, was at work in the tack room. He helped her to saddle Guinevere and led the horse to the mounting block. Flora paused only to clip back her obstinate hair and to pull on gloves, before clattering out of the yard and into the drive.

Half-way down she spotted Matty walking across the lawn with a trug in her hand, on one of her mysterious expeditions. Flora waved and Matty waved back and disappeared. Guinevere's haunches rolled lazily, the saddle was old and comfortable and Flora's bottom settled into it in a familiar way. She forgot about Matty, about Rupert and sick rooms and gave herself up to the day.

Guinevere tossed her head and proceeded at a dawdle. Flora let her; it was too nice to hurry. A mist was clearing up by Jonathan's Kilns, trees were an optimistic green, a couple of peonies — blowsy ladies — bloomed in Mrs Riley's garden, and a few bluebells still flowered on the verges.

She had been meaning to ride up to the Reeves' shop in Dippenhall Street for cigarettes, a habit acquired in London and now rather necessary. She knew the shop as well as her own room, with its flitches of bacon, chunks of butter and lard, flypapers black with victims and boxes of sweets. Fred Reeves handled the vicious bacon cutter as easily as a butter knife and coughed and smoked over the bread and the famous lardy busters, and Sally kept her hair in curlers all day Saturday ready for Sunday.

But instead, Flora rode up the Well Road and turned towards Jonathan's Kilns. The corn was well advanced and she stopped to squint down at it. Then she turned Guinevere's head towards Horsedown Common and Matthew Potter's land. He had just lost his wife, and poppies and corncockles had gained an upper hand in the south corner of his field. Poor chap, she thought. He never used to let that happen.

A thud of hoofs coming in her direction made her turn sharply.

'Hallo, there.' Robin Lofts cantered up on a respectable-looking bay a shade too big for him, which did not like being reined in. Dressed in a tweed jacket and breeches, Robin looked better on a horse than in a car and his pallor was tinged with pink from the gallop.

'Hallo.' For all her newly acquired worldliness Flora, who was all too conscious of their last meeting when she had wept into his handkerchief, suddenly felt shy.

'Do you mind if I join you?'

On horseback, the difference in their height was cancelled, and Robin appeared bigger and bulkier than Flora remembered.

'I didn't think you rode—' Flora bit off the rest of the sentence realizing that she might be considered rude.

'You mean village doctors don't ride for pleasure. Only the family in the big house.' Robin's lightly dealt irony took the sting out of his words. Almost.

'No. I mean, yes. Of course I don't mean that.'

Robin laughed but entirely without malice. 'You did mean it,' he said disarmingly. 'It's quite all right, and Rolly keeps Aesculapius in his stables for me.' He raised his whip and pointed towards Horsedown Common. 'Shall we go?'

But Flora had dropped the reins, and down went Guinevere's head. 'Dr Lofts, I've done it again.' She collected Guinevere, eager to put the situation right. 'I didn't mean to insinuate anything.' Although, of course, it *had* crossed Flora's mind to wonder if Robin liked his sister being married to the blacksmith, and where exactly that left the doctor in the social scale.

He laughed again. 'Of course not, Miss Dysart.'

Hoofs sinking into a carpet of last year's leaves, the horses picked their way through a clump of beeches.

'My sister-in-law tells me you have some interesting and advanced ideas,' said Flora. 'I would like to hear about them.'

'Goodness, I'd no idea I'd made such an impression.' Robin seemed pleased, and Flora smiled secretly to herself.

He began to explain to Flora his views on the politics of medicine. He was in favour of a national health service where no one paid and rich and poor received the same treatment, he said, and admitted he was a Labour voter. Flora, who had not encountered many Labour Party supporters and who had been

242

warned they were closely related to the devil, tried to maintain a suitably adult expression.

'What else?' she invited.

Never slow to talk about his interests, Robin treated Flora to a digression on mortality figures, diet, and his plans for Nether Hinton. With his grammar-school-masked Hampshire accent, his trick of jabbing the air with a finger to emphasize a point, his insight, his gentleness, and his almost shocking matter-of-factness over birth, death and sex, Robin introduced another dimension to his listener.

'Why here, Dr Lofts?' she asked at last. They had reached the edge of the wood and were idling around the perimeter. 'Why Nether Hinton? Surely the city would be better for your schemes?'

'Good question. And the answer is, I may have a few ambitions but I'm not a martyr. I love this bit of the world, and I don't like the city very much.'

'Nor do I.'

'Anyway, Nether Hinton has its share of horrors. It's still recovering.'

'From what?'

'From the war.' He seemed astonished she should ask. 'Bert Stain is minus a lung, Tom Dart an eye, and old Hal Bister had the privilege of losing most of his mind.'

In a couple of sentences, Robin made Flora see what had been staring at her for most of her life and she went bright red. 'Yes,' she said in the flat way which indicated she was upset. 'Of course.' It was followed by the unworthy thought that it did not matter what the local doctor thought of her – and that made her feel worse.

Robin's bay manoeuvred around a fallen branch. 'Miss Dysart,' he said, 'I've just been a first-class bore, and you've allowed it.'

Flora followed him. 'But you're not, Dr Lofts,' she protested. 'Certainly you're not.'

She was overdoing it. Robin was not stupid and heard the false note. He grabbed hold of Flora's reins. 'Yes, I have. Confess.'

This time, his accent grated and it occurred to her that his tweed jacket was a bit loud. 'No, you haven't,' she said crossly. 'And you're only suggesting that because you think I haven't the wit to take in what you're saying. That's insulting, not boring.' Which was precisely what Robin had been thinking. 'I'll tell you if you're boring, if you wish, Dr Lofts, it would give me pleasure, but on condition you stop looking at me as if I was five years old.'

They gazed at each other across the horses, Robin rueful, Flora flushed and indignant.

'Done,' said Robin at last. Then he grinned and the atmosphere changed. With a queer, uncertain feeling inside, Flora returned the smile. 'You were saying?' she said.

Thus it was that Robin Lofts began his wooing of Flora Dysart, with a lecture on mortality rates in babies, the utter necessity of family planning and the place of green vegetables in diet. And Flora, never previously aware of a thirst for knowledge, drank it in with the fervour of the dehydrated.

'Hallo again.'

It was a week later, and Robin trotted the bay up to where Flora, yo-yoing between hope and dread, loitered by the beech trees.

'Hallo.'

A brown butterfly danced past the bay's nose and Aesculapius performed a good imitation of an unbroken colt. 'I've been looking for you,' said Robin, struggling to keep his seat. 'I thought this might be the best place.'

'Have you?' said Flora airily. Since she had last seen him she had been into the village at least twice a day for no reason and had developed an obsessive interest in overseeing Rupert's medicines. 'I was at the house.'

Robin wheeled the bay round in a tight circle. 'Actually not like that,' he said. 'I wanted to get you on your own.'

He could have had no idea of the effect of his words for, suddenly, Flora was conscious of pulses beating in her stomach and groin. She felt hot, cold, radiant and pale, all at the same time.

'Why don't we ride up towards Snatchanger's?' she said.

At Snatchanger's they cantered up to the top of the grass mound fringed by trees. Robin dismounted and tethered the bay. Then he held up his arms to help Flora down. She swung her leg over Guinevere and slid, more or less gracefully, down to the ground. Skylarks sang in the clear air and the sun continued to climb to its noon position. To the north, the land dipped and then rose, patchworked with fields, chalk outcrops and pinkish houses. Beyond lay Odiham, to the east Farnham, to the west Winchester.

They faced each other: Flora, plump-hipped, wild-haired and a good inch taller than Robin; he, freckled, slight, a little drawn from overwork, with a hairline that was beginning to recede.

Breathing more quickly than normal (and the doctor in him calculated the adrenalin rushing through his bloodstream), Robin put out a hand and brushed the renegade hair from Flora's face. Unsure of how to respond, she remained quite still.

'I shouldn't have done that,' he said. 'Will you overlook it?'

Only a few months previously, Flora would have gabbled off some answer, but she had learnt a few things in London. She smiled and said nothing. After a moment because she couldn't think what to do next, she sat down on the grass. 'When did you decide to become a doctor?'

Robin picked up a stone and tossed it from hand to hand. 'When my sister died of diphtheria.' The stone disappeared into the grass and he bent to retrieve it. 'She was ten. Luckily my parents made sure I went to the grammar school. We were seven, of which only four survived, so you see they had a vested interest.'

'Was it hard?'

'For my parents, very. We didn't have any money and medical school was expensive.'

'But worth it?'

'Yes.'

She leant back on her hands, and her breasts jutted full and beautiful through her cotton shirt. The sight tipped Robin over into wanting Flora much more than he had anticipated and to stop himself he looked instead at her brown-booted feet stretched in the grass. They, too, were big and well made, but less tempting.

'What about you, Flora?' He said her name for the first time. 'What are you planning to do?'

No one had ever asked Flora that question because it was considered neither necessary nor suitable. Everyone knew what Flora would do, including Flora.

'I'll get married probably.' She shrugged. 'Providing someone will have me.'

'Nothing else?'

Flora thought of tea by the fire, of hunting through a frosty landscape, of chatting to Danny in the twilight, of wet dog tongues on her hands and horse smells, of the rustle of a taffeta ballgown and the sensation of champagne fizzing at the back of her throat, of the tick of the clocks in the house, and the sun chasing dust motes across the windows. What they made up was not a bad existence.

But perhaps they did not amount to very much. She shook her head: talking to Robin confused her.

By now his imagination was seriously out of control. He went over to adjust a strap on the bay's saddle.

'With a bit of luck I'll get married quite soon,' she said and pulled up a blade of grass.

He pulled the strap tight with a jerk. 'Have you found anyone?'

'No,' said Flora, nibbling on the sappy part of the stalk, dismissing Marcus without a thought, and scrambled to her feet. Their hands brushed accidentally. Flora's fell to her side and, the breeze whipped at her blouse. After a moment, Robin placed his hands on Flora's shoulders and pulled her towards him. Abandoning every rule she knew, Flora did not resist.

Since she was taller, Robin was obliged to strain upwards and Flora to bend her knees before their mouths coincided. For an instant, she wanted to laugh at the picture they must make; then it became obvious that Robin meant business when he kissed the corner of her mouth and moved onto her lips.

'Close your eyes,' he said. 'It's better.'

It was. By degrees Flora relaxed. Robin's fingers were warm and gentle on her flesh.

'You are lovely, Flora.'

She felt a sensation running up from her stomach into her head. 'No, I'm not.'

'Take a proper look at yourself.'

He pushed his leg into Flora's and kissed her again, and Flora, terrified that she would do something wrong, began to understand about passion. It was an extraordinary experience – extraordinary in every sense – to have another body so close to hers, to worry, and yet not to worry, about what her own was doing. Sighing with pleasure, Robin pushed up her chin and kissed the sensitive bit beneath her ear and Flora stretched like a cat and closed her eyes.

Eventually, she began to wonder what, after such intimacy, happened next. What could she possibly say? Embarrassed, stirred, aghast, and full of singing joy, she pulled away.

Robin defused the situation. 'Next time I shall have to arrange not to kiss you standing up, Flora. Or grow an inch.'

Gratefully, she seized on the point. 'I used to dread being measured each year. Robbie . . . Miss Robson, you know . . . lined us up in the nursery and marked off the heights on the wall. Lucky old Polly was always the smallest.'

'I dreaded it, too. But for the opposite reason.'

'Obviously you didn't eat your greens.'

He pulled down the corners of his mouth. 'There wasn't that much to eat.'

'Oh, sorry,' she said. 'I've done it again.'

'Why don't we agree to stop apologizing to each other?' he said, and looked across at the rebellious hair, the bony nose and Dysart blue eyes, and felt hopelessly entangled by her freshness and genuineness. 'Will you see me again?'

She hesitated only for a second. 'Yes.'

When Flora returned to the house, Robbie was waiting for her and demanded to know where she had been. Flora said she was not going to tell Robbie, and Robbie put her hands on her hips and replied, oh yes she was.

247

No, Flora reiterated, and felt the familiar dread in her stomach. Obviously someone – one of the men up in the fields? – had ratted on her.

'Excuse *me*, Miss Flora,' Robbie's hands appeared glued to her hips, 'but it's my business to know. I promised your mother.' Here, Flora hissed that she did not wish to discuss *anything*.

Robbie clicked her tongue against her teeth. Apart from childish tantrums and battles of will over rice pudding, sensible knickers and saying grace before elevenses, Flora had never challenged her. She pushed her broad, pale face in front of Flora's and said, 'You were with that doctor. I know you were. What were you thinking of, Miss Flora? The doctor, indeed.'

A new loyalty twisted in Flora at the words 'that doctor' and she told Robbie to be quiet. Robbie said that Flora would do exactly as she was told and promise never to see the doctor again, otherwise she would tell Rupert and Miss Flora knew what effect *that* would have on a sick man.

'You wouldn't do that!'

Robbie smiled. Yes, she would, she said. It was for Flora's own good and she was the only one who could keep an eye on Flora. 'It's for your own good, pet,' she said, and added that Flora's hair needed a good brush.

After that, Flora took care to be discreet. All through that June and July she saddled Guinevere and rode out to meet Robin secretly. Sometimes over at Paradise, sometimes at Caesar's Camp or Powderham Castle or away up Itchel Lane where the wind rippled the crop into waves and the poppies were too thick to be counted.

To the observer – and there were a few – nothing much happened. The new doctor and Miss Flora rode and talked. Once, it was reported back to Ellen Sheppey, they held hands. Another time Sam Prosser swore he saw two shadows merge under the oak tree by Lee Wood, but he couldn't be sure.

CHAPTER NINE

H ER GARDEN apart, Matty had set herself the task of sorting
out the contents of the attics, which had been left during the
renovations. The rooms had originally been used as servants'
sleeping quarters, but after the war and Hesther's death the
number of servants had dropped and they were turned over to
attics.

The rooms ran east–west along the top floor, each one stuffed
with boxes and trunks, furniture and paintings. The sight set
Matty's organizational antennae quivering.

Mrs Dawes had other ideas. 'Oh, my Lord,' she said gloomily.
Not only was the task formidable, but Matty had declared she
was going to work alongside her. She surveyed hat boxes, garden
chairs, shooting sticks, boot scrapers, trunks bulging with linen
and cupboards piled with God knew what, and mentally girded
her loins. Matty held out her hand for an apron and with the air
of a condemned felon Mrs Dawes gave it to her. But once set to,
they enjoyed themselves as women often do in such situations.

'What *are* these?' Matty held up a couple of poles encased in
leather at one end.

'Crutches, I think,' said Mrs Dawes.

'And these?'

'More crutches. From the time when the house was a hospital.
I thought all that stuff went back long ago.'

Matty cradled them in her arms. Someone had used these to
shuffle his way painfully down the corridors and out into the rest
of his life. 'I see,' she said and laid them down.

The piles grew and so did the list in Matty's notebook.
Progress was not as fast as it could have been, for every so often
Matty pounced on an object and went into lengthy discussion
with Mrs Dawes as to its history and use. Both women were

feeling more positive about each other, and Matty enjoyed the sensation of bringing order into chaos.

The best of her haul was discovered behind a scrap screen which partially obscured a stack of paintings. Matty pulled out one, looked at it, said, 'Oh,' and then went quite pale. It was of a little girl sitting on a woman's knee having her feet washed, ordinary people painted with an insight that made them extra-ordinary. She stared at it, both fascinated and pained by it, and loved it. After investigation among the family papers in the Exchequer, it was pinpointed as a Mary Cassett.

'How could you let it sit up there?' she tackled Kit over after-dinner coffee. They were in the drawing room where the Cassett had been hung between the windows. 'It's a wonderful thing. Look at the way the foot is so real in the mother's hand and how she cradles its weight.'

Matty drank her coffee and scrutinized her find for the hundredth time. Kit got up and came and stood behind her. Matty had her head on one side and her coffee cup at a precarious angle. He put his hands lightly on her shoulders and Matty felt his touch like a burn through her dinner gown. 'I think it came from Boston. Mary Cassett was an American,' she said without turning round.

'Was she?' From habit, the muscles in Kit's jaw tautened. 'Perhaps . . . perhaps my mother brought it on one of her trips to see my grandparents.'

But Matty, absorbed in the contemplation of the brushwork and colours, apparently did not hear him.

'Here,' said Kit, rescuing the coffee cup and restoring it to the tray. 'You'd better let me have this.'

Matty had heard, but she had chosen not to respond.

When she returned to the grand clear out, she went in search of a trunk she had noticed on a previous foray. It was stored in the smallest attic, in which the kitchenmaids had slept, and which was now filled with discarded nursery furniture and toys. Claus-trophobic and cramped, the roof sloped at a sharp angle and every surface was covered by a layer of dust so thick it had curdled. Their life over, toys lay on shelves and in boxes: a teddy bear with torn paws, a dolls' house which said 'Flora's House' in tiny writing above the door, a French *bébé* doll on her face, limbs corkscrewed under her skirts. The *bébé*'s coat was trimmed with squirrel fur and its hair was real. White Surrey, the rocking horse named after Richard III's horse, was under the window. 'We won the Battle of Bosworth on White Surrey,' Kit said, when Matty mentioned she had seen him in the attic. 'He wouldn't have allowed us to ride him otherwise. You had to be careful not to hurt his feelings', and he told Matty about games he, Polly and Flora had played. 'We always rewrote history,' he said. 'We never liked to be the losers.'

White Surrey had a painted snarl and chipped teeth and as her dislike of horses extended to the wooden variety, Matty found herself giving him as wide a berth as possible. The initials 'HKD' had been embossed on the leather cartouche on the trunk, which had labels all over it. 'Boston', read one. 'P&O' another. 'Don't touch me,' said the whole trunk. Don't tamper; the past can never be understood.

That isn't true, thought Matty, and knelt down. The keys on an old-fashioned wire hoop were cold and heavy in her hand and clinked softly.

To examine the things that belonged to a dead person was, in many ways, unfair. Suddenly, you achieve mastery, even over someone you feared – and Matty did fear Hesther. You acquire power to see where it was not permitted in life. She hesitated, and then pushed back the lid.

A petrified forest of tissue paper lay on top of the contents and released a powerful odour of mothballs. It made Matty sneeze. She pushed the paper aside – and her hands froze. A glance was enough to show her that the dead woman's effects had been piled pell-mell into the trunk, without care or consideration. With spite, even. She sat back hard on her heels.

No maid would have dared to leave the oyster satin beaded bodice to crack over the breast as this one had been left. Or scattered the contents of the glove box, or ripped the lace from the muslin blouse sandwiched between a striped skirt and matching bodice. No maid would have allowed the ostrich fan to catch in the handles of a glove stretcher. Matty put out a finger and stroked the feathers.

Why?

The mothball smell pricked at her nose and made her eyes water. She wiped them with the back of her hand, knowing without being told that she was witness to a desecration as deliberate as an ancient Greek despoiling the tomb of his enemy.

A blue leather-bound book lay near the top, gold-edged, made with thick and expensive paper. Matty picked it up.

On the first page someone, she imagined Hesther, had pasted in a postcard of the harbour at Honfleur in Normandy, taken from one side of the square through a forest of masts. On the opposite page there was a second postcard, this time of a farmhouse silhouetted against the crest of a ridge and a flat horizon beyond. Solid and unfussy, it was a substantial building with wooden shutters, ironwork gates, hens in the yard, a decaying outhouse and praetorian guard of poplars. At the bottom of the card, the caption read, 'La ferme Boromée'. An arrow had been inked in pointing to a room on the top floor. 'My bedroom', someone had written, with difficulty, on the shiny surface.

Other pages in the book were blank except for greenish-yellow vegetable-like stains. The marks were puzzling, but when a dried rose fell out and disintegrated in her hands Matty realized the book had been used to press flowers. Underneath one of the blotches the unknown hand she was now sure was Hesther's had written in jerky, urgent-looking script, 'Konigin von Danëmark' and 'General Klèber' and put in the accents incorrectly. Under 'Général Kléber' was written: 'A damask-hybrid moss rose raised by Robert in 1856. Vigorous and upright. Scented. Named after the general who commanded Napoleon's army.'

There was a space and then Hesther had written, 'Lovely, lovely.'

Matty smoothed the page. This was Hesther, a bit of her at least, and there was a strong answering echo in Matty to the woman who had written 'Lovely, lovely' about her roses.

Because her eyes were still streaming, she nearly missed the letters. They were tucked into the back of the book, tied into a packet with black ribbon, creased from being tied and untied. She opened the first and read:

My Darling,
    Nothing is in its proper place. Ideas, things, humans. The world has gone crazy, and we are crazed with it.
    Shall I tell you the worst thing? It's not the blood nor the mud, nor the sights, nor the boredom and discomfort, nor the blasted stiff upper lip of Rupert. No, it is none of those things, bad as they are. It's the knowledge that this war is so terrible and so senseless that anyone who is not in it cannot understand. The war will make a gap between us . . . we will be on different sides.

Matty could not read the signature.
Written in the same hand, the second letter was shorter and to the point.

I am going with Rupert tomorrow to Amiens. Can you send some sewing things, socks, extra handkerchiefs and a fruit cake . . .

The third letter began,

My darling, did I ramble in my previous letters? If I did I am sorry, particularly if it cost my dearest most sweet flower any pain. Write to me soon, my heart, for we are ordered back to the front. Tell me about the garden and what you have been doing to improve it. I want to hear everything, down to the last leaf. By the way, I think you should plant the lilies where the sun warms them, and the climbing rose (as white as your skin) on the wall. I enclose a sketch to show you what I mean. Corporal Stevens tells me that 'Tuscany' (he pronounces it Tooscani) is the old velvet rose. Nothing to beat its colour he says, as 'dark as blood'.

253

Here there was a competent pen sketch of the garden, which Matty immediately recognized, criss-crossed with arrows and labels, followed by, 'goodbye, darling'.

Underneath that Hesther had written: *his last letter*.

And underneath that someone else had written: *Bitch*.

Whose last letter? Who did Hesther love so much, and was it Rupert who, having found out Hesther loved someone else, had thrown her things into a trunk after her death?

Matty did not read any more. She folded the letters and put them back into the book which fell open at the page where the rose had been.

Lovely, lovely.

An unease slid over the room, stretching over silent objects, over White Surrey, the *bébé* doll and the pensioned-off teddy bears. Matty piled Hesther's things back into the trunk. She knew without question that the letters spelt muddle, pain and disorder, and that they affected everyone in the house. Banging down the lid, she fled.

This, then, was the focus of the family into which Matty had married, the secret map.

Since Rupert's accident, Kit had taken over the financial affairs of the household. Things were worse than he had imagined but, hostile as he often felt towards Rupert, Kit did not blame his father. Before Matty came with her rescue package, it had required fiscal brilliance to balance the outgoings of Hinton Dysart with its modest income from rents and crops, added to which there were always pinpricks: nail fatigue in the roof, an outbreak of dry rot in the stables, vets' bills, new fencing.

Matty's money was not only welcome, it was vital. Kit found himself in the position of a beggar whose wish had been granted, which drove him to several conclusions he had not considered when he accepted Matty's proposal. Money smoothed and effected, but it also shackled. It brought choice and comfort but not, necessarily, happiness.

Nevertheless, he was grateful to Matty, truly he was grateful.

The Verral lawyers had transferred capital in favour of Hinton Dysart and he was careful to use it only on the upkeep of the house. Naturally, the lawyers sought to safeguard Matty and Kit supported them, despite her wish to settle capital on him.

'You're quite generous enough,' Kit reiterated to his wife. 'I wish I could show you how grateful I am.'

They were taking a morning walk up Croft Lane towards the church. Minerva, the Clumber spaniel (Matty's birthday present to Kit), rooted excitedly in the undergrowth. The verge was thick with corncockles and rosebay willowherb, and sprays of china pink dog rose arched above their heads.

'It's nothing,' she replied, repressing a reply that he was quite able to show her, easily, then dismissed the thought as absurd. 'I have the money. You need it.'

'Even so,' Kit insisted. He sounded calm but Matty was aware of Kit's ambivalent feelings and, since she had learnt a thing or two about managing him, deployed evasion tactics. 'The fence up by Lee Wood. Have you decided on which kind?'

Kit clicked his fingers at Minerva. 'Sycamore,' he said. 'Nothing else is any good.'

Kit wished to generate money of his own and began to shake off his obsession with the East, to look out at the rest of the world and take an interest in what was happening there. The scenery was complicated. The American stock-market crash, towering unemployment figures, an expensive British empire, an economy at odds with itself, these factors released forces no one understood. Raby had done his homework and Kit purchased stock in vacuum cleaners and a business that made wireless sets to a new, stream-lined specification. As yet, there was no return. 'If only I'd waited until I'd tried a Hoover,' went an advertisement in a magazine Kit had picked up in the dentist's waiting room. 'Don't be rushed or persuaded into buying any old vacuum cleaners.'

No, indeed. The great British public had nothing to spend and nothing to wait for. In this manner, politics crept into Kit's life.

'Patience,' said Howard Raby. 'Patience, Mr Dysart.'

Raby was right. At this point, Kit made a second discovery. The Bible had dealt with only half the problem of charity. As he signed the bills with his wife's money he understood with blistering clarity how much easier it was to give than to receive.

Meanwhile, at Hinton Dysart, two decades' worth of papers in files and drawers required sorting – and that was only the beginning. After the Season had ground to a halt in London, in a flurry of stained satin shoes and ruined reputations, Kit came home. Very quickly he established the routine of retiring to the Exchequer after breakfast. A cigarette burning nacreous rings into the ashtray, a congealing cup of tea, and he was more or less content.

There was little to surprise, but quite a lot to intrigue, for the Exchequer contained the record of the house's life. In 'Stables' he found bills for oats, bran and linseed, horse rugs, saddle soap and a chaff-cutting machine, in 'House', bills for soap, blacklead and furniture polish, which his mother had ordered once a year from the Army and Navy Stores. Where these industrial quantities had been stored Kit was not sure.

The file that interested him most was thick, buff-coloured and labelled 'Hesther Dysart, née Kennedy'.

On the top were letters and Kit found himself making the acquaintance of the grandfather he had never met. Charles Kennedy showed himself to be rich, bluff and decisive, anxious to make a substantial marriage settlement on his daughter. Figures on a balance sheet showed how much he had donated in capital and stock, and the dates when Rupert realized the cash. Nothing untoward about that, except for the abrupt cessation of the support. Judging by the correspondence, the relationship between the American and his English son-in-law had not been cordial, but it did not explain the thick black line drawn under the date, 30 September 1916. After that, there were no entries in the accounts, nothing.

Kit dragged deeply on a cigarette. His mother died in September 1916. Charles died in early 1919, followed by Euphemia, his wife and Kit's grandmother, a year later. It was odd that neither of them had made any provision for their grandchildren. In fact, his grandfather had gone out of his way to cut them off.

Kit pushed the letters aside. Of course he knew why.

He leafed through the statements of account from Messrs Coutts and the summary of stock-holdings, and compared them with the list that Raby had compiled. They were consistent and depressingly accurate.

At first Kit took no notice of the modest-looking document attached to the back of the file. The pin had rusted and left marks on what turned out to be a share certificate. Apparently, in June 1910, Hesther had acquired 100,000 shares at the cost of one cent each in a company specializing in real estate in a suburb of Los Angeles called Hollywood. It was thought, read the accompanying prospectus, that the climate and scenery would attract home-dwellers.

That was clever advice, thought Kit, draining his cold tea. The film industry is there. He replaced the document in the file, dropped it back into the desk drawer and locked it.

At exactly four o'clock in the morning, he woke up. There was no noise, and he was comfortable. Puzzled, he rolled over onto his back and bunched up the pillow. Gradually, it became clear to him that his brain was moving round a fixed point. Kit had never seen those Hollywood shares ticked off on Raby's checklist.

In the adjoining bedroom, Matty was also awake and heard Kit come out of his bedroom and go down the stairs. Woken by her demon, who always chose her most defenceless moments to attack, she had been staring into the dark. Determined to dislodge him, she swung her legs over the bed.

As usual in summer the house seemed warmer at night than during the day. Kit padded down the staircase and along the passage towards the Exchequer. The room was acrid and un-aired. He switched on the light, emptied an overflowing ashtray into the bin, and threw wide the window. The night air poured into the room. He opened the drawer, pulled out the buff file and spread it in front of him.

He worked through the first column of figures before he allowed himself a lift of excitement and was checking the second when a footstep in the passage made him leap to his feet. The chair went crashing over and Matty appeared in the doorway.

'Matty! For God's sake. What are you doing?' Kit picked up the chair and inspected it.

Matty advanced into the room. 'Sorry, Kit. I didn't mean to alarm you.'

'It's all right. Couldn't you sleep?' Kit leant against the desk.

Matty nudged her chin at the papers. 'No. I couldn't. What's all this?'

'Fortune-hunting.'

Her eyes opened wide. 'How?'

Kit explained he had found some unaccounted-for stock and intended to track it down. As he talked, his face wavered in and out of the circle of light cast by the lamp, and Matty was reminded of the photograph of the twelve-year-old Kit. She was tactless enough to say, 'Don't we have enough money, Kit?'

He went over to the cupboard by the door and flung it open. 'I think I have some whisky in here,' he said. 'Want some?'

'Yes, please.'

The whisky was excellent. Kit hugged his glass and said, 'If I explained that I cannot be in your pay all my life, would you be hurt, Matty?'

Yes, she wanted to say. Is it so awful? Instead, she drank more whisky and replied, 'I suppose not.'

'I don't expect you to understand, but please believe me when I say I am grateful for everything you have done.'

'Yes,' said Matty from the wilderness.

Kit stared at his wife. 'No, I don't think you do, Matty, but it doesn't matter. Look. I want to make a little money of my own and I want to use it to go into politics.'

'Oh,' said Matty.

'Times are changing,' said Kit. 'And I want to be in on the changes.'

'Yes,' she said. 'I think I understand.'

'Matty, I'm going to make a short trip to America to chase some business I've found that needs finishing. Is that all right with you?'

'If I said no?'

'I'd still go,' he said. 'But I wouldn't like it.'

'Go,' said Matty, a little drunkenly.

By now, the dawn chorus was in full throttle. A pencil of light appeared through the window and spread over the room's grubby interior. Kit talked on and Matty listened, feeling rejected and in the position of a benefactor who had wanted to be loved but had been used instead. Common sense then pointed that Kit had not asked for her money and he was, at least, talking to her.

The whisky glugged as Kit refilled the glasses. He clinked his against Matty's. 'Cheer up.' More footsteps echoed down the passage.

'What are you doing?' A hairbrush in her hand, Robbie appeared in the doorway. Husband and wife looked at each other and Kit shrugged. Matty's bottom lip twitched.

'Sorry, Robbie. Did we wake you?' said Kit. 'Have some whisky.'

But Robbie had been frightened and her heart was beating a violent tattoo. She was also annoyed that her gallantry was for nothing. 'I thought there were thieves in the kitchens and murderers on the stairs.'

'Poor Robbie.' Kit scraped back his chair and stood up.

'You make me so angry sometimes, Mr Kit.' Robbie moved towards him to berate him further, and her dressing gown fell apart, revealing a voluptuously scalloped, lace-edged nightgown. The sight was so unexpected that both Matty's and Kit's eyes widened in surprise.

'You must get up to bed at once, Mrs Kit.' Robbie snatched at the dressing gown, pulled it across her chest and one large breast sprang into relief under the blue flannel. Above it hung her angry face and pepper-and-salt plait. 'You have no business to be up frightening the life out of me.'

'Robbie,' said Kit, 'my wife will go to bed when she wishes.'

'It was very thoughtless, Mr Kit.' Robbie cut him off. 'There I was, scared to death. I shall feel quite dreadful later.'

'Robbie,' said Kit. 'Go back to bed. Take a sleeping draught or something.'

259

He looked impatiently at the figure who, throughout his childhood, had bullied, exacted, cajoled and, through no fault of her own, failed to give him comfort.

Robbie may have been thick-skinned but she was not immune to pain and the figure inside the protective dressing gown seemed to dwindle. Matty took pity. 'Kit, Miss Robson has been frightened,' she said, frowning at him. She turned to Robbie. 'Actually, I could do with a hot drink before I go back to sleep.'

Robbie brightened up at once.

Arrangements for Kit's trip were quickly made: by the end of the week tickets had been booked and business appointments in New York and Los Angeles hooked up.

'I won't be away long, Father,' Kit informed Rupert.

'I suppose it's no use asking what you're up to,' said Rupert, directing his gaze on his son.

'No. It's a surprise,' replied Kit. 'If it comes off I'll tell you when I come back.'

'I'm not senile yet,' said Rupert.

'Tea?' asked Matty. The family had formed a habit of taking Sunday tea in Rupert's room – less of a party and more of a mass sacrifice, Flora privately informed Matty. Father likes to study the entrails. Matty laughed and told Flora that Rupert did sometimes have the look of a Roman senator.

As cluttered as ever, the room was hot, filled with a curious sweetish odour and Matty made a note to sort it out. Rupert was flushed and irritable.

'Any crumpets?' Flora had been out riding and was hungry.

Matty lifted up the lid of the silver chafing dish. 'You're out of luck, Mrs Dawes has sent up teacakes.'

'Shame,' said Kit from his position by the mantelpiece. 'There's a strong possibility you'll starve.' He looked excited, which made Matty feel miserable because she knew he could not wait to go.

'Rotter.'

'Why aren't you going with him?' Rupert jerked his head in the direction of his son, and the loosening skin under his chin folded like an accordion.

Matty put down the teapot. 'I think I'm better occupied here,' she said.

It was a touchy point, for Matty had hoped that Kit would ask her to go too.

'Sensible girl,' said Rupert, surprising his daughter-in-law. 'I never went anywhere unless Hesther forced me. And that was only once.' He pushed his teacup from side to side over the embroidered tray cloth. 'Never liked abroad much.'

Flora bit into a teacake. 'I don't see why you shouldn't go with Kit. After all, there can't be much more that needs doing to the house, you've done everything possible to turn it inside out.' Flora realized she had blundered again the moment she looked into Matty's face. 'Oh, Lord,' she said. 'Don't put on the wooden look, Matty. I didn't mean it like that. Everything's lovely.'

Kit came to the rescue. 'Matty's done a wonderful job.'

'So she has,' said Rupert unexpectedly, and demanded to know if he had to wait any longer before he was given more tea.

The point was taken up again at lunch the following day. The guests included Mr Pengeally and his wife. Mrs Pengeally stabbed genteelly at her castle pudding with her spoon. 'Such a delicious lunch, dear Mrs Dysart. But, then, it always is these days. You work so hard and you deserve a little holiday. But I gather you'll be staying behind when your husband goes on his trip.' Her gaze wandered in the direction of Matty's midriff, hovered and moved on.

'It's a business trip,' said Kit. He smiled his charming, lazy smile and Mrs Pengeally wilted.

She shifted tactics. 'Are you quite well, Mrs Dysart? You have, if I might say so, been looking a bit pale.'

Try as she might, Matty could not stop a wave of red creeping up her cheeks. 'Perfectly,' she said, knowing that her body, its health or productiveness, was public property in Nether Hinton.

Mr Pengeally had a habit of being a step behind in

261

conversations. 'We can't have you missing the village show. It's the high point of the year. In fact . . .' he leant towards Matty, 'I think we shall be calling on you, Mrs Dysart, for a spot of ribbon cutting.'

'Actually,' said Matty, who was now an attractive pink, 'I would hate to miss the Nether Hinton show.'

To her surprise, she meant it.

Kit was aware that Matty had feelings about not accompanying him on the trip to the States, and he wanted to reassure her. The night before he left, he came to her bedroom.

'You won't overdo it, will you, Matty, when I'm away?' He sat down in the chair by the window and shook out a cigarette from his case.

'If you mean,' said Matty a shade tartly, 'that I might do things in the house while you are gone that you might not like, say so.'

'No, I didn't mean that.'

'Good.' Matty set down her hairbrush with a crack and, because she looked so indignant, Kit grinned.

He watched her fuss with pots of night cream and it occurred to him that, in her way, Matty gave a lot. It was years since the house had been run so well, or felt so comfortable – and who would have thought that funny, scared Matty was a born house-keeper, with a capacity to smooth and domesticate with the lightest of touches?

Kit was getting to know her: her shyness, her sudden with-drawals when he hurt her, her astringent sense of humour. There were coldnesses between them – often – irritations, and the open knowledge that they walked divergent paths. There was also the suspicion that she loved him and the fact that he did not her. Kit felt no merit in that, only distress for Matty. But he was intrigued by the things that made her up: her often surprising views, and passionate ideas on design and painting, her love of the East. Kit liked always to turn a corner to discover a fresh landscape, and Matty had something of that unexpected quality.

He tapped the cigarette on the case and became serious. 'You must think we're very ungracious,' he said at last. 'Don't you?'

'Do I?'

Kit floated behind a smoke-screen. 'I want to make you understand. For as long as we can remember the house has been the same. Decaying, yes, in need of paint, yes. We got used to it like that. So . . . when you came and began to put things to rights we needed time to adjust. That's all. Like my father must have adjusted when he married my mother. It doesn't mean to say we don't like what you have done.'

Silence.

'You do understand, Matty?'

She made a noise in her throat and wondered if she would tell him about Hesther.

Kit stubbed out the cigarette and went to sit down on the bed. 'Matty, will you come here?'

Hesther forgotten, Matty got up from the stool and sat beside him. It was a warm night and Kit was sweating slightly in his cotton pyjamas. To Matty he smelt of tobacco and the whisky he had drunk after dinner and the faintest suggestion of fresh male sweat. He was as alien as anyone could be to her, and she loved him.

As usual, his hair had fallen forward and, before she could stop herself, Matty did something she had always wanted to do. She reached up and brushed it back over the damp hairline. Her fingers twined in the fair hair for longer than necessary and pressed into the skull underneath. Before she had let go, Kit's hand had trapped hers. Slowly, he forced it on a path downwards and she felt the hammer of excitement beat in her own body. When her hand had reached its destination, Matty looked up at her husband.

'You can go to America with a clear conscience,' she told him.

In reply, Kit kissed her on the mouth and pushed her back onto the pillows.

The drive to Southampton did not take long. The road sliced through downland, past Chawton and Alton, Alresford, crammed itself through the centre of Winchester and out again towards Chandler's Ford.

It was a kind, confident landscape. Nourished by the smooth slopes, productive earth and soft winds, English civilization had begun in this country of downland and watermeadow.

Matty watched villages come and go through the car window. Neither she nor Kit spoke very much. From time to time, Kit enquired after her comfort and then fell silent. She rehearsed how she would say goodbye: friendly, contained. Sometimes she sneaked a look at him and wondered why the longing to possess a person was like physical hunger, why sex did not appease it and whether feeling dulled with age.

'Don't wait,' said Kit as Tyson drove into Southampton docks.

Even so, Matty insisted on inspecting the suite on the *Mauretania*. The bathroom gleamed with zinc, there was polished wood in the sitting room and a hush emanating from a deep pile carpet in the sleeping area.

'Goodbye,' said Kit, and held Matty in his arms. He kissed her forehead and took one of her hands. 'Please take care.'

'And you too. Will you write?'

He patted her shoulder. 'Of course I will.'

The car seemed empty without Kit. 'If ever a ship had a soul,' Franklin D. Roosevelt said of it, 'it is the *Mauretania*.' Matty thought of the famous dive and swoop of the ship's pitch taking Kit away with her.

HARRY

Summer . . . and the gardens are swarming. In contrast the rooms of the house seem cold and silent; only the patient guardians moving to and fro breathe movement into the stillness. Occasionally, I walk through them to remind myself that nothing has changed: the white dining room, the comfortable, chintzed drawing room hung with its dramatic oil paintings, chosen by my mother. The bedrooms where satin eiderdowns sit primly on top of the beds. I look at them, so daunting, so correct, and it seems impossible that they were ever rumpled or cast aside by passion.

I wonder what people think as they shuffle through? What impression do they receive from the things here – Worcester vases, marble-topped washstands, chamber pots patterned with roses, a double bed with a railed mahogany head and foot, a crocodile dressing case? Do they gain an impression of the life that flowed through the house from photographs in worn leather frames, or my father's footwear lined up in the boot cupboard, or the gold half-hunter on the dressing stand? Possibly not.

Why should they?

But they do understand the garden. It is easier to read: to feel what happened without searching for words. For me, the garden is the leveller, the constant with infinite variety, and the passion which has no messy repercussions. After all, mistakes in a garden can be pulled up and put onto the compost heap. Its triumphs can be repeated.

How many have walked through the white garden at Sissinghurst or here, for example, and decided, 'We'll do that', and gone home to Balham, Croydon, Basingstoke, Manchester and Prestwick and, in true democracy, altered a suburban setting or a

265

northern viewpoint to take on board another's passion and vision? Hundreds, thousands of gardeners.

Imagine seeing this, my latest scheme (concocted in the December fallows), for the first time.

The first ingredient is the dark mass of a yew hedge. Plant white delphiniums well away from the greedy roots (mice nest in yew) to form a contrast with an arching spiraea. Thread the huge, nodding flowers of a 'Marie Boisselot' clematis through the spiraea. Scatter white and cream foxgloves and in front of them position a grey-leaved plant, cotton lavender perhaps.

Magic, would you not agree? Better, unlike most magic it is obtainable magic.

After thinking about it for years, I have come to the conclusion that the Miss Jekyll style of planting is too cramped. Like the spirit which must be allowed room in a life, so plants should sprawl, infuse and self-seed in natural patterns. It has taken me almost a lifetime to arrive at this point.

A warning. The white convert will rapidly discover that nothing is pure white. If you examine any white flower you will see tiny green spots, blue veins tracking through the snowiness, dramatic orange anthers. But once rooted, the idea drives a rigorous and demanding bargain. For the disciple seeks the cleansing properties of white – the desire, I submit, for the innocence that we lost in the Fall. Vita Sackville-West was right. Who can pass by pale massed blooms in a twilit garden – a memory that nourishes the spirit during winter? Who can ignore a poppy created in buttery cream, or ice white, or the stained, rumpled blooms of the *Paeonia suffruticosa*? Who can remain unmoved by the lily's pure seduction?

I confess I *am* seduced by the paradox of the lily: by both its purity and wantonness and so, I must tell you, was my father ('Unbalanced,' says Thomas, but smiles all the same), and we spend the evenings consulting the books: Thomas to his antiques and paintings, myself to plants. Each to his own Holy Grail.

These are the busiest months in the nursery and in June the roses come into bloom. All through the day and into the evening the visitors come: in coaches, cars, even on foot. They crowd into the walled garden to gaze at 'Adelaide d'Orléans', 'Blanchefleur', 'Duchesse de Montebello', 'Jeanne de Montfort', 'Louise Odier', at 'Maiden's Blush', 'Perle d'Or', 'Rambling Rector', at 'Souvenir de la Malmaison', 'Tuscany Superb' and 'Zéphirine Drouhin'. They come with notebooks, hats, sticks to lean on, with babies in rucksacks and slings, in high heels and sensible shoes, driven by love, by possession, by the knowledge that if they make the journey they will arrive, at the end, immeasurably comforted and enriched.

CHAPTER TEN

THIS YEAR Ellen Sheppey decided not to enter for the boiled potato prize at the Nether Hinton–Well–Yateley annual horticultural show (held this summer at Nether Hinton). After all, she had won it two years running and it never did to be greedy, else fate took a hand. She would miss the triumph and, it had to be said, a feeling of superiority at the sight of her potatoes, boiled to floury perfection, sitting beside the square of cardboard emblazoned with a copperplate 'First'. As Ned said, 'Life moves on, girl.'

Instead, this year Ellen was tackling the two-pound fruitcake competition and, fired by the additional challenge, the egg entry. After long discussions with Ned, she narrowed her sights down to the whitest egg class as being the most taxing and worthy of her skills. Last year – the year of the Great Egg Scandal – had been a lively one, and Mary Prosser's reputation was stained as dark as the eggs which she had allegedly dipped into coffee solution. Too bad for Mary. She, Ellen Sheppey, had no need for such tactics, for she was the proud owner of the Leghorn and no other fowl laid such pearls.

Show day dawned with a mist swaddling the village. It was going to be fine and Ellen was up early, her hair crimped in curl papers. It was already warm, and her upper lip was speckled with sweat. On days like this, Ned knew better than to be helpful, so he waited until the final egg had been eased into place in a sugar box, the cake wrapped and Ellen's sweet peas laid reverently in the basket.

'Not bad, eh,' she said at last, pleased with herself and the world. She bent over to pull her stockings straight and prodded the lump on her knee, which had never been the same since she knocked it at Blane's. 'Bloody thing,' she said.

'I keep telling you to get it looked at, girl. And you won't listen. You never listen to me,' said Ned. His tone expressed concern. 'You just go your own sweet way.' He reached up to the mantelpiece for the brown Coronation mug, which was full of coins. 'Here. Take this and go and see that doctor, just to make sure all's well. Do you hear me?' Ned took Ellen's hands and wrapped her fingers around the coins. 'Yes?'

'Yes.'

Ned helped himself to a good dollop of beer money and put the mug back in its place.

'But not today, Ned,' said Ellen, counting the change. She turned to the mirror to tackle her hair. 'Lay off today.'

He smiled at his wife's reflection. 'Done.'

At ten o'clock, Ned bicycled off with the exhibits, and Ellen took off her print overall and put on her hat.

This was it.

At Hook Meadow a flood of bicycles and carts loaded with flowers and produce was making an efficient job of blocking the entrance, resulting in a fair amount of free interchange. At one end of the meadow, the Fair people had set up their stands: catchpenny stalls, a bran tub and a roundabout. In between were stalls selling lemonade and cakes, and tea for the ladies. At the other end was the marquee, a stalwart of village life. The air inside it was thick, redolent of warm canvas, flowers, grass and sweat. The judges had made their rounds earlier and cards were propped up beside the exhibits: vases of dahlias, phlox, montbretias and asters arranged on tables covered with white cloths. Contrasted with the mould-spotted canvas of the marquee, their colours were fresh, startling.

Ellen began the wide circle designed to avoid the thing she wanted to look at most until last.

'You're daft,' said Ned. 'Always were.' He went away to look at his own entries.

Several of their rivals from Yateley were grouped together making loud comparisons among themselves. Ellen ignored them and inspected the gentlemen's buttonholes before moving on to the vases of mixed perennials and annuals. Outside, the brass

269

band began an oompah tune which made her feel excited. She studied the children's section – as always the wild-flower arrangements in two-pound jam jars were the biggest entry. On to the vegetables: carrots weren't bad, onions only fair. Beans ... well ... Only then did Ellen allow herself to look towards the egg table.

The first quick squint did not tell her much.

'Looking to a first, then, Mrs Sheppey?' said Fred Stevens, whose own garden was famous in the village.

'I might or I might not be, Mr Stevens.'

The air in the marquee grew even thicker and, feeling a little as if she was pushing through water, Ellen drifted towards the egg table. Now she was at the point, she had not realized quite how much she wanted to keep up her record.

But it was all right. 'First' said the copperplate legend on the stiff card beside her Leghorn pearls and she sighed with satisfaction. Then she shuffled her handbag from her left hand to her right, and tried not to look in the direction of Mary Prosser, also peering at the eggs, because, at heart, Ellen felt herself to be a merciful woman.

Hooking her handbag over her arm, she moved over to the Women's Institute stand to discover that her fruitcake had been bested by Mrs Chandler's, ranking only second.

Later in the afternoon, when the men had removed their jackets and rolled up their shirt sleeves, Ellen sat beside Madge on a fold-up chair in the shade by the marquee and drank her tea. They talked about Alf and Blane's and poor little Simon Prosser, and the government's attempt to cut dole pay from fifteen to thirteen shillings. Despite dry mouths and raging thirsts, the band oompahed stoically on.

The sun blazed onto the red- and blue-painted roundabout and the gaudy colours of the tombola stall, on glass bottles, half-finished cups of tea, bags of marbles, sticks of twisted rock, and onto hissing tea urns, plates of curling sandwiches and fairy cakes, whose icing had lost its anchorage in the heat.

The sun also picked out the ruby in Matty's engagement ring. Flanked by Flora in green and by Dr Lofts (Ellen nudged Madge to look at that), the young Mrs Dysart moved through the crowd dressed in a straw hat and pink cotton. She was a nice little lady, Ellen told Madge, a good girl who didn't get what she deserved from the family.

Madge agreed and asked Ellen if she liked working at the house. Ellen told her she did, but missed the chat.

'Funny lot,' said Madge. 'Always thought they'd lost a bit of their plumbing myself.'

'Tell you what, Madge, I could give up work tomorrow.'

Madge made a face as she bit into an extra sweet cake and her teeth jumped.

At four o'clock, Mr Fielding rang the bell to announce that Mrs Dysart would pick the winning ticket for the grand raffle, and, with a good deal of flourish, guided an anxious-looking Matty through the motions. Silence fell. Mrs Dysart seemed willing enough, thought Ellen, wondering whether if she nipped round the back she could get a refill of tea without having to queue.

The raffle announced, Mr Fielding launched into a peroration which welcomed Matty to her first Nether Hinton–Well–Yateley show, mourned the absence of Mr Dysart in America and concluded by sending respectful greetings to Sir Rupert and all good wishes for his health. A little girl lurched forward with a posy of sweet williams and marguerites and, over-eager and under-rehearsed, stuck them in Matty's face. Matty's hat dipped above the posy and hid her face, and Ellen had the impression that she was laughing. That's right, she thought. You enjoy yourself.

Later still, when the edge of everyone's high spirits had worn off and Matty had gone home, the band left off the oompah and settled into waltzes and foxtrots. The long afternoon drew to its close, and evening threw mauve and violet light across the meadow. Skylarks wheeled high in the sky, and over by the river swallows dived for their evening dip.

Beer and local cider were being sold from the tea-stand and the lads were now at it. The marquee had emptied: its vegetable exhibits filmed over in the heat, flowers drooped and the boiled potatoes had lost their floury eat-me quality. Family parties sat on rugs under the trees, and over by the bushes which led into the field, shadowy figures indicated couples who had gone in search of privacy.

Occasionally, the cry of a tired child sounded above the music. Tom Hudson was drunk quicker than normal, Alice Bugg was sick behind the school wall and Ma Barnet got stuck on her sticks and needed hauling over the mud by the gate. Ellen enjoyed that drama. During the day a smudge of potted meat had appeared on her dress and under her hat her hair was a disgrace. For once she did not mind.

Ned was locked into a group of men by the beer table, and he looked up to check where his wife was. The gesture made Ellen feel safe. The familiar life of the village: the familiar stuff of *her* life. Looking round, she concluded how little everything changed; each year it was the same, and each year it would remain the same. She did not wish it any other way.

After much negotiation, Robin Lofts had settled his surgery on the ground floor of Iris House. The house was damp and there was some question as to whether the sewage had backed up from the pipes running nearby, but it would do. Jock and Ethel Turner had lived there for years, arthritic shadows, and previous to that, the Boysells had struggled to survive and died, in due course, of damp-induced illnesses.

The siting of the surgery, therefore, was not auspicious. Ellen knew it well because she had often shared a pot of tea and charcoal biscuits ('good for the back end') with Ethel. They had shared the same brittle, sometimes bitter, sense of humour.

Ethel was a sharp one. Children grow up, she told Ellen. Don't pin your hopes on them.

No trace remained of the souvenir shell boxes, knitted patchwork rugs and general clutter that Ethel had favoured in Robin's freshly whitewashed surgery. Instead the room was clean and bare except for several wooden chairs arranged by the wall and a desk, at which sat Flora Dysart.

'Hallo, Ellen.' Flora looked up from an account book at the

clock on the wall. 'You're just in time. Surgery closes in five minutes.'

'Miss Flora! I didn't expect—'

'No. Why should you?' Flora closed the book. 'I'm sorting out some of the records for Dr Lofts as things have got in a bit of a muddle.'

Aha, thought Ellen. Dr Lofts's attendance on Flora had not gone unnoticed at the village show – that and the sightings that had been reported of the two of them began to make sense. 'Good for you, Miss Flora.'

Flora flipped open the ink well and dipped in her pen. 'Um. I'm also going to work in a new clinic for Dr Lofts.'

Ellen adjusted her expression into one of polite interest.

'Yes.' Flora's pen clunked against the pottery lip as she wiped off excess ink. 'He wishes to set up a family planning service.' Flora had not quite mastered carrying off this announcement and found herself observing the inkpot with the fascination of a naturalist watching a praying mantis eat its mate. She raised her eyes and correctly interpreted the appalled expression on the older woman's face. 'Only for married ladies, Ellen, of course.'

Apart from the determinedly modern, who adopted it as a rubric, in a village such as Nether Hinton family planning ranked on a level with satanism and incest. Ellen found herself looking at the floor and, for the first time in many years, was at a loss as to what to say.

'Think of it, Ellen. No one need have children unless they want them.'

Ellen thought of the years of good tries and near misses, and the bleeding and weakness that always followed – and of the two small graves up in the churchyard. Of Betty who had left home at seventeen. Of the years that had gone too quickly.

'Does Sir Rupert know about this?' she asked.

Flora became very busy with the papers. 'Actually, no, Ellen, not yet. I would be grateful if you didn't mention it to anyone, particularly Miss Robson.'

'I won't have to, Miss Flora.' Ellen recovered enough to point out with her usual tartness. 'It'll be over the village like wildfire.'

'Oh dear,' said Flora. 'Still, I promised Dr Lofts I'd do it.'

At this point it occurred to her that Ellen was looking worn. Conscience-stricken, she pointed to the chair by the fireplace. 'Ellen, please sit down and I'll search out your records before Dr Lofts sees you.'

When Ellen emerged from the surgery, all colour had drained from her face.

'Oh dear.' Flora leapt to her feet.

Ellen hunched herself away.

'Can I help?' Flora's voice sounded somewhere in the ether in which Ellen was floating. In the vague hope that things would return to normal, Ellen squeezed her eyes shut and moisture oozed onto the weathered skin beneath them.

'Can I help?' said the clear voice again.

Ellen shook her head, words reduced to a useless buzzing. After a minute or two, the habit of a lifetime asserted itself and she said, 'If you don't mind I want to go home.'

'I'll take you,' said Flora. 'I was just packing up. Can you wait five minutes?'

The walk to Clifton Cottage usually took fifteen minutes or so but Ellen, frightened by Robin's gentle reassurance that there was *nothing* to be frightened about, moved awkwardly and without impetus. Flora offered her arm and, silhouetted between the cornfields, they moved slowly onwards, Flora keeping up a flow of talk. Ellen screwed up her eyes now and then, but would not look at Flora.

At the cottage, Flora said in the false-bright voice she hated but could not stop herself using, 'I insist on making you a cup of tea.'

The crocks in the scullery were scoured and placed in height order on the shelves. A pile of laundry had been folded in a manner that creased it least: flapping shirt tails, tucked night-dresses and expansive knickers. The same skill and inventiveness was evident in the kitchen for Ellen had collected glass stoppers from Blane's bottles and crocheted them into a mantelpiece covering.

Flora assembled cups and saucers and masterminded the

making of the tea with difficulty. Eventually, she placed a full cup in front of Ellen. 'Would you like . . . would it help to talk about it?' She peered at the liquid in the cups. 'Sorry about the tea leaves.'

Ellen did not look encouraging. The clatter of their cups emphasized the silence. Flora asked about the crocheted rugs covering the backs of the two chairs. Ellen straightened herself.

'I made those.'

'And the jug?' Flora pointed at a fat-bellied object painted with shells.

'Ned bought me that on an outing to Brighton.'

'How pretty.'

Ellen roused herself. 'You're thinking, Miss Flora, that you've never seen anything quite so ugly. So it is.' Ellen's mouth twitched. 'But Ned gave it to me and it means a lot.' She got to her feet. 'More tea?'

Greatly daring, Flora asked, 'Is it your knee, Ellen?'

Ellen picked up the kettle. 'The doctor *says* there's nothing to worry about. He thinks the lump on my knee is just a cyst. Even so, it's got to go and I don't like it.' She poured hot water into the teapot. 'I don't like the notion at all.'

It puzzled Ellen sometimes as to why she was the anxious type when her childhood had been so safe. You're a fusser, Ned accused her over the years. Always nipping and tucking at things.

'I'm sorry.' Flora recognized terror in Ellen's eyes and felt inadequate to deal with it.

'I asked him if it would hurt.' Ellen pulled the cosy over the teapot. 'Last time I cut myself with a knife carving up the rooks, it hurt something rotten. Funny,' she said, almost to herself, 'me mum used to say I was as sharp as a knife.'

Flora fumbled to give some kind of comfort. 'It's not so terrible, Ellen. Hospitals are very good these days.'

Ellen transferred her gaze to the flowerbed outside the window. '*You* can say that, Miss Flora.'

Flora was trying to cut through the barrier of the healthy talking down to the sick and pushed her hand towards Ellen. As she did so, she made a typical Flora muddle and knocked over

275

her tea. A puddle spread over the wooden surface and dripped over the edge of the table. 'Oh, I'm so sorry, Ellen. Let me get a cloth.'

'Oh no!' said Ellen. 'I've just scrubbed it.'

'Quick, then. Tell me where the cloth is.'

'Don't bother, Miss Flora. I'll do it much better.'

The last was true. Flora subsided and it was obvious to Ellen that she wanted to get out of the confining cottage: away from the china jugs and crocheted mantelpieces. Away from her guilt that her own body was young and healthy and Ellen's was neither.

'Look,' she said. 'I'm not doing any good here. I'm just in your way.'

Ellen crouched painfully and scrubbed at the floor. 'If you wouldn't mind, then I could get on with Mr Sheppey's tea.'

Flora met Robin letting himself in at the gate. He took one look at her face.

'Not good, I imagine.'

'I'm afraid I haven't helped, Robin,' said Flora. 'Is it serious?'

Robin hesitated. 'It's possible,' he said cautiously. 'But I don't think so. Poor Mrs Sheppey. Knees hurt and she's never had an operation before.'

Flora kicked at a stone on the path. 'Oh, Robin,' she said. 'She's scrubbing the floor because I knocked over the tea.'

'Well, it's no use you getting in a state.'

Flora looked up at the sky bright with July sun and felt the breeze on her face. 'How do you cope with things like this? Particularly when they're really bad.'

'I'm not sure that I do.'

When Robin put his head round the kitchen door, Ellen was still chasing tea puddles on the floor. Because it was an effort to pull herself upright, she called out, 'Come in.'

He closed the door gently behind him. 'I've arranged a hospital bed for you, Mrs Sheppey. I'm pleased about that. Only a few years ago I would have been operating on your kitchen table.'

Ellen glanced up at her things: the jug, the rugs, the kitchen range where Ned's supper was cooking. If I have to be carved up, she thought, I'd prefer it here.

Robin made no attempt to help her up but asked if he could sit down. 'You know,' he said, 'it's often the little things that bother patients when they go into hospital. So I thought I'd come and see if there's anything I can tell you.'

Ellen spotted a suggestion of tea on the floor and bent to annihilate it – and a disconcerting flash that she had had her life made her heart beat harder.

'What's the morgue like?' she said, groping for the edge of the table and hauling herself up.

'Freshly painted, as it happens.'

Her laugh grated on both of them. 'That's one up on us. Ned has promised me for years that we could repaint.'

'Well, he'd better do it, since you won't be seeing the morgue.'

She twisted the floor rag between her hands. 'Do they look at you with nothing on?'

'Not unless they have to. You must remember that they're trained to look at bodies differently.'

'What happens if I talk in my sleep?'

'They are under oath not to repeat confidences.' Robin felt in his pocket for his pipe. 'I would almost think you had a con-science, Ellen.'

Ellen flashed back at him, 'If you're trying to winkle my secrets out of me, Dr Lofts, you'll get nowhere.'

'Now, why would I do that?'

She stood, hands on hips, and smiled for the first time since she had gone into the surgery. She understood Dr Lofts and she fancied he understood her. 'You look in need of tea, Dr Lofts.'

Robin Lofts knew that most people carry secrets, that Ellen would not be exempt – and he had no intention of ever asking . . .

At night, things are not so ordered and Ellen's memories twisted a skein of disorderly echoes through her sleep and half wakings. Doused in sun, for it had been high summer, or in the magic of a summer dusk, the memories pulled Ellen back to the time when she lived with an unaccustomed exhilaration in her breast.

Oh, nothing had happened. Nothing bad, that is. Nothing that Betty — who had already left when Bill came into Ellen's life — or Ned could accuse her of.

Nonsense, said the shadowy figure (which she thought sometimes was God or a queasy conscience), who hung over her sleep. You have sinned with your mind if not with your body, all because of a slow, serious smile and a cap of fair hair above a stocky body which turned her guts to water.

Among other things, that was what the war had changed.

Bill and his men had been on a route march: down Jackall's Hill, past the Horns, left at the watercress bed and fallen to up Redlands Lane. Pulled by mules, the soup kitchen trundled behind them and came to a halt by the stile.

The men were queuing with their mess tins when Ellen lifted her skirts and swung a leg over the stile. She met Bill's gaze full on. Steam from the soup kitchen meandered upwards and the cabbage in the boiling liquid was as pungent as she had ever smelt it. And Bill smiled.

After that, Bill had often walked up to Redlands Lane in his spare time where the women were working the osiers. White osiers, Ellen explained, had been soaked in the pond over the winter and stripped. The dries were used to give contrast in the baskets. Brown ones were kept for bicycle or dog baskets and garden chairs. These were boiled in the hop kiln by the Plume of Feathers and steam often blotted out the bottom end of the village.

White were the nicest, she said. Just like your skin, he said, and touched the inside of her wrist with the tip of his finger. Her forty-year-old heart jumped as if it had had an electric shock.

How many children have you got? she asked. Only one, he replied. And that made a bond between them.

Ellen never dared to ask what happened to Bill and the boys after they had been ordered out, almost certainly to the front in France, leaving her heart to beat normally again and her emotions to rearrange themselves around a space in her life.

Dreams won't be ordered. Occasionally Ellen went with Bill to France, and dreamt of the horror there. She saw him, in a water-filled trench shouting at his men, watched him go over the top and weave over the pocks and dents, past the petrified remains of the trees into the gunfire.

She never got further than that. Bill and she were unfinished business, and she never questioned that it had to be so.

That night Ellen woke up in the dark. Beside her Ned breathed noisily. The doctor had said *not* to worry and she set herself the task of controlling her fear.

CHAPTER ELEVEN

Telegrams backed up by letters arrived from Kit at regular intervals.

GONE TO CHARLESTON STOP THEY STILL TALK OF
CIVIL WAR AND YANKEES STOP NEW ORLEANS NEXT
STOP

'Where's the atlas?' Flora asked. 'I thought Kit was only going to visit New York and Los Angeles.'

'He was,' said Matty.

'New Orleans is in the opposite direction.'

'Correct.'

'Then why?'

'Obviously the mood took him,' replied Matty, who wanted to ask the same question.

'Oh, well, he always did have the luck.'

NEW ORLEANS HOT HOT STOP JAZZ STOP GHOSTS
RESTAURANTS AND DECAY STOP DOUGHNUTS AT
CAFE DU MONDE STOP DINNER AT ANTOINES STOP

Flora looked down at her hips. 'At least it won't be me getting fat.'

'No,' said Matty.

As always, Kit's letters were stuffed with observation and topographical information and said nothing about himself. America was not one country, he scrawled in one. It's many. Down South, he went on, they are still living the great days when the Mason–Dixon line held and General Sherman had not yet burned his way through Georgia . . . slave cabins behind moss-draped antebellum mansions and people have very long memories.

It's hot, reported a letter begun boldly in New Orleans and finished irritably in Los Angeles. (Kit was nursing an almighty hangover and a paradoxical relief at having let his hair down at last.) The New Orleans hotel was in the French quarter and boasted wrought-iron gates in the shape of a cornstalk fence and the ghost of a slave woman tortured to death by her mistress. The city reeked of history, voodoo and sex.

In California it was hotter still and heat massed in walls over the cotton fields. News was not good. The crash and the depression had dealt near death blows to the country. The value of stock was rock bottom. Buildings were empty. Rich men had turned into tramps and, as ever, the poor starved. For many, the diet consisted only of corn, nuggets of fatback pork and a few vegetables. On the prairies, the bread baskets of America, a drought had set in and the sky billowed with black dust rollers – or, as the locals called them, he said, 'the wrath of God'.

The film industry, however, was flourishing. Which, Kit finished, was extremely good news and he would explain why when he returned. He signed off by saying that he looked forward to seeing Matty, hoped that Rupert was stable, and he would be home in mid-August on the *Île de France*.

Matty read the last letter in the garden. A light wind ruffled the onion-skin sheets covered with Kit's impatient writing. She looked up. Some of God's wrath was gathering over Hampshire and a summer storm threatened to break the long spell of fine weather which had held through July.

She folded the letter and put it away in her jacket pocket. Kit seemed remote and, if she was truthful, Matty had enjoyed the break. For a little while she could be herself, free from hungering, free from watching Kit, from puzzling out ways to reach him, from trying to plait together the threads of a marriage. On a summer afternoon in a garden with plenty to do, there was everything to be said for the ease of solitariness.

Matty leant back against the statue. The corner of the plinth stuck into her bottom and made a greenish mark on her skirt.

Too bad, she thought. She had put on weight and under the material her thighs splayed against the stone. How satisfactory that was, and she poked one experimentally in the soft upper part and admired the indentation.

Direct as ever, Flora had already told Matty how much better she looked. 'Pinker and less breakable. Less lost.' (Less like a doll, Flora had wanted to say but desisted.)

A little self-conscious but pleased, Matty put up a hand to her hair and tugged at it. 'Do you like my hair?' she asked.

Flora took half a minute to answer. 'No,' she said. 'It's too crimped and too short. I think you would look better with long hair, Matty. Why don't you grow it?'

'If you think so, I will.' Always well dressed, Matty's confidence and flair for design did not always extend to herself, and she liked to ask advice. As she feared, the hairdresser in Farnham had not been up to the challenge of limpish hair but Matty did not mind Flora's bluntness – rather, she was pleased that her sister-in-law felt close enough to be honest.

'By the way,' Flora stopped prowling, 'where do you go to in the afternoons, Matty?'

Tempted by the idea of exchanging a confidence, Matty's resolve wavered before Flora's interested gaze. Then the habit of secretiveness asserted itself. No, she thought. The garden is mine. 'Nowhere,' she answered. 'I walk a lot. To get healthy, you know. Dr Lofts said.'

'Divine,' said Flora, who was not fooled. 'A woman with a secret.'

'Very funny,' said Matty.

'Aha,' said Flora in a knowing way, and went off for a ride singing Al Jolson's 'You Ain't Heard Nothing Yet' to the tune of 'Hark the Herald Angels Sing'.

Matty smiled at the recollection and felt in her other pocket for the list she had made earlier. According to the catalogue issued by the Old Rose Garden in Colchester, 'Transom', an apple-scented coppery rose, would climb to fifteen feet or so. Matty levered herself upright from the statue and squinted at the wall behind the flowerbed. She knew that the orange–red spectrum in roses was fashionable just now and Ned approved them. ('They warm me up,' he said. 'I like flowers with a bit of bottom, like.') Matty saw his point, but could not match his enthusiasm and crossed 'Transom' off her list. Blush-pink 'Himalayan Musk' sounded nicer. She wrote that down instead and added to a second column 'Metro Sulphate' which *Popular Gardening* assured her was 'Gentle Dame Nature's Favourite Plant Food', now available in dried crystals.

Underneath that she wrote 'trowel' and 'Eureka weed killer', decided that enough was enough and returned the list to her pocket.

'Watch Out For Disease In Your Roses' also figured in *Popular Gardening*. Matty was taking the warning seriously for her roses had been chosen with care, obtained with effort and planted entirely by herself. Ned had also given her a lesson on the subject and, mindful of his warnings, she knelt down beside the newly planted roses to search for the exotica of mildew, black spot and leaf scorch.

Something else Ned had said came back. Matty examined a leaf on the 'Fantin Latour'. What was it? Her finger hovered over a colony of greenfly massing on the underside. 'They were very alike to look at,' he had said. 'Lady Dysart was not the same after he was killed. Very fond of him, she was.'

Matty swept her finger over the greenfly and a mass of dead and dying insects clung stickily to it. She stared at the massacre, surprised that she did not feel any remorse.

Those letters. They must have been written by Edwin who loved his sister, and she him . . . Had they always been so fond of each other? Was *that* why Hesther had been sent to England to find a husband?

If that was the case, how stupid, Matty thought. Hesther would have been lonely over here in a foreign land. Exile is no cure for anything if you are not happy. Had Rupert known? And was that why he had written 'Bitch' on the letter and thrown his dead wife's effects into the trunk?

Did loving your brother over your husband (over your children?) count as a disease, and how did you exorcize it?

283

Two ounces of soft soap in five pints of water, with one ounce of permanganate of potash crystals stirred into the lather killed the rust spore. Matty had that formula off pat: Ned had made her learn it. She had sat on the bench in his gloomy office, legs swinging, until she was word perfect. Ned's garden lore was precious, and Matty was not going to waste any of it. Anyway, she could tell Ned liked teaching her, and pleasing an elderly man who missed his daughter was simpler than most things in her life.

Matty moved on to the problem of rose suckers. The sucker may look good to the inexperienced gardener, warned *Home Gardener's Year*, but they are briar growths, stronger and more vigorous than the cultivated rose grafted onto them. Leave a briar shoot unchecked and it will kill off the rose proper whose place it is usurping. In other words, *Home Gardener's* doom-tinged prose suggested, the rose will revert to the wild. Once that has happened, it is too late to save it.

Never, thought Matty fiercely, forgetting about everything else. I'll never allow that to happen to my beautiful *grandes dames*, my 'Fantin-Latour', my 'Queen of Denmark', my Jacobite rose, my 'Comte de Chambord'. My tamed, thorned, crumpled beauties.

Every reason, then, to search for the invader. How could she tell? she asked Ned. He replied that suckers usually produce seven leaves to the spray instead of the normal three or five. 'You can spot 'em a mile off, like,' he said. 'Be on your guard, Mrs Kit.'

Gouge out stem suckers with a penknife, said the murderous-minded *Home Gardener's Year*. Merely to break them off is to invite their reappearance.

Matty's secateurs closed around one stem sucker and clicked shut. It fell to the ground and that was that. Easy to kill the invader when you knew how.

She stood up and rubbed the palm of her right hand where new blisters punctuated the skin. It was late afternoon, the sun had shifted and she was thirsty for tea. A heap of prunings lay at her feet ready to gather up into her trug. It was quiet. This was England: cool, damp, full of hidden life, her garden here a speck in the flowing continuum of growing things. And she was a part of this process which was as physical, as spiritually satisfying, as *felt* as any love affair.

'Matilda?'

'Aunt Susan. How lovely.' Matty's voice always rose when she lied on the telephone.

'I haven't spoken to you for months, Matilda. How are you?'

'Actually rather good.'

An impatient sigh came down the line. 'I always said you fussed too much. You shouldn't think so much about yourself.'

There was silence while both women digested the exchange so far. Although it was tea-time Susan was not at her best, having imbibed one too many White Ladys at luncheon.

'How is Uncle Ambrose?'

'Well, but very busy.'

Another silence. Susan reached for the cigarette box. 'Matilda. I would like to come down for a Friday to Monday visit. How about next week?'

Matty searched frantically for inspiration in her diary, which was deliciously blank except for entries such as: 'Visit the Craddocks' rose garden', 'Send off for bulb catalogue', and 'Take cuttings of pinks'. Get out of this one, Matty Dysart, and you are in line for the Foreign Office . . . The sighing had been replaced by exhalations of expensive Virginia tobacco. One thing was certain: Matty did not want her aunt Susan anywhere near her for the time being.

'I am afraid it isn't possible, Aunt Susan. I'm booked up until the first week in September. Would that do?'

'I see.' Susan mustered the chilling note that, in the old days, had never failed to shrivel Matty and glared at the telephone, impatient that the new Matty irritated her as much as the old one. 'Couldn't you manage a little sooner?'

Matty lied with a sense of relief that she felt free to do so. 'I'm afraid not, Aunt Susan. September really is the earliest. You are welcome then. Shall I write it in?'

'Goodness, we *are* busy.' Susan had been looking forward to relaxing at the Dysarts' expense – after all, Matty owed her an upbringing. A desire to wring her niece's neck hardened. 'But if you say so, September it is. Write us in, please.' She stubbed out her cigarette and lit a new one immediately. 'Have you and Daisy been in touch?'

Matty pushed the diary away. 'No.'

'You know she's in America? In New York, actually. She was run down and a little depressed and wanted a holiday. I packed her off for a change of scene. One of Marcus's friends invited her to join the houseparty at Great Neck and they went down to Charleston and New Orleans for a week. I must say they appear to have had a very good time.'

'Ah.' Matty noticed that the knuckles on the hand holding the earpiece had gone white.

'So you didn't know? Of course you wouldn't if you haven't been in touch.' Susan was going to enjoy her revenge. 'Funnily enough, she met up with Kit at a dinner party. Wasn't that a coincidence? I wrote back at once and told her to be careful which, I think you would agree, Matilda, was the right thing to do.'

How can she be so cruel? Matty thought. Both to me *and* to Daisy.

Susan went on smoothly, 'In the letter that came yesterday, Daisy said that a party of them were planning to travel back on the *Île de France*.'

Matty groped with her free hand for the pile of letters on the desk and pulled the top one towards her. Working her fingers into the folds, she spread it across her knee. It was dated two weeks before and headed 'Fifth Avenue Hotel'. She skimmed the contents: apparently the Dewey arch beside the hotel took its inspiration from the Roman arch of Titus and Vespasian, Delmonico's was *the* restaurant, Tammany Hall was named after an Indian chief, etc., etc. Her eye travelled over the page. Kit's face filled her vision and her ears rang with the sound of his voice.

There was no reference to Daisy.

'Oh, really,' she said weakly. 'What a surprise for them both, Aunt Susan.'

Susan smiled at Daisy's silver-framed photograph on the table beside her. 'Yes, Matilda, wasn't it?'

Matty clattered down the stone steps and ran across the lawn. The yew encircled the grass in a dark grip, and beyond it flowed the river. She stumbled on towards the mound that hid the remains of the earlier Tudor building.

It seemed to Matty that she was back where she had started.

At the river bank, she paused, turning blindly this way and that, not sure where to go.

'Mrs Kit . . .' Ned came into sight with the wheelbarrow full of prunings, but she brushed past him.

'Not now, Mr Sheppey.'

Slipping on the dry summer grass and hardened mud, Matty half ran, half walked up the path towards the boathouse.

It was tiny, hardly more than five feet wide, with a door that hung on one hinge propped shut with a length of wood. Mould and decaying wood showered her face and hands as she pulled it open and plunged inside. Constellations of dead flies lay on the floor and the single paned window had turned green.

No one had used the boathouse this year. Matty surveyed the decay, shrugged, picked up the oars, manhandled them outside and lowered them into the rowing boat tethered to the wooden post.

'We used to go out in the boat a lot as children,' Kit had told Matty. 'With Mother. We'd take a picnic and Tyson would row us up to the big field. When I was old enough I went out to fish, particularly when I felt rattled. It was soothing.'

When they had returned from honeymoon, Kit had taken Matty out once or twice and taught her the rudiments of handling oars. It will toughen you up, he had teased. Develop muscles which you didn't know you possessed.

Bugger you, Kit, she thought, using the strongest language she could muster. Bugger you. Trapping the oars in their cradle, the rowlocks screeched from disuse.

Rocking from side to side, the boat, only just in Matty's

control, swung out into the river and brushed through the reeds. Her blisters stung and wept, but she rowed on, away from Hinton Dysart. Slowly, shining in the sun, its freshly painted windows like royal icing, the house diminished.

The handles of the oars slipped and bucked in her hands. The boat rocked and the water made slippity-slap noises against the wooden sides.

Kit and Daisy. Dancing together. Talking together. Eating together. What else were they doing together? Matty rowed harder until the boat glided through a bed of bulrushes and shuddered to a halt. There she crouched over the oars and gave herself up to the agony in her heart.

It was hot and quiet. Hogweed and blackberry bushes rampaged over the banks, and above stagnant caches made by fallen branches, trees spread green canopies over root boles. Mayflies skimmed over the water, and a cloud of midges nipped and stung Matty's flesh. Marbled in greenish brown and patched by sunlight, the water looked cool. Here and there a ripple betrayed a fish. The river bed was full of hidden things and washes of underwater reed. Matty raised her head. There was nothing civilized here, she thought, no depilation of grass and plant, only the natural vigour of wild things competing for the right to exist.

Like the deceptive sucker on a rose.

Jealousy was a cruel emotion. Matty should know, for it was tearing her in two. She looked up at the sky. She wanted Kit to love her. She wanted to be his wife, and the mother of his children. She wanted peace, contentment, domesticity.

She wanted to be old so that none of this mattered any more.

After a while, she manoeuvred the boat out of the bulrushes and rowed back, listening to the thump and squeak of the oars in the rowlocks. At the boathouse, she stood up. The boat tipped and the river came up to meet her. She grabbed the edge of the rudimentary jetty with her stiffening hands and, groaning, pulled herself up onto the bank and tied up the boat.

It was too much effort to return to the house, and Matty sat there with her feet hanging above the water. A chill crept into the breeze, as it often did at this time of day, and she shivered.

She turned her hands palm upwards, stared at the blisters burning her skin, before inspecting the backs. Ned said you should always put soap under your nails if you garden, otherwise they will never be clean. True. Next time, she must take his advice. Deliberately, Matty spread her fingers wide and bit her lips when the raw skin cracked apart.

You have to be taught happiness – and Matty had not been taught, either by parents or husband. Contentment she had taught herself, and had rejoiced in the pleasure she took from a painting, a fire on a winter afternoon, her garden. Her borrowed garden.

When they rode up the sand dune and out of her life, the Verrals could have not considered the legacy of loss they bequeathed to their daughter. 'Just be patient, littly darling,' Jocasta told Matty, her eyes already fixed on the horizon. 'You'll be fine by yourself and we'll be back soon.'

Perhaps, then, it was right that Matty would never bear a child because how could she, so inadequate, teach it what she had failed to teach herself . . .?

The touch on her shoulder was the lightest imaginable, and Matty barely registered it. It came again – tentative, and as nebulous as thistledown. She raised her face from the dark shield made by her hands.

A familiar little figure stood on the river bank a couple of feet away from Matty, twisting the skirt of her dress between her fingers. The material was powder blue and heavily tucked, and the face above it was sunburnt.

Matty shivered. 'For God's sake,' she begged, and knelt on the rotting wood, 'for God's sake, tell me who you are?' She raised her arms and held them out to enfold the child into her empty, hungry body. 'Tell me . . .'

Her arms encountered no resistance. Light streamed over the river, swallows swooped over the water, the breeze gathered force and sent ripples out from the jetty. High above, a curlew sounded.

There was nothing.

PART THREE

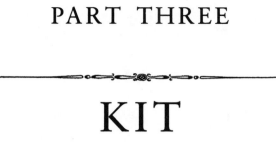

KIT
1931-2

HARRY

A woman who loved her brother more than her husband? A husband who both knew and did not know. A war. An economic crisis. A house that had been allowed to die on its feet. A broken love affair and an ill-advised marriage . . . A garden.

These are the ingredients of a story. They may be familiar, they may not. For families often share similar experiences – but not quite, for each family, as Tolstoy said, is different in its unhappiness. Because I am no longer young, I like to mull over the memories, the stories, the gossip, the residue of anguish and passion left by yellowing papers and I ask Thomas (with whom I discuss most subjects): Was this really us?

Each family is marked, I suppose, with a canker peculiar to itself.

The best ones survive. Like Alba roses which, for all their beauty, are extraordinarily tough. Albas thrive in semi-shade or against a cold north wall, and cock defiance at mildew and black spot. 'Queen of Denmark' is my *favourite* favourite, and I admire her strength and purpose. (Her one fault is straggliness, but that can be rectified by a hard prune in December.) Ruffled rosettes, the flowers are the colour of raspberries mashed into double cream, served on elegant grey-green leaves.

A feast, my friends.

293

CHAPTER ONE

'H ERE LET me.' Kit extracted Daisy's crocodile dressing case from her grasp. 'The stewardess can deal with it.'

'Goodbye, New York,' said Daisy, relinquishing the case into Kit's care.

'Exactly,' said Kit, 'you mustn't miss a second.' He went off to see to the disposing of the luggage and left Daisy to make her way through the crush on the gangway up to the first-class deck. He rejoined her there within ten minutes and informed her that at least five bouquets were already in her cabin and more arriving.

'The wages of flirting,' she said, with a delicious laugh. 'How nice.'

She lifted her face to the sky in an effort to gain some fresh air. New York had been as hot as hell, so hot that Daisy fancied the marrow had boiled in her bones. But fun. New York had been fun.

It was early morning, and already the haze around the Empire State Building and across the famous skyline was shredding. On the river, at least, there was the pretence of a breeze. Kit drew Daisy towards the rail and manipulated a space for them both in the crush. 'OK, as they say here?'

'OK.'

'Good girl.'

'Look. There's Sally Allsop and Monty.' Daisy pointed at the spectators lining the quay. 'Beside the woman in the yellow dress.'

'*And*, if I'm not mistaken, your admirer the Gurney chap is loitering in the hope of attracting your attention.'

'Oh dear,' said Daisy. 'I gave him strict instructions not to come.'

The *Île de France*'s funnel emitted a shriek and Daisy jumped. In her cotton dress and jacket and white straw hat she looked every inch the fashionable woman, but Kit, watching her from under the brim of his panama, knew from the way she held her head that she was very tense. 'Don't you want to go home?' he asked suddenly.

Daisy rubbed at the deck rail and left a smear. 'Not much, if you must know. There are things that need sorting . . .'

'Tim Coats?'

She glanced at Kit, raising an eyebrow. 'I suppose so. I owe it to him. I've kept him waiting too long.'

'I don't like him.'

She went quite pale and twisted her head away. 'Stop it, Kit, and say goodbye to New York.'

Kit did as he was told, and watched luggage being wheeled on board, passengers clogging the gangways. A few cars had edged close to the ship, and their horns mingled with the chorus of farewells. It was a noisy scene: brash, cheerful, with the high gloss of American efficiency.

'You shouldn't be here with me, you know.' Daisy waved at Sally Allsop. 'Mrs Guntripp might leap to conclusions.'

'Hardly. Where is she?'

'Settling the daughters in their stateroom.'

'Then she won't know.'

Daisy sighed and lowered her eyelashes, hiding her expression. 'No.'

Kit fastened on details: a strand of hair had escaped from behind one ear and lay on Daisy's cheek, and one sleeve pressed into a tiny fold of flesh under her arm. Daisy's beauty was growing more assured and settled, and although he hankered for the wilder Daisy with whom he had fallen in love in France, it still maddened him. She shifted, cupped her chin in her hands, and crossed one long leg in front of the other. Kit returned to his contemplation of the quay.

Neither had intended to meet up with the other. But they did, at a Mary Sopwith's weekend houseparty at Great Neck where they drank cocktails on a terrace overlooking the sea. Mary was rich and liked new faces and Kit, fresh from the unfriendly reception of his Boston cousins, accepted her invitation to go south with the same houseparty to visit Charleston and New Orleans where he had drunk too much planter's punch and danced to a Creole band under the dripping Spanish moss. Nevertheless, he and Daisy behaved in exemplary fashion, and never held a conversation alone. Looking back over the games of golf, sailing expeditions, cocktail parties and dances, it had been an intensely aware time – the stretched glove waiting for the hand, the senses climbing to a pitch of acute sensitivity.

Like New York, the week had been fun . . . fun – but painful, and, if he analysed it truthfully, addictive.

Daisy marched white-gloved fingers along the rail and touched his wrist lightly.

'I'm pleased you're here, Kit.'

Kit forced himself not to return the gesture. It might trigger the unstoppable. For here was Daisy: a breathing canvas of skin, pores, hair, of secret, folded flesh and blue vein and he wanted to devour her as once he had devoured sugar mice. He was afraid it would take only the flick of the beautiful mouth for him to hustle her to his cabin, spread her wide and use her until he was quiet.

Instead, he concentrated on the ropes being uncoiled from the tenders by the crew, and listened as goodbyes tuned up to crescendo. The woman next to Kit began to cry noisily and the child beside her jumped up and down, screaming, 'Daddy!' The pilot tug bucked its way towards the river mouth and, with a second eerie hoot from her funnel, in which was distilled a history of departure, the *Île de France* burst the forest of streamers between her and the quay and eased away from her berth. A ribbon of water between land and ship widened into a canal, a river, then a channel.

The engines made the deck hum underfoot. Daisy put up a hand to shade her eyes and watched as the cityscape was lost to the mist. Past Battery Park the breeze sharpened, and Daisy pulled her jacket round her shoulders and stood with her arms folded over her breasts.

'I've forgotten what it's like to feel cold,' she said.

297

'Goodbye, Statue of Liberty.' The child had stopped crying and bounced up and down in front of his mother. The statue loomed close and then drifted away. New York was behind them.

Daisy pulled her jacket even tighter so it strained the material, and flashed Kit a determined smile. 'Let's go inside,' she said. 'You'd better say hallo to Mrs Guntripp and Chloë and Peggy. They'll expect you to dine with them. Beware Chloë. She's terribly nice and innocent.'

'I'm a respectable married man,' said Kit.

Silence.

'Married, yes.'

They stared at each other for a full five seconds. In the end, it was Daisy who pulled away her gaze. 'What are we waiting for?'

At the Guntripp table during the first-night dinner, Kit played up, with the right degree of skill, to the Guntripp daughters' expectation, which was to be treated as adults. Freshly shaven, hair sleeked back, and folded loosely into a chair ready to talk, he was a débutante's dream. As Daisy had warned, Chloë was at the awkward stage: too innocent to check her enthusiasms and not clever enough to mask her inexperience. But she was charming and pretty, with a hint of an inner life, and Kit listened as she chatted on to the accompaniment of silver clattering on porcelain. Particularly as artless Chloë supplied him with titbits about Daisy.

'Miss Chudleigh was *so* kind to us when we met in New York. She arranged outings, and never let us get stuck with difficult people. And all when she was so busy herself.' Chloë's tone was a compound of how-does-she-do-it? and will-I-ever-be-like-that? (No, thought Kit.) 'Miss Chudleigh's cabin is awash with the most exquisite flowers, some of them quite rare. Orchids and lilies and things. Mother says if we're ever half as popular . . . doesn't she, Miss Chudleigh?'

Kit may have been talking but he was also watching. Every move of Daisy's acquired significance: the way she drank or picked up her fork, turned to her neighbour or wiped her mouth with the napkin. Across the maidenhair fern in the table centre-piece Daisy said, 'Chloë is exaggerating. Chloë, I do think by now you know me well enough to call me Daisy.'

'Have you enjoyed your trip to the United States, Mr Dysart?' Mrs Guntripp was dressed in eau-de-Nil satin with a matching turban pulled low over her forehead. Her plump fingers scuttled over the glasses at her *placement* and selected the water tumbler.

'Weren't you on business, Mr Dysart? You probably had no time to enjoy yourself,' Chloë cut in, earning a reproving frown from her mother.

Kit began to light a cigarette and realized it was too early in the meal. 'Yes, the trip was for business but I've also enjoyed myself.'

'Was it successful? The business? Should we drink to it?' Daisy raised her wine glass.

'Not really, no.' Kit thought there was no point in disguising the results. 'I thought some property shares I held might be valuable. Still, I'll hang on to them for the moment.'

Mrs Guntripp was surprised. Everyone knew that Kit Dysart was bankrolled by his wife, so why the bother of a trip to the other side of the world? But she raised her glass and smiled ingratiatingly.

'Well,' said the irrepressible Chloë, who had no idea as yet of the Machiavellian reflections of Society mothers, 'you can make up for the business bit with pleasure during the next few days. The band is supposed to be simply something.'

Sitting beside her sister, Peggy blushed for Chloë's forwardness.

Watching Daisy's fingers curl around the stem of her wine glass and the fascinating way her upper lip stretched over the rim, Kit was, at last, at liberty to smoke a cigarette.

'They're very sweet,' Daisy said later, meaning the girls, when she and Kit were walking round the deck. It was midnight and the lights of the liner shone like gold coins in the blackness. 'Do be careful – they'll develop a frightful crush on you.'

'No harm in that. All's fair, etcetera, etcetera.' Kit was amused. 'I'll dance with both tomorrow.'

'You're in danger of becoming very conceited,' said Daisy mildly. 'Are you going to flirt with them all the way to Southampton?'

'Probably.'

Daisy wandered across the bleached deck to the rail. 'What will you do when you get home?'

'Pick up the reins. What else?'

'No trips with Max to somewhere no one has heard of?'

Kit laughed. 'Maybe.'

In the dark her voice floated back to Kit, seemingly careless and dreamy. 'Is Matty happy, do you think?'

She did not deceive Kit, who propped himself against Number Six lifeboat and felt for his cigarettes. 'Matty?' He had forgotten about his wife and the sound of her name gave him a jolt. 'To be honest, I don't know if she is or not.'

'That *is* honest, at least.' Daisy's pale green dress shimmered as she swung round. The rail pressed into her back and she curved her body against it, which emphasized the full breasts. Kit wondered if she was doing it on purpose. He drew in a deep lungful of smoke.

'Would you know if I was happy?'

He joined Daisy at the rail, keeping three feet or so between them. 'I don't know. But I like to think I might because I would recognize it from my own experience.' He finished his cigarette, threw the stub overboard and then said, 'I shouldn't be saying these things to you.'

'Do you know what I think, my Kit? I think you rub along nicely with your wife and your home.'

'Rubbing along is quite different from being happy.'

'It's what most of us do,' she said, surprising him. 'Some people are grateful to rub along because they don't like hurricanes and tempests. I suspect you might be one.'

An entwined couple walked past. The man had his arm around the girl and she was whispering to him. They did not notice Kit and Daisy. As they rounded the lifeboats, the breeze hit them and the girl gave a soft shriek. Her lover drew her even closer and they disappeared. Watching them, Kit felt a pang of envy to be like that again. 'And you, Daisy?' he asked. 'Are you rubbing along?'

With a jingle of bracelets, Daisy reached up and brushed her fingers across Kit's mouth, and he found himself snatching her hand and pressing kisses into the palm.

'Kit,' she said, low and anguished, and retrieved her hand. 'I have to ask you again. Why did you marry Matty?'

He considered a long moment before he answered. If he was absolutely truthful, Kit was not sure. 'Why did I marry Matty? Drink? I went on a blinder that night and I wasn't thinking properly. I believed you when you said you had someone else. I was angry with you. Fear of my father . . .'

'I'd just thought I'd ask,' she said. 'To see if the answers were the same. Can I have a cigarette?' She bent over Kit's lighter. 'I've thought and thought about this, Kit. You hesitated over me, who you said you loved, but jumped at Matty, a virtual stranger.' She inhaled smoke with a gasp. 'I don't think I'll ever understand.'

The water slapped loudly against the ship's side and Kit had to confront the extent of the wound he had inflicted on Daisy – and himself.

'I'm sorry, Daisy.'

She turned away, and he watched the glow of her cigarette tip in the gloom. 'I forgive you, Kit. Of course I do. I was to blame as well, you know. But I want to tell you something which is very selfish. I don't want to bury our love affair . . . so it's conveniently forgotten.'

'No chance of that.'

'Of course there is. It's the easiest thing to do and everyone likes things smoothed over, including you, my darling.'

'Daisy . . .'

She shook her head at him. 'I think you broke my heart, Kit, and at one point I thought I'd never recover. In a sense I won't. But I've learnt. Life is about broken hearts and disappointment. Everyone has to deal with those from time to time. With a bit of luck . . .'

'Yes?'

'With a bit of luck you come out stronger.'

The *Île de France* ploughed onwards. A light swung towards them and illuminated the davits holding the lifeboats. A gull screamed into the night. Heavy with guilt and appalled at his mistake, Kit said, 'We must leave it alone, Daisy.'

She moved away from him, but she had drunk a quantity of champagne at dinner. 'No. For once we will say what we really mean, Kit. I am tired of thinking about you, of hurting. Of puzzling at it. Of *hating* you. And you might have the decency to explain. Really explain.'

'I have.'

Their faces were almost touching. Kit felt Daisy's breath on his lips and smelt clean skin and face powder, overlaid with expensive perfume. He closed his eyes and imagined taking her lower lip between his teeth and worrying it until her mouth opened under his.

'All right,' he said, sounding so anguished that Daisy almost made him stop. 'I suppose I must have married Matty for her money. I don't know. I really don't know.'

She let out her breath with a sigh. 'I'm sorry, Kit,' she said, regretting her belligerence. 'I shouldn't have asked.'

'Don't.' He grabbed one of her wrists, then backed her against the rail. A satin shoulder strap fell down over her arm.

'What do you think I feel?' he said, bending to kiss the white hollow between shoulder and breast. 'How do you think I like my own stupidity?'

Terrified yet exalted with emotion, Daisy moved her hand up to cradle the back of his head and held it for a second to her breasts.

Almost immediately, Kit straightened. 'I'm sorry, Daisy. I shouldn't have done that.'

'Kit . . .'

Very slowly he adjusted the fallen strap. Daisy made no move to prevent him. Unable to stop there, Kit ran his finger over her collarbone to her breast, and she shivered uncontrollably at his touch. Suddenly afraid to lose control, she said, tough and flippant, 'Making up for lost time?'

302

'Now it's you being stupid,' he replied. 'You must see, I didn't understand the power of you and me. I also thought I had no choice, but of course I did.'

'Ah . . .' Daisy's unhappiness folded round her like a cloak, and with an odd little sound, she began to cry.

'Daisy, you're only twenty-three. There will be others.'

Angry with herself, she wiped a hand over the tears, then, because she did not have a handkerchief, held it awkwardly in front of her. 'There have been others.'

Kit dug in his pocket for his. 'Real lovers?' he asked, and dried her hand, regretting the question.

A door opened onto the deck from the first-class saloon and band music filtered into the night: a sweet, spun-sugar confection.

'Yes, real lovers,' Daisy said. 'One or two. And you?'

He thought of his wife and of the bed he occasionally occupied with her. 'No. I owe Matty that much.'

'Damn and blast Matty,' said Daisy suddenly. 'Damn and blast her.'

The big ship pounded and strained through the water, travelling between two shorelines and liberated from both. In the saloon the band played on.

'Goodnight, then, Kit,' said Daisy, and anchored her shoulder straps firmly back into place.

Infinitely gentle, infinitely tender, Kit wiped away the residue of tears on Daisy's cheeks.

'Goodnight, Daisy.'

'Tell me, does Mrs Guntripp always arrange her hair to resemble a doormat?' Kit nodded in the direction of the well-upholstered figure sitting under the awning.

Daisy giggled. 'Kit, don't be so rude.'

'I was only asking.'

'Go and get me a drink for a penance. I'm parched.'

Daisy dropped into a deck chair and let her arms flop over the sides. Tennis in this heat sapped energy and she and Kit had played hard. During the night the wind had freshened, dropped at dawn and left the sea running a swell. It was now afternoon and Daisy was getting used to the movement. The air was clean and fresh and the sun was burning her cheeks, comfortably so. Daisy closed her eyes. When she opened them again, Kit was standing above her. He squatted down beside the chair.

'Drink up. Fresh orange juice.'

Eyes narrowed against the dazzling light, she looked at Kit over the frosted rim of the glass. Gone was the contained, older — married — Kit of the previous evening, replaced by a suntanned youth in shorts that had seen better days, a cotton shirt with rolled-up sleeves and hair stuck to his forehead by sweat. Daisy had a disconcerting vision of what he must have looked like as a boy, somehow vulnerable, with the power that little boys have to tug at the heart.

'You look like you did in France,' she said.

'So do you.'

She drank the rest of her juice and sighed with pleasure.

'That was a good game,' Kit said as he drew up a chair beside Daisy's.

The breeze lifted the hem of her tennis skirt and tugged at the orange scarf she had tied round her hair. The ocean seemed bluer than ever: an enamelled, impassive expanse that ran into the horizon. Two other couples were playing tennis.

'Makes me tired to watch them,' Daisy commented, hardly bothering to move her lips. Without lipstick, they were pale pink and dry-looking from sunburn and spray.

'Indolent creature.'

The sun was still high, and the swish of backwash from the liner settled into a regular rhythm. Rocked by its comfortable roll, both Kit and Daisy fell asleep.

Daisy awoke to a tight feeling across her nose and cheeks. 'Oh, Lord,' she said. 'I'm burnt.' Only then did she realize that Kit was watching her with a mixture of tenderness, possessiveness and baffled fury. Unguarded from sleep, she smiled at him and Kit was shaken by an onrush of desire so strong that he was forced to look away.

'Did you know that you mutter in your sleep?'

Daisy sat up. 'No. I don't, do I? Nothing incriminating, I hope.' She touched her sore nose experimentally. 'Kit, is it bright red?'

'Ships could steer by it.'

'*Kit!*'

'If you come with me, I'll give you some cream I've got in the cabin. It's good for sunburn.'

She got up groggily, shot an exploratory look in the direction of Mrs Guntripp who was also dozing, and rubbing her nose, she followed Kit.

After the brightness outside, the corridor leading to Kit's cabin was dim. The ship lurched and, staggering, they clutched at the rail and groped forward.

'Steady.' Kit grabbed Daisy as he unlocked the door and, as the floor rose, they fell through it together. He closed the door. Suddenly, they were cut off from everything else.

It was hushed and quiet in the cabin. Kit went into the bathroom and rattled among various pots. 'I was ill in Damascus once and my friend Prince Abdullah ordered a medical arsenal from his doctors designed for every contingency and gave it to me. I must say, it's been very useful. Here you are.' He held out a glass jar.

'Thank you.' Daisy was sitting on the bed looking through Kit's reading on the bedside table. '*Arabia Deserta*, *The Seven Pillars of Wisdom* . . .' she read out the titles. 'Escaping?' she teased. 'Shouldn't it be *Husbandry in Hampshire*?'

'Ever heard of the armchair traveller?' He opened the pot and scooped out some of the ointment. 'Here.' He rubbed it into her nose and cheeks. 'Does that feel better?'

'Yes,' she said, as it soaked into her skin. 'Will you do my arms? They're burning too.'

He obeyed and concentrated on his task. When he had finished he looked up. Daisy was watching him and a smear of ointment remained on her cheek: icing on the hot skin beneath. It was too much for Kit.

'Daisy.' Kit jerked her roughly to her feet, took her head between his hands and kissed her mouth. Then he licked away the smear, savouring the texture of her cheek. Daisy remained absolutely still.

'Say something,' he begged. There was no marker in her eyes to Daisy's thoughts, no light to guide him, nor invitation to her body, only an intense blue in which he could read neither acquiescence nor encouragement.

She disengaged herself and, as a form of defence, wrapped her arms across her chest. 'What do you want me to say, Kit? That I want you? Of course I do. But that's not enough, and I have Tim to consider, and you Matty.'

'Daisy. Come here.' Incensed by the mention of Tim, Kit pulled her to him, picked her up and dropped her onto the bed, sweeping *Arabia Deserta* and the pot of ointment to the floor.

She struggled hard for a moment then, suddenly, went limp. Kit caught her legs and tore off one tennis shoe, then the other. They fell with a thud into the silence in the cabin. Then he wrestled with the mother-of-pearl buttons on her blouse. Underneath she was wearing a soft cotton chemise through which were visible the curves of her breasts. With a groan, he pushed her tennis skirt up her sweat-glossed thighs, hooked his fingers into the elastic of her knickers and dragged them down.

There was no partnership in what happened next. On the bed in the hot, dim cabin it was Kit, only Kit, demanding that his need be met. He was not prepared, could not wait, for Daisy.

Later, when Kit was beyond caring, she gave a cry which he was to remember for the rest of his life. Afterwards there was silence, except for the slow, rhythmic roll of the pot of ointment over Daisy's orange scarf on the cabin floor.

Daisy lay with her skirt crushed around her waist, her blouse spread over the pillow and her arms stretched out over the crumpled sheets. 'Oh, Kit,' she said, lit up both by love and despair. 'I love you.'

Kit propped himself on an elbow. 'You lied to me, Daisy.'

She laughed and touched his cheek. 'Yes, I did, didn't I?'

'Why?'

'Because . . . because . . .' Daisy could not tell him – she did not understand herself.

306

Kit gathered her into his arms. 'Why didn't you tell me, Daisy? Why didn't you tell me?' he murmured into her hair.

'Did you know, there are eighteen items on the breakfast menu in third class?' Peggy Guntripp had been busy with the ship's literature in order to woo Kit's attention at dinner. She attacked her lobster with the subtlety of a blacksmith. Opposite her, Chloë, struggling to engage an elderly gentleman in conversation, clattered her fork in suppressed frustration.

'No,' said Kit, amused despite himself. 'Tell me more.'

'Bathrooms are available at all times.'

'Thank heavens,' said Kit.

'What's more, the *Île de France* represents the face of victorious France reborn and the glory of France personified.'

'If only I had known when I booked,' said Kit.

'Her three hundred and ninety first-class staterooms are each furnished differently—'

'Peggy,' interrupted her mother, 'would you pass me the salt?'

'Only two more days,' said Daisy, who wanted to keep on staring at Kit. She addressed Mrs Guntripp. 'What are your plans when you return?'

Mrs Guntripp patted her fringe. 'We'll spend some time in the country and then we'll be coming up to town to prepare for Chloë's coming out.' She took a sip of wine. 'The thought exhausts me.'

Peggy was made of stern stuff. She did not relinquish her hold on Kit's attention for the entire dinner and he, touched by her perseverance, rewarded her efforts by dancing with her twice, and once with Chloë.

The band struck up 'Hot Nights' and Kit turned to Daisy. 'At last,' he said, and held out his hand. She took it.

'Since we have been on the subject, do *you* like the décor?' Kit indicated the tubular lighting and blond wood veneer, a style that could only be called advanced Odeon.

'I don't notice that sort of thing, really. But I like the way it creaks. My bathroom is a perfect orchestra.'

It struck Kit that Matty would have noticed the décor of the ship. The thought made him feel ashamed. 'At least you haven't got monkeys painted in yours,' he said.

'How do you know?'

'Nobody could ever repeat that mistake.'

The ceiling over the dance floor was low and suited the intimate atmosphere. The *Île de France* was a popular ship whose passengers, preferring her elegance to the speed of the P&O liners, were faithful and the saloon was crowded. Tonight, ostrich feathers predominated, in fans, sewn round waistlines, drooping off hemlines. Silver, gold lamé and eau-de-Nil shimmered, and the panelling, which was painted in soft colours, was reflected in the mirrors. Rising above the cultivated English voices were the swooping French tones, and an occasional American drawl. For a while, Kit and Daisy danced in silence, and although they did not look at one another her body was pressed into his.

'Remember France?' she asked.

'What do you imagine?'

'Do you think that that Bill woman is still there? Propping up the bar and dishing out dubious cigarettes?'

'Probably. She had, as they say, the habit.' He moved his hand so that it lay in the curve between waist and hip. Daisy's hand rested on Kit's shoulder and her bracelets rattled gently in his ear. Uncontainable joy swept over Kit. He looked down at Daisy, at the chestnut hair and sunburnt cheeks, and remembered his passion of a few hours ago.

'Daisy,' he said into her ear. 'About this afternoon.'

At that she twisted closer into him, an intimate gesture that delighted him.

'Shush,' she said.

There were red patches on her thighs where Kit had rubbed her, her chin was sore from his beard. When she dressed for the evening, Daisy discovered a bruise on her arm, and was aware of an unaccustomed ache between her legs. When she considered the theorizing about love, the books that had been written and the poetry composed, Daisy concluded how strange it was that in the end, it was condensed to physical sensation: soreness, wet thighs, a bruise.

'I want to say I'm sorry,' said Kit. 'For acting like I did.'

'Hallo,' said Chloë, circling past them in the charge of a youth who looked out of control. 'Isn't this fun?'

Daisy roused herself. 'Yes, isn't it?'

Kit waited until Chloë was out of earshot. 'Daisy,' he said, 'this is serious. I want you to know that what happened this afternoon isn't what usually happens.' An image of Matty's small, willing body in the bedroom at Hinton Dysart forced its way into his mind, and shocked him. He bent over Daisy. 'Listen . . . I . . . I don't know that much about it . . .' His confession touched Daisy in a way that nothing else had. 'I haven't been a great lover for all sorts of reasons, but I do know it can be better for you, Daisy. I was wrong to make you . . .'

The music switched to a slower tempo. It was hot and smoky in the saloon, and the crush was uncomfortable.

'Oh, for Christ's sake,' said Kit. 'Let's get out of here.'

'Swim?'

'*No*,' he said emphatically.

Daisy took two seconds to make up her mind. 'Come with me.'

This time, it was Daisy who led Kit into her cabin and shut the door behind her, feeling light-headed with her own daring. Then she held out a hand and said, more to herself than to Kit, 'What am I doing?'

Kit took her hand and bent to kiss her. Frightened by what she had initiated, she turned away at the last minute and his mouth fastened onto a corner of hers.

The music had followed them down to the cabin and filtered in through the porthole. The lilies in Daisy's bouquets seemed very white, and with each movement of the ship indelible orange pollen rained onto the carpet.

Daisy reached up and tugged at Kit's tie. He allowed her to do so — both of them thinking about Matty which, paradoxically, intensified their desire. Tentatively, she undid the studs that secured his shirt.

That night Kit, the outsider, was not alone. For the first time in his life, he breached the barriers between himself and another and found the completion he had been seeking. Riven with gratitude, he buried his face in her neck and whispered, 'I love you, Daisy.'

Daisy's face hovered over Kit as she said, 'I love you,' back to him. Moonlight played over her shoulders and full breasts bestowing on her an unearthly beauty, and Kit ran his hands up the white body in a frenzy to keep it so for ever.

'I love you,' she said, intoxicated by passion.

The smell of lilies permeated their sleep, sweet, disturbing. Kit dreamt of the garden at Hinton Dysart with its ravages and despolation and woke to an overcast dawn. Daisy stirred and turned over, puzzled by the unfamiliar arms wrapped around her. Kit stroked her cheek.

'I'd better go.'

'It's all started again,' she said.

'Yes,' said Kit, and sat up. He leant over and brushed his hand down the long, lovely shape lying beside him. 'The same but quite different.'

What have I done? Daisy silently addressed the dawn and the aftermath of the night. She reached up and traced Kit's eyes and nose with her finger. He kissed the sunburnt lips and each breast.

'What have I done?' she said aloud.

That day the weather changed, bringing rain and a strong wind. The deck was no longer inviting, the swimming pool, abandoned, sloshed on the swell, and passengers consoled themselves in the bars.

At the Isle of Wight, the *Île de France* turned and ploughed through grey seas past the Calshot coastguard station towards Southampton where it docked in a fanfare of hoots, and shrieks from spectators.

'Goodbye, Kit.'

Their party had come on deck to watch the proceedings. Daisy was once again dressed in her smart dress and jacket. Her hair was tucked under her hat and she held her crocodile dressing case tightly to her chest. She looked exhausted and distant.

'Goodbye,' said Kit.

This is worse, he thought, far worse than he had imagined, and he could tell from the taut line of her lips that she was thinking that too. Last night, after hours of talking it over, they had agreed to end the affair, to consider it an episode that happened between America and England, not to be repeated in either. Although it was a mutual decision, despair and regret drifted between them.

'Daisy.'

'Yes.'

'I didn't deal with it very well,' said Kit, 'but I love you.'

'Nor did I,' she said. 'Deal with it, I mean. And I love you.' She bit her lip. 'I do, Kit.'

The bustle of docking intensified. He moved forward as if to gather her into his arms, but stopped himself. She took an involuntary step towards him and Kit, catching a whiff of jasmine scent, felt the back of his throat tighten.

'I didn't know,' he said with difficulty.

'Didn't know what, Kit?'

'I didn't know what it was like to feel . . .' She gave him one of her quick, slanting looks, a question in her blue eyes. '. . . so intensely,' he finished. 'Such joy.'

'Yes,' she said, and smiled. 'I wanted to thank you for that.'

Kit swallowed. 'I wish . . .' he said.

'I know,' she said quickly. 'I know.'

For the last time he traced every line, every fold, every warm, beating part that was Daisy and breathed in the essence of what lay between them, as if to imprison the ecstasies of willing flesh now burnt into his memory.

The wind ruffled his hair and Daisy almost cried out with longing to hold him.

'I'll see you in September.' She turned away because she was not going to let herself cry. 'Mother wrote and told me we're coming for a Friday to Monday.' She hesitated for a second. 'Tell Matty I'm sorry about the baby.'

Kit picked up his briefcase. 'Yes.'

The future stretched out and neither of them could bear to think about it.

CHAPTER TWO

DURING THE last week of August, Danny made his annual visit to the kennels in Odiham.

'Does he still live in the house opposite the stocks?' Flora was helping Danny give the hounds their evening meal, and the air was thick with their squeals.

'Yup.'

'Down.' Flora pushed Lady's paws off her bare leg. 'You're in fine fettle, old girl. Did you have any luck getting a new bitch, Danny?'

'Yup.'

'Ellen tells me the sole topic of conversation in hospital was how awful it was that the RAF is going to set up a base in Odiham.'

'Don't blame 'em,' said Danny. 'More noise.' He dished up the boiled meat and broth cooked in his cottage, apparently unperturbed by its vile smell.

'It wasn't the noise, stupid,' said Flora. 'Ellen says they're worried the girls will be swept off their feet.' With a grimace, she stirred the slop with a spoon: hounds liked it.

'Pass me the bowls, Miss Flora.'

Inside their casing of corduroy, Danny's legs resembled sticks, and the freckles on his face and arms appeared etched onto his pale skin. Danny was a neatly made, wiry man, normally quite healthy-looking and quick of movement. But today he was slow and lethargic and Flora sighed at the whisky signs. She took a deep breath.

'Danny. Why don't you go and visit Father? He'd like it. He asks for you all the time and you've only been once since the accident.'

Danny shovelled out the last of the meat and slapped down

the bowls. A tan and white tank division promptly launched itself towards them and they retreated. Flora let herself out of the pen and waited while Danny fastened the gate.

'Won't you?' she persisted.

'See 'ere.' Danny dropped the keys into his pocket. 'Your pa doesn't need me in the sick room. Anyway, that woman stands there checking every breath I take. I don't 'appen to like it, that's all.' Danny's jaw assumed a gin-trap look, which it did at times.

'Robbie's not that bad.'

Danny opened the gin-trap and released the information, 'She wants 'im.'

Flora was not sure she had heard correctly. 'What a funny thing to say, Danny. What do you mean?'

'She wants 'im,' he repeated, the Cockney exaggerated.

Shocked by what she thought he meant, Flora pushed open the gate into the cottage garden. Danny was implying that Robbie wanted her father like a woman wanted a man . . . like she wanted Robin. The idea of her sick father as such a target left Flora speechless. Perhaps if she said nothing further the subject would drop. But Danny's hangover was bad this morning and it pricked him into telling a few home truths.

'Listen, Miss Flora. 'As no one ever told you it goes on all the time? *She*,' he emphasized the word in a flat, unfriendly way, 'is entitled to the same wantings as you or me.'

What are your wantings, Danny? she asked herself. And the memory of him naked flashed through her mind.

It had been a revealing speech for Danny, given matter-of-factly and without embarrassment, and it left Flora bewildered. She also felt betrayed. It had never occurred to her that Robbie might put anyone other than her charges first in her affections.

'Why?' she asked faintly. 'Why are you telling me this now?'

'You're a big girl now, Miss Flora.'

Out of her depth, she said uneasily, 'Even if it's true, what difference does it make to you, Danny?'

Danny's bloodshot eyes narrowed. 'She won't want me there with your father,' he said. 'She doesn't like it and it makes me fidget. Anyway, I don't belong in the 'ouse, so I'd rather stay 'ere with the family.'

'Ye gods.' Because she was at a disadvantage, Flora felt rather irritated. Even so, her loyalty to Danny was deep-rooted. 'Listen, I can make sure that Robbie is out of the way, if that's what you want.'

Danny watched the whirlpool of tails, claws and tongues inside the cage with professional detachment and a hint — just a hint — of softening. Flora tried again.

'You'd be doing me a favour, Danny.'

'Bugger off, Jupiter.' Danny always pitched his voice a shade higher when talking to the hounds. 'Let Juno 'ave some.' Flora tapped his shoulder lightly. Danny shrugged, but she knew he was not displeased.

Flora raised her voice above the din. 'Think about it, Danny. Please. You'd do him so much good. I know he gets bored and Robbie does drive him mad. So do his other visitors. You know, the family and neighbours.'

Danny cleared his throat and spat phlegm into the yard. Flora made a hasty detour. He unfastened the back door to his cottage. 'Don't you worry, Miss Flora. Your pa will do. So will I. You must learn to let alone. 'E knows I'll come when 'e needs me. Now that's a promise.'

'Oh, Danny. You're infuriating.' Flora picked up her bicycle and threaded her leg through the frame. 'I'll get rid of Robbie. Promise.'

From habit, she looked back over her shoulder when she reached the end of the track. Danny was leaning against the pen smoking, a thin blue trail wreathing above his head.

Flora cycled through the Borough and along Dippenhall Street towards Turnpike Lane. It was watercress time again. Fed by a pipe from the river Hart, the bed had been cleared out after the spring crop and replanted. Tilly Prosser and Ellen's friend, Madge, were packing dripping bundles into baskets. A couple of harnessed pony carts were waiting on the grass verge to take the cress down to Aldershot and North Camp.

'Morning, Miss Flora.' Tilly held up a pair of wet hands, and scratched at the bites on her fingers.

'Hallo, Tilly.' Flora spotted a small figure over by the ponies. 'Hallo, Simon.' Dirtier and more hopeless-looking than usual, Simon was crooning a monotonous song to the ponies. He turned his blank gaze on Flora. 'How are you, Simon?'

'Not very talkative today.' Madge looked up from her work. 'His mum went on a blinder up at the Horns last night.' She plunged her hands into the bed to cut another bunch. 'Wish I had.'

'I'll take six, please.' Flora helped herself to a sheet of newspaper and lined her bicycle basket. 'Mrs Dawes wants to make soup.' She slapped at a gnat that had landed on her cheek and counted out the money. Tilly tossed the coins into an open tin on the wall.

'Waste of good watercress, Miss Flora,' said Madge. 'Soup.'

The fresh, peppery smell of the cress made Flora's nose tingle. Rogue drops of water splashed onto her knees. On the way back, she cycled past the church with its distinctive avenue of limes: up that avenue sometimes rode the ghost soldier of Nether Hinton. Mrs Dawes had seen him as a girl, a Parliamentarian doomed to endless, unresting re-enactment as he fled from battle through the wall of the church in a flurry of leather and jingling spurs. As a child the story had made the hairs rise on the back of her neck.

Then it was down Church Lane towards the Dysart path. The threshing machines were busy up in the fields – they were threshing early, Kit said, because no one could afford to wait for better prices in the autumn. Sam Prosser and his team were up there, silhouetted against a clump of elms. Flora rang her bicycle bell and Sam gave a thumbs-up.

Soon the hop-pickers would be here from the East End, bringing their noise, their unfamiliar Cockney and their dozens of grimy children. The Hall family had been coming for generations, and Flora wondered if old Ma Hall would make it this year. She'd sworn she would, but who knew?

She cycled across the river by the bridge and over the lawn, leaving wet tyremarks in the grass. Matty was on the terrace talking to Ned and Kit appeared round the side of the house in boots and breeches.

'Can you wait for me?' she called. 'Fifteen minutes?'

Kit lifted his whip in reply. 'I'll be in the Exchequer.'

Only then did Flora permit herself to look at the drive. Robin's car was parked by the stables and he was scrambling out of the awkwardly tilted driver's seat. Flora let out a sigh, braked and the bike slowed to a wobble while she watched. Robin had a habit of pulling down the back of his jacket and patting his pocket cuffs, which, for some reason, she liked. Sure enough, he patted them and Flora found herself grinning like Alice's Cheshire cat.

During those rides up on Horsedown and Caesar's Camp, a sickness had infected Flora. The symptoms were gradual: a wish to be with Robin; a greed to watch him. With an onrush of fever she had succumbed. To what?

One day she had woken up and realized that the old Flora had been cast off and, newly tender, newly awake, she had stepped out of childhood. When she reflected on the change, she supposed it began in France and continued in Miss Glossop's tea-less lodgings. There – or in the ladies' powder room watching Matty pull herself together while her husband danced with another woman in the ballroom.

The bicycle scrunched on the gravel, Robin turned and she skidded to a halt by the wall.

'Flora.' She was still grinning when he joined her and she held out her hand to say hallo. Above them, on the first-floor landing, a curtain twitched back and Robbie looked down on the scene.

'I like you like this.' Robin rubbed Flora's hand, which was flecked with watercress and rubber from the perished handlebars. 'All tousled and warm.'

'Drat. That must mean my hair's terrible.' Flora attempted to run her hands through it and then recollected how filthy they were.

'I was paying you a compliment,' said Robin.

Feeling odd, shivery, and curiously breathless, Flora extracted the cress from her bicycle basket. 'Mrs Dawes wants this as soon as possible.'

'Flora.' Robin repossessed her hand. 'I want a serious talk with you.'

She moved towards him and their shoulders brushed. For an instant before he stepped away she felt his imprint on her. Upstairs, the curtain at the window dropped.

'What about?' Flora thought she knew perfectly well. The eagerness of two seconds ago was replaced by dread that things were going to have to be resolved and, all of a sudden, she was not sure . . . 'I was going riding, can it wait?'

Robin paid no attention to her hesitation. 'I've got to do a post-hospital check on Mrs Sheppey after visiting your father. I thought you might like to walk up to Clifton Cottage with me. Please.'

Flora's heart began to behave in an extraordinary manner, bumping about in her chest.

'Well?' Robin took his black bag out of the car. 'Yes or no?'

Flora looked up at the landing window. 'I think Robbie's been watching us,' she said.

'What's wrong with that?' Robin followed her gaze. 'She's probably waiting for me – I'm a bit late.'

'She's seen us talking.'

'Well, of course she's seen us. We're standing here in full daylight.'

Flora did not answer, but began to walk towards the house. Robin followed her and, as they went through the front door, said, 'I'll expect you later.'

He left Flora to drip watercress water over the Persian rug.

Matty waylaid Robin at the top of the stairs. 'If you have five minutes . . .' she asked, and led him into her private drawing room. The Valadon blazed at him from above the fireplace and Robin halted in his tracks.

'How extraordinary,' he said, not sure whether he liked it.

'Yes, isn't it?' Matty seemed pleased that he had noticed.

The room surprised Robin: he would have expected chintz and ruffles and knick-knacks but instead, it was full of cool touches, creamy white and primrose yellow. The chairs were upholstered in Puritan calico, their only concession to frivolity the antique braid with which they were piped, and the cushions looked as if they were made from antique tapestries. (Robin was correct: Matty had taken pains to search out tapestries that were past repair.)

'How can I help you?' he asked, and forgot about the room, for Matty's face, which had been rounding up nicely, wore its old pinched look and a haunted expression in the brown eyes. Disappointment? Anger? Not getting on with her husband? Robin ran over various permutations.

In one hand Matty clutched her handkerchief which she rolled between thumb and finger, pinching out the lace border between alarmingly cracked fingers.

She held out the other hand. 'The rash has come back,' she said. 'I think I need more of that cream.'

In his professional grip, her hand had no substance. He turned it over to examine the palm. Angry and invasive, the condition had worked its way into the cracks.

'That must hurt,' he said. 'Are you washing in soda or anything like that? Anything you don't normally use?'

Matty used carbolic soap to scrub her hands after gardening which, these days, was frequent. There was also Gentle Dame Nature's Plant Food, but she was not going to go into all that. 'Kitchen soap?'

'Might be the offender if you're not in the habit of using it. Any special face or hand creams?'

She shook her head and Robin fished in his bag for his notebook. Some patients liked to seek reassurance in their doctor's face, others required a little privacy while they talked. Judging Matty to be in the latter category, Robin kept his head bent as he asked, 'Is something bothering you, Mrs Dysart?'

'No.'

'Are you sleeping well?'

'Yes.' Matty's tone was one she adopted at afternoon tea parties.

Robin wrote a sentence. Then he looked up at her and tried

319

the direct approach. 'I am going to ask you again, Mrs Dysart. Is anything bothering you? Very often the sort of condition you have recurs when a patient is anxious.'

The girl is sitting by the statue in the garden, crying. She looks up as Matty approaches . . . and melts away.

Matty cleared her throat and repressed the urge to spread out her fingers until they cracked. 'You remember our last conversation, Dr Lofts? About something you called the unconscious?' Robin nodded and she continued, 'Well, I was wondering. A friend of mine is . . . longing to see someone who is dear to her. But this person is far away. The strange thing is that she keeps seeing this person, usually in a particular place, but not always. Like a ghost.'

'What are you asking me?'

Matty kept her hands flat on her thighs. 'I don't know, really.'

Robin wrote 'Hysteria?' in his notebook. 'I would have to read up on the subject to be absolutely sure, Mrs Dysart, but from what you tell me it appears that your friend is projecting her dearly held wish outside herself and that it's taking a physical form. So she . . . I take it she is a she? . . . she is seeing what she wants to see.'

'I see.' Matty looked at Robin and laughed awkwardly. 'Sorry that's the wrong word to use. I think I understand.'

She gave Robin the impression of being huddled up inside.

'Does anyone else see what your friend sees?'

There was a long pause. 'I don't think so.'

'Well. That's not necessarily significant.'

'Doesn't it seem very odd to you?' asked Matty painfully. 'Mad, even?'

Robin wrote 'Delusion?' beside 'Hysteria?'. He searched in his mind to possible clues as to Matty's condition and wrote 'Childless at present. Wish for a child?' He looked up.

'Unusual, yes. But I don't think, unless your friend is displaying notably antisocial tendencies, that she could be called mad. I think it is quite possible that a deep, unfulfilled longing can manifest itself physically.'

320

And the misery, Matty asked herself silently, the misery that comes with the sightings. Is it all mine? Or someone else's?

'Has your friend suffered a loss?'

Matty hesitated. 'Not that I know of.'

'It's an odd thing, but well documented.' Robin thought aloud and addressed the Valadon. 'Sometimes when someone has lost something or someone very important the grief only comes out later, after a second loss perhaps, or a period of great tension.'

'I see.' And Matty did see. A long, sloping line of desert dune and the child waiting by the window.

Robin transferred his gaze back to Matty and closed his notebook. 'The more I practise, Mrs Dysart, the less surprised I am by what I see and hear. It's important to keep one's mind open.'

'May I tell my friend what you said?' Matty seemed less pinched and huddled. 'I know she'll be grateful.'

'Please do. If she would ever like to come and see me, I'm always available.'

The black bag was another useful prop in stage-managing consultations. Robin hunted through its compartments for nothing in particular while he waited to see if anything else was forthcoming. Nothing was, and he fastened it up.

'Do you mind if I ask how old you are?' said Matty.

Robin's eyebrows shot up, and then he grinned. 'Patients often ask me that. Not much older than I imagine your husband is. I'm twenty-nine. Why?'

'I just wondered. I apologize if that was a rude question.'

'Not at all.' Robin made for the door and turned to face Matty. 'Mrs Dysart. I'm going to be rude. Are you very unhappy?'

The pinched look was replaced by one of acute embarrassment. Matty fluttered her hands.

'Goodness no,' she said. 'I'm awfully happy.'

Predictably, Robbie offended Miss Binns and no apology would mend the situation. Miss Binns therefore departed, leaving Robbie to reign undisputed.

Outwardly, nothing changed. A hoist had been installed to help Rupert change position, but papers still lay in heaps on the table and dust blanketed his war memorabilia. A strange odour also lingered and, once, Matty and Flora horrified each other by asking if it was Rupert's flesh rotting?

Appearances are deceptive. The balance in the sick room lay in Robbie's favour and she, experienced by years of ruling a nursery, took control. She knew – the family knew – that the family needed Robbie. Who else would cajole, bully, and care for Rupert with a devotion that no one else could give?

She was not a subtle person, her tactics were often crude, but they were effective. Along with the dust, Robbie's *imprimatur* now lay on the room; unmistakable, almost stifling and, as Danny had so shrewdly concluded, designed to beat off the intruder.

For his sins, Rupert was forbidden wine, pork and sticky suet puddings, and made to eat cabbage, fresh fruit and to keep the whisky down to a tot a day. To give Robbie credit, he looked better. She insisted also that the family only visit him at agreed times in the morning and afternoon. Fair enough, conceded Flora to her brother, it gave Robbie time to manage the complicated business of washing, dressing and feeding an immobilized patient.

'Now, now, Sir Rupert, you know you get tired so don't go on about the rules.'

'Bloody hell, Robbie. Do you have to cut a chap's balls off?'

'Tsk, Sir Rupert.' Robbie thrust her face over his as she brushed the greying fair hair. 'So vulgar.'

'You haven't heard anything yet.'

'Well, sir, I shall have to ask you to make sure I don't.'

'I want Danny to come and see me, Robbie. Send him up.'

'That man is not setting foot in this place again, sir. Not until you are better.'

'If I order you, Robbie.'

'Well, you can, sir, but that is the day I leave this house and settle with Miss Polly.'

Rupert's tongue, his only weapon, was no match for Robbie's cast-iron devotion. In the end, *faute de mieux*, he grew to rely on it.

For her part, Robbie grew thin and exhausted as a result of vigils kept over Rupert during his bad phases. Wrapped in a shawl, she sat enfolded by stillness, broken only by the rustle of trees outside or the high, startling call of a fox, and watched all night over the dreaming, twitching form in the bed. Every so often she administered medicine, or patted the pillow and her hand lingered on Rupert's forehead or held the thick wrist and its increasingly unpredictable pulse. At last, she knew what it was to possess.

When Robin knocked on the door after leaving Matty, Robbie was standing by the bed talking to Rupert. Propped on his pillows, Rupert's skin matched the linen and his eyes were angry and inflamed. One hand was raised as if to make a point, and Robbie was listening with her just-leave-it-to-me expression. Between them stretched intimacy.

At the doctor's entrance, Robbie looked up and it was quite obvious that the subject of their conversation had been Robin. Liberated blue serge wrinkled at Robbie's waist as she advanced towards Robin.

'Sir Rupert wishes to speak with you and I'll thank you not to upset him. I'll be back in ten minutes.' She departed with a click of her lace-up leather shoes.

The interview granted by Rupert to Robin proved a revelation to the latter. Too shrewd not to perceive that he was part of an upward progression in a society where antecedents mattered, Robin had grown a thick skin as far as his background was concerned. It did not matter to him that his brother-in-law was the blacksmith and that his father had been a village school-teacher; that his ancestors had dug in the chalk pits and banded together in tithings to farm the land. It may be that the chasms presented by the English class system were impossible to ignore, but as far as he was concerned they could be negotiated around.

Nevertheless, by the time Rupert, savage with frustration and discomfort, had finished, Robin's thick skin had been well and truly flayed.

If Dr Lofts wished to transgress his professional ethics, went Rupert's message, then it was Lofts's own affair. Rupert neither minded nor cared. However, when the doctor took it upon himself to trifle with Rupert's daughter, then the doctor should watch out. Rupert pronounced the word 'doctor' as if it levelled with 'Piccadilly pimp'. Either Dr Lofts cut off all contact with Sir Rupert's daughter from this moment forthwith, or his services would no longer be required. There was no discussion.

For a man who was seriously ill, it was an impressive performance.

White to the lips, Robin took refuge in professionalism. 'Sir. I need to check your pulse.' And it took an effort of will not to grip the thick wrist and squeeze it until it bruised.

The sound of raised voices floated in from the passage outside and the door burst open. Flora thrust herself into the room. She pushed the door shut and leant back on it, ignoring Robin's signals to go away. 'Father,' she said, 'I gather Robbie has been talking to you.'

Robin released Rupert's wrist. 'A little raised,' he noted on the chart that hung at the end of the bed. 'Have you been doing the exercises I recommended, sir?'

'Father!'

Rupert ignored Flora. 'If you mean that damned toe-wriggling and wrist-waving, no, I have not. I don't believe in it.'

'Father.' Flora went up to the bed and looked at Robin's set expression. 'What's Robbie been telling you?'

Rupert made a sawing movement with his head, and the loose flesh subsided into his neck. 'My dear Flora, Robbie has only your best interests at heart . . .' No, Flora contradicted silently. She has yours. 'Robbie was perfectly correct to come and tell me if she saw you carrying on with someone unsuitable.'

Flora made a huge effort to keep calm. 'May I remind you that you rely for your health on this so-called unsuitable person with whom I am supposed to be carrying on, Father.' Robin looked up from his position by the medicine bottles and smiled his sweet smile. The charge between them leapt across the room, inescapable and provoking. Flora's hands clenched and she thought how unfair her father was — unfair and unbelievably hurtful. She took a deep breath and made the most daring statement of her life.

'You're friends with Danny, Father. You spend more time with him than you have with us. Always have done. What's the difference? Why can't I be friendly with Dr Lofts?'

'Flora don't—' Robin sounded sharp.

For a second or two, Flora thought she had won. Then Rupert replied, 'You are more ignorant than I thought, Flora. I don't carry on with Danny. That's the difference. Do you wish me to spell out what I mean?'

'Father . . .' Flora made the mistake of glancing in the direction of the pier glass and was confronted by her own reflection: unbrushed hair, lumpy skirt, a wrinkled stocking. Suddenly her bravado drained away, leaving her unfocused and unsure. How could she take on her father? The entire family?

'I had thought, Flora,' Rupert sounded so like the cold, angry man who had dominated her childhood that she wanted to run out of the room, 'that out of a pair of witless daughters you were the one with common sense and a sense of fitness.'

The tips of Robin's ears had gone red and the sight dug a hollow somewhere in Flora's middle which churned with panicky fear at the scene. In the bed, Rupert moved restlessly.

'Are you listening to me, Flora?'

The temper note was strengthening in his voice. Flora looked at Robin for help but he shook his head. In that second, Flora understood the power that the sick exert over the well.

Robin wrote directions on the label of a new bottle of pills and placed it on the tray with the other medications. 'I will leave you now, sir,' he said. 'Please take the pills as directed. I will remind Miss Robson.'

'Get out,' said Rupert.

Panic turned into desperation and spurred Flora. 'Father, please stop.'

A flush stained Rupert's pallor. 'Dr Lofts is leaving now.'

At certain points in her childhood, Flora had been conscious of a muddle of anger and guilt in the house, no less punishing for

325

not being understood. Perhaps it was something to do with growing up? Or with her mother, whose death had bequeathed bitterness to her children? Less so to Flora than to Kit and Polly who had been older. But however Flora ducked, wove and ran, the muddle always claimed her at crucial moments.

She gazed down at the man who had ruled her life and to whom she was bound, a solid, injury-raddled and, she realized, wounded man. Rupert stared back at his daughter and Flora was appalled to see that lurking in the depths of his eyes was a plea. Then she looked at the man she loved, quietly folding up his stethoscope and stowing it in his bag. Only the tips of his ears and the hunch of his shoulder indicated just how barely he was containing his rage.

The battle was too big for Flora to fight.

'Get out, Lofts,' repeated Rupert. 'Flora, I'm cold. I want the fire lit.'

To her eternal shame, Flora let Robin go.

Kit discovered her first. Flora was crunched up on the window seat overlooking the garden. She had cried until her eyelids felt as if they had peeled away from her eyeballs.

'Budge up.' He pushed Flora's legs aside and sat down. Then he reached over and took one of her hands in his. 'Can I help?'

She turned her face towards him and Kit was shocked by her unhappiness. 'I'm so angry,' she said, pulling at her ungovernable hair.

'You look awful. Who are you angry with?'

'With Father. With you. With everyone in this – this family. With myself,' she added.

Kit sighed. 'Robbie told me about it.'

'Did she also tell you that she sneaked on me to Father?' Flora spoke through gritted teeth.

'Sooner or later,' said Kit practically, 'something would have come out. The question is, old girl, has it forced you into action you didn't want to take?'

'I don't know.'

'Try and see it from that angle, won't you? If you want to do something, make sure you want to do it.'

Flora concentrated on her face. Everything was sore. Her eyes, her mouth, her skin. 'Bloody, bloody hell.'

Kit's eyebrow shot up. 'We're two of a kind. Rotten love affairs . . .'

'Don't.' Flora moved restlessly. 'Rotten love affairs for bad eggs.'

Kit squeezed her hand. '*You*'re not rotten.'

She looked sceptical and then relaxed a trifle. 'Scrambled, rather,' she said and blew her nose.

'Rotten joke, though.' Kit dropped a kiss on her cheek. 'Poor old girl. Are you going to tell me about it?'

'There isn't much to tell.'

That was true, Kit thought. When you boiled down into words the feelings and sensations, probings, speculations and dreamings of a love affair, they did not add up to anything much. That was the paradox. Or was it tragedy?

They sat in silence for a minute or two. The sun cast a shadow over the house. Beyond it, exposed in the full sunlight was the circular lawn with the river beyond. As they watched, Matty came into view pushing a wheelbarrow. She stopped to adjust the load and bent to retrieve something from the ground. Then she lifted her face to the sun for a moment before hefting up the wheelbarrow and turning in the direction of the old rose garden. A few seconds later Ned came round the side of the house, dressed in the corduroy suit which never varied from summer to winter. His trowel was stuck into his belt and he carried a pair of shears. Matty saw Ned, stopped and they fell into conversation. Both seemed interested in the path on which they were standing. Eventually, Ned went down on one knee and began to scrape at the ground with his trowel.

Flora turned to Kit. 'What are they doing?'

'I imagine,' said Kit, 'they're trying to trace where an old path crossed that one.' He pointed to the path which led from the old rose garden. 'I found a map of the garden as it was in Mother's time and showed it to Matty this morning.'

'Really,' said Flora. 'Why? And what on earth is Matty doing with a wheelbarrow?'

'Well,' said Kit, 'Matty wants to be let loose on the garden. She seems to have made a conquest of Ned and they spend hours discussing it.'

'Matty's clever,' said Flora. 'She's found something to do.' Flora's bottom lip began to quiver again.

'So have you,' said Kit pointedly. 'Family planning?'

'Oh, that,' said Flora. 'That's over now.'

'Matty's right,' said Kit. 'We will have to tackle the garden some time.'

Flora shot her brother a look. The habit of reticence between them was ingrained, but they understood each other well enough. Flora suspected that Kit still thought about Daisy – although it had not occurred to her that he had been adulterous. With unconscious irony, she said, 'Eases the conscience, Kit?'

By this time, Matty had joined Ned on the ground and their heads were close together.

'If only it was so easy,' said Kit bleakly, but Flora was too busy contemplating her own predicament to take note.

She blew her nose. 'Kit, I'm not angry with you.'

'I know.'

'How do you know?'

'I've been through it all myself.'

It was Flora's turn to take Kit's hand. 'Sorry, I didn't mean to bring it all up again.' She pinched the tanned fingers. 'But you're quite happy now, aren't you? I mean, Matty's all right. I like her.'

'Good. So do I.'

'Then it is all right?' She searched her brother's face for reassurance. 'Do you suppose all children are in hock to their parents' wishes?' she asked.

'Listen, old girl,' said Kit. 'Only you can make the decisions, don't forget that.'

Flora thought that she had never felt so alone. 'Not if you are an unmarried daughter you can't,' she came back tartly.

'True. I'll not deny that.' Kit took her chin in his hand and swivelled her face close to his. 'Remember, you don't have to accept what Father says. You can fight. If you wish to marry this man, I will back you. Don't make the mistake I did.'

'But . . . you said Matty and you . . .' said Flora.

'Don't,' he said.

She broke in again. 'You don't understand, Kit. What I hate most of all, what I can't bear about myself, is that I wasn't sure. I wasn't sure if I was brave enough to stand up to Father if Robin asked me to marry him and I just let him go when Father was so rude. Really rude and abominable to him.'

'I know,' said Kit.

'No, you don't know,' she said, rearing up from the seat and staring wild-eyed through the window. 'There is something worse about it which makes me feel awful. It's been bothering me for a long time. You see, I wasn't sure if I could give all this up to become a doctor's wife in a tumbledown cottage. That is what was awful about it. Don't you see?'

'Oh, yes,' said Kit from behind her. 'Oh, yes, Flora, I do see.'

CHAPTER THREE

ROBIN PRESENTED his bill to Rupert with his compliments, wrote out detailed notes for his successor and sent them up to Hinton Dysart. He did so with misgivings and anger, for he had been wounded far more deeply than he cared to admit.

In one sense, however, he had been hauled back from a precipice. He suspected then, as he certainly knew now, that opposition to his marrying Flora would have been formidable and, having tasted the battle, even Robin shrank.

Nevertheless, his treatment at Rupert's hands gave him a jolt and he castigated himself for having grown smug. One look at Flora's half-defensive, half-terrified expression as she stood between her father and her lover had been enough to convince him that he had misjudged the affair. Flora was not ready to make that kind of choice, worse, perhaps never would be. There had been – was – no point in pressing the issue.

Since then, Robin had caught glimpses of her at odd intervals, riding towards Horsedown, but he made no effort to join her. Neither did she him and that hurt. Robin did not want to see her, but he wanted to know that Flora wished to see him, and he wanted the pleasure of denying her. Once she sent him a note, saying she would no longer be helping out at the surgery. Robin threw it in the wastepaper basket and did not reply – which made him feel ashamed and about two years old.

He made enquiries in the village to recruit a helper, and, since there is never any shortage of applicants to assist marriageable village doctors, was able to employ Anna Tillyard from Eweshot, to the fury of the Nether Hinton maidens.

Anna was tiny, efficient and a hard worker. She had a mass of red hair, a good complexion, and a giggle which echoed through the surgery door. She was an efficient employee and perfect for a doctor's wife. In due course, word of Anna filtered back to Flora and she found herself saddling up Guinevere for long, solitary rides which achieved nothing except to try Tyson's patience.

August came to a close with gales and floods, in which fourteen died, and with freak synchronicity the country was plunged further into financial crisis. A run on the pound reached desperate proportions and national bankruptcy was considered by the governor of the Bank of England to be only a hair's breadth away. Amid the dust of soured promises, the Labour government collapsed and a government of co-operation was formed to deal with the emergency.

' "In all modern times",' Kit quoted from *The Times* over the breakfast cups at Hinton Dysart, ' "there has never been such a party convulsion." ' He looked down the table at his wife who seemed particularly pale this morning. 'No, I suppose there hasn't. God knows what's going to happen.'

'That's what politics is,' said Matty, making one of the statements she made from time to time. They always surprised Kit. 'Convulsion, I mean.'

Kit folded the newspaper and shoved it across the table. 'Aha,' he said. 'A political philosopher.'

' "New York bankers agree to give Britain sixty million pounds in short-term credit," ' he read out some days later and, by the end of the month, reported to Matty that Ramsay MacDonald had been ousted as Labour leader.

'Money,' said Matty, ticking off dishes on Mrs Dawes's proposed weekend menu. 'Money, money.'

'Yes, money,' said Kit.

'Don't forget Aunt Susan and Daisy are arriving on Friday,' she said, as Kit headed for the Exchequer and the telephone.

'No,' said Kit, who had not.

'Dust to dust,' said Daisy to her reflection. Since the storms, a heatwave had settled on the south of the country and her hand felt burning hot as she traced the violet circle under her right eye. 'Do I see wrinkles?'

331

She spread her fingers across her cheek and pulled at the flesh under her chin, which was perfect. 'No,' she said to the image. 'I'm afraid, desperately afraid, I see something much more serious.'

There was a knock on the door and Ivy Prosser edged into the second-best guest room at Hinton Dysart with a pile of towels. The floor was a little uneven: the door banged shut and made Daisy jump.

'Sorry, Miss Chudleigh.' Ivy glared at the door. 'Mrs Chudleigh is now finished and ready, and she sent me to you.'

Ivy was now Matty's personal maid and Matty frequently lent her to her Friday-to-Monday guests. For this weekend, she had sat up late ironing her uniform and goffering the frilled apron and cap. Early that morning, half stupid with fatigue, she had set off from the cottage in Church Street to a chorus from her envious sisters – bring back any empty scent bottles or cast-offs. Ivy was now at home in the world of the well-to-do and experience had brought about in her a sea-change. It was now a confident Ivy who wielded a hairbrush and rolled stockings up sleek thighs, dreaming of the day when she would be independent.

Her capable hands smoothed and patted Daisy's underwear into folds and stowed it in lavender-scented drawers. Ivy was going to make sure that Daisy had never been served so well, for Ivy's sights were set on London.

Pretty, hard-working Ivy. Daisy's gaze drifted to the cut-glass bottles on the table. Distorted in the curve of a silver top, her face slid into vision. Hard-working Ivy, who would probably never take a silly risk or fling a challenge at established order.

Sensible Ivy.

'Shall I draw your bath, miss?' Ivy asked, grave and important.

Afterwards, Daisy sat down again at the dressing table. Her discarded underclothes lay on the chair, and she avoided looking in their direction. She felt sick and nervous.

She waited until Ivy had laid out her evening dress on the bed then asked Ivy to brush her hair. The brush strokes were soft and reverential.

'Oh, Miss Chudleigh,' she said. 'Your hair is lovely.'

Daisy's eyes slid back to the knickers. Fear rubbed in her mind, like sand in a shoe. Her throat felt dry; she swallowed and asked Ivy for a glass of water.

It helped a little, but not much.

What did you do in such circumstances? How did people cope with the outside world when inside was chaos? How would she know which of the choices in front of her was the right one? How could she be sure that her courage would see her through? For the first time in her life, Daisy was at a loss and, also for the first time, wished she was religious. 'How nice you are, Ivy,' she said mechanically.

Later, Matty knocked and put her head round the door. 'Do you need anything?'

Cyanide, thought Daisy savagely. Failing that, morphine.

Gowned in a black Dove creation, which suited her rather well, Matty checked the room for biscuits and writing paper before turning her full attention on Daisy.

For once, the sight of Matty flattened Daisy's fighting spirit. Go away, she thought. Matty made her feel both guilty and angry – particularly with herself – and she did not want to deal with either at this low moment, between her bath and the first cocktail.

Matty felt the old apprehension slide into her stomach and settle: how much less clever, less interesting, less beautiful than Daisy she was. Would always be.

Kit and Daisy together on the *Île de France*, hooted her demon, and wrenched at the softest part of her heart. What had they been doing? Kit had not mentioned the voyage at all – nor had Matty asked.

Emma, Emma, *make* me stop it. Matty smoothed the black dress over her hips and asked, 'Are you sure you don't need anything, Daisy?'

'No, thank you.' Daisy dipped a swansdown puff into the powder. 'You have made it all perfect.' She dabbed gracefully at her face.

'Hold the scarf so,' Matty instructed Ivy, 'so the powder does not go over Miss Chudleigh's clothes.'

And stop being such a damn perfect hostess, Daisy screamed silently.

'Isn't it hot?' Daisy began to apply her lipstick.

'Just like France was, do you remember?' said Matty and checked herself. Why had she mentioned France? She took refuge in the mirror, assessed her reflection and adjusted one neat diamond earring.

Daisy had a vision of snatching them off the small pink ears. 'What happened to your mother's earrings, the ones I liked?'

'They're in the bank. You were right, Daisy. They were too big for me. Do you want to borrow them sometimes?'

'No.' Daisy sounded savage. It struck Matty then that her cousin looked odd: brittle, anxious and white round the lips.

'Are you feeling all right?'

No, went Daisy's private monologue, I have never been so frightened in all my life. She looked up at Matty's image in the mirror and forced a smile. 'Absolutely fine. Never better. Who's coming tonight?'

Matty stepped back from the mirror and swooshed out her skirt in a circle.

'Not bad,' said Daisy, powdering her shoulders and arms.

Matty sat down on the pretty French *bateau lit* and crossed her legs. A high-heeled sandal dangled from her foot and Daisy focused on the perfectly applied squares of nail varnish on Matty's toes. How civilized they were, and how she detested them with an uncivilized passion.

'Who's coming? Well, it's a sort of celebration of Kit being back, the house being finished, and you and Aunt Susan being here, of course—'

The cosy domesticity of Matty's plans was suddenly too much for Daisy, and she cut Matty off. 'Excuse me. Ivy, could you pass me the jewellery case in the corner there.'

Matty took the hint and stood up. Matty was learning, thought Daisy, and it occurred to her that her cousin – the moulting cuckoo – was, had been, more formidable than she had allowed herself to imagine.

Matty's hair was growing and tonight she had pulled it back

from her face with a pair of enamelled combs. The style suited her, and forced the observer to take account of the soft brown eyes so often hidden by her hats.

'Since it's so hot, cocktails are on the terrace,' she said.

Daisy was left staring at the contents of the top tray in her jewellery case. A diamond brooch shaped like a bee. A pair of diamond clips, not very good. An emerald pendant on a gold chain. She picked up the bee, which caught in the light slanting through the window, and heard Ivy's indrawn breath at the glitter. Daisy pinned it onto her bodice. Beneath the exquisite, powdered surface, grains of sand rubbed and buffeted, and hurt.

Kit ripped off a ruined collar and reached for another. He hated them. Starch was unnecessary and it was the middle of a heatwave.

What was it Prince Abdullah used to say? Calmness was achieved through inner discipline. Through the contemplation of a chosen object of beauty – like the rose, my friend, or the lily. Look at them, hold them in the mind, and examine their perfection cell by cell, then all things will fall into place.

Take a look at yourself, rather, Kit addressed the shaving mirror. What do you see? The face and eyes of a man who is not satisfied and knows he should be. The face of an adulterer.

Last night, Max had telephoned and said, Come to Iraq. Kit had said no, there were family commitments. Max had been adamant. There's plenty of time, I don't plan to go until next spring, he argued. And it won't be for long, a couple of months. Surely your wife won't mind. Give her a chance to do her own fluttering.

Matty would mind, but probably would not say anything for that was not Matty's way. Don't ask her, said Max unfeelingly. Marriage, Kit felt obliged to point out to his bachelor friend, did not work like that. He was not entirely joking. I'll expect you, said Max, and cut off the call.

Kit tackled the collar again, successfully this time. Did Matty suspect anything, he asked himself, and keep silent because that was her way? Guilt had a strange way of dressing things up.

Sometimes he caught his wife looking at him and immediately concluded: she knows.

She knows.

What? That each moment of loving Daisy intensified every sense in his body. Brought him wonder, tenderness and awe. Passion and profound joy. That Daisy had given him the sharpest pain, the sharpest happiness, and an understanding that the human spirit was divided into compartments, each separate from the other.

The knowledge that he had given these things to her.

Oh, Daisy. He sought to absorb her, all of her, into himself, down to the tiny crease of flesh under her arm.

Kit pulled on his jacket and went in search of his wife.

A White Lady in one hand, Geoffrey Handal turned to Archie Ritchie, a fellow hunter. 'Gold chip, did you say?' he articulated into Archie's ear, meaning Matty.

'Absolutely.'

Handal was about to say something when Daisy made a late entrance onto the terrace. 'Good God,' he said instead. 'Who is she?'

'Daisy Chudleigh. Mrs Dysart's cousin. And that chap's sister.' Archie held out his glass for a second head-slugging dose of cocktail and indicated Marcus. 'From London.' Archie nursed his refill and observed Kit stand up from the stone balustrade and Harry Goddard, who was sitting beside Susan Chudleigh, leap to his feet. 'And all that means,' he added.

'Daisy darling.' Harry barely knew Daisy, but he surged forward and kissed her. Laughing, Daisy kissed him back, and then Kit's hand rested briefly on her forearm as he made the introductions.

A whiff of lavender and thyme drifted up from the parterre below the terrace where Matty had placed pots of both, mixed with the exotic evening smell of *Nicotiana*. During the day, heat had settled down over the valley as it had for days now. Up by Whitebridge House the stream was reduced to a trickle, and at

Long Copse the leaf mulch under the trees was dry and powdery. Desperate for their evening drink, swallows dipped and swooped over stubbled fields at Itchel. A milky white light tipped with red stretched across the low horizon as the sun slid below the tree line.

'Dinner, Uncle Ambrose,' said Matty, and waited for her uncle to take her in.

Thirty guests sat down to eat at the rectangular table, polished to mirror brightness. The walls were painted buttery cream, and set off the gilding on the plasterwork. Candles had been placed on the sideboard and at the centre of the table and wall lights cast a pale yellow glow across the curtains.

'Very, very advanced,' said Tufty Bostock as he saw Susan into her chair.

'Yes,' replied Susan tightly, comparing it to what she now perceived as her dull dining room at Number 5 Upper Brook Street. Truly, if consulted, she would have had no idea that Matilda had it in her to decorate a laundry basket, let alone a country house, and she suppressed an urge to say something cutting to a wilting youth lucklessly assigned to her left hand.

Matty had Archie Ritchie on one side, and Harry Goddard, the scamp, on the other. Daisy sat between Geoffrey Handal and Harry – Matty had played fair with the seating. Kit, however, had Susan on one side, and Archie's mother on the other. Flora sat beside Marcus who was making a flourish of unfolding her napkin and bringing her up to date on the latest movements of his regiment.

Matty looked round. Cracks no longer spidered the ceiling. Mould had been banished. Pictures hung in the right places and experts had restored their resonance. Somehow (an effort of will?) Matty had brought this about with a sentence uttered on the Calais–Dover ferry.

I think you should marry me.

She unfolded her napkin. The candlelight burnt into the corner of one eye and suddenly she was reminded of a stage set, ringed by darkness.

'Mrs Dysart?' Archie enquired, alarmed by Matty's eyes which had grown dark and tense. His heart sank for he did not relish the plod of a neurotically inclined female for several courses.

Matty turned to him. 'Mr Ritchie,' she said, sending a puff of rose scent in his direction, 'I must have been daydreaming. Forgive me.' She checked that the soup was being served and then, 'Tell me,' she said, 'I hear your record is unmatched out hunting.'

Archie relaxed, but before he could answer Tufty Bostock's loud voice rose over the conversation. ' "Threadbare Thirties"? Did you read that in the newspaper?'

'Bolsheviks,' said Archie to Susan. 'I always said Ramsay MacDonald was a Bolshevik.'

'Come on, sir,' said Kit with a smile. 'The Bolsheviks are quite different from pleasant Mr MacDonald. I should warn you Labour's base is solid and growing.'

'Don't be too sure, my boy.' Tufty gave discreet encouragement to the hired wine waiter. 'The red peril will end with another war.'

'Good God, we haven't recovered from the last one,' said Susan. 'Only last week we took a party to see *All Quiet on the Western Front* at the cinema. Very trying, I thought.'

'I haven't seen it,' said Kit.

Daisy quoted at Harry, not quite accurately. ' "Weary, burnt out, rootless, we shall be superfluous even to ourselves." That's how the soldier saw himself when he came home. But I'm sure that does not apply to any of us here.' She gave one of her irresistible smiles and the men's gazes fastened on her. 'You were all heroes.'

Kit imagined his father lying upstairs listening to the hum of their conversation. Had he seen himself as superfluous?

An echo sounded in Matty's memory. Of what, and of whom? Of Edwin, she remembered, Hesther's brother, who wrote such passionate . . . *feeling* letters. He had said something like: 'The war will make a gap between us. When I return we will be on different sides.'

'People do drone on about the war,' Marcus muttered to Flora. 'It's unhealthy, all this looking back.'

For the first time in weeks, Flora laughed. 'You're right, Marcus,' she said.

At her end of the table Matty asked Archie, 'Have you heard about a series of paintings in the memorial chapel at a village called Burghclere? By an artist called Spencer. He's painting the war as he saw it.'

'No,' said Archie, his fears taking a new turn.

'I thought I might visit them one day. I hear they're remarkable,' said Matty.

Across the sweet peas, Kit met Daisy's troubled eyes. I am at one end of the tunnel, she seemed to say. And I want to join you at the other. Hold on, said his. I can't help you, but hold on.

Because it was so warm, the guests were invited to take their coffee out onto the terrace. Some elected to stay away from the midges and remained in the drawing room, others sat outside in wicker chairs and balanced coffee cups on their knees. A few strolled over the lawn towards the river. The coffee was strong and bitter, the way Kit preferred it, and Mrs Dawes had produced excellent *petits fours*.

Hot and still, the night layered mysteriously over the garden, in the way of Indian-summer nights. Light streamed out from the drawing room and cut into the darkness. From the garden filtered the aroma of tobacco, a murmur of conversation, the quick flurry of an animal, and an occasional splash from the river.

Daisy sat next to Kit. She picked up a marzipan apple, and Kit watched her bite into it. Her teeth were white against the red dye.

'Daisy. Can we talk for five minutes?'

She leant back in the chair and her bracelets clinked. The light from the drawing room caught her face and, with a flash of self-hatred, he realized she was suffering. 'Daisy?'

'I'll come.'

Once across the lawn, Kit tucked his hand under her elbow and drew her close. They walked in silence, the yew a dark crescent. Despite the heat, Daisy shivered.

'The garden feels strange at night,' she said. 'I'm not so sure I like it.'

'What's wrong?' he asked. 'I can feel something is wrong.'

339

She shook her head. 'Nothing. It's just the garden.'

'You're lying, Daisy.'

'I never tell lies.'

'Yes, you do.' The memory of crumpled sheets, an orange scarf, a rolling pot of ointment and the evidence that Daisy had been a virgin flashed through his mind like a film sequence.

'Let's go this way,' said Daisy. She slipped past him and ran down the stone steps.

'Daisy,' he called as the white shimmer of her dress caught in the moonlight.

'Here,' she answered, from the opening in the yew circle.

They passed Marcus and Flora coming back from the river. Daisy waved at them. The heat made Kit sweat into his dinner jacket and he took it off.

'Not that way,' he called to Daisy as she reached the scrub. 'Don't go through there.' His patent leather shoes slipped on the dry lawn. 'This bit hasn't been touched for years.'

But he was wrong. Daisy pointed at the path. 'That's been used recently. Look.'

'No,' he said and tried to grab her. 'Don't, please don't go there, darling. No.'

But Daisy was not listening. She walked through the opening where the scrub had been used to conceal the path and along the birch avenue.

'Come back,' he called, but when he saw it was useless, he went after her.

Daisy's high heels were much less suitable than Kit's shoes, but she scrambled somehow over dry lumps of earth and arrived at the edge of the garden. Down she went, down the slope towards the stone woman eternally guarding her stone child.

'Daisy, where on earth are you?' Kit ran into the clearing and looked down. He stopped in his tracks.

'My God,' he said, as the moonlight revealed the roses, the clematises, the foxgloves and the flaring, dying trumpets of two late lilies. 'My God.'

Daisy disengaged the hem of her dress from a trailing stem of catmint. 'I thought you said no one came here.'

340

'Matty!' said Kit slowly, and stared at the restored garden. 'This must be Matty's work. I should have known. This is exactly the sort of thing she would do.'

He searched in his pocket for his cigarette case and Daisy, pitying his evident shock, laid a hand over his. Kit's was unsteady and she waited a second or two before opening the case for him. 'Tell me what's wrong.'

'Thank you.' Kit inhaled and blew out smoke.

The smell made Daisy feel nauseous and she moved away. 'Do you have a handkerchief, by any chance?'

He passed her one and she blew her nose hard and retched into its folds, but he was too preoccupied to notice. After a while, he threw away the cigarette.

'Daisy. I'm sorry.' He folded his arms around her body and she could feel him shaking. 'None of us ever come here. I'll explain one day.'

She was puzzled, but made no move to break free. 'How long is it since you were here?'

He pulled her tighter and inhaled her smell. 'Ages. Years.'

'How long?' He dropped his chin onto her shoulder and was silent. 'How long, Kit?'

The answer dragged from him. 'Since I was eleven.'

'Why?' she whispered and looked up at the flowers peacefully enshrouded in the darkness.

There was no answer except for a sharp, indrawn breath. Daisy reached out to touch the statue's face. It was cold and grainy under her finger. She traced the roundness of the woman's maternal haunch and her own needs resurfaced. She swivelled in his arms to face him. 'Kit. I've got to talk to you.'

But he was looking over her shoulder at the statue, anguish and horror fighting in his face. Daisy felt her own tighten with disappointment.

'Oh, Kit,' she said, realizing that he was going to let her down for a second time. Then with the self-abnegation of love she asked herself, What does it matter? 'I love you, Kit,' she said and pulled him towards her. 'Tell me what's wrong.'

With an inarticulate sound between a groan and a sigh, Kit

buried his head in her shoulder. 'Nothing, Daisy. Nothing at all. Just a goose over my grave.' He muttered something else into the nape of her neck, which she did not hear, and held her so tightly that her breasts hurt. He had not meant to touch her ever again. But shock, the darkness and the flowers removed his defences. After a minute, he pulled free and cupped her chin in his hand.

'I wasn't going to do this,' he said. 'It's all over as we agreed. It has to be.'

'Is it?' she whispered.

'I can't bring myself to say it,' he said.

'It is,' she said.

Frightened, exhilarated, disappointed, Daisy's hope died.

Kit pushed down her shoulder strap, peeled away the damp silk chemise underneath, and bent to kiss the exposed breast that gleamed lily pale in the moonlight.

'Delicious coffee,' said Archie who had forgotten his initial doubts about Matty. In fact, he had enjoyed the evening: Matty had been ready to agree to all his opinions.

'I can't live without good coffee.'

'Quite right,' said Archie. Matty tucked her handkerchief into her evening bag. 'You are not at all like your cousin, Mrs Dysart.'

'No,' said Matty, rather sharply for her. 'Not at all.'

Where was Daisy? Matty looked up and realized that neither she nor Kit was present and nerve ends sent a warning. She got to her feet and smoothed the Dove gown over her hips. Like a doll, thought Archie idly, but when she looked down at him he found himself looking into the undoll-like eyes of a real woman who was angry.

'I must check that there is more of this delicious coffee to give you,' she said.

Is that the way of it? thought Archie, having worked out that both his host and the girl from London were missing. Dear, dear, how predictable things were.

Matty held the skirt of her gown in one hand and ran down

the kitchen passage, past the Exchequer. The door was ajar revealing piles of paper on the desk and a forgotten teacup on the window sill.

It should have been cleared away, she thought.

In the kitchen Mrs Dawes was busy decanting left-over food at the table. She looked weary, and Matty knew she should go in and say something. But not now. Not now.

She let herself out of the back door. Away from the terrace, it was quiet outside in the kitchen yard and Matty caught the sharp, feral smell of a fox which had been rooting in the compost buckets. Something, someone, moved, and Matty turned her head sharply. The moon shone directly onto the path leading into the garden. Dressed in a blue smocked cotton dress, hair shining, the girl ran ahead of Matty.

And Matty, knowing that she should be with her guests, knowing that she was courting disaster, that it was best to leave alone, knowing all these things, followed the figure, her heart soft with fear.

'Wait for me,' she called, stumbling down the cleared path towards the garden. *Her* garden. 'Wait for me.'

The moon drew pointed fingers on the path. There was the spot under the beech trees where Matty had knelt and grubbed up laurel roots with splitting fingernails. There was the place she had dug until her back shrieked in protest, filled the hole with compost, steadied a hornbeam's roots and driven in the stake. There she had slashed, cut and trampled on the nettles and weeds, and there she had planted anemones, daffodils and a scented viburnum.

At the edge of the garden, the girl stopped and turned. Matty gasped. The patched light had turned the small face almost transparent: a curious, deathly bloodlessness that filled Matty with a sense of unutterable waste.

'Who are you?' she asked desperately.

Anguish darkened the blue eyes, tightened the childish mouth and traced lines between the thin nose and golden hairline. Seemingly irresolute, or casting deep within herself, the child hovered at the edge of the garden. Then she glided down the slope, flitting on booted feet with a swish and a swing of blue cotton.

The sexual parts of a lily are obvious. Huge, swollen and sticky with pollen, they wait for the bee's attention or the gardener's cross-pollinating brush. The Madonna lily – *Lilium candidum* – has a strong claim to be the oldest domesticated flower, and the loveliest. It is found on Cretan vases; it was known to the Assyrians and carried west by the Phoenicians. Possibly the Romans brought it to England and, possibly, it was the poet Virgil who gave this lily its name. The Venerable Bede made the lily the symbol of the Virgin's resurrection but also the bulbs were used for the most earthbound ailments: boils, baldness, dropsy, erysipelas and quinsy.

Stainless white through which shines the likeness of gold. Pure and yet carnal. Beautiful and gross. Obedient to cultivation, yet eluding the cultivator – for the scent of the lily has never been captured. And dies with the flower.

Like the slug who flings himself over the sand to feed on their white and gold and suffers a thousand razor slashes to do so, Matty, who had dug their beds, guarded them, staked, cherished and fed the lilies, was drawn by the child towards their dying trumpets and their heavy, selfish perfume.

The child dodged around the stone statue. And vanished.

Under Kit's, Daisy's long, slender body seemed even more so than Matty remembered. Her dress lay sloughed beside her on the grass, her long arms were twisted around Kit's neck and her legs raised to take in his body.

Kit's face was hidden, but Daisy's was thrown back on the turf. Dizzy from the heat and from running, Matty, nevertheless, saw clearly the parted mouth and the beautiful face on which was mixed passion, shame and triumph in equal part.

HARRY

I like to think that at the cusp between two seasons, time pauses: nothing changes, one plant is suspended in dying, another in taking its place. Such is the moment between high summer and that cool displacement of air in the evenings which warns that the wheel has turned a ratchet towards autumn.

Shakespeare, who had these things right, chose the image of two buckets passing one another to illustrate the anatomy of power. First one king is up, then the other. So it can be said of the garden.

September's cool nights and dew-drenched gardens suggest winter — only to up-end our ideas with a succession of hot, luscious days. I don't object. The lilies are dead, blackberries ripen in the hedges, the scent of windfall apples in the orchard fills the air, and the sun feels hot and strong on my back as I pick fruit crops and fuss over flowerbeds with secateurs.

In September, I dispatch Thomas outdoors to plant bulbs in the cottage garden, which he does with a reasonable grace. Full of content, and the memory of the good years we have shared, I watch him potter up and down the path and give thanks that I have been dealt with so generously by life.

Up at the house, I contemplate the stars of the September garden. Pink nerines, autumn crocuses and the powder blue of the agapanthus. I take out my notebook and record that we should move this hosta, or that iris, try this experiment . . . grow the clematis 'Étoile Violette' through a dull green tree . . . eradicate the marigolds . . . I write it down because memory is never as precise as you imagine. Certainly not my memory.

Last year I forgot to put in the asters, so essential to prolonging the autumn flowering season. The autumn spectrum tends to red and gold but with their whites, pinks, lavenders and mauves, the perennial asters (introduced from America in the seventeenth century) nicely contradict this rule. They are obliging plants, offer themselves in a range of heights, will grow in both light and shade — and Thomas will tell you I never like to bypass a willing flower.

My last thoughts for September rest with the sedum. The most generous and showy form is 'Autumn Joy', whose flat pink plate-like blossoms act as a beacon for bees. (If you leave the dead flower heads till the frosts you will be rewarded by an ice-sprinkled fantasy in the flowerbed.) I love watching the bees cloud the flower; busy and pollen-filled. The young sedum is no trouble, but the older plant tends to splay outwards — a bit like myself, I always think.

CHAPTER FOUR

A FTERWARDS MATTY could never be sure how she came to be lying on the river bank. She was wringing wet, hair trailing over her face and her mouth tasting of rot, gravel and sour vomit. Mud spread into her eyes and ears.

She remembered only the hot scent of lilies, Daisy's sudden cry as she saw Matty, Kit's bent, absorbed head and running. Running away. Running on high heels up the river path towards the splintering jetty. She remembered the crunch of stone, a splash and the piercing cry of a disturbed bird. There was a smell of wet vegetation, the slap of water on her skin and mud sprouting silkily through her fingers. Then, she had spun round and round, the black Dove gown billowing, and plunged into the matching blackness.

Above all, Matty remembered the stones pressing into her face as someone thumped hard on her back. Danny shouting, 'Get 'elp. There's been an accident' – and of how it did not surprise her to be hovering between death and a ridiculous desire to ask if her guests had been offered more coffee.

Matty had known all along that she did not deserve happiness.

'My goodness, you gave us a fright.' Robbie plumped up the pillows and wedged Matty upright. 'Open your mouth now, please.' She inserted a spoon between Matty's lips and then pushed Matty's jaw shut. 'Swallow, please.'

If ever I have sinned, thought Matty, wearily picking her way back to consciousness out of drugged sleep, this surely must be my punishment. Robbie and a medicine spoon. 'Time?' she whispered through a throat so sore it was raw.

'Four o'clock in the afternoon. You've been asleep for some

time. Very natural, considering.' Robbie did not refer to the hideous business of resuscitation, the bowls and tubes, the sounds, the touch-and-go of the first half-hour.

'What happened?'

Robbie pulled down her sleeves, fastened the cuffs and sat down heavily on the bed with the determination of a professional interrogator charged with a mission to gather information. 'You tell me, Mrs Kit.' She leant over and Matty's vision was filled by the moon face and hedge of hair. 'Did you trip in the dark? Those high heels? You can tell me, Mrs Kit.'

Matty closed her eyes and ran her tongue over her sore lips. 'I don't know.' Fragmented memories sifted like blown dust through her mind.

'Mr Kit can't make out why you were up by that part of the river in the first place.'

'Who found me?'

Robbie pursed her lips. 'That Danny person,' she said. 'I don't know why he was in the grounds. He said he heard a noise and came to check up. He found you floating in the water by the boathouse.'

Deceptive and incomplete, the first recovered memory drove a needle into Matty's chest. I can cope with that, she thought. Then, as the rest assembled – the hot night, the girl . . . Kit and Daisy twined together – the needle turned into a sword which smashed through bone and nerve. Matty closed her eyes: somehow she had to endure it. Finger on Matty's pulse, Robbie checked off the pulse beats against the watch pinned onto her chest in the way she had observed Miss Binns doing it.

'There, there,' she said, her tone a mixture of curiosity and excitement at the drama. Matty's eyes remained closed and she continued, 'Fancy. I'm going to have my hands full with two invalids. I haven't been so busy since Mr Kit and the girls were young. I don't know how I'm going to manage.' She meant exactly the opposite.

Because she knew it was important to put the record straight, Matty summoned the remnants of her energy. 'I must have fallen in,' she croaked – and allowed herself to believe it. She opened her eyes and willed Robbie to look directly at her. 'Wasn't that silly of me?' Robbie was silent. 'Wasn't it, Miss Robson?'

The older woman gave in. 'Yes,' she said, reluctant to bypass drama but aware of her duty, which was to preserve the Dysart reputation. 'You must have done. That landing stage is a disgrace. I've warned Sir Rupert about it for years.'

Half an hour later when Robbie went downstairs for her tea, Flora came and sat by Matty's bed.

'Poor darling,' she said, in her best conversational manner to conceal her shock and concern. 'Father sends his regards and says hurry up and get better as no one reads to him like you. He says you and he are two of a bloody kind. Careless.' Flora took Matty's hand. 'How are you feeling?'

'My throat is hellish.'

'Aha.' Flora nodded. 'That must have been the tube Dr Lofts put down.' Conscious that her interest made for a certain ghoulishness, she supplied the medical detail. 'Robin had to make sure you hadn't swallowed anything terrible in the river.' She rubbed Matty's hand hard. 'Awful for you. You might have died.'

'Dr Lofts?' Matty's croak was awful. 'How did ... I thought ...'

'Well.' For the life of her, Flora could not prevent her eyes brightening. At the same time she managed to look both shamefaced and defiant. 'It was an emergency and he *is* the nearest doctor. Besides, I thought you liked him. Don't you?'

'Yes.' Flora was forced to bend over to hear Matty properly. 'I do.'

A flush stormed into Flora's cheeks and she ducked her head. 'I mean, he's so good with people, don't you think? Not that it's any of my business. So gentle, though.' Too preoccupied with the reappearance of Robin to ask questions, Flora would have continued in the same vein but Matty interrupted.

'Flora. Listen. Please.'

Flora edged the chair closer to the bed. 'What is it, old thing? I don't think you should be talking too much.'

Matty took a deep shuddering breath. 'Daisy?' she asked. 'Aunt Susan and Uncle Ambrose? Have they gone?'

Flora's hair was a halo in the evening sun; beneath it her blue eyes were perplexed and affectionate. 'They went this morning,' she said. 'Daisy felt they should get out of the way. Besides, she wasn't feeling very well. It was the best thing and, frankly, they were a nuisance. Did you . . .?' Flora hesitated to ask Matty because it did not seem likely, but perhaps a brush with death made people feel different. 'I don't suppose you wanted to see her.'

'No.'

'That's all right, then. I didn't think you would. And Daisy did look very odd. Perhaps she's sickening for something.'

'And the other guests?'

'They left as soon as possible. I think they were all very shocked. I must say, Matty, it *was* quite dramatic. Picture the scene. Kit was holding you in his arms. You were dripping all over the terrace looking like Ophelia and Kit was as white as a sheet. Your aunt Susan screamed, Daisy chose that moment to faint, and Danny was staggering around, because he'd been at the whisky, leaving wet footprints all over the carpet. Naturally . . .' Flora could not resist an opportunity to bring his name into the conversation, 'we telephoned Robin, I mean Dr Lofts. There was nothing else for it.'

'Kit?'

'He's been in and out while you were sleeping. I think he's all right. I can never tell with Kit. Would you like to see him?'

'What do you think people are saying, Flora?'

Flora struggled between honesty and the lessons she had learnt from Robin on patient care. 'Nothing too terrible. After all, it was an accident.'

'Yes. It was.'

'Did you wish to see Kit?'

Matty turned her head towards the window and did not answer. Troubled by the undercurrents, Flora watched her for a minute and then tiptoed away.

During the night, Matty's temperature rose sharply and Robin was again called in. He diagnosed acute shock, possibly pneumonia, perhaps a recurrence of rheumatic fever, but it was too

350

early to tell. The following day she was no better, and Robin began to talk about hospital.

In the early hours of the second night, Robbie was roused from her chair by Matty's groans and mutters. She sponged her down, gave her lemonade to drink and, with an effort, Matty raised her head from the pillow where, in her fevered fancy, nightmares clustered on the lace edging waiting to leap.

'There,' said Robbie almost tenderly, and her plait of pepper-and-salt hair swung over her shoulder. 'There's a good girl.'

And because she was ill and lonely and hurt beyond words, Matty forgot she did not like or trust Robbie, and clung to her hand for comfort.

'Robbie . . .' she whispered. Robbie's expression took on a tinge of triumph, for Matty had always called her Miss Robson. 'Robbie. I can't get to sleep unless I know.'

Robbie spooned more lemonade between Matty's lips. 'What do you want to know?'

Matty's bird hands plucked at the sleeve of Robbie's uniform. 'Why does no one go into Lady Dysart's garden?'

A drop fell onto the sheet and Robbie made a fuss of fetching a towel. She scrubbed at the patch. 'Don't you know, Mrs Kit?' and Matty could tell she was enjoying her advantage. 'Surely you do? Hasn't he told you?'

'No. He hasn't.'

Robbie paused for fuller effect. 'Lady Dysart died there.'

'Mother.' Daisy knelt by the chintz armchair in the drawing room of Number 5, Upper Brook Street. 'Mother.'

Susan put down her fountain pen, looked up from the account book and, alerted by Daisy's tone, which did not suggest good news, stiffened. 'What is it, Daisy?' she answered, anxious to avoid unpleasantness.

As she talked, Daisy clung to the back of the chair for support. 'Mother, I'm going to have a baby. It will be born in the spring. May, I think.'

My God, thought Susan, her eyes snapping shut with shock,

this is the result of all my efforts. She sank back onto the cushions. 'You little fool,' she said softly. 'You little thankless fool. I thought I could have trusted you.' She opened her eyes. 'If you couldn't control yourself, why at least weren't you careful?'

'You've got to help me.'

Her mother's eyes refocused. 'Of course I have to help you, Daisy. What else would I do?'

'I didn't know,' said Daisy truthfully, and let out a sigh of relief. She pressed her hand to her stomach which, these days, was permanently at war with itself, levered herself into the chair, decided that made her feel worse and stood up again. 'I had no idea what feeling sick all the time was like,' she said, one hand on the mantelpiece. 'It's impossible to think of anything but your body.'

'I thought there was something odd about you.' Susan reached for her address book and began to leaf through it.

Daisy picked up the box of Bryant and May matches lying beside the reproduction statuette of Canova's *Three Graces*, and rolled it between her fingers. Round and round. 'Aren't you going to ask the obvious question?'

'Be quiet, Daisy. I want to think.' Susan did not look up.

'Don't you want to know who the father is?' Daisy had a hysterical thought that she was participating in some madly modern play where no one connected with anyone else.

'It's irrelevant who the father is,' said Susan. 'You won't be having it. But I imagine Kit Dysart isn't a million miles away from the problem. And I suppose all that nonsense with Matilda in the river was something to do with it. It would have been too much to hope that Tim was the culprit who at least could have married you. Now, I'm not sure that Brayfield still practises.'

'Practises?'

'For goodness sake, don't repeat things.' Susan marked the 'B' section in the address book with her finger. 'Harley Street, Daisy. Don't be stupid. You must know what I mean.'

Feeling better now that the confession was over, Daisy stood upright. 'I'm not stupid, Mother, and I have no intention of paying a visit to your man in Harley Street.'

It took a minute or two for the implications to sink into Susan. 'Great God,' she said, staring social ruin in the face. 'Have you gone mad?'

'No, I don't think so,' said Daisy. 'But I am frightened. About coping. About having it.'

'I have never heard such nonsense. You can't possibly keep a baby. You'll be branded a trollop, admittedly by women who are no better themselves, but at least they're discreet about this sort of thing.' Susan seldom appeared agitated – in fact Daisy could not think of one instance when her mother's shiny carapace had been breached – but Daisy's news had succeeded in making her manicured hand shake as she reached for a cigarette. 'You have no right to think of exposing us like that.'

'I can't kill it,' said Daisy flatly.

'My dear Daisy, you won't be the first or the last.'

Daisy walked up and down the cluttered drawing room. 'How much did you love Father when you married him?'

'Very much.' Susan was an expert liar but, in this instance, she did not sound convincing, so she repeated it. 'Very much.'

'Describe what you felt.'

Susan threw her daughter a look which said, I'd better humour you. 'Well. Your father was very suitable. He promised to look after me. He was pleasant and good-tempered and I wanted to be married. Your father has been all of these things, of course, and considerate.'

Daisy thought of her stiff-collared father, his perpetual frown and the half-hearted conversation made over breakfast in a concession to fatherhood. Yes, Ambrose had been a father who did his best, and she was not ungrateful.

Daisy stopped prowling, and held her stomach. 'Did you feel as awful as I do when you were having Marcus and me?'

'Yes.' Susan was not one for sharing intimacies and she did not elaborate.

'The sickness comes in waves. Like being on a boat.'

Like being on a boat.

'Will you be quiet, Daisy.'

Daisy moved away from the cigarette smoke and stood

under the open window. 'Matty doesn't know about the baby, Mother.'

'Daisy ...' All Susan's cleverly acquired, cold-heartedly applied social arts went into her plea. 'This is serious. You have *got* to be sensible. Listen to me. I am your mother and I know the world. It will kill your father, give him a heart attack or something, and the scandal will affect business. You can't keep this baby.' Susan perceived she was not making progress. 'You can't be so thoughtless.'

'Do you know what happens when I see Kit?' Daisy asked the window pane. 'When I see him across the room, at Ascot, at a ball, wherever, the breath leaves my body, Mother. That's how it is with me.'

'Oh, Daisy.' The armour-plated Susan almost sobbed. 'This is suicide. This is selfishness—' She seized on a straw. 'Does he know about it?'

'No.'

'Then tell him, for God's sake. He'll tell you what's what.'

'No.' Daisy was in the grip of a combination of exaltation and nausea, which had worked on her until she was light-headed and dizzy from the notion of sacrifice and the world well lost for love. 'Falling in love freed me, I think.' Daisy faced her mother, still rolling the matchbox over and over in her hand. 'It freed me from myself, and all the torment and anguish I have felt since cannot take that away. I will not do anything to harm his baby.' She touched her stomach. 'And I've decided not to tell him either.'

'Think of Marcus. It will ruin his standing in the regiment.'

Daisy raised her head and Susan was reminded of a saint imprinted onto stained glass at the moment of religious ecstasy – impassioned, tunnel-visioned and immovably obstinate.

'Get rid of it,' she repeated. 'Marry Tim and have another one quickly.'

Daisy shook her head and there was pity for her mother in her face. Slowly, the address book slipped from Susan's grasp onto the carpet.

'Perhaps I will marry Tim in the end,' Daisy said thoughtfully.

'But I am not going to kill Kit's baby. That's where you're going to have to help me.'

'You are a fool, then,' said Susan bitterly. 'A weak, selfish fool.'

Churned up, frightened by her own daring, Daisy said, 'Don't you see? It isn't weakness at all. In choosing this way, by giving myself a choice, I have become strong.'

'No,' said Susan. 'I don't see.'

Guilt has several effects and one leads into another. Each long day while Matty lay burning with pneumonia ratified this uneven mental state for Kit. His first response was an evasion, a shabby hope: perhaps Matty had not seen Daisy and him in the garden and it *was* an accident. His second was anger. How dare Matty make such a public act – such a destructive act? His third was a despairing acknowledgement that certain events recycled, repeated, resurfaced, and were inescapable.

His fourth was to put as great a distance as possible between him, Matty and the house. Of course, he could do no such thing and Kit's dreams were jumbled with images of smooth-branched gum arabic trees, of sand and raging thirst.

Instead guilt drove him into the sick room to watch over his restless wife and to share the night vigils with Robbie. Left on his own for those troubled hours, he nursed a tumbler of whisky and read. More often than not, he found himself staring at nothing. Details of the bedroom – rose chintz curtains, satin eiderdown, lace-edged sheets – etched onto his memory for ever.

Thus Kit experienced the catharsis of watching over a sickbed where every priority except one is leached away. In the shadow of the nightlight, he picked over the past and saw how blind he had been, saw how passion had made him selfish. But why, he asked himself, endlessly, had he not married Daisy?

Would he do the same again? Kit stared into his glass and tried to piece together strands of truth in the muddle, understand the motivations that drove him. Of course, whisky did not give good answers. It never does.

'Robbie?' Matty usually woke up for a drink and she was stirring now.

Kit put down his glass and got to his feet. Matty never asked for him when she woke. Why should she? But sometimes he hoped that she would – because it would make him feel better. 'It's Kit, Matty. Hang on. I'm coming.'

Kit poured barley water into a glass and moistened her lips with his fingertip. 'Be a good girl and drink this.' He eased a teaspoon of liquid between the drained lips. 'Just a little.' Matty swallowed. 'And again.'

He eased her head gently back onto the pillow and pulled back the sheets. Matty's nightdress had rucked up round her thighs and, very gently, he pulled it straight.

'You shouldn't be doing this,' she croaked. 'But thank you.'

'Why not?' Kit brushed damp hair back from her cheek. 'Do you want some more to drink?'

Matty shook her head and closed her eyes. Kit replaced the netting top on the jug and went through to the bathroom to wash the glass. She had felt so tiny in his hands. So light and brittle – and he thought how much he had done to break her. He returned, checked Matty was still, sat down in the chair, adjusted the light and tried to reread the final passage from *The Seven Pillars of Wisdom*. It failed him.

'I'm sorry, Daisy,' he had said when the Chudleighs departed in haste the morning after the furore. 'I'm sorry for the mess and the waste.'

They were in the hall at Hinton Dysart, and she looked up from her dressing case with that quick slanting look that held him enchanted. Her cheeks were dead white. 'This *is* the end, isn't it, Kit? We must not see each other again.'

'No. I mean, yes.'

He must have looked as desperate as he felt, for she touched his hand and said, 'You must not worry about it.'

He permitted himself to gaze at the beautiful face, a little mysterious under one of her hats, he couldn't remember which one. She returned his scrutiny then turned away.

'Goodbye, Kit,' she said in a matter-of-fact way . . .

'Why aren't you in bed, Kit? Can't someone else take over?' Matty whispered from the bed.

Kit slid *The Seven Pillars of Wisdom* onto the table and got up. 'I thought you were asleep.'

'I can't see you very well.' Matty was fretful. 'Can I have the light on?'

He switched on the bedside lamp. Matty sighed and seemed easier. 'It's less frightening,' she said. 'I don't like the dark.'

'Are you feeling better?'

She moved jerkily under the bedclothes and winced because moving hurt, especially her chest. 'Not much.' She experimented with a smile, which proved too much effort. 'Everything hurts. My hands hurt.'

He took one of her hands and examined it. 'Wait a minute,' he said and disappeared through the connecting door to his room. He returned with a pot of ointment.

'I should have given this to you before but I didn't think about it. Do you remember I told you about Prince Abdullah? Well, this was supplied by his personal physician.' Kit unscrewed the lid and gently rubbed the paste into Matty's skin. 'That should help.'

The irony of the gesture did not escape Kit and it made him feel worse: everything he gave Matty was second-hand.

But it pleased Matty, and she held up her other hand. When he had finished, Kit pulled up the chair and suggested that he read to her. But Matty wanted to get something straight.

'Are you going to leave me for Daisy?'

Dr Lofts had issued stringent warnings about tiring or exciting the patient and Kit leant over Matty. 'No, I'm not going to leave you.'

'I need to know so I can fix my mind on what I'm to get well for.'

'Matty, don't.'

'The truth?' Her fever-ridden eyes stared up at him. Robin's orders forgotten, Kit slipped to his knees beside the bed.

'Matty, I am so sorry, so very sorry.' He cupped his hand around her face and his thumb rubbed gently against her cheek.

The blood pounded through Matty's frame, releasing rivulets

357

of poison into her flesh. Sweat gathered in her armpits and between her legs, vanishing before it had a chance to cool her heated skin. Her lungs laboured. The bedroom wavered between eyelids that had grown too heavy, and Kit's face, with its blond lick of hair, hung disembodied above her. Despite the fever, though, the lump of grief and outrage in Matty's chest refused to dissolve.

'I'm sorry, I'm sorry,' Kit was saying. 'I'm sorry I hurt you.'

Matty closed her eyes. 'I don't want to talk any more.'

After a while her breathing deepened. Inexpertly, Kit pulled the sheet up over her arms, and got to his feet. Stiff and chilled, he went over to the window and lifted the curtain. Dawn was breaking and the garden wore the dewy, soft look of autumn. Kit caught his lower lip between his teeth: he wanted to punch his fist through the glass because he had hurt someone so badly, because he had blundered.

Curiously, of all the emotions Kit experienced when his mother died, the strongest had been the sense that his body did not belong to his mind, that both operated at a distance from one another. He felt that now. Kit raised his hand, looked at it, balled it into a fist and pushed it towards the glass where it came to rest. His feeling of loss was so great that he felt he would never recover.

A child was crying in Matty's ear, a heartbroken sound, and Matty could not understand why. Determined to find out, she walked down the path towards the garden, *her* garden – only to find it had vanished. The garden was not there, and where there had been beauty and peace there was nothing.

The sobbing went on and on.

'Hush now,' said Robbie. 'You're crying in your sleep again, Mrs Kit. It won't do. It upsets me, and Mr Kit here.'

Matty woke with a start and lay blinking at the ceiling. It was late afternoon and tea-time. Each time she woke, she was forced through the process of remembering. She had been ill, very ill, for six weeks, but was now better. To be more precise, without knowing how or why, Matty had willed herself to recover. Yesterday she had been allowed out of bed to sit by the fire.

'Tea,' said Robbie firmly, 'and here's Mr Kit to read to you.'

Behind Robbie's back, Kit raised an eyebrow at his wife. 'You'd better be a good girl and eat up all your bread and butter.'

Matty smiled. 'Do I get sent into the corner if I don't?'

She pulled herself upright and allowed Robbie to help her on with her dressing gown. Robbie tucked the folds modestly around Matty's legs and pulled back the sheets. Matty held out her arms and Kit lifted her up from the bed and placed her in the chair by the fire. Robbie tucked an army's supply of rugs around Matty and went over to attend to the bed which apparently required an inordinate amount of pillow banging.

Kit held up a copy of *Time and Tide* magazine, which was currently serializing *Diary of a Provincial Lady*. 'More?'

'Yes, *please*,' said Matty.

Kit read: ' "Call from Lady Boxe who says she is off to the South of France next week as she Must Have Sunshine. She asks me Why I do not go there too . . ." '

Kit was a good reader and Matty gave a sigh of pleasure.

' "Why not just pop into a train, enquires Lady B., pop across to France and pop out into the Blue Sky, Blue Sea and Summer Sun. Could make perfectly comprehensive reply to this but do not do so, question of expense having evidently not crossed Lady B.'s horizon . . ." '

Not France, thought Kit. Not a good subject.

' ". . . Reply to Lady B. with insincere professions of liking England very much in Winter, and she begs me not to let myself become parochially minded . . ." '

Kit read on to the end of the extract, both of them enjoying the satire. No one regarding the scene by the bedroom fire would imagine that it hid a fault line. Not even Robin Lofts who looked in to be greeted by the sight of Kit's legs splayed out in front of the fire. Matty was sipping tea from the best tea service which Mrs Dawes insisted on using – 'As if that's going to make her feel better,' said Robbie.

'Ah, Lofts.' Kit got up and brushed crumbs from his lap. 'I think my wife is better, judging by the giggles.' He held up the magazine. 'It's excellent stuff. I'll come back when you've finished with her.'

'Dearest darling Kit,' he read, in the privacy of the Exchequer, for the twentieth time. The letter had arrived two days ago, addressed in Marcus's handwriting.

I cannot go without dotting 'i's' and crossing 't's'. I mean, I cannot say goodbye without giving some shape to what has happened between us. If you like, I want to put it in a frame so I can look at it properly – and then I will have done with it.

Now, Kit darling. Both of us understands that one phase is over. We took risks that should not have been taken. I am sorry, truly sorry it resulted in such disaster, and I am sorry Matty had to know. But, and it is a big, big but, my love doesn't stop there. It keeps on growing like Matty's garden. It grows through me. I breathe with it. I sleep with it. It gives me happiness I never thought possible, and pain that is too intense to describe.

I would not have it one drop the less. I am not a martyr and I wish desperately it had not turned out as it has. Despite the anguish I feel I would not go back, even though I can never have you, that I know I have hurt people, even Matty. For falling in love with you, Kit, has rescued me from being a silly and blank person. I believe that. Truly.

When I was with you, Kit, and learnt to love you, I was never sure where I ended and you began. That is no small thing in a life and now I have time to reflect, I know just how precious it is.

Listen, Kit. I am going away to France because I want to make a fresh start. I don't know how long I will be

360

there and I am not going to tell you where. You know
how I love France. I will be perfectly safe and content.
  For always, Daisy

Kit folded the letter and put it back into the file labelled
'Fencing'. Then he lit a cigarette and smoked it.

Upstairs, Robin turned his back while Matty adjusted her dressing
gown. 'Progress,' he said cheerfully. 'Did you eat lunch?'
  'Huge helpings.'
  'You've done well, Mrs Dysart. I'm proud of you.'
  She gave him an unusually direct look. 'If I can get through
this crisis, I can get through most things.'
  'Yes, I think so.' Robin did not insult her by pretending he
had not heard the gossip. 'Can you remember more yet?' he asked
carefully.
  'No.'
  'It's no matter. These things take time.'
  'The funny thing is . . .' Matty hesitated. 'You might think
this fanciful, but I think this illness has cleansed me in a strange
way.'
  Robin did not understand what she meant, but he stored the
remark away in his memory. Outside in the corridor he met Kit.
  'Your wife is recovering,' he reported. 'I don't think we will
ever know what happened the night of the accident, and perhaps
it is best that we shouldn't. There is no point in remembering, if it
brings distress. People do that, you know.'
  'Do they?' said Kit.
  'Yes, they blank out what they don't want to think about.
However, Mrs Dysart seems very calm.'
  The two men sized each other up. There was a query in
Robin's eyes and, Kit fancied, a hint of disapproval, but he was
not prepared to answer any questions.
  'I see,' he said shortly.
  'Under the circumstances, you won't be requiring my services

any more,' Robin said. 'I'm sure Mrs Dysart will be able to use Sir Rupert's doctor.'

'I'll talk to her. I think it should be her choice.'

'Of course.'

They parted, not exactly in accord, although they had come to be almost friends during the last weeks.

Matty was sewing when Kit rejoined her. Her hair was freshly brushed and anchored into combs, and she had put on her rose scent. Tea was cleared away and the fire freshly banked, and she was enjoying the solitude. With true English contrariness, the weather had turned raw and cold and it was difficult to imagine that only six weeks ago the house had sweltered.

She held up the canvas onto which she was tracing in *petit point* a fantasy of fruit and flowers. 'See, I've put a ladybird on the hollyhock.'

Kit smiled at the poetic conceit. 'You should embroider the garden here when you've finished.'

She put down the canvas. 'Kit,' she said in the light conversational tone she had recently adopted with him, 'I know now why you didn't want me to have anything to do with that part of the garden, so perhaps you would like to tell me the story.' She folded the canvas. 'In the end I found out, like I found out about you and Daisy.'

Kit sat down opposite and fingered the fringe of a Paisley shawl that lay over the back. Matty persisted. 'You owe it to me, Kit. In fact, I insist.'

He was taken aback by this new Matty. 'Yes, I do owe it to you,' he replied. 'But it is a long story and a difficult one.'

Kit hesitated but Matty was ready for that. She handed him the tortoiseshell cigarette box and the lighter. 'Go on.'

'My father married my mother in 1900. She was an American, and rich, and my father met her when she was over here doing the Season. Lady F. had been taken on to present her at Court. For a fee, of course. Lady F. made a living presenting girls who were just wide of the mark, or from the colonies or America. It's often done. Her father had made a lot of money importing cotton from the South and making it up into cloth. My grandparents were generous with their children. Uncle Edwin went to Harvard, and they thought that if my mother did the Season in England it would add to her social standing. That's how she met my father. At Ascot. They were forced to share an umbrella in a rainstorm.'

Kit pushed the chair back and got up. 'As you know, Matty, things are not always simple. Perhaps in those days expectations were different. People wanted things differently. I don't know.' He turned to Matty, an eyebrow raised as if she might know. She didn't. 'My mother and my uncle were very fond of each other. Extremely fond, and they didn't like being separated. Mother constantly referred to Uncle Edwin and they met frequently. He was often over here and they wrote to each other most weeks. I think it irritated my father. They understood each other so well, you see, that I think he felt left out.'

Matty remained quite still.

'Their marriage wasn't happy.'

Yes, she thought. She loved another man. Her own brother. A man who told her that things would never be the same again after the war. And did not come back himself. Matty wanted to tell Kit what she knew – but it was not her secret.

Kit tried to describe what he meant by not happy. How the edginess and unease between his parents had infected him, the child. How he knew it was there, but thought it was normal.

'They rubbed each other up the wrong way, although you would never guess from their behaviour in public. Then the war came and Father returned from it a changed man. That was after Uncle Edwin was dead.'

Kit cut himself off and was silent. After a few seconds he went on, 'Did you know they had four children?'

'*Four* children?'

'Yes. We had another sister called Rose.' It was growing dark and Kit moved away from the window. His voice was very bleak. 'If you don't mind, Matty, I don't think I want to talk about this any more.'

Matty dropped her detached tone. 'Please, please. If you have one ounce of affection for me, *try*.' He was silent. 'You must try, Kit.'

'Rose drowned,' he said, after a long minute. 'In the river, by the boathouse, like you nearly did. She had been playing on the jetty by herself and Mother told Robbie that she would watch Rose for half an hour or so. But she didn't, she went down to her garden and left Rose alone.'

'Ah.' Matty's heart was beating hard and she expelled a long breath. 'Yes?'

'That was after my uncle was killed in the Somme. I've always thought the deaths drove her mad. She blamed herself for both. Firstly for badgering Father to wangle a commission for Uncle Edwin. He shouldn't have, you see, but it's always possible to fix things if you know the right people. Then Rose.'

'In the garden?' Matty whispered. 'That garden?'

'In the garden.' Pause. 'By the statue.'

'How?'

'She took a knife from the kitchen. She was so desperate to die that she slashed herself more than twenty times.'

The pause this time was longer. Kit ran a hand over his hair and his shoulders hunched. He seemed to be gathering strength for what he had to say. His gaze swung back to his wife, and locked onto hers.

'Matty, she was so desperate to leave us that she even stabbed herself in the face.'

CHAPTER FIVE

'Why didn't you tell me?' Matty sat motionless while she listened. Like many people on hearing shocking news, she fastened on trivia. 'I've just ordered more roses for planting.'

Kit looked at Matty as if he did not understand a word she said. 'It's not important,' he said. 'Really.'

'But it is, don't you see?' Matty had got into the habit of cradling her hands in her lap to give them maximum protection. She did this now. 'It meant we were approaching each other from the opposite ends of a pole. You should have told me, Kit. I would have understood, however things are between us.'

Kit relaxed his shoulders and lost the hunched look. 'I find it incredibly difficult to talk about,' he said and spread his hands out in a gesture which said: Forgive me. 'Nor do I want to. Neither did Polly nor Flora. We didn't discuss it, but there was a sort of tacit agreement we wouldn't talk about it. I was only twelve when Mother died, Polly a bit younger and Flora was four.' Matty made a noise at the back of her throat. 'The girls know Mother killed herself, but I've never told them the details. I thought it was unfair.' He paused to tuck in a stray edge of rug around Matty's bottom. 'It's the old reaction to this sort of thing, I suppose. I told myself if I ignored it, pretended it hadn't happened, I would forget about it.'

'I understand about losing a parent, parents,' said Matty. 'But not about the . . . the other thing. I can't imagine.' She was beginning to make some sense of the puzzle; the wounds of children deprived of their mother in such a fashion. 'What about your father?'

'You know how we are with him, and he with us,' said Kit flatly. 'He was never the same when he came back from France — he was invalided out in 'sixteen and sent off to Craiglockhart hospital in Scotland. Shell shock. He returned to find Rose dead. Uncle Edwin was dead. But I think he gave up on us, and Mother. Gave up on life.' He balled one of his fists and punched it into the palm of the other hand. 'How can one stand in judgement knowing one's own shortcomings? But I do, I do. I know it's unfair, Matty, but I felt Father should have known better. I think he should have tried harder with us, not retreated. I think he should have tried harder with Mother.' He went silent. 'I blame him.'

It was impossible to digest everything at once, and Matty did not want to. Later she would have to think over what he had told her.

'After Mother's death,' Kit said, 'my grandparents cut off contact, which left the estate considerably poorer. You know about that, too.'

'Do you know why?'

'No, I've never discovered. They died soon after and left their money to a third cousin. I don't think my grandfather liked Father very much.' Kit flashed a look at Matty. 'He probably regretted selling his daughter off like a prize heifer.'

I think I know, thought Matty. They must have found out about Hesther and Edwin.

'From then on, Father ignored us, really. We were a reminder and a nuisance. It's funny. He cut quite a figure in those days and I wanted him to be proud of me. But he wasn't. He preferred Danny to us, certainly he gets on better with him. You must have noticed.' Matty nodded. 'They fought through the war together, you see, and he rescued Danny from some hospital or other and brought him to Hinton Dysart.'

Kit had lit another cigarette. The strain of remembering and talking showed clearly in his face.

In killing herself, thought Matty, Hesther had committed more than an act of self-destruction. She had left the survivors, the children, the knowledge that she had not loved them enough to live. She remembered her flight from the garden – her expulsion from Eden – after she had seen Kit and Daisy and went hot with the realization that she, too, might have done something similar.

'Poor Hesther,' she murmured. 'But I think she was wrong.'

Kit flashed Matty a look which she thought was dislike and she knew she risked this new-found intimacy between them. 'I don't think you should blame my mother,' he said.

'She was wrong,' interrupted childless Matty fiercely. 'Don't you see? Whatever she felt. Whatever she suffered. Because she had children, Kit. Don't you see?'

Her conviction got through to him and his touchiness subsided. He returned to his stance by the window and stood looking out over the garden. 'I might as well tell you that I found her,' he said.

'Oh, my God.' Matty pushed back the rugs and heaved herself to her feet. Knees trembling with the effort, she edged her way towards him. 'Oh, my God, Kit. I'm sorry. I'm so sorry.'

He was standing with his arms pressed up against the window. Matty tugged at his sleeve forcing him to turn round and then, sweating with weakness, clumsy, she pulled him into her arms. 'Tell me,' she insisted.

'I'd been looking for her all morning,' he said into the space above her head. 'There had been a disagreement with Father earlier, and I was going off to stay with a friend from school and I wanted to ask if everything was all right. She had not been well since Rose's death . . . and we were worried. The house was full of convalescent officers because Mother had wanted to do her bit. In a way, I think that had something to do with it, too. Everywhere you turned in the house there was a limping or bandaged man. Some of them had been blinded, others were scarred or mutilated. They gave Polly nightmares. The worst ones sat for days on end without moving and were carted about by the nurses like lumps of meat. One of them went mad, and began to howl and twitch and nobody could shut him up. He was sent off somewhere, Craiglockhart, I think, where Father had been . . .'

Kit, Polly and Flora sat on the main staircase and every so often pressed their faces to the banisters to hear better. The door to the morning room was open and their parents were quarrelling.

Polly had been thinking. 'Couldn't Mother have another baby?' she asked Kit. 'That would make her happy again.'

'I expect so,' said Kit, who was not entirely sure.

Kit and Polly thought about the proposition while Flora sang a song on the stair below. They missed Rose, of course, but death was not much more than a curiosity and they dealt with it briskly.

'How do babies get here?' Polly was aware there was a gap in her knowledge.

'They just arrive,' said Kit, who did not want to lose face, especially with his sister. 'Through the stomach.' He picked impatiently at the black armband on his jacket.

'Oh,' said Polly. 'That doesn't sound very nice.' She added, 'Poor Mummy,' and ate the end of one plait as she contemplated the problem.

Nurses shepherded patients in and out of the dining room for breakfast. Kit watched Maggie, the under-housemaid, lug a bucket of hot water onto the front steps and begin the scrubbing. It seemed a pointless activity to him as the steps were dead white already.

'I think I ought to shut the door to the morning room,' he said. 'We don't want people to hear.'

The sound of his mother's sobs rose above the mêlée in the passage. Before Kit could do anything about it, Hesther emerged in a swirl of black lace and muslin, a black-edged handkerchief pressed to her cheeks. She stopped, dropped her hand and revealed the face that Matty was to pore over in the photographs, ravaged and wet with tears.

'I know it was my fault, Rupert,' she said through the open door. 'I know, I know, I know—'

'Mother!' Kit hissed.

But Hesther did not hear her son, and she vanished down the passage towards the kitchens. Rupert emerged from the morning room after her, a younger, slighter version of the thickset man he was to become. His colour was up which meant he was angry and even four-year-old Flora knew better than to advertise her presence. For thirty seconds or so, Rupert stood at the bottom of the

368

stairs, his children frozen into statues above him, visibly pulling himself together before stepping past Maggie onto the main steps and out of sight.

That point marked, as precisely as a line on a map, the end of Kit's childhood. And when, later that morning, he discovered his dying mother who, despite her efforts with the knife, had not done the job cleanly, he knelt down and took her bloody hand in his and screamed at the horror of the adult world.

'She was too far gone to talk to me,' Kit said. 'I held her hand and I begged her, I begged her not to leave us. But she did. I had never seen anyone dead, but I knew when she was. She sort of collapsed inwards and her body stopped fighting the terrible injuries. Then I ran away and left her there, by the statue. I have never told anyone I found her first.'

Not even Daisy? Matty wanted to ask. She held Kit tightly until he had finished speaking and then she raised one of her half-healed hands and, daring him to shake her off, brushed away the tears under his eyes with her thumb.

'Better?'

He squinted down at Matty and managed, half shamed, half defiant, a weak, lopsided smile. 'Matty, I don't know what you've made me say. Yes, I do feel better.'

'Kit . . .'

'Yes?'

'Kit, I think I have to sit down.'

'Good God,' he said at once. 'What have I been thinking of?' He picked her up and carried her back to the chair and fussed. Matty sat back and concentrated on willing the stuffing back into her knees which had turned into the consistency of Mrs Dawes's aspic jelly.

Kit knelt down in front of the chair. 'I shouldn't be upsetting you, Matty.' With a gesture that took her breath away he laid his head in her lap. She breathed a life-giving gulp of air and ran her fingers through his hair, luxuriating in its thickness. He raised his head. 'Enough, I think.'

369

His hair was soft on her fingers. 'Just one more question, Kit. Please.'

'If you wish.'

She gave the nervous jerk of her head. 'You really love, Daisy, don't you?'

'Do you want me to answer that question?' Kit raised his head, puzzled by her directness and when Matty nodded said, 'Yes. I cannot deny it.'

'And me?' she asked, greatly daring.

He searched her face for a clue. 'It's different, Matty.'

With a sigh, Matty slid back into the chair and parts of her heart that she had considered dead stirred. But the feelings were too exhausting, and she closed her eyes, content just to be at that point.

'I'll ask you a question,' said Kit. 'I wouldn't ask it now if the answer didn't matter to me very much.' She waited, braced, knowing what it would be. 'Did you throw yourself in the river deliberately? Or did you slip?'

Matty's eyes were extra large and brown as she looked down at Kit still on his knees by the chair, and their expression was stronger and more assured than he remembered.

'Forgive me, but I need to know.'

'Kit.' Matty gripped his head between her hands and looked straight at him. 'I have to be honest with you. I don't know. I don't know what happened after I saw you and Daisy in the garden.'

Later, when Kit had gone and Matty was eating supper on a tray by the fire, she realized she had got something wrong. Charles Kennedy, Kit's grandfather, had not cut off the Dysarts because he had discovered the truth about Edwin and Hesther. That wouldn't make sense.

No. It was far more likely that, after Hesther's death, Rupert had written to his in-laws and told them what he suspected about their children, and they – church-going, God-fearing pillars of the community – had been so outraged by the accusation that they ceased all contact with their son-in-law.

That was one possible version of the truth.

Matty knew – she was sure – that Rupert had read Edwin's letters to Hesther and had bundled them away with Hesther's possessions and what he had read of their contents had driven him to write to Boston. Perhaps he had concluded that the worst had taken place between his wife and his brother-in-law. That would not necessarily be correct. People loved each other without even touching.

Unless Charles and Euphemia Kennedy had sent Hesther away for precisely that reason?

Matty would never know.

CHAPTER SIX

B Y NOVEMBER the shooting season was in full swing and the gamekeepers at the Redfields, Itchel and Eastbridge estates were frantic. Most of the land in the area was arable and running with partridges and hares, as well as pheasants. Itchel Manor and Redfields reared their own birds, plumped out with buckwheat, and with the aid of dummy eggs a good tally of partridges. The pheasants this year were so fat they had grown cocky and sat in rows on farmyard walls and ran along the lanes in front of the horses.

It was early in the morning and a breeze blew down the valley from Alton way into the village. In Clifton Cottage Ned was out in the garden checking the crop of the red-cheeked harvest apple which had ripened at last. The harvest apple was a funny one: it cropped every other year and, compared to other varieties, was rather small. Still, he could rely on it until Christmas – unlike the Rhymer, a pretty striped cooker, which he suspected had developed canker.

The curtains at their bedroom window puffed through the open window in the draught. Ned looked up. Ellen lay behind them under a patchwork quilt, trying to sleep. He sighed and turned away.

That blasted knee of hers had brought them bad luck. First, the discomfort and dislocation of the operation, although Ellen had got back into her stride quick enough after she had learnt that the lump was only a cyst. But then it had introduced a warning note into their unity. Ned brushed a hand down the trunk of the apple tree. If you like, from now on, he and Ellen were prey to black spot, mildew and rust. And canker.

A week ago, Ellen tripped over his fork in the garden, and cut open the scar on her knee on the sharp edge of his trowel lying beside it. Now, she was back in bed with an inflamed leg and a temperature.

Its red breast looking as though it had been spread on with a palette knife, a robin hopped up to the back door and on to the step.

'And bad cess to you, birdy, if you come in,' said Ned automatically. Robins brought bad luck if they came indoors. The bird preened itself with a twitch of its head and hopped inside.

Ned sighed again and sat down on the stone by the doorway to lace his boots. Good tools were his life blood and he took care of his.

'You'd sell me for a good pair of boots,' Ellen said into his ear, her voice from a long way back, around the time they had married.

'If you let me down, girl, I would, I would, girl, just try me.'

The boots were made with thick, soft leather and had that right degree of tackiness from incessant polishing but, just to be sure, Ned dipped a rag into the pot of dripping by the door and smeared it over them.

The fob watch that had belonged to his father said five to eight. Ned looked up at the sky to check the light and get a feel of the air. About now, the birds came down from their roosts, and he needed to get a move on.

He stood in the doorway and shouted up the stairs, 'I'll stop at the surgery and leave a message for the doctor.'

Ellen roused herself and called, 'Keep your backside out of the target area.'

'You take it easy, girl.'

Ned picked up a bundle of old newspapers, checked his handkerchief was in his pocket and went down the garden path.

It was still fairly dark, but light from over Jackall's Hill way traced a pattern in the sky to the east. He was going over to Redfields to work as a 'stop' on the shoots, and by the end of the day six extra shillings would fill up the Coronation tin on the mantelpiece.

The trick was to prevent the birds breaking out of the wood and running across the fields, especially as the Redfields' shoot bordered directly onto the Eastbridges'. And vice versa. Like anyone else in Nether Hinton, Ned had learnt with his mother's milk that shooting your neighbour's birds ranked with murder.

Across the ploughed field a winter dawn hung over the elms. The light was pearly, the air damp and fresh and the trees wrapped in mist. Ned liked this sort of day. Beautiful, but no nonsense about it.

'Mornin'.' Jo Fisher, the ratcatcher, out with his dog, ferret and gun, raised a finger to Ned. Winter was falling, the rats were sneaking back into barns and Jo was busy.

'Mornin', Jo.'

At nine thirty the guns, mostly elderly gentlemen, twelve beaters and Ned, straggled out from the grounds of the big house and across the fields. Wet earth sucked at boots and splattered gaiters, slowing their pace. The world smelt cold, and wet cobwebs glinted between branches lit by a weak sun.

At the edge of Falkner's Copse, the head keeper handed out cartridge bags to those boys chosen to earn the extra sixpence, and the beaters fanned out into their positions behind the guns.

'Rattle yer sticks,' ordered the keeper.

'Hey, hey, hey . . .'

A drumbeat sounded against the tree trunks and with a flurry and a beating of wings, three pheasants rose into the air.

'Hey, hey, hey . . .' sounded the beaters.

'Forward left,' sang out Ned, as a fourth pheasant struggled into the sky.

'Hey, hey, hey . . .'

Two guns cracked in unison and a pheasant swooped in a dying arc to the earth. It fell at Ned's feet, a red-brown bundle, streaked with scarlet, one eye fixed on Ned in an accusatory glare. Noses down, the spaniels wheeled in and crashed up towards him.

'Go and find the others,' he said, picked up the bundle and, for the first time in his life, felt a distaste for the killing. It reminded him of Ellen, somehow. The scar on her leg under her lisle stocking. The way in which her eyes had followed him around the room at Clifton Cottage this morning, begging him for reassurance. Ned stuffed the bird into the bag.

At lunch-time the keeper called a halt near the house. Ned and the beaters ate their sandwiches in the shed, and drank Blane's ginger beer and beer from the barrel. The shed smelt of sawdust and wet corduroy, and the dogs lay in untidy muddy heaps on the floor. Mr Brandon had arranged to send out Blue Prior cigarettes, and the men smoked and exchanged gossip about the coming general election, the row over the council houses in the Croft and the whist drive to be held in the church rooms. Ned drank his beer, forgot about Ellen, and enjoyed himself.

Flora heard the guns as she walked down Hyde Lane, past the Turnpike towards the Horns pub (best beer in the village, Danny told her). But before she reached it she turned right into Bowling Alley and up towards Pankridge Street. Minerva pattered around her heels.

Flora hoped that long rides, long walks, long everything, would tire her out. They did not. She was sleeping badly, thinking badly and – the only advantage in the mess of her love affair – eating badly.

To her right, fronted by trees and a field which proclaimed its status, was Eastbridge House. Further on, the street showed less respect for the buildings and ran close to the walls of the cottages. Flora stopped to look back at the big house. Then she transferred her gaze to Vine Cottage opposite, flanked by dahlias and a rough stone path. Plaster peeled away from an eave in the front, there was a damp patch on the side wall and weed was growing high up by the lead guttering.

Flora stared at the weed, the contrast between Eastbridge – or Hinton Dysart – and Vine Cottage very sharp in her mind.

The plain fact was, whether she wanted it or not, Robin was back in her life. He had returned, not with a whirl of sword and a clatter of a destrier, but in a Ford motor car wielding a rubber tube to stick down Matty's throat. If Flora had ever imagined that her capitulation to love would be romantic, her witnessing of Matty's battle with river water in her lungs, the appalling vividness of vomit and choked airways, rid her of that notion.

That battle for life had been real, conducted in a bedroom with the smell of disinfectant rising over that of stagnant water, as romantic dreams were never real. The sounds of Matty being dragged back from death – the pitiful crying through the bruised throat. Horrified, Flora saw that this was real life. Hard. Difficult to take in. She had wanted to run away. Throughout, Robin had been there, in charge, gentle, and concentrated. He had anchored her.

Intent on a smell, Minerva cut in front of Flora and she was brought to a halt. 'Careful, old girl.'

Not that Robin had specially acknowledged Flora, or made any move to speak to her other than when it was necessary.

It seemed a lifetime ago since she had stood in the Throne Room at Buckingham Palace in a roll of drums, dipped and swayed to Their Majesties, felt ostrich feathers trail over her face, drunk iced coffee from 'G.R.IV' porcelain and eaten savouries off *Honi Soit Qui Mal Y Pense* plates. Far longer than the pile of torn-off days from her calendar suggested . . . a decade since she danced with Marcus in a green gown at Londonderry House and felt thorns of excitement and desire press into her flesh.

A childhood ago. If she was truthful, Flora had arrived at a point where a weed growing in a cottage's gutter indicated the choices more accurately than any green silk gown.

Flora looked down at her muddy shoes and tweed skirt.

The crack-crack of guns and beaters' cries sounded faintly from the valley. At the bottom of Redlands Lane the sun shone directly into the windows of the basket factory and licked them into gold. The rays lay across the piles of baskets stacked by the entrance and over the roof of the Wesleyan chapel further down the road.

On the spur of the moment, she decided to visit Ellen who, according to Robbie, had not been in to work this week.

At Clifton Cottage a faint 'Who is it?' answered Flora's knock. Flora left Minerva whimpering on the step and went inside.

'It's me Ellen, Flora Dysart,' she called up the stairs. 'I've come to see how you are.'

Dust lay over Ellen's furniture, which surprised Flora for she knew disorder would grieve Ellen more than anything. Ned's breakfast things were still on the table, and the stove was almost cold. Puzzled, Flora set her hand on the post at the foot of the stairs and took the first step.

The bedroom was tiny. Ellen was sitting in a chair by the window watching the dying light. She looked awful with yellowish, fatigued skin and eyes burning with fever. The chatter that Flora had planned, the message from the healthy to the getting-better, died on her lips.

Clearly, Ellen was very ill. The unwashed smell of her was enough to warn Flora. She bent over, took one of Ellen's hands in her own and felt a twist of panic.

'Hallo, Ellen.'

With an effort, Ellen returned from the place where she and Bill were walking up Redlands Lane to inspect the newly dug practice trenches. Every so often, Bill stooped to pick up a discarded sardine tin or an empty cartridge. Betty was there too, young and bright-haired and full of talk about her new life in Winchester.

This was no source of shame for Ellen, for she had nothing to be ashamed of. There was no worry either because she knew it was possible to love both her men. There was no grief, because she had done with that a long time ago. Ellen watched as Bill and his men marched off down the lane, the sun shining into their faces, mess tins clattering in time to their boots.

Someone was talking to her. 'Ellen. Are you all right? How long have you been like this? Has Ned asked Dr Lofts to come and see you?' Someone was stroking her hand. She made a huge effort to focus.

'Miss Flora.'

'How long have you been ill, Ellen?'

'Three days,' she said, confused. 'Four. I fell on the knee, you know, and cut it open. On the scar. 'Bout a week ago. It's made me feel odd.'

The curtains at the window blew in with the breeze, and Flora got up to fasten the latch. Ellen's eyes followed her.

'I don't like you to see the room like this. You must excuse me.' Ellen struggled to explain. 'Ned always did like living in a pig's ear.'

'It doesn't matter at all.'

Ellen looked at Flora. 'It matters to me, Miss Flora.'

'Would you like me to tidy it?'

'Certainly not.' Shades of the old, tart Ellen resurrected smartly.

'Have you eaten anything today?'

'I can't say I have, Miss Flora. I couldn't get up this morning as I thought I would, and I told myself to sit here until I felt more like myself.'

'Let's see if you can manage some soup.'

Flora leant over to rescue the cushion behind Ellen's back, and nudged her leg. Ellen groaned. 'Careful, miss.'

'I'm sorry.' Flora backed away, and to over-compensate for her clumsiness rather bossily straightened the wool patchwork blanket on the bed.

Ellen watched her efforts. 'You've missed a corner, Miss Flora.' Flora plumped up the pillows. 'Miss Flora,' said Ellen, 'please don't. I don't think I can bear watching you making another pig's ear. If you don't mind me saying so.' Then she went silent.

Flora felt even more inadequate. 'Look,' she said. 'Is Dr Lofts coming to see you?'

Ellen muttered something about the extra expense, but Ned had promised to drop in at the surgery.

'Ellen, what did they say about your knee at the hospital? Did they manage to get rid of the problem?'

'Oh, yes.'

Flora was more successful in imposing order downstairs. It was a simple matter to stoke up the stove, to run a duster over the sideboard and to clear the table and boil the water. Then she set about chopping an onion and a carrot which she discovered in the scullery.

She took the soup up in one of Ellen's prized china bowls with unnatural pink rosebuds all over it and sat down on the bed beside Ellen's chair. She dipped the spoon into the bowl.

'Can you swallow, Ellen?'

Ellen sighed and Flora saw her mask slip. The older woman's bottom lip trembled. 'What's the point, Miss Flora? I say, the quicker my carcass is on the heap, the quicker it's over.'

'You're only saying that because you don't feel well.'

'Yes,' said Ellen. 'It's only a touch of that nasty flu.'

Between them, they struggled to get a few spoonfuls down Ellen. A trickle ran down the side of her mouth and Flora dabbed it away. Once Ellen retched it all back, and they had to start again.

After a while, she lay back against the cushion and closed her eyes. 'I don't fancy much,' she said.

Since it was cruel to continue, Flora put down the spoon.

Ellen opened her eyes and looked directly at Flora. Thoughts of death floated through her head, and she grabbed at the one that bothered her most. 'You mustn't worry,' she said, interpreting the expression on the girl's face. 'I don't mind if I have to go.' Then Ellen paused, and rethought what she had said. 'That's not quite true. I don't want to leave the party, but if I have to, I'm going to do it well.' She paused again and opened her eyes wide. 'That's the twisting bit.'

Flora told her not to talk if it was difficult, but other thoughts were processing through Ellen's tired mind. 'Ned will never manage on his own, you know,' she said. 'He looks the kind of person who'll cope, but he won't. I'll have to find him a floozy before I cock my toes up.'

There were many platitudes Flora could have trotted out, but Robin and she had often talked about patient care. 'Ellen,' she said. 'You are *not* going to die.'

Ellen smiled properly this time. 'An old goat is Ned,' she said. 'Stubborn old goat in thick boots.'

'Could your daughter come home to help nurse you?'

'Perhaps. For a little.' Ellen seemed to tire of the subject.

The room grew dark. Ellen dozed and Flora sat on the bed and watched her, listening to Minerva whimpering downstairs. Ellen stirred in the chair.

'I'm frightened,' she said, and Flora was not sure whether

Ellen knew if she was still in the room or not. Then Ellen's eyelids flicked open and for a scalding second Flora gazed into terror that she had not imagined possible.

'Why's it gone wrong, Miss Flora?'

She sat and stroked Ellen's hand.

Flora heard the Ford nose along the track, and, heart thumping, ran downstairs.

Robin started when he saw her standing at the kitchen door but did not comment on her presence.

'Robin, Ellen's not at all well.' Flora rushed over the words. 'I didn't realize how bad she was, and I think someone should be with her.'

He dumped his bag on the table and avoided the blue Dysart gaze. It had been a long day with a stroke, a broken leg and a nasty cut, and he still had to get through evening surgery before his supper. He did not suppose his lacklustre mood would last for ever, but these days he felt as though chips were being knocked off his optimism and he resented the change and missed feeling well and good-humoured.

He missed, also, untamed flaxen hair, plump hips, a straight-forward mind and a friendship. Very much.

'Can we talk afterwards?' Flora asked, doing things to the saucepan on the hob.

'If you like,' he said indifferently, for he did not imagine anything was going to change. 'But I warn you, I am in no mood to play games. I've accepted the situation as regards you, me and your father. I don't want to go through it all again.'

The idea that Robin was getting over her was enough to frighten Flora silly. In that split second she was spurred into frantic action.

'Please, Robin,' she said. 'I'm not playing games.'

'Flora! You have rotten timing.' Unsmiling, Robin lifted the bag, and she saw then how badly she had hurt him.

'Please.'

He shrugged. There was iodine on his finger and the leather patch on his elbow was torn. 'All right.'

Flora busied herself with straining the rest of the soup. Then, knowing she was being presumptuous, she laid the table for Ned, and covered the bread with a clean rag. She put on the kettle and made a pot of tea.

Upstairs, Robin moved around the bedroom and conducted a conversation with Ellen, which was sufficiently muffled by the floor to be unintelligible. Eventually, a squeak of shoe leather told her he was coming down. She poured tea into a mug and shoved it at him across the table.

'She's not dying?'

'God forbid,' he said. 'But she's got an infection in the knee, and I'm arranging for her to go into Fleet hospital.'

Flora thumped down into the chair. 'Have the Sheppeys paid their insurance, do you think, Robin? Ellen's operation must have taken up a lot of their funds.'

Robin sat down in Ned's wooden carver chair and cradled his mug. 'A good question. I don't know Ned's position.'

Flora spread her hands on the scrubbed table where they appeared obscenely full of life. 'If Ned has run out, I'll pay for Ellen to go to hospital,' she said.

'That would be seen as charity,' said Robin, retrieving the teapot from her and helping himself to a second mug.

'But it is.' Flora had grown tense with the excitement of the idea. She leant over and poured some milk into his tea. 'Look, we're told every week in church to have charity.'

'Shush.' Robin jerked his head towards the ceiling. 'You don't want Ellen to hear. Think about it, Flora. Every time anyone else falls sick in the village it will be remembered you helped the Sheppeys. Are you prepared for that kind of finger-pointing?'

The tea had burnt her tongue. Robin was not being helpful, nor did he look in the sort of mood to be talked to. Her charity was found wanting. Disappointment and anti-climax brought Flora close to losing her temper.

'Heavens above, Robin.' She leapt to her feet with a scrape of

chair. 'I made an offer in good faith and you are niggling because
. . . well, because.' She seized her coat from the peg behind the
door and thrust her arms into the sleeves. 'Nobody has to know
if the money comes from me. Pretend there's a fund in the hospital
or something.' She tied up the coat belt in as contained a manner
as she could muster, and ruined the effect by jamming her beret
down on her head. 'I'm very, very sorry for what has gone wrong
between us, but I don't think you should let Ellen suffer for it.'

'You don't have much money yourself, Flora.'

She went very cold. 'No, I don't, Robin. But enough.'

She was tempted to up-end the dregs in the teapot into his
mug, but thought better of it. Instead, she opened the door and
let loose her parting shot. 'By the way, your jacket is ripped at the
elbow. Perhaps Anna Tillyard could mend it for you.'

Robin swivelled his arm to have a look. 'I'll ask her,' he said,
white with anger. 'Thank you.'

'Goodbye, then.'

Flora trudged down the path and along the track, hoping,
hoping, that she would hear him call. There was silence.

Minerva hugged the ground by her heels, criss-crossing in
front of Flora until she snapped at the dog to get out of the way.
The rain that had threatened in the west all afternoon now chose
to fall. It seeped under her coat collar and damped her wayward
hair. Like yellow seaweed, Flora reflected, and just as attractive.

Futility and disappointment washed her, and she struggled to
beat them back. Nineteen was not so old to begin again, was not
so awful, hardly unusual. After all, she had constructed a very
good case for *not* marrying him.

Point one. Marrying Robin would create an awful, gut-
churning rumpus in the family. Point two. Flora herself was not
at all sure if it was the right thing to do. Point three. She and
Robin unquestionably annoyed each other sometimes and it
would only get worse.

It was all for the best.

Relieved, stiffened by a dose of martyrdom (obedient daughter), Flora plodded on through the wind and rain. She did not
hear the car draw up beside her.

'Get in.'

At the sight of Robin, warm, dry and holding the advantages, Flora's emotions did an abrupt volte-face. 'No,' she said furiously, and splashed on.

Robin raised his eyebrows heavenwards and steered the car alongside the stubborn figure half shrouded by the dark. 'Don't be silly,' he called through the rolled-down window.

Flora snapped back, 'I will be silly if I want to.'

Owing to the engine noise and the rain, Robin missed that remark. He was tired, hungry, fed up and lonely. 'For God's sake,' he shouted, 'will you stop. I spend my life talking to you through car windows.' No answer. Robin tried again. 'Flora,' he yelled. 'Be sensible. Listen to me. Let's not waste our lives.'

At that she stopped. 'Is that Labour government policy?'

'For pity's sake.' Robin ground the car to a halt and scrabbled out of the bucket seat. Then he grabbed Flora. Blazing with anger she resisted. 'Flora, you idiot, beloved, idiotic Flora.' Robin pulled her against him, so roughly she gasped. 'Listen to me, you stupid girl. I love you. You love me.'

She threw up a hand to ward him off, and he seized it in one of his own. 'Say yes,' he ordered, turning it palm upwards. 'Say yes and damn the rest.' He bent and kissed the soft dampened area where her artery ran close to the surface. It pulsed under his lips.

She gazed down at the bent head now slicked with rain, felt his lips possess her flesh. Inside her chest, her heart began its now familiar banging and bouncing. Robin kissed her again, and raised his head and looked at her, an eyebrow raised and mouth pulled into his tired, sweet smile.

Points one, two and three were buried so hastily that it was indecent. Incoherent with relief, Flora turned her face to Robin's, and clung to the damp tweed of his jacket. Robin kissed the tip of Flora's aristocratic nose before he kissed the lips underneath. Rain slid down their cheeks.

'Oh, yes,' she said between the kisses, her tears mixed up in the rain. 'Oh, yes, Robin.'

Both of them talked at once.

'You never came back,' she said. 'Not once.'

'I'm sorry.' Robin took a strand of her hair between his fingers. 'You hurt me so badly.'

'I know,' said Flora. 'I shan't forgive myself.'

'I warn you,' Robin took a step back, placed his hands on her shoulders, 'it's on my terms. You will come to me, into my life, to live and work as I do. I shall not try to ape yours—'

'I wish you'd stop talking,' said Flora, 'and kiss me again.'

Later, she asked him, 'What made you change your mind and come after me?'

'Do you really want to know?'

She pressed her body against his and felt the warmth of his blood and bone through the slick of rain on her skin, and wanted to absorb all of him into her. 'Yes, I do.'

He nuzzled her neck. 'Really?'

'Yes.'

He said quickly, 'The thought of Anna Tillyard doing my mending,' and stopped Flora's cry with his mouth.

How curious [Matty wrote to Susan the following morning in her private sitting room]. How intriguing. Why on earth would Daisy wish to spend a year in France? It is not like her to miss the Season. Perhaps she will come over from time to time? Has Tim Coats left the scene? . . .

Yes. I am much, much better, feeling cheerful, and occupying myself with drawing up plans for renovating the main garden next year. Kit has agreed.

Now that I am so much better, he's decided to go on the trip to Iraq with Max Longborough in the New Year. He didn't feel he should go, but I persuaded him it would be good to get away for a bit. I shall have plenty to do . . .

Letters to Number 5, Upper Brook Street were always a chore – and recently a bore. She knew they were stilted and, equally, that they were thrown into the wastepaper basket at the first opportunity.

Matty glanced at the drawings of the main garden littered over the writing desk. She planned to plant a wisteria tunnel and twine a white variety into the mauve . . .

'Anyway, I hope you are well, Aunt Susan,' she finished, and scrawled her signature as it had occurred to her that she had forgotten to talk to Ned about planting the primulas in the pleached lime walk.

A bellow sounded along the corridor. Matty dropped her pen.

The cry came again. This time she got to her feet and went to investigate. Kit came bounding up the stairs.

'What is it?'

'I don't know.'

A door flung open and Robbie appeared from Rupert's bedroom holding Flora by the wrist. 'Do something,' she said to Kit. 'She's a wicked, wicked girl.'

'Robbie, let go of Flora.' Kit shook his sister loose. 'Tell me what's happened. Quick.'

Flora was defiant. 'It's no use bullying me,' she announced. 'I am going to marry Robin Lofts.'

Kit relaxed temporarily. 'Is that all? I thought something awful had happened. Father, I take it, is signalling his disapproval?' Kit ran his hand through his hair. 'Seriously, Flora, before I go into battle, are you quite, quite sure?'

Quick as a flash, Flora rounded on him. 'You said you'd back me. Remember?'

He pressed her arm. 'Of course. I did and I will.'

Flora let out a gasp of relief and smiled at her brother through her fright.

'Help,' she said. 'I feel rather sick. Can you deal with Robbie?'

Kit looked to his wife for help. 'Matty, take Flora, would you?'

Matty led Flora away and Flora explained that she was not going to change her mind, so Matty was not to try to make her. No, she wouldn't, Matty said. Why should she?

Robbie blocked the door into Rupert's bedroom. 'How *dare*

she do this? You go and tell him you're not going to allow it,' she said.

Kit removed her hand. 'Robbie, I'm sorry to say this, but whom my sister chooses to marry is no concern of yours.'

Robbie gasped and jerked back her head. The movement exposed her thick white throat and emphasized her waist and breasts. In the half light of the landing, her body turned fluid, almost seductive, and for the first time Kit registered Robbie as a woman.

'It's Flora's business,' he repeated. 'Not yours.'

Her reply startled Kit so thoroughly that he was silenced. 'Oh, yes, it is,' she said. A flush spread over the white skin, red ink through water. 'Your father is very upset. He told her he would forbid it and Flora said she didn't care what he thought. Her life was hers to do with as she wished. Then, he said, she wouldn't get her bit of the money, and Flora said it was hardly anything, anyway, because he had lost it all. She stood there, by the bed, like a big cat, blazing away.'

'Robbie?'

When he was tiny, Robbie had rocked Kit on her lap, held his hand, spoon-fed him rice pudding so he would grow. She had listened to a child's litanies, and applied sticking plaster to cut knees and bruised spirits. She had written to him at school, chastized him in the holidays and sat by his bed after Hesther died.

For old times' sake, he spoke gently. 'I think you forget yourself.'

'Your mother, your silly, helpless, wicked mother, left you to me to bring up,' said Robbie. 'And I have done what she asked, though I didn't ask for it and I didn't do it for her.' Robbie inflected her years of loving Rupert hopelessly into the *her*. 'You can't cut me out now, Mr Kit.'

Kit was about to reply when a snorting, animal sound which none of them had ever heard before came from the bedroom. It was followed by a second.

Robbie's eyes widened. 'Oh, my Lord,' she said, and the red drained from her neck.

They pushed their way into the bedroom.

HARRY

Thomas and I met two years after my mother's death. I was travelling in Italy and bidden to dinner with a well-known figure in the art world. Thomas sat opposite and looked at me through the candles and I knew at once that he would fill the gap in my life. After that dinner, he telephoned. He was writing a book on English interior decoration through the ages and he wanted to look at Hinton Dysart. The rest, as they say, is history.

He brought with him a knowledge of porphyry stone and blue john, marble, ormolu and giltwood. He knew about glazed tiles, and stained-glass windows, about painters, furniture and the things that belong in great houses. It was Thomas who persuaded me to hand it over. 'It won't survive otherwise, my dear,' he said, over and over again. 'I've seen it all too often.' When I protested he said, 'You are the last of the line: be practical. What will happen when you die?' And so it was, on 7 November 1980, that I gave the house away to the Trust. There was a small crowd of well-wishers from the village, a formal handing-over ceremony when I surrendered the key and then it was down the drive to Dippenhall Street where we had chosen to live.

Some things are too difficult to speak about, almost to write about. This is one of them. It might have been different if Polly's son had lived, or Flora had had sons. But it wasn't so and, as Thomas said, one has to be practical. I accept the necessity now as I was persuaded to accept it then, and out of that decision I have made my life.

I left the house surrounded by dying embers of the autumn plants; withering rose hips, the brittle remains of the autumn crocuses, whirling seeds, and the dark, shadowy blocks of the yew and the evergreens. My children . . .

But at night I return to the silent rooms and beautiful garden, to join the ghosts from the past.

CHAPTER SEVEN

RUPERT SURVIVED the stroke brought on by the shock of Flora's news, but it left him speechless and paralysed down the right side. After consultations with Dr Williams, who had replaced Robin, and a specialist from Harley Street, it was agreed that it would be best to leave him at home since it was unlikely that treatment in hospital would improve his condition. It was the signal for Robbie to redouble her efforts and she placed herself on duty round the clock. Miss Binns was also summoned back to ordeal by terror under Robbie's jurisdiction.

Throughout the next difficult weeks when Rupert, at last, appeared stable and relatively comfortable, Robbie did not address one word to Flora and ignored her when she met her in the passage.

'This is awful,' confided Flora to Matty, seesawing between hysteria and hilarity. 'It's as if I'm a murderess. The dreadful thing is, I was always her favourite, and I didn't care two twopenny hoots. But I do now.'

'Leave Robbie to me,' said Matty, basting the hem of Flora's wedding dress. 'I'll try and talk to her about it. You concentrate on your wedding.' She snapped the scissor blades shut and tried a joke. 'If Robbie is difficult, I'll cut her plait off.'

'Lady F. telephoned after she saw the notice in *The Times*.' Flora sat down beside Matty. 'She said some awful things about letting down the family.'

'Oh dear,' said Matty.

'I was tempted to say that she should give thanks that I hadn't inflicted a James on you all.'

The pressure was on Flora: unspoken criticism from tactful relatives was just as telling as more forthrightly expressed views. Marcus was especially curt in his congratulations and Susan

Chudleigh had written a masterpiece of discreet *Schadenfreude*. It was not, Flora thought, sewing savage stitches into her dress, as if Polly had made a good marriage – or that her father had followed his own rules. After all, he had spent more time with a London Cockney than with anyone else.

Delivery vans crunched their way up the drive burdened with butter dishes, paper knives and various exotica, including a lizard-skin umbrella stand and a Chinese lacquer hall table. Flora surveyed the booty laid out in the library and took fright. They would never cram it all into the cottage in Dippenhall Street – and somehow the haste and the pell-mellishness of the wedding seemed wrong. She begged Robin to wait until Rupert was better.

She had taken him upstairs to show him the old nursery where she had been made, so to speak, and, as gently as he could, Robin had pointed out that Rupert would never get better.

'More than likely the stroke would have happened, anyway.' Robin was careful to be absolutely honest. 'It was possible that a blood clot was floating around his body waiting for a chance to block up an artery.'

'We – I – gave it the chance,' said Flora bleakly.

'Thank you,' said Robin with more than a tinge of irony. He flicked the ugly central light with his fingernail and its metal shade rattled. 'Flora, we can't take responsibility for your father. You mustn't.'

'No,' she said uncertainly, feeling that nothing would shift her guilt.

'Look at me, Flora. It's important you mean it.'

The light swung to and fro. With a little cry, Flora flung her arms around him. 'Anything might have done it,' he said into her neck. 'Anyway, it *has* happened. We have to go forward from there.' He retrieved his tie from Flora's stranglehold. 'Do you see what I mean?'

'No and yes.'

'I thought you didn't like your father very much?'

'Even if I hated him, I wouldn't want to be the cause of his death.' Flora released Robin. 'In a way, loving or hating has nothing to do with it. I'm attached to Father in spite of those feelings. Now he's so ill and I've made the break, I feel more, not less, bound. Does that make sense?'

'Perfect sense.' Robin leant over and kissed the soft bit at her temple. 'All the more reason for you and me to get married as soon as it's decent and then everyone can get on with their lives. Including us.'

A fortnight later, Flora and Robin were married very quietly in the church. Up the lime avenue she walked like her sister before her, but on Kit's arm, her veil blowing in the wind and her hem dragging along the wet stones. Except for the blaze of candles in the aisle and on the altar, which Matty had insisted on providing, it was dark inside the church. The smell of hot wax mingled with that of the white freesias and narcissi that she had also arranged to be flown in from the South of France.

The guests bunched in the front pews – rangy Dysart relations on one side, short, sandy-haired Loftses on the other. Rolly was in his best suit and Ada had sewn bunches of artificial cherries onto a green velour cloche.

Wearing her funeral hat, outraged and stony-eyed, Robbie sat as far back as she could manage, beside the nativity tableau in pipe-cleaners and cardboard that the children had put up for Advent. Smelling of dog and spirits, Danny sidled into a pew opposite and stared straight ahead throughout the proceedings. Only Matty, soft, tawny and wearing dusty pink silk, looked really weddingish – better, in fact, than she had at her own. Under her hat, she smiled gently.

Flora was happy. The light filtering into the chancel was tinged with December murk, the church was cold and the carpet frayed, but Flora felt cradled in its antiquity, part of a chain of men and women who had stood in the same place, saying the same words, full of hope for the journey ahead. For change.

Mrs Pengeally touched the keys of the wheezy organ and Flora turned to her bridegroom, the waistband of her dress pinching her sturdy frame. The corners of Robin's eyes narrowed as he smiled at his bride, whose scraped-back hair under the Honiton lace veil

391

was doing its best to escape. It will be all right, he tried to say silently to her, and Flora was at peace.

'Danny.' Back from three days' honeymoon in Bath, Flora ran up the path to the cottage at Jonathan's Kilns and banged on the door. 'Danny.'

'I'm coming, Miss Flora. I'm coming.' Danny stood blinking on the threshold with a glass in his hand.

It was a dark afternoon in the week before Christmas. In the distance the gas lights in the village shone a hazy yellow. It was cold and the temperature was falling. Flora waved her torch in Danny's face.

'You must come, Danny. Dr Williams says Father's getting worse. You said you would.'

'Dying?' Danny glanced at the thick gold band on Flora's finger and she flushed.

'Come on, Danny. Don't waste time.'

'Wait, then.' Danny's mouth did its gin-trap trick. He pulled down his corduroy jacket from the hook and slammed the door behind him. 'That woman'll be there?'

'My brother promises that there will be no trouble.'

Matty was keeping watch in Rupert's bedroom while Robbie snatched some rest. Rupert appeared to be sleeping, and she shuffled through a pile of his books on the table – *Decisive Battles of the Western Front*, *Mr Britling Goes to War*. Rupert had annotated the margins of the latter with black ink. 'Youth and common people shone,' she read. 'For the sons of every class went out to fight and die, full of a splendid dream of this war.' Further on, there was a heavy underscoring: 'It is a war without point, a war that has lost its soul . . .'

She put down the book. If the war had not finished off the body of this soldier, it had done a good job on his spirit.

Earlier, Matty had helped Robbie to wash the body that no longer had jurisdiction over itself, and rubbed it with alcohol to avoid bedsores. Then they made Rupert as comfortable as they could. Robbie had arranged his hands so they rested on the sheet

– like the disembodied marble hands so favoured by Victorians. Rupert seemed mummified and inert from the inside out but Matty wondered, with panic for him, if it was true that the comatose were cursed with a mind that was still active.

Flora poked her head round the door. 'He's here.' She ushered Danny in and went over to the decanter on the table. 'Have this,' she said, and poured him some whisky.

Danny drank it. Matty had not seen him for some time, and he seemed more lined and red-eyed than she remembered.

'I've rung Polly,' she told Flora. 'She'll try and get down tonight, if not first thing tomorrow morning. Apparently she's expecting again and not feeling well.'

'*Again?*' Flora drew up a chair beside the bed. 'Here, Danny,' she said. 'Talk to Father.'

Danny reached over and took Rupert's limp hand in his own. 'Sir?'

Not surprisingly, there was no answer.

'He's normally a little more responsive,' said Flora. 'That's why Dr Williams thinks we ought to say goodbye. He's slipping away.'

Danny said nothing, but rubbed his fingers gently to and fro over Rupert's palm, and Matty was touched by the tenderness of the gesture.

'How long did the doctor give 'im?' Danny asked at last.

'Dr Williams couldn't be sure.' Flora poured out two more glasses of whisky and gave one to Matty. 'It might be a long night.'

The phone rang in the hall and Flora went down to answer it. She returned to say that there had been a bad car crash the other side of Odiham, Dr Williams would not be able to come as he had promised and, Flora silently dared Matty to contradict, she had telephoned Robin to tell him to come instead.

'Of course,' said Matty.

Suddenly, Flora covered her eyes with her hand and sat down.

'You must have known Sir Rupert well,' said Matty, standing beside Danny.

393

'You could say that, Mrs Dysart.' Danny fixed his gaze on the figure in the bed. 'We saw things together.'

Over Danny's head Matty and Flora exchanged glances, aware that they were not admitted to what Rupert and Danny had shared – a world narrowed down to a trench or a mud track through a wood, a penny whistle playing in the twilight, a damp cigarette, the creak of leather harness, the smell of wet documents in a canvas message pouch. To fat, sated bluebottles.

'Yes,' said Danny. 'We saw some things, Sir Rupert and I. I saved 'im and 'e saved me. After it was over, when I'd nowhere to go, 'e brought me 'ere and gave me an 'ome.'

'You never said,' said Flora. 'Why didn't you tell me?'

Danny shrugged.

Later, when it was almost dark, Kit came in and refilled the glasses. Because she liked catching the very last drop of light, and partly because she did not want to intrude, Matty stood by the window. Kit came over and slipped his arm around her.

'Not too tired?'

She shook her head, enjoying the weight of his arm on her shoulders.

'You will tell me if you are?'

The afternoon quickly turned into evening and Matty drew the curtains across the windows, shrouding the room in red velvet. Kit built up the fire, and it became very warm. Danny remained at the bedside. Flora played Patience opposite him on a portable card table and wished that Robin would come. The whisky was making them light-headed.

Shortly after eight o'clock – Flora knew that because she looked over to the clock – the form on the bed seemed to twitch. Then Rupert made a definite sound and his eyelids flickered open. Flora's card table collapsed with a crack.

'I wish Robin was here,' she said.

Slowly and with obvious effort, Rupert swivelled his eyes and made a noise from the corner of his mouth that might have been 'Danny'. Danny dragged his chair closer to the bed.

'Talk to him, Danny,' said Flora. 'He wants you to talk to him.'

'Do you remember, sir . . .?' Danny was jumbled with whisky and emotion. 'On the Somme, sir? The big push? Twenty companies of us, shoulder to shoulder. Remember Plugstreet Wood, Tram Car Cottage, Kansas Cross? Do you remember the beer and 'ow the locals could never get the 'ang of making tea?'

Flora made encouraging signals to Danny with her hand. 'Go on.'

'. . . Marguerite Trench where the bloody Frogs 'ad let the flowers grow because they never went over the top? Like a bloomin' flower shop it was. 'Ow we marched, sir, through streams, culverts and woods. I remember you sayin' it was good 'unting land.'

'Keep talking, Danny.' Kit's glass shook in his hand.

'They loaded us up right and proper. I don't know what they thought we were. Bloomin' camels. Empty sandbags, shovels, grenades, rockets, cable, pigeon baskets and shittin' pigeons. We woke on the morning it began and it was raining through a mist. We stood and watched the early mist ripple from the 'owitzers' shells. It was just like a lake with stones being thrown into it. Wasn't it, sir?'

Again Rupert made a strange sound. Kit bent over him. 'Father?'

'The eighteen-pounders and four-sevens made us think, didn't they? So did the fifteen-inch 'owitzers coming down on Gomme-court Wood. Whole trees were being flung into the air, and the bloody 'Uns sat in their dug-outs, waiting.'

Dear God, said Matty, spare that *ever* happening again. She reached up, snapped on a second light, and the bed was illuminated like an enormous painting.

'Near as pickled, weren't we, sir? From the rum, seeing that we never went into battle on a full stomach.'

Danny's soft voice flowed on like a stream, pausing here and there, and Kit watched at the bedside as another man saw out his father's life.

'We did all right, sir? Didn't we?' Danny's voice rose, an aching, keening note.

Matty watched Kit, and suffered for him.

Flora's gaze riveted on her father's hand. Slowly, with infinite effort, a finger uncurled, a white slug looping out from its leaf, hoping for anchorage. She hissed, 'He's moving.'

Once again, Danny took hold of Rupert's hand and this time the bulging eyes obviously recognized him, for they widened and softened.

' "We are the dead",' said Danny lightly. 'Do you remember? We laughed at the bloke who read us that poem. I liked it. But I always liked the poems, though, didn't I, sir? This one was a real Percival poet, even I laughed at 'im. Still, it's a good 'un and 'e died quite soon after. You always said, sir, my taste in poetry was rotten.

> ' "To you from failing 'ands we throw
> The torch: be yours to hold it 'igh
> If ye break faith, we who die,
> We shall not sleep, though poppies grow
> In Flanders' fields . . ." '

'Don't,' said Flora, tears falling down her cheeks, too proud to wipe them away. 'Don't, Danny.'

By midnight Danny was drunk, Kit verging on it and the others chilled and stiff.

'If ye break faith . . .' The line was tailor-made for Flora's germinating guilt. She longed for the comfort of Robin's presence. He had promised to come as soon as Violet Girdler in Croft Lane had produced her baby. The images that Danny conjured clung stickily in her mind, and she wanted to cry out that they should, all of them, forget these memories. Life could not be driven – *they* could not be driven – by this terrible war any more.

Robin arrived at last. He looked weary, with dark circles under his eyes. Flora took herself off to get him some tea and sandwiches.

In the corridor, her heart somersaulted and she stopped abruptly. Someone lurked in the dark wedge made by the shadow between two windows. Then she realized who it was.

'Robbie,' she said sharply. 'What on earth are you doing? There's no need to hang about on the landing.' She felt along the wall with her hand and turned on the light.

Robbie's face was blotched from crying. For the first time in many weeks, she addressed Flora. 'I'm keeping watch in my own way.'

For a dreadful moment, Flora thought Robbie had gone mad – and the cold, the dark and the creaks of the floorboards in the landing heightened the fancy. Then she pulled herself together. 'Please, Robbie. You mustn't get like this. You mustn't mind about Danny.'

Extremity made Robbie reckless, and, from her self-imposed exile, she attacked. 'I don't trust him. He has some sort of hold, knows something about Sir Rupert.' Robbie caught Flora by the arm. 'I've known what it was, Miss Flora. Do you?'

Because Robbie was so distressed, Flora stopped herself from pushing her away. 'No, Robbie, of course not. I can't think what you're talking about.' She felt her temper slipping and thought to herself that Robbie was quite ridiculous to make a scene at such a moment. Besides, Flora's first priority was to get her tired husband some tea and, as far as she was concerned, Robbie and Danny would have to fight it out between them. 'I wish you wouldn't be lurid, Robbie,' she said crossly. 'They're two comrades from the war, admittedly rather odd ones, who like a drink and have kept up their friendship, that's all. Now, I suggest you come downstairs with me and have a cup of tea.'

Robbie moved down the passage and the electric light trapped her face in its glare. Fresh from her discovery of physical love, Flora was suddenly alerted by the expression in the older woman's eyes. I have nothing, it said. And I wanted more. I wanted what most women have.

Ye gods, she thought. And I have everything.

'Robbie,' she said and slid her arm around the older woman's waist. 'It's no use you going to pieces. We rely on you to get us through.'

'Yes,' said Robbie, after a moment. 'Yes, pet.'

'You should go to bed.' Kit bent over Matty and pulled her to her feet.

'I'm fine.'

'No.' Kit was deadly serious. 'It would be very difficult if you got over-tired and had a relapse.'

She looked up at the fair head she had spent so long trying to see inside, and saw that the shutters were closed against her. Rupert's dying was private, and Kit did not want her there. For a second, the demon squeezed her chest and then she said, 'If you like,' and went.

'Danny.' Rupert managed to get out an approximation of the word.

'Sir.'

Kit took up a position by the window. Wrapped in a tartan rug from Ardtornish, Flora knelt at the foot of the bed and Robin drank his tea by the fire.

The logs hissed. Flora really ought to be holding a lighted candle, Kit thought with the irreverence that catches the mind at important moments. Then she would resemble one of those plump, worldly women in a medieval Dutch painting who kneel in adoration of the Christ-child in a welter of household goods.

It was cold by the window, and his thoughts drifted. He recollected his escapes from the home he often found intolerable, riding into Damascus with Max in blazing heat, of pure blue sky, of peach and almond blossom, of the tinkle of water in courtyards. He thought of Daisy.

He remembered, too, held until not so very long ago, his dislike and distrust of his father . . . the blame he attached to Rupert for Hesther's suicide . . . his anguish that Rupert never noticed him, never appeared to care. They were fading now, those feelings, in the shrouded room, leaving Kit curiously empty.

'Remember the marching we did up to the line,' said Danny. 'Through the mud. Feet all soft from the trenches. Up Tin Pan Alley. "Don't look round," you said to us, sir. "Just keep going." We knew that an 'ard time lay ahead but you say, "There's an omelette waiting for each chap at the depot if you get through." Cigarettes, too. Letters, perhaps. "Look, chaps," you say to our lot. "We got through the Marne, le Câteau. Wipers. Let's get through this bloody awful one."' Danny paused. 'And we did, sir . . .'

In June 1916, Kitchener's New Army assembled to fling itself at a German army that had already been dug into French soil for two years — a first, second and sometimes third line that had snatched every high spur and chalky ridge of the Somme downland for its advantage and disappeared into a labyrinth of underground bunkers.

Kitchener's boys had to make do with the terrain they had.

Mixed in with the New Army were the remnants of those who had fought in the north and east. The 'old 'uns'. Blooded, experienced soldiers, unlike the new recruits who didn't know nothing from nothing. Among them Lieutenant-Colonel, formerly Major, Rupert Dysart, Danny Ovens, Bill Cranstone and Jack Oakley from the Hampshires. The 'old 'uns', who knew a thing or two, rested up and waited, assembled their kit and their thoughts, wrote letters home and watched the raw recruits fling themselves around. Rupert struggled to get a grip on his unstable nerves.

These days Danny stuck to Rupert. They had come to an arrangement. Danny made Rupert's tea, shone his boots and shaved him. He liked having an officer to look after, and Rupert wanted a batman. He was a Londoner, Danny confided to Rupert during the long evening twilights. I never would have guessed, said Rupert with a rare flash of humour, I thought your dropped aitches were from Manchester. Danny explained he had joined up with the Hamps after a couple of beers on a day visit to Farnham to see his sister and one regiment was like another. Anyway, he was thinking of moving to the country. 'Course, there's not much left of us Hamps now, is there, sir?'

'No,' said Rupert, white-faced, his head in his hands. 'No, there isn't, Danny.'

On 1 July the 19th Wilts — the Butterflies — which had been held in reserve moved up to the left of those who still survived, dug into positions overlooking the village of La Boisselle. Nearly a thousand men slogged down the line towards the front, and the Germans, bunked up on their higher vantage point, picked them off like targets in a shooting gallery. By the time they reached the assault trench, the men were sweating from the physical effort – and from fear.

'I'll need me fucking Danny's Cockney luck today,' Danny said.

Crouching in the dirt among writhing telephone cables, the men settled in for the wait. A long line of them. Bombers. Snipers. Mopers. Messengers. Signallers. Sappers. But all fodder.

Rupert sprinted along the top of the trench and ordered, 'Fix your bayonets and get ready to go over when you hear the whistle.' A German machine gun screamed, there was a volley of bullets and Rupert's water bottle was hit.

'Get down, sir,' shouted Danny.

Rupert threw himself over into the trench.

'Don't think you'll do that again, sir,' said Danny.

'Shut up,' said Rupert, who agreed.

The worst of waiting in the assault trench was the machine guns, which arced backwards and forwards, cutting the sandbags to pieces on the parapets. Going over the top was a joke, going over with your eyes and nose full of sand was hilarious.

It was midday and hot. The men had to ration use of the water bottles and Danny's tongue swelled to twice its size.

'Tell you what,' said Rupert, unhooking his water bottle from his belt. 'Take some of the sandbag rags, put them in this tin with some candle grease and see if you can't boil the last of the water and we'll have some tea.'

An hour later, they had warm, wet liquid but not much else.

A colonel came in from the 19th and requested Rupert for a signaller to go down the line to help get the troops into position. Rupert detailed his man. Pressed down into the earth, Danny watched the signaller's flag dip and wave, and the companies shuffled forward, bayonets fixed. Then it was up and over.

The German guns began in earnest.

The stretch of land that the Hamps and the 19th Wilts had to cross lay in front of a huge mine crater. Beyond that lay the second German line, which they had been ordered to take.

When the whistle went, Danny threw his rifle on top of the trench, pulled himself up, grabbed it and surged forward. Underfoot was pitted with shell holes, and treacherous. He stumbled, fell, got up, ran, fell, and was never sure if he was going down with a bullet in him or not.

From the third German line on the higher ground, the machine guns hammered out hell, the guns tore the sky apart and the shells burst like burnt-out stars.

Weaving, dodging, Danny ran. Rupert was behind him, bringing up the rear. Then Danny caught his foot, fell, and Rupert ran on past. Danny flung himself to one side, and caught a glimpse of his face from which emotion had been stripped.

He struggled upright. Ran. Reached what he thought was the parapet of the German trench, hovered on the edge and, with a crump, a shell exploded. For a second or two, the world coloured black. Danny felt his spirit rise out of his body and watch while his body rolled and bumped down forty feet or more with a dozen or so of the other men following him.

'Bloody fuckin' 'ell.' He spat out chalk and earth and tried to sit up. 'It's a fuckin' mine crater.' That was the last thing he said for several minutes, for he passed out. When he woke, it was quiet except for a loud buzzing. Then the guns started again.

'Bloody fuckin' 'ell.'

One of the men had clambered up the opposite side of the crater and lay under cover keeping watch. Bill Gunstone wriggled on his stomach back to Danny, sending a shower of chalk over his face. 'All right, son?'

'Where've I got it?'

'Thigh, I should say.' Bill fiddled in his bag for a dressing and did his best to tidy up the wound which was bleeding heavily. 'Not like Jack over there.'

Danny squinted. Jack Oakley lay twitching in a pool of drying red. One of his legs had been mashed up and, by the look of it, his shoulder had gone. Bill shoved the neck of his water bottle into Danny's mouth. 'Here. Looks like we're stuck here for the time being. We'll have to wait till dark.'

'Nice 'otel,' said Danny, and the pain in his leg hit him.

The shells kept coming. How they kept coming. Every so often the crater took a hit and a man cried out. The summer sun blazed like the Day of Judgement. One by one, the sweltering, islanded men were picked off. Bill first, then the others. Then Jack began to scream.

'*Will someone shoot me.*'

His cries scrambled Danny's nerves until he, too, was shrieking inside his useless body. Only his eyes were capable of movement, sliding from side to side, watching the darkening sky while he listened to Jack die. In the end, Danny knew he had to make himself move. If it was the last thing he ever did, he *had* to move. He couldn't go out, just like that, with no effort.

Inch by gasping inch Danny pulled himself up the side of the crater on what he hoped was the British side. A body lay at the top, and he heard machine-gun bullets rip into it. They made the same sound when they tore into sandbags.

Didn't matter to the poor bugger now.

With a final effort, Danny raised his head above the rim of the crater and peered through the stifling grey smoke. Through it he could make out men stumbling to and fro as the battle raged for the line, reeling from the fumes of the gas-soaked earth and smoke.

But Danny became conscious of only one thing: the buzzing of a thousand million flies settling over the bodies that lay between the lines in the Flanders' fields.

That Danny dreaded most, dying in no man's land in gas-infected crater water, in pain. Alone. With no one to see him out.

Danny wept into the foul-smelling earth, and then fainted.

When he regained consciousness it was dark. Moonlight played over the scorched landscape. Mercifully, it was quiet, the lull while more reserves were brought in. There was the merest hint of a moon in the sky, and from time to time an odd flare spat yellow light. Perhaps I'm dead already, he thought.

Creeping with infinite care, morphia pills tucked into his jacket, aching, exhausted, Rupert launched himself from the dug-out in the British line to where he and the men had retreated, and slithered towards the crater having ordered the others to keep cover.

Somehow he got himself over the top.

He owed Danny a debt. He knew some would say that the carnage cancelled it out: it did not matter one way or the other any more. There was no time for such niceties. But Rupert did not agree. He could not, would not, let go of the idea that he could do something right, that it mattered he tried. That he owed a man the honour of being buried with his own kind. He could not let go. Despite the shattered nerves, despite the failures, he would pay his debt, and if he had to crawl over the hellish landscape until he dropped, so be it.

So Rupert crawled, the dust coating his Dysart hair, freezing into the ground every other foot, willing himself forward. A gun spluttered. A burst of German from the trenches in front of him was quickly hushed. The instant dazzle of a match. Then silence and darkness.

At the top of the crater where Rupert, turning to look back in battle, had seen Danny throw up his arms and fall, he rolled his body over and spiralled down to the bottom. Seconds later a machine gun splattered bullets where he had been.

'Ovens.' Rupert lit a match and cupped his hand around it. 'Ovens,' he whispered. The flare lit a huddled form half-way up. 'Danny Ovens?'

And Danny waking from the nightmare of pain and fear heard the Angel of Deliverance.

'Here,' he said. 'Over here, sir.'

Rupert crawled his way back up the side of the crater, hanging onto the chalky earth with his clawed hands. By the time he reached Danny earth clogged his nostrils and he was dizzy from the exertion.

'Sir,' said Danny and felt fresh blood welling on his leg. 'You're a fool . . .'

Rupert's hand crept precariously over the earth and grasped Danny's.

'I wouldn't let you die on your own, Danny.'

Danny cradled his whisky and blew into it. 'Somehow, he got me across that piece of land. He stuffed me with morphia pills, and he dragged me on his back, I think.'

A log broke in the grate.

'Your father kept faith,' said Danny. ' "Let's get through this bloody awful battle, Danny," 'e said. And we did.' Danny paused. ''E knows I won't let 'im go out alone. 'E knows I'm 'ere.'

As Danny talked, Rupert opened his eyelids and, ignoring his son and his daughter, gazed at Danny with eyes as clear and lucid as a Highland burn. Right at Danny, through him and beyond. Then he died.

After Kit had come, told her the news and gone again, Matty read through the night, a cone of electric light from her lamp illuminating the page. *Papaver* – the poppy – she read, the flower of sleep and oblivion. In mythology, it is said to have been created by Somnus, the god of sleep, its juice the pathway along which flee wild and fanciful dreams so seductive that the dreamer never tires. Therein lay its fascination and its danger.

Matty pushed back her hair and studied the illustrations: the violet poppy . . . the carnation poppy . . . the curled poppy . . . the fringed poppy. The French call the wild poppy *coquelicot* because it is a persistent scarlet tease that returns time after time to thread its brilliant pinpoints through the corn – the corn that Rupert and Danny, and those hundreds of thousands of men, those Tommy Atkinses, now dead and gone, trampled through in their rotting boots.

'The Poppie procureth sleepe,' wrote Gerard in 1567, 'it mitigateth all kindes of paines.'

404

So it did, so it does, thought Matty. Laudanum. Loddy. Opium. Pathways to the waters of the river Lethe where Rupert now swam.

He was at peace, she was quite sure, free from the wrapping of a body that no longer functioned, free from the past.

She closed the book and thought about her garden. That also contained the past, and she had been fearful of going back into it. For Hesther was there, Rose was there, and she was afraid that Kit and Daisy had left their imprint over her flowers.

But finally, the memories had not mattered. What bothered Matty was the neglect of the past weeks, and that she could – and did – do something about.

Matty rolled back the bedclothes, stood up on the freezing floor and, light-headed from lack of sleep, shivered. The house was quiet and Robin's car was no longer parked in the drive.

She opened the wardrobe door. Hanging undisturbed at the back were the clothes that had become second nature, a little dusty from disuse. With a sigh of pleasure, Matty took them down from their hangers – her daring breeches, blouse, green corduroy jacket – and dressed, bundling on two vests under her blouse because of the cold. Then she pulled on her boots.

Wearing breeches made her feel free and uninhibited – as if she had put on another Matty. The Matty who had come to accept things about herself and her life: who could see ghosts; whose husband would continue to love another woman; who was childless.

She wound a scarf round her neck and looked at the clock in the shagreen case. Seven thirty. Barely light, but light enough.

Rupert was dead and she was glad for him – and she, who was alive and now well, was going out into the dawn to indulge a passion that would not fail her.

Saddened but exhilarated, Matty smiled at herself in the mirror.

As she filled the kettle in the kitchen, Matty remembered that she had to cancel the Christmas guests and arrange Rupert's funeral. She put the kettle on the stove, got out the tea caddy and raked up the coals. The kettle would be boiling by the time she came back.

'Get up, you lazy lump,' she said to Minerva in her basket.

She let herself out of the house into the freezing air. Breathing in gusts of it, she walked across the frosted lawn towards her garden.

HARRY

During the early days of the year, the weather sometimes flings us a bonus of warm, sun-filled days smelling of frost and iced berries. I suppress my fussy urge to cut and tidy, for frost must not get into open wounds.

Once winter depressed me. The gloom and fog of November and December, the rawness of January, February's bleakness. There is nothing there, one is tempted to conclude, peering out into the dead brown and buff, the rattling skeleton of the garden.

But there is, you know. Tiny stirrings of life. Unexpected bursts of blossom and glorious scent. Winter stars are, of necessity, isolated, but when they come one can concentrate on them. Ah, when they come . . . I wait for the pink blossoms of the *Prunus autumnalis* with the impatience of a child, or for the scented honeysuckle, the starbursts of daphne, the first snowdrops, the first crocus . . . These, in many ways, give me more pleasure than the profusion later.

This is the time when you know if you have chosen your evergreens well, when ivy comes into its own, when the pleasures of a box-edged bed deepens, when the spurge, *Euphorbia characias wulfenii*, will repay many times over the trouble you have taken with it.

This is the time to dig deep into yourself and to swear to do the things that you omitted to do the previous year. For winter exposes the soul of the gardener and the garden. In its retreat, it is possible to see the traps which are laid for every gardener, however prudent.

That is why it is such a great leveller.

CHAPTER EIGHT

WHEN SHE went back into hospital, Ellen stopped dreaming – except for one strange instance. Afterwards she was never sure if it *was* a dream or a twist of mind brought on by the drugs. In it, she struggled with a monster, a black, formless shape that pressed down on her whichever way she turned, smothering and implacable. Ellen recognized the monster. It was fear. Fear was no stranger and over the past few months she and it had become well acquainted. Restless, she tossed and turned in her starched hospital sheets.

Then Bill stood before her, as clear as the day she had swung over the stile and smiled into his eyes. 'Don't run, love,' he said. 'You must face it.'

'I can't,' she told him. 'It's too much for me.'

'No, it isn't, love. Go on.'

'I just want some peace, Bill.'

'*Go on*, love.'

Still in her dream, Ellen slowly turned a half-circle, spread wide her arms and looked into the heart of the monster.

After that, the dreams ceased. Ellen responded to the sulphona-mides, her fever dropped and she began to get better.

Matty and Ned discovered her in the women's surgical ward of Fleet hospital dispensing mid-morning tea from the trolley. Sister led the way down the polished no man's land dividing the beds. Matty was wearing a sable-trimmed jacket with a row of pearls and there was a rustle as the regimented occupants in hospital gowns sat up to get a better look. Ellen's standing shot skywards.

'Hallo, girl,' said Ned awkwardly.

Sister intervened at this point. 'Mrs Sheppey's our helper. She's done so well,' she explained, as if Ellen was not there.

'Mrs Lofts is very sorry she can't come today,' said Matty, and allowed Sister to usher her into a chair. 'How is the knee?'

Sister nipped in. 'Mr Staine has seen to that, Lady Dysart. And it's all tickety-boo. And, in a trice, here Mrs Sheppey is dispensing tea and sympathy.'

'Ned,' said Ellen with her old fierceness when Sister had moved on, 'if you don't get me out of here soon, I'll kill that woman.'

'No need for that kind of talk, girl.' Ned shot a distressed look at Matty, who came to the rescue. She told Ellen about Rupert's funeral service at the village church and the tea at the house afterwards, about the short obituary in *The Times*, and how the family, Flora in particular, had been forced to keep a close eye on Danny, who had set about drinking himself to death. Luckily, the hunting season was in full swing and he had been forced to pull himself together.

'How was your daughter, Mrs Sheppey?' she asked, at last. 'Ned tells me she came to see you as planned.'

Ellen smiled a smile from which all worry had vanished. 'She was fine, wasn't she, Ned?' Ellen looked at him. 'And I wanted to thank you for having Tyson drive her up. It was a kind thing to do. Seeing Betty means everything to me, and Ned here.'

'That was Mrs Lofts's idea,' said Matty, fiddling with her handkerchief.

Plainly, Ned was ill at ease: polished floors and disinfectant did not agree with him. His eyes shifted around the ward – he was unable to stop himself searching out sights he would rather not see – and lingered on patients who were clearly very ill. 'When are you coming out, girl? Have they told you?'

'Monday next,' said Ellen, 'providing I behave. I am grateful for what they have done, sure, but I tell you, Lady Dysart, the women that run this ward are enough to send a saint round the twist. Our helper, indeed. I'll give her help.'

'She looked so indignant,' Matty reported to Kit later, 'I almost took her home there and then.'

She had been in bed writing up her garden notebook when Kit had knocked on the bedroom door.

'Can I come in? I know it's late.'

'When planning a garden,' she had written, 'you must make a path along the line which people will always take. That is, the shortest route, unless you mislead them by planting shrubs.' Under that she had put, 'All young plants (and trees?) require feeding and watering for their first two years. N.B. Must build that into the plans . . .'

'Do you mind?' asked Kit, sitting down on the bed. He was wearing his striped dressing gown and down-at-heel slippers and seemed restless and preoccupied. He squinted over her knees to the notebook. 'Are you writing a diary?'

Matty surveyed her husband. Once upon a time her heart would have beaten a tattoo at his entrance, but it had got tired of doing so – or perhaps Matty had given up hoping that Kit would love her. 'Do you need an aspirin powder or something?' she asked politely.

'No. I came in to see you and to say goodnight.'

Then she told him about Ellen, and after that a silence fell between them. Matty asked if Kit had been in touch with Max over the final arrangements for the trip to Iraq the following week. Kit replied that all was under control.

Another silence.

'You do understand why I'm going?' he asked out of the blue.

'Max asked you.'

He leant forward with his elbows on his knees. 'Just one more time, Matty. That's all. To drive it out of my blood. The smell of leather, sun on your back, the smell of it. Cleanness.'

'Yes,' she said.

Still Matty was not sure why he had come.

Suddenly, he reached over and touched the collar of her nightdress. 'I am glad you don't wear frilly, slippery things,' he said. 'You're so comfortable and soft.'

It flashed on Matty that Kit was telling her that she looked motherly, and perhaps this was what he had been wanting all along – after all, she knew now that Hesther was the key to Kit. She said nothing, but nor did she push him away as he undid the first button. A childish horn button, sewn on tightly. Kit undid the second button.

'Stop me if you wish,' he said, and slid his hand inside to cup her breast. At his touch, her feelings awoke, green and surprisingly strong, and she caught her breath as Kit eased the nightdress down her shoulders. 'I don't expect anything after all that has happened.' She remained motionless under his hands. Then he removed the combs that were still in her hair, shaking them free so that her newly grown hair framed her face in a cloud.

'You're very pretty,' he said, and he meant it. He stood up with his hand on his dressing-gown belt and looked down at Matty. 'Shall I go on?'

As he kissed and stroked the small body, Kit seemed to be searching for something and Matty was wary of being hurt. But, in the end, the habit of loving Kit was too strong, and she strove to give him what he searched for. But an edge was missing, or perhaps, Kit thought as he moved above her, it was trust. And who could blame Matty? Afterwards, they lay in the dark, with their separate thoughts.

He drew Matty into the circle of his arm and for a moment she allowed herself to relax against his shoulder. 'What were you writing when I came in?'

'Notes for the garden.' Kit's flesh was smooth and muscled under her cheek. Her lips tasted his saltiness. She turned suddenly and propped herself on one elbow. 'Kit,' she said, 'I was going to wait, but perhaps we should discuss something now. We both know that our marriage was a business arrangement . . .'

She felt him tense. 'Go on.'

She slipped away from him and sat up on the pillows. 'What I am trying to say is, that I want you to think very hard on this trip whether or not we should continue. Or whether it would be better to finish the marriage.'

'Why now, Matty?' Kit switched on the light and both of them blinked. From habit, Matty looked for her nightdress in the bedclothes and Kit for a cigarette in his dressing gown.

'Because of what we have just done. That.' She beat the space that they had occupied with the flat of her hand. 'Both of us want something other than the original bargain provides for. Don't you see?'

'Matty what are you driving at?' Matty was trapped in the neckline of the nightdress and he reached over to ease it over her head. 'You love Daisy, and you should have married her,' her voice was muffled by the material, 'and everything you have done since has convinced me of that. Your going off with Max is one example. I thought I wouldn't mind but I was wrong.' Matty's face and tousled hair emerged. 'I do, Kit.' She stuffed a pillow behind her and sat up straight. 'You know I love you, and there is no use pretending.' She picked at the lace edging of the sheet and then raised her eyes. 'I don't want half measures any more.'

'I see.' Kit was very quiet. He looked into familiar features — and concluded, with a surprising jolt, that he would mind very much not seeing them again.

Unaware that she had unwittingly chosen the best tactic — that of threatening to take something away — Matty pressed on. 'If we part amicably, the fuss will die down after a bit and then you can marry Daisy. You mustn't worry because I have lots of things I want to do.'

'What things?'

She reflected for a moment as if, he thought wryly, deciding whether to allow him access to her thoughts. 'I would like to breed roses and develop a garden. I'd buy a house somewhere, near Winchester, perhaps. I like the country and I like the country life.'

Kit got out of bed, grabbed his dressing gown and took up his favourite stance by the window. With a mixture of weariness and hunger, Matty gazed at him. 'If divorce is unthinkable,' she said, 'maybe we could get an annulment.' She added painfully, 'Because of no children.'

Kit shrugged on the dressing gown. 'Do you really want a divorce?'

'I think it might be the best thing. But what I want, Kit, is to know your feelings. I never know. You never tell me. I feel I am living in a one-sided world, or with a block of wood.'

He spoke with his back to her. 'We have never discussed this, Matty, but have you ever considered the lack of children may be my fault?'

'No,' she replied. 'Dr Hurley was adamant on that point.'

Kit tied a knot in his belt. 'I mind, you know, Matty.'

'Oh, Kit.' Matty's heart gave its lurch of pain. 'I didn't know.'

'I thought I didn't, but I find myself looking into prams to see what's inside.'

Half tearful, half angry, thinking how typical it was that Kit had never said anything, Matty said, 'And I spend my time not looking into prams because I can't bear it.'

Kit undid the knot in his belt and retied it, and then he said with an obvious effort, 'I'm sorry if I never let you know what I'm feeling. I find it difficult.' Pause. 'I have told you some things, though, Matty.'

Although it was an apology, the hint of justification in Kit's tone made Matty see red. She beat the pillow with her fist. 'You may find it difficult, but you don't know what it's like to wake up every day and know that your husband wished another woman lay under your roof. Do you? You don't, so you can't possibly understand.' The pillow sagged under its pummelling and she shoved it towards him. 'You don't even like taking anything from me. Not even a pillow, I daresay. Although, I note, you take it in the end.'

In a detached way, Matty noticed she was operating on two levels: an upper level where she shrank from the scene, a lower level where a surge of astringent emotion washed away the detritus in her mind. 'The worst thing is that I asked for it. I arranged this marriage.'

She clamped her full bottom lip shut. Kit stood absolutely still, his face unreadable, and lit another cigarette.

Anger having temporarily lanced the wound, Matty felt relief at having spoken out at last. But, before she subsided completely, she threw one last missile at her husband. 'What's more, you standing there, Kit, is going to make me say I'm sorry, and I promised myself I wouldn't. There is no need for me to apologize. It's a habit. So would you please go away.'

He shrugged and said quietly, 'I imagined what we have was what you wanted. You seemed so self-contained, Matty. I didn't realize.'

413

'Well, you're blind and unfeeling, and you never bothered to ask. Now please go away.'

'That's not very kind, Matty.'

It wasn't, but Matty summoned all the anguish of the past two years and threw it at him. 'I don't care.'

Incredibly, Kit gave a snort of laughter, and checked himself. 'Matty, I shouldn't laugh. But you looked so furious and . . . it rather suits you. Sorry,' he added when he saw he had gone too far.

'That is unforgivable.' Matty now began to shake with hot, releasing rage. 'How *dare* you?'

Kit suddenly became very serious. He finished the cigarette and stubbed it out. 'You're quite right, Matty, things do need to be sorted out. And I am to blame, I know that.' He pulled back the curtain with a jerk. 'You love this garden, don't you?'

'Yes,' she answered from the bed. 'More than anything.'

He twitched the curtain further back. 'Go to sleep, Matty,' he said roughly. 'Go to sleep.'

To her surprise, Matty did just that and was woken only by Kit slipping into the bed in the early morning. He was shaking with cold, and his hands beat a frozen path up her body as he pushed up the nightdress.

'Don't go, Matty,' he whispered into the hollow of her shoulder and kissed the *café-au-lait* eyes. 'I know I've hurt you and I didn't know how much. Wait a little. I'll go on this trip, and when I come back things will be different.'

'Kit,' she said, sleepy and bewildered. 'Why? Why are you doing this?'

'Because—' Ice-cold and urgent, Kit made love to Matty with a passion that she had not experienced before. Afterwards he pulled her to him and kissed the soft hair, and she cradled him like a child on her breasts. 'Listen, Matty,' he whispered. 'Promise me not to decide anything until I get back. I've never asked you anything before, and in many ways I don't have the right, but I'm asking now.'

Did she trust Kit? Did she care any longer? Had Matty become so weary with her great, heavy, burning love that she wanted only peace?

'Matty?'

'I agree.'

With a groan, Kit turned on his side and fell asleep.

Kit's letters arrived at irregular intervals. From Basra, after he and Max had come back from an expedition into the marsh Arab territory. From Baghdad, where they acquired pack horses and a donkey, plus a wayward Bedouin called Kiaszim as a guide. From towns on the trek between Baghdad and Damascus where, Kit wrote, sandstorms came and went like spring showers and the insects in their lodgings were the size of sharks.

'In a strange way I feel cleansed,' he wrote from Ghaymin in late March, after a bout of fever and the death of the little donkey. 'Perhaps it is the experience of thirst and exhaustion.' He added the PS, 'I don't think I'll ever eat another boiled egg in my life.'

On 20 April, Kit wrote from Damascus.

> Here we are, Matty . . . we have made it. The impressions
> are overwhelming, almost too much after the sparseness
> of the desert: almond blossom and the sound of
> fountains. Burning hot coffee in tiny cups, nut-filled
> Turkish delight and a scent of spices filtering from the
> bazaar. Squalor mixed with exquisite and civilized
> delights. Peace and noise. Comfort and terrible poverty.
> The luxury of surrendering my aching, blistered body to
> hot water and a soft bed. Kiaszim is heartbroken because
> he knows he will have to say goodbye to us, although
> Max is thinking of staying on.
>
> I am coming home via Marseilles. Cable or write to me
> there, *poste restante*.
>
> Dearest Matty, it is time I came home from the desert.

Ten days later on a lovely spring afternoon, Ivy laid out, as instructed, Matty's new crêpe wrapover dress in navy blue. The hem reached almost to her ankles and the skirt flared out in a satisfying *frou*. Matty studied her reflection – she did not want to look swamped in the new-style length.

'So pretty, Lady Dysart,' said Mrs Pengeally, sizing up the dress, when she was ushered into the drawing room for afternoon tea. 'But perhaps not terribly practical.'

While Mrs Dawes spread a tablecloth and anchored it with plates of scones, raspberry jam and Madeira cake, Matty and Mrs Pengeally discussed Spain, the awful kidnapping of the Lindbergh baby, the bun-throwing incident at the Odiham–Nether Hinton Scouts meeting and the mass break-out of Mr Sparrow Wilkinson's day old White Wyandotte chicks.

A snippet of gossip had reached Mrs Pengeally about the Dysart marriage and she was curious. She ate two scones and asked, 'Sir Christopher will be back soon?'

Matty smiled politely. 'He's due back in a couple of weeks. He does like to travel.' Before she could stop herself she added, 'I might go with him one of these days. I'd like a trip to the East. I used to live there, you know, when I was very small.'

She wondered why on earth she had said that. Perhaps the glue made by habit and association in a marriage, however patchy, was stronger than Matty had supposed. She fumbled up her sleeve for her handkerchief and then stopped herself.

Ivy knocked, came in with a telegram. 'Telegram for the master, madam. I thought you would like it straight away.'

'Thank you.' Matty turned the envelope over in her hand. Years of administering to the flock had toughened Mrs Pengeally. 'Do open it, please, Lady Dysart. Don't take any notice of me.'

'Thank you, Mrs Pengeally.' Matty crossed over to the desk by the window and picked up the paper knife.

The telegram was postmarked Cap d'Antibes in Provence and it read:

COME STOP ASK AT THE BUREAU DE LA POSTE STOP
DAISY STOP

416

When she relived the moment, Matty congratulated herself on her self-control. She did not cry out, or gasp, or crumple the paper into a ball. She merely blinked a little faster than normal, tucked the telegram under the edge of the blotter and said, 'A friend of my husband's wishing to arrange a meeting.

'An old friend,' she reiterated, and smiled vaguely in the direction of Mrs Pengeally's inquisitive gaze.

When she had gone, Matty rushed upstairs to change out of her frock and went running down to her garden.

It was there, waiting.

If nothing else did, her garden needed care. The weeks of her illness in the autumn had set back her plans for it, smothered as it now was in spring abundance.

It needed Matty.

Half expecting to see Rose, she hovered by the statue and for an awful second imagined she saw the dying Hesther. She turned and skimmed back over the lawn, puffing breath through her cheeks to steady herself, across to the river, past the blue and white of the chionodoxa and anemones that she had planted, to the bridge and looked into the water, where acid green, stringy weeds floated. She made her way through the gap in the yew, across the circular lawn towards Ned trimming the box edging in the parterre below the terrace steps.

His tools were beside him on the path: a trowel whose handle had worn smooth and shiny with use, a slatted seed tray with a dibber, a battered trug, a galvanized watering can and a sack reeking of creosote.

Above Ned, the sky spread a blue wash of colour, and the breeze brought a smell of new life and growth. The sun was pale and not warm, but it was out.

The F sharp throbbed in Matty's ears, plangent and ominous.

Ned did not notice her at first. He was concentrating hard, moving with economical steadiness, a spare figure with weather-beaten hands. Matty wanted to fling herself at the tough old chest under the rough jacket and cry until she was dry.

'I'll help you, Mr Sheppey,' she said instead, and got down on her knees on the stone path.

Comfortable and easy with life now that Ellen was better, Ned said without looking up, 'You do that, Lady Dysart. I could do with some help, like.'

There were so many ghosts in this garden. Matty trowelled at a dandelion forcing itself up through a crack in the flagstones, failed and resorted to her hands. The ghosts of wounded soldiers trying to put back the pieces of their lives. Irritatingly, the dandelion snapped at the top of the root, leaving a white circle wedged between the stones, ready to grow again.

She moved on to tackle a second growing between the angle of the path and the wall.

The ghost of Hesther, who had once written 'Lovely, lovely' about a rose and then killed herself. Of little Rose, the shade that teased and tormented Matty because she knew Matty was empty and burning with longing. This time, the dandelion root yielded with a snap and earth rained over her face and down her front. Matty tackled the rogue clump of grass beside it. Of an eleven-year-old boy who had found his dying mother and, at a stroke, lost his childhood and had searched for it ever after. Of herself, who came to Hinton Dysart wounded and frightened, and discovered both a centre and a spirit.

The scar made by the uprooted grass was alive with woodlice and earthworms.

'Easy,' said Ned looking up. 'Don't waste your energy.'

The F sharp swelled, drilled through Matty's ear until she wanted to cry out and then, as suddenly as it had begun, died.

'Matty, can you hear me? The line is terrible.'

'Just about, Kit. Where are you?'

'Marseilles.' A pause. 'Thank you for sending me the telegram. It was generous of you.'

She spoke crisply into the mouthpiece. 'Of course I sent it, Kit. What else would I do with it?'

Her tone obviously worried Kit. 'Matty, listen to me,' he said. 'I know Daisy must be in trouble, she wouldn't send for me otherwise. I must go and see her.' There was a silence at Matty's end of the phone. 'Matty,' he said. 'Are you there?'

'Yes,' she replied, eventually. 'I'm still here.'

'Do you understand what I am saying?'

Matty ran her fingers up and down the telephone cord and looked into the drawing-room fire. She considered cutting him off. 'Kit, what can I say? I don't want you to see Daisy, but I cannot stop you, and there is no reason why I should. But if you do, I can only think that I should begin to pack.'

'That's why I'm ringing you, Matty.' Kit's hotel room in the *vieux port* looked out over the seafront in Marseilles. A wind stirred the palm trees and whipped the sea into beaten cream. 'Please don't do anything until I get back. Please wait. Listen, I've got a rose for you. A beauty called "Blanchefleur" raised by someone called Vibert early last century . . .'

'Goodness.' Matty was startled. Kit must care something for her if he'd found her a rose.

'Do you understand about seeing Daisy?' Static intruded on the line and turned his words into nonsense.

'What did you say, Kit?'

'Do you understand about Daisy? If she's in trouble I have to go.'

'No, I don't see.' Matty clung to the telephone. 'All right, I do see, but you must understand how I feel about it.'

Kit wanted to thump the table with exasperation. Instead he turned his cigarette case over and over in his hand.

The static intensified and in the background an operator talked in a monotone. Someone speaking in rapid French cut across their conversation.

'For God's sake, this is ridiculous,' Kit shouted. 'Wait until I get home, Matty, and then we can talk about it. If you want to go then, I won't stop you.'

Because she could not bear to hear any more, Matty dropped the earpiece as if it had burnt her hand.

419

CHAPTER NINE

K IT ARMED himself with a map and plenty of cash, just in case. It took him some time to find a garage in Marseilles that would hire him a car but, eventually, he tracked down a Dion, heavy but roomy, with a reasonable-sounding engine. He settled behind the wheel for the drive over the aromatic, breast-shaped headland to Antibes.

At Brignoles he stopped for lunch, and ordered an omelette flavoured with shavings of white truffle. Half-way through the meal he regretted it and pushed the plate aside, his appetite drained. He lit the umpteenth cigarette of the day.

Smoke drifted upwards into the still air as Kit pondered on the nature and complexity of his feelings. He knew he was risking the relationship he and Matty had begun, so painfully, to build. Which . . . Kit drew in a lungful of smoke . . . he *wanted* to build. On the other hand, Daisy had called him, and he was responding. With no shadow of doubt, no hesitation.

He stubbed out the cigarette and got to his feet.

The car surged over the road and bucketed over occasional pot-holes. A breeze blew in at the window with the hint of rain in it that spring winds often have. It cooled his cheek. As he drove, Kit reflected at length on the stepping stones that had brought him to this point: the hesitations, the epiphanies and false turns, the moments of rapture and despair, and motives that were less than clear.

At Antibes he drove to the post office and procured the address that had been left there for him. Unfamiliar with the town and its narrow thoroughfares, he had difficulty finding it and it was late evening before he drew up in front of a typical town house, in a dismal state, with wrought-iron balconies.

The concierge was fat and bad-tempered, and Kit's enquiry

after 'Miss Chudleigh' made her even more so. She heaved her bulk out of the minute office cluttered with knitting, newspapers and a large board for hanging up the keys, and sighed at the prospect of the climb in front of her.

'Bad thing,' she informed Kit. 'This *mam'zelle*. Ill, too. She owes me money.'

'Has she had a doctor?'

'We had to get one, and his bill isn't paid.'

The concierge assessed the Englishman in his rumpled linen suit. How much would *he* pay? How did he fit into the story upstairs? She was not to know that Kit had taken one look at her and lapsed into appalled silence.

What had happened?

On each floor the atmosphere grew frowsier, with the staleness of trapped air. On the half-landings, the *cabinets* gave fair warning of what it would be like when the summer heat took over.

Kit's mouth tightened. What was Daisy doing here – fastidious Daisy – in a peeling lodging house with bad smells? He did not know, could not imagine.

A faint odour of anis overlaid all other impressions as Kit entered Room 2 on the top floor. It was small with a sharply angled ceiling and Kit ducked. The concierge shuffled in behind him and observed Kit blench visibly as he surveyed . . . what?

A room with a single bed, a chair and a heavy, rather good, chest of drawers from better times. There was no mirror, no decoration to speak of. No carpet. Nothing except for Daisy asleep on the bed in a garish kimono.

She lay with one cheek turned into the pillow and her hair, less chestnut than he remembered, trailing in strands across the linen. A tin bowl and a rumpled towel lay on the bed beside her.

At the sight, Kit's heart turned inside out with love for Daisy, with pity, with a sense of ineluctable loss.

'Go away,' he said to the concierge, pushed her out into the corridor and shut the door. He stood still for thirty seconds or so then went over to the window and tugged at the *étincelette*, releasing a shower of rust from the rotting iron balcony above. Salty air streamed into the room, and Daisy woke with a start.

'Kit,' she said, articulating through the tail-end of sleep. 'You took your time.'

'If you will send me telegrams when I'm at the other end of the earth.'

With an effort, she held out her hand. 'Joke.'

'I know.'

He sat down on the bed and took her hand. 'Daisy, what have you done? Is this my fault? Tell me.' He gestured at the room. 'Why here?'

'Why not? It's an experience.' Daisy seemed lethargic and reluctant to talk much. She put up a hand and tugged at the hair that had fallen over her face. 'But if you insist on explanations, you could say I have mismanaged my life. It happens to a lot of people.'

Under the pulled-back hair, her face sprang into relief. It seemed to Kit that all her brightness had drained away, leaving only a wan imprint. Daisy dropped her hands and wrapped the edges of the kimono over her breasts. 'Miss Daisy Chudleigh's diary of a social outcast. From Number Five Upper Brook Street to rue de la Coin, downtown Antibes.' Abruptly she changed the subject. 'Where have you been?'

Kit concentrated hard on the kimono because he could not bear to look anywhere else. 'Iraq.'

'Matty? Does she know you're here?'

'She sent on the telegram.' Kit flicked up an eyebrow. 'Does that surprise you?'

A smile curved the pale mouth. 'Well, life is strange, isn't it, my Kit? Will you prop me up, please?'

He bent and slid his hand under Daisy's shoulders. Obviously weak, her head fell back and Kit was forced to support her with his shoulder. Automatically his hand sought, and found, the bump at the base of her spine. 'Are you going to tell me what has happened?'

'As you see I became ill.' Daisy sighed with pleasure against his shoulder. 'For a variety of reasons. Not much food and perhaps . . . lately, a little too much to drink.'

'I can smell it.' Kit chose his words with care. 'Daisy. Anis —

any spirit for that matter – isn't a good drink. It mashes the liver. If you want to drink you should tipple on something less punishing to the system.'

'Experience learnt in the kasbah?'

'Something like.'

'Don't lecture, my darling. It doesn't suit you.'

His fingers closed over her shoulder and gripped it. 'Why are you here? Do your parents know? Why didn't you call on me sooner?'

'What? And be bailed out with Matty's money? Now, that would be too much, Kit.' Daisy's hand crawled slowly up her body, found and covered Kit's.

'Don't avoid the issue.' Privately, he acknowledged the point. 'I have the American shares. I'm told by Raby that I've made a bit from wirelesses.' His fingers bit into her flesh and she yelped. 'Why, Daisy? What's going on?'

'The money ran out after I was evicted from my respectable lodgings in Nice.' Daisy's eyes slanted away to the window and looked beyond. 'Very character-forming,' she added softly.

'Bloody hell, Daisy.'

She shifted in his arms. 'Don't, Kit. I haven't the energy to deal with the recriminations and the whys. These things happen. Just be here, that's all.'

So Kit gathered his frail, white, ill Daisy to him, and buried his face in her hair. Close to, her skin had a yellowish tinge, there were tiny lines at the corners of her eyes and a thumbprint of fatigue below them. What disturbed him most was that her kimono was unwashed. Perhaps that more than anything raked up the old feelings which flared, caught, and blazed with the intensity of what had been – and what might have been.

Kit eased Daisy's head back onto his shoulder, cupped his fingers round her chin and smoothed the damp, sticky hair that he would swear had not been seen by a hairdresser for a long time. There was a tidemark at the base of her neck and her fingernails were cut inelegantly short . . . evidence of her suffering which washed Kit in an ache of desire that went far beyond the physical.

He gazed down at her, understanding that once and for ever the power to love had been unleashed in him by Daisy – and thus, unknowingly, she had given him reparation for the wounds dealt by Hesther.

He wanted to tell her. He wanted to thank her.

Instead, he held her so close that again she was forced to protest and he loosened his grip. 'Why didn't you send for me sooner?'

'I don't know,' she replied tiredly. 'I thought about it, but somehow I didn't. I can't explain. Perhaps I like extremes. Perhaps I need them.'

The days – even more the nights – had been long ones for Daisy and she drifted in and out of sleep, dreams flickering across an interior landscape menaced with shadow.

'I can't explain, Kit,' she repeated. Then she said, 'Yes, I can. At least I can show you the reason.' She tugged at his jacket sleeve. 'Kit, I have a present for you. It's over there.'

He frowned, and Daisy's mouth lifted in one of its quick, teasing smiles, edged with tenderness. 'Before I give it to you, there's one thing. You must think hard before accepting.'

Puzzled, Kit eased Daisy back onto the pillow and straightened up. He smiled down at her in the old manner. 'A present?' he said.

He went to look into the open drawer of the chest – and everything was understood.

'Your son,' said Daisy. 'He was born two weeks early.'

'*Trente secondes, Monsieur. Attendez, s'il vous plaît,*' said the black-robed portress at the door. She snapped shut the grille and was gone a long time before the huge, nail-studded door opened and Kit was allocated a space to enter. He followed the silent, gliding figure, who stopped every few yards and beckoned him on.

The sanctity in the convent was almost palpable, flowing over the Romanesque arches and worn flagstones. Impatient as he was, Kit found himself both curious and impressed. This was a place where outwardly nothing happened but where beneath the ordered fabric he could sense a pulse, presumably directed at God. The idea intrigued him.

They halted in front of a door. 'If you will wait here, Monsieur.' The nun spoke in heavily accented English. She disappeared through it, and Kit was left alone in the corridor.

He had not seen Daisy for a week, not since he had peered into the face of his son and staggered with the shock of the encounter. And as he had stood there, reeling and disbelieving, Daisy slid down the bolster into unconsciousness, and there was no time to think.

Within an hour a doctor had come. He pronounced Daisy under-nourished and still weak from the birth, ordered that she should return to the convent where she had had the baby, and stay there until she recovered her strength. Telephone calls were made. An ambulance arrived and Kit, scooping Daisy up in his arms, carried her down to the waiting vehicle. Behind him, on her swollen feet, shuffled the concierge, a smile softening the outer reaches of her mouth at the prospect of the bills being settled.

At the convent, Kit had been banished because Daisy was too ill for visitors – and because his relationship to her had been detected at once as scandalous.

Inhaling town smells of garlic, tobacco, fresh bread and watered dust, Kit spent most of the week in the Café Oriane in the centre of Antibes, drinking wine and brandy, absorbing the fact that he had a son and considering what was to come next. Twice a day, at noon and at six o'clock, he abandoned his table and made his way to the convent to enquire after Daisy. For a week the answer was the same: improving, but not yet, Monsieur.

It was a long wait, in many ways, and Kit journeyed deep into himself, as he had never managed when journeying across Iraq.

The portress reappeared and stood to one side to allow Kit into the room. He blinked at the contrast to the dim corridor outside: painted stern, unyielding white, the room was scrubbed very clean. There was a chair, a painting of the Madonna holding a bunch of lilies, a bed with a cradle beside it, a wooden table with a crucifix, but the sparseness was entirely different in its essence from the poverty at the rue de la Coin.

At the sound of the door, Daisy turned her head. She looked much better, but still alarmingly pale. 'Hallo, Kit.' He proffered a bunch of mimosa. The heavy scent wafted over her.

'Kit,' she said, with a trace of laughter but with her hand over her mouth. 'I'm sorry, but the smell makes me feel sick. Don't worry, lots of things do at the moment.'

Kit threw the flowers into the cloister outside the window and Daisy laughed properly.

'Oh dear, and they were so beautiful. The sisters will be horrified.'

'Too bad,' he said. 'It's nice to hear you laugh.' She held out her hand and he took it, rubbing each finger gently in turn. 'I've spoken to your parents on the telephone. Your mother is on the way.'

Kit did not elaborate on the conversation, but he was quite sure that he and Susan Chudleigh would never willingly speak to each other again. We gave her money, Susan had protested to him, and Daisy never got in touch. Of course we were worried. Very worried, but Daisy is not a fool, nor is she a child.

Kit terminated the conversation by informing Susan that she was contemptible and that, if she could not bring herself to visit her daughter, then at least she could have ensured that someone else did.

'It's none of your business,' retorted a sharp, bitter Susan.

'But it is,' said Kit. 'I just didn't know it.'

'The only business of yours,' said Susan, slashing back at him for having put her in the wrong, 'is to pay up. Daisy will need it.'

Kit was silenced and put down the telephone. It was not so much Susan's coarseness or, even, her grasp of the essentials, it was that, in the end, always, always, he and Daisy came down to money.

Daisy retrieved her hand and tucked it back under the sheet. She searched Kit's face for clues. 'It's all right darling,' she reassured him. 'I'll live.'

He drew up a chair. 'Tell me about it.'

'You really want to know?'

426

'Don't be silly.'

Daisy told him. Not everything, but enough. Of staying with the respectable acquaintances, contacted by Susan, on the outskirts of Nice, who were, so they said, very broad-minded and willing to help. Unfortunately, Madame Fauçonnier's broad-mindedness had not extended to her husband, who had pursued Daisy with the logic which held that since the ship was already in port why did she object? Turned out, Daisy was unwilling to contact friends – partly because she now understood precisely how far friendship stretched when it came to unmarried mothers, and partly because a voice in her head was urging her to see her Gethsemane through alone.

Daisy sent letters to Susan informing her that she was fine, the money would last. Of course it did no such thing, but Daisy made no effort to contact Ambrose for more.

'These extremes, I suppose,' she said. 'A test I set myself.'

'How did you eat? Where did you live?'

'I remembered Antibes and how much I liked it. It's modest, but full of what I love.' The pale skin stretching over the cheekbones developed a touch of pink as Daisy talked. 'Colour and heat. Good food. My French has improved, you know, not Versailles French, street French. I worked at a local *boulangerie* for a couple of weeks, then I helped out at a café until I became too big to be of use. I got good tips.'

For God's sake, thought Kit.

'Pregnancy didn't suit me.' Daisy's eyelashes hid the expression in her eyes. 'One of God's little tricks on women. I felt dreadful quite a lot of the time, and I got into the habit of having a drink in the afternoon and I shouldn't have done. And in the evening,' she added. Her eyelids snapped up and she directed her quick, slanting look at Kit. 'Do you know what, Kit? And I can only say this to you because I know you understand me in a way no one else does.'

'What?'

'I liked the sensation of going down. Slipping. Leaving everything behind. Not caring much.' Not caring at all, she thought, remembering the afternoon when, desperate for francs, and also

427

any human contact, she had gone with a tall fisherman to a hotel room. The give and take of the episode – her giving of her thickened body, which was not very expert in the business of undressing and sex, and taking the money in consequence – seemed ridiculously easy.

Because Daisy did not have the strength to shield Kit and because her predicament had made her impatient with false pride, she told him.

His chair screeched along the stone floor. 'Don't tell me any more,' he said, punching his fist on his thigh. 'I don't want to know.'

'It didn't matter, Kit. Truly. It was over in fifteen minutes and I ate dinner that night. A good one. *Coq au vin*,' she added, echoing Susan in a way he had never imagined.

'Is that meant to be funny?' he said bitterly.

Afternoon sun streamed into the room from the cloister. A couple of the sisters were pacing round it, the rosaries at their belts swinging in time to their bodies.

'In the end, I had enough to rent rue de la Coin. The sisters were kind and let me have the baby here, but I didn't want to stay because I could tell they didn't approve, so I went back to the room. But I didn't seem to recover very well.' Daisy slid over the nightmare birth, the bleeding afterwards, the chilly expression of the nun attending her, the impatient doctor, the fear, and the freezing sensation of being alone.

'How long ago?'

'Two weeks. A bit longer.'

The thought flashed across Kit's mind that he had been a father for all that time.

'So you see, my darling, why I had to ask you to come because it is all very well me behaving for *me*, but now I have your son, my son, to consider.'

Kit did not reply for a long time, and Daisy thought of the letter she had written telling him she would love him for ever, and reflected that promises like that had a way of spoiling lives – and that was why events like the fisherman did not matter.

The baby stirred in the cradle, puckered his face and moved

428

his head from side to side. Daisy watched him, rather as she might a small, furry animal in the zoo. 'I suppose he needs feeding,' she said. 'Do you think you could lift him up for me?'

The baby rooted unsuccessfully at his mother's breast, but failed to find what he wanted and began to yell. Daisy tried to help him, but she was still too weak. 'I don't like this bit,' she said. 'I don't think I'm a natural mother, but the sisters say this way is the best.' She made an attempt at a joke. 'It's not like me to be unfashionable.'

Uneasy with the crying, Kit abandoned his scrutiny of the cloister and helped to position the baby's head against Daisy's breast. The crying broke off into blissful silence. Daisy raised her face to Kit. 'He's greedy, your son,' she said.

Later on, the nun came in and dismissed Kit in a swish of cheap black cotton. '*Vous pouvez revenir demain, Monsieur.*'

'Can't I stay, Sister?'

'*Monsieur, je suis désolée . . .*'

Kit got into the Dion, and drove down to Cap d'Antibes where he walked along the cliff above the sea until it was quite dark. As dusk fell, a fresh breeze blew up and the sea grew dark and winy. He pulled off his hat and, in characteristic fashion, ran his fingers repeatedly through his hair.

He looked back at the town. The lights in Antibes flicked on and, from that distance, threw a sparkled enchantment. Behind one of them lay Daisy. Love for her welled through him and spilled over: passionate, longing, filling both body and soul, generous and complete.

Love had given Kit wholeness and transcendence; but love also brought the threat of fracture and madness, and those things had to be avoided. Daisy appeared to know that instinctively. Kit had been slower to learn.

But what of Matty? How much could Kit expect of her – knowing that by his behaviour he could expect nothing at all?

'Darling Kit.' Daisy was sitting up, looking better. The nuns had washed her hair, and there was more colour in her cheeks. 'You would be proud of me. I ate a whole plate of soup and some bread.'

He put a couple of yellow-wrapped novels and a bottle of brandy onto the table with the crucifix. 'I don't think you looked after yourself at all, Daisy.'

Daisy tried to remember exactly what she had done, and failed. 'I think I just drank,' she said.

The baby began to cry. Daisy gestured to a bottle standing in a tin jug. 'Why don't you give him his bottle?' she said. 'I've given up the other business.'

'Me?'

'Don't look so surprised. I imagine some men somewhere in the world give bottles to their babies. Pick him up, darling Kit, and sit down. He *is* yours.'

The baby was surprisingly light and, expertly wrapped into a papoose by the nuns, easy to hold.

'Go on,' urged Daisy, and lay back to watch him struggling to hold the baby at the correct angle and to deal with the bottle. Eventually, the rubber teat was in place, the baby sucked and a runnel of milk snaked down his chin and onto the shawl. Daisy was amused.

'I never thought,' she said, 'that I would say the things I am going to say to you over a baby's bottle. I imagined a serious, dramatic talk with a lawyer or something.'

Milk was seeping into Kit's jacket sleeve. The baby sucked and nuzzled and grew heavy with contentment. 'What have you called him?'

Daisy rolled the edge of the sheet between her fingers and said carefully, 'I thought perhaps you would like to choose since I would like to give him to you.'

Kit stiffened, the baby lost the teat, and it was a good half-minute before he replied. 'I didn't think you meant it when you first said it.'

'But I did. I'm giving him to you to do with what you think best. You must decide. That is both my punishment and yours.' She reflected. 'Nothing is without its consequences, is it?'

'And what about you, Daisy?'

The sheet rolled back and forwards in her fingers. 'What will I do? I will stay here for a while. You know how I like France. I like the food, the sun and the people. Who knows, I might find a rich man at one of the hotels.'

'Stop it, Daisy.'

'Don't worry. Perhaps, after a decent interval, I'll come home and see if Tim will still marry me. I don't know. I don't see my way quite yet. But don't worry about it.'

Kit's sleeve was sodden. Trapped, he could only stare at Daisy and say, 'Of course I'll worry.'

'That woman we met in the *boîte*, wearing a striped jersey and a fringe – you didn't like her but I've often thought about her and wondered if she and I had something in common. If you like, she had cast anchor.'

'Daisy, will you please stop talking such nonsense.' Kit had had enough. He got up, dislodging the baby, and thrust him and the bottle at Daisy. 'I can't bear to hear you say things like that.'

To the baby's wail and Daisy's cry of protest, he left the room and let himself out through the convent door. On the seafront, he walked into the Bar Leduc where he ordered a double brandy. Three glasses later, Kit tottered back to the hotel and flung himself onto the bed.

When he woke up it was ten o'clock in the evening and his mouth was so dry and furred it was painful to swallow, but that was nothing to the pain that thumped in his head. Moving like an old man, he found the bathroom and plunged his head into a basin of cold water. When he looked up, a stranger's face regarded him from the brass-framed mirror. Daisy's voice echoed in his ear. 'Extremes.' And Kit shivered. He knew about extremes. He put his face into the cold water for a second time, and knocked his nose on the brass tap. Eyes streaming, nose throbbing, head pounding, he got dressed as quickly as he could and snatched up his hat.

The convent was in darkness when the Dion drew up in front of it. Kit hammered on the door and when no one appeared hammered louder. A light went on in the house opposite and a man poked his head out through the shutter.

'Go home, *salud*. That is a house of *réligieuses*, not *poulettes*.'

'Monsieur.' When she finally opened the door, the nun was so outraged by Kit's presence that she stammered. '*Allez-vous-en* . . . This is not the time. Leave us in peace. This is a house of God.'

'I'm so sorry, Sister,' he said and, placing his hands on her shoulders, pushed her gently to one side. The nun's hands flew up to her chest and she sagged against the wall.

But Kit did not care. He ran down the long stone corridor with its shadowy spaces and plaster saints, through the murmurs of sleeping women, and the half-coughs and groans of patients, until he reached the door of Daisy's room.

'Daisy.'

She was awake, watching the moonlight stream at an angle through the window, her face half in the dark, half in the light. As it had once before, in the garden at the Villa Lafayette, the moon lit her hair and skin. She seemed not of this earth and it frightened him.

'Daisy.'

Kit slid to his knees beside the bed. 'Have you forgiven me?'

She turned her brilliant eyes on him. 'Oh, Kit. Only you would organize a break-in at a convent in the middle of the night. Of course I've forgiven you.' Her gaze returned to the door. 'We won't have much time before they come clucking in.' She thought for a moment. 'Perhaps this is the time to say goodbye.'

'Daisy—'

'When I left you in the garden that time at the Villa Layfayette, I made a choice, Kit, though I didn't know it then. You remember. The day you agreed to marry Matty *you* made a choice. I'm not saying yours was the wrong choice, because I think Matty gives you something you need, Kit. Somehow you knew that.'

He cherished her hand against his mouth and kissed each finger one by one.

'You must do what you think fit with the baby.'

'He's your son, too,' said Kit. He brushed their entwined fingers with his lips. 'Don't you want him?'

'Yes I do, very much. More than I can tell you. But how could I keep him? Think of the whispers and the finger-pointing. The

432

innuendo that will always follow him. In the playground. At school. I would never get away with it. People are inquisitive and children are cruel . . . I was cruel to Matty so I know. You see, when I refused to visit the convenient doctor in Harley Street, I didn't understand that bit of it. And now I've got him and I love him, I can't let that happen.'

Kit was silent, and Daisy stroked the bowed head with her free hand. 'Please, darling. Take him for me. Please. I will abide by whatever you decide.' She tugged at his hair and Kit raised his face – an older, haunted face. Daisy ran a finger along an eyebrow, which had turned almost white from the sun, along the thin nose, and down to the mouth.

'Anything,' said Kit.

Several pairs of rapid footsteps came down the corridor and Kit, burying his head in the curve of Daisy's arm, turned his face into her full breast and inhaled milky maternity. 'I will love you for ever.'

'Yes, of course,' she said, catching her breath. 'But one part of it is over, Kit. And I've promised myself not to become a mass of regret, otherwise it won't have been worth it. Nor should you.'

There was a gabble of whispered, excited French outside the door.

'I managed it badly,' muttered Kit into the soft roundness, 'didn't I?'

'So did I.'

With the passion and possessiveness of one who knew that neither was permissible any longer, he pressed kisses onto the breast beneath the starched cotton, desperate to imprint her flesh on his.

'Monsieur. I must demand that you leave at once.' Flanked by her flock of nuns, the Mother Superior held an oil lamp high above her head. It cast a long shadow over the room. 'You have insulted our trust, and our hospitality, and I hope you will leave at once. Your behaviour is not that of a gentleman.'

Kit got slowly to his feet and looked down at the figure in the bed. The black shapes by the door shifted and closed on him.

Daisy lifted her hand and whispered, 'Take him, won't you?

Please. I trust you, Kit. You'll know what to do. Don't worry, I won't ask for him back.' She paused and said, 'Goodbye, Kit.'

'Daisy.' Kit bent over and kissed her on the lips. For the last time, her arm snaked up around his neck.

He took Daisy's hand, held it cupped in both his own and then laid it gently on the sheet.

'Daisy,' he said to her, full of longing. 'Daisy. I may not have loved you very cleverly, but I loved you. Whatever happens, I won't forget.'

'I know.'

'Monsieur. *At once.*' Mother Superior's voice was shaking with anger. 'This is a sick patient. I will be forced to summon the police if you do not leave at once.'

As he went obediently through the door, Kit turned and looked back through the accusing faces. Under the picture of the Madonna with the lilies, Daisy was lying motionless, watching him, her hand where he had placed it. The moonlight lit up the pale mouth and long neck, and the tears that poured in a stream down her face.

'Smile, darling,' she said. 'Otherwise I can't bear it.'

CHAPTER TEN

I N THE third week of May, Hurricane Betsy slipped her moorings at her Caribbean birthplace and hurled herself, screaming and dust-filled, into the atmosphere. Growing bigger and darker by the minute, she waited until she was ready to unleash her fury on the land below.

After that, growling like an animal, leaving grievous wounds in her wake, she whirled out over the Atlantic and headed east.

Carrying a bunch of dew-soaked lily-of-the-valley and a string bag, Matty walked up the avenue of limes in the churchyard. Sappy and fresh, the flowers smelt of spring and soaked her cotton gloves. She left them on the wooden ledge inside the porch alongside a collection of drums and bugles left by the Odiham–Nether Hinton Scout band who had been practising for the June parade. (Matty always meant to ask the vicar what the ledges were for – sinners who were not allowed into the service or latecomers?) and went inside to say good morning to Mr Pengeally whose bicycle she had spotted.

Looking hairier and more stick-like even than usual, he was inspecting the wood in the main doors. 'Dear, oh dear, there is always something that needs repairing,' he said, after greeting Matty. He refused to meet her eyes and wrote a line of muddled-looking script in his notebook. Something in that polite evasion told Matty that this was a preamble. She was right.

'We have also got to the point, Lady Dysart, where we must tackle the stonework in that arch.' He pointed over-dramatically. 'And there.' Obediently, Matty looked. 'Shocking decay, Lady Dysart.'

Exuding the odour of mothballs, he swivelled in the direction

435

of the arch above the main window and flapped a hand at the south transept wall, which did, indeed, bulge. What can we do? said his gesture. We need help. The implication was clear.

Matty observed that Mr Pengeally had tufts of hair on his fingers as well as in his ears. 'Yes, indeed, Mr Pengeally,' she said, fascinated and repelled, wondering if she sounded as she did to herself: a parody of the lady of the manor, one in the long line of good ladies who presented a befrocked, united Anglican front, and hid yearnings and griefs under Sunday hats. 'We must talk about it. Perhaps we should draw up a plan of action. I am sure my husband will have a view.'

'It's not so much ideas, Lady Dysart,' said Mr Pengeally pointedly, risking a great deal – but, then, God was worth a risk.

Having agreed to contact Mrs Pengeally about the Women's Institute cake-making contest, Matty murmured a platitude and left him gazing fixedly at the structure of his church, feeling treacherous. Perhaps if she had found the vicar more sympathetic, Matty might have been tempted to confide a little of her turmoil over her marriage.

The lily-of-the-valley had stained the wooden ledge. Matty picked them up and trod over the grass to Rupert's grave, pausing to pick up a stray cigarette card of the sort that the boys in the school opposite collected. It was a colourful card depicting the new Sunbeam car and she could not bear to waste it. She put it in her pocket, intending to dry it out and send it over to the school for their noticeboard.

Rupert's grave was situated in the south section of the churchyard, and the earth heaped over it was still raw and unsettled-looking. The headstone that Kit had chosen was grey and inscribed with Rupert's name and his dates. That was all.

Mrs Pengeally had questioned its brevity – dear Sir Rupert, she said, had done so much more, should they not suggest his standing, his rank? – but Kit had been unexpectedly stubborn. Privately, Matty felt Rupert would have minded not having his army rank indicated; but no inscription could make up for . . . not so much the loss but the space left by Rupert, around which tiptoed his remaining family.

Someone had visited the grave recently, someone who had tidied the straggling grass, pulled out weeds, left a bunch of lily-of-the-valley in a pot and driven a small wooden cross of the sort seen in war cemeteries into the earth. On it was printed in block capitals: 'Boisselle, July 1916. He kept faith.' Matty dropped down onto her haunches and touched a faded petal.

Danny.

She arranged her flowers in the vase she had brought, and filled it with rainwater from the butt. Then she stepped back to consider the effect. The grave looked neat and ordered, unlike her father-in-law, who had tried to contain his life within a slot, only to find that, tangled and unpredictable, it escaped from the tag written above it. Now that Rupert's uncomfortable presence was no longer there, Matty could see that.

The Scouts were playing tag in the field below the church, shouting at each other, pounding over the grass like young horses. The sound floated back to Matty. High-pitched. Excited. Young.

She took one last look at the grave and picked up her string bag.

At home in Dippenhall Street in her freshly painted morning room, Flora was working at household accounts. She was dressed in a terrible old tweed skirt and an overall from a stall in Farnham market. Matty eyed it with disapproval, but lack of elegance could not hide Flora's happiness.

'Goodness,' she exclaimed on seeing Matty, jumped up and ripped off the overall. 'I wasn't expecting callers this morning.'

'I thought you wouldn't mind. I've walked over from the churchyard.'

'No, of course not. You're family.' Flora rang the bell. 'Elevenses?'

While they chatted, the phrase 'You're family' resonated like evening bells in Matty's head. It was such a simple phrase to indicate such a complicated arrangement of people and associations. The ease with which it had slid off Flora's tongue made Matty feel sad when she reflected that soon it would no longer

437

apply. She was going, of course she was going. After Kit's latest telephone call from Antibes, there was no question.

Daisy's in trouble, he had said. Understand, Matty. Please. I have to help. I'll be home as soon as I've sorted it out. When she went silent, he said, You have *got* to understand. The old demon gave the reply. There's no 'got' about it, Kit.

Please, Matty.

I don't understand.

'Did I tell you Kit has been in France and is on his way home?' she said.

Flora took a large bite out of her second biscuit. 'Lucky chap.'

Matty sat back on glazed cotton and sniffed at the lingering paint smell. 'Did you write to Polly about the new baby?'

'Ye gods.' Flora clutched her head. 'I didn't. And a miffed Polly is more than I can bear. As for her children.' A thought struck her. 'If I have children, I suppose Polly will come and stay more often.' She reached for the teapot. 'I don't think I can bear the thought.'

Too late, she saw Matty flinch at the mention of children. 'Oh, Matty,' she said. 'That was tactless of me.'

'Don't be silly. I brought up the subject.'

Flora drank more tea. 'Can I ask you a searching question, Matty? Do you mind very much? About . . . about no babies.'

'Do I mind?' Matty folded her hands and pressed them into her stomach. 'I'm not sure how to explain it, but if I said that I minded like a river not having water, or a garden not having rain, would that convey what I mean? Does that sound very silly?'

Flora looked remarkably like her brother when put on the spot, taking refuge behind dropped eyelids, embarrassed, trying to understand. 'I'm sorry, Matty,' she said, clearly feeling inadequate to comment. Without the usual clatter she replaced her cup on the saucer. 'Don't talk about it any more.'

Matty's lower lip made her look very young. 'Funnily enough, Flora, it's a relief to talk about it. I've bottled it up for so long.'

'Is it?'

'Sometimes, I've found myself hating women with babies and wondered if I was going crazy. Once when I went into a shoe shop in Farnham there was a woman in there with twins. I hated her. And I hated her so much, I had to leave the shop.' Matty's eyes widened at the recollection. 'Stupid, really.'

Flora examined the delicate face in the chair opposite – not so delicate now that country living had freshened Matty's skin and plumped her out a bit. 'Matty, I'm going to be very tactless, but it might appeal to you.'

'Go on.'

'You know my pet project, the family planning clinic for the village.' Flora had practised the words and enunciated them with care, watching for Matty's reaction.

'Oh, yes.' Matty also made a brave attempt to sound at ease with the idea. The two women stared at each other solemnly and then Matty flopped back in her chair and began to laugh. 'You'd think we were talking about murder, Flora.'

Flora pulled herself together. 'I want to get it going in Nether Hinton. I *know* it's a good idea.'

'Go on,' said Matty.

'It's important that the clinic is easy to reach but reasonably tucked away. No one wants to be watched as they go in and out. I need help running it *and* to make it respectable so that the wives will feel easy about coming for help and advice. That is where you could help.'

'I see.'

'Besides, there aren't many people I dare discuss it with.'

It only needed one more request to make a hat-trick for the morning, thought Matty. Stone arches, Dutch caps, what would be next? The requests pleased her, though.

'It will be uphill work, I don't doubt,' said Flora. 'Possibly we could find ourselves very unpopular. Jezebels in tweeds.'

'What does Dr Lofts think?' asked Matty.

'Why don't you call him Robin?' Flora looked soft, happy and released. 'He and I agree absolutely.'

As they spoke, Hurricane Betsy was half-way across the Atlantic, gathering speed and force. She sent out forerunners of thick cloud which spread over the morning sky and curdled into black junket. Gradually, under the quickening breeze, the new leaves on the trees turned their silvered backs to the onlooker.

Ned was in the walled garden, checking the cloches. He looked up at the sky and made a mental note to tie in plants at risk from the wind. Do it now, boy, he told himself and got rather stiffly to his feet.

'Weather looks odd to me, Lady Dysart,' he said when he saw her later. 'You don't get a sky that colour unless something's brewing.'

She looked up at the sky. 'I hope you're wrong, Mr Sheppey.'

'I'm right.' He paused and wiped his fingers on some sacking. 'I drive Ellen hopping mad because I'm always right.'

When Ellen had been ill, Ned never mentioned her in conversation. Now that she was better he dropped her name in frequently. Matty helped Ned to lift the heavy cloches into place, leaving footprints in the green-speckled, spring earth.

Ned settled a cloche and collected up his tools. Matty handed him the dibber and his trowel.

'I'm so pleased that Mrs Sheppey is better,' she said, running her fingers along the smoothed handle.

Ned sighed gustily.

By tea-time, the sky looked worse and the wind picked up. Thankful there were no afternoon callers, Matty retreated into the drawing room and ate her tea in front of a fire of applewood logs. Mrs Dawes did her conjuring trick with the tablecloth and placed a plate of scones wrapped in a napkin on top.

To her surprise, Matty ate three and washed them down with Lapsang Souchong. Sleepy and full, and content just to be, she watched the fire and listened to the house creaking with the wind. Odd bangs filtered through to her as it blew into corners and caught at loose objects. She almost made the effort to telephone

Tyson in the stables to check that the horses were under control, but felt too lazy.

She supposed that none of these things would be her concern in the future.

Minerva had taken to following her about, and whimpered in the basket Matty had had placed in the room. Matty snapped her fingers and the dog pattered over and settled beside her chair. A little later, she concluded drowsily that the weather was how she felt about Kit and herself, lashed and turbulent. She imagined him as she had last seen him three months ago – pale and irritable because it was five o'clock in the morning, a cut on his chin from a too-hasty shave, surrounded by a mountain of luggage. But he had been eager to be off, quivering with the prospect of the East.

Then, in a wilful rubbing of salt into wounds, Matty picked over the puzzle as to why Daisy had sent for Kit. Perhaps she was in trouble, or had quarrelled with Susan . . . It was possible. Perhaps Daisy wanted Kit to leave Matty and was going to persuade him in person. Although Matty was thinking of doing precisely that it did not stop her from feeling outraged, and her face burned with indignation.

The fire shifted over the logs and, half sleeping, half waking, Matty was aware of a change. A ripple of gooseflesh over her skin, a surge of blood at the base of her neck. With it, Matty's conscious perception of the room and its objects altered – as if she had flowed through a mirror and was looking at herself and the room from inside out. Heavy and inert, her body was anchored into the chair but her brain spun.

At Matty's feet, Minerva twitched and whimpered.

The air felt charged with an electricity Matty could not place. She looked down the length of her legs to her feet and went very cold. Winging in from another dimension, a familiar note pricked and reverberated, needle-sharp and foreboding. Matty willed it to stop, rolling her head, which felt as heavy as stone, towards the fire.

Outside in the garden, the wind swelled and whined around the corners of the house. Rattling in counterpoint was the slap, slap of branches against other branches.

441

A flash of colour, a movement, something, caught in the corner of Matty's eye and hung, frozen. As if pulled by an unseen puppet master, Matty turned away from the fire, eyes wide and brilliant with unease. The wind screamed down the chimney and she heard herself cry out, sharp and despairing, 'I know who you are.'

The girl sitting quietly in the tapestry chair by the window looked up from the needlework in her hand, and Matty stared into a version of Kit's face. A long, thin nose, thick, fair eyebrows, flaxen hair caught back in a severely neat plait. The sort of plait a nanny might make.

'You're Rose, aren't you?' asked a wooden-lipped Matty from her chair. 'Why do you keep coming back?'

Rose bent her head and pulled the needle through the half-worked canvas. The steel glinted and made a popping sound as it pierced the material. Rose's childish bones were outlined under her skin with each movement. Matty swallowed. At the point where the child's chin met her cheek, in the confluence of fresh skin, soft hair and uneven hairline, there was innocence – and a suggestion of later beauty in the features which neither Flora nor Polly possessed. Absorbed in her task, Rose pulled the thread through the canvas, her head cocked to one side.

'I won't see you again, Rose.' Matty had to force her lips to move. 'I'm probably leaving here. But I would so like to think you are at peace.'

The child looked up, and Matty made out the letters R O S and a half-formed E outlined in pink silk against the canvas. Oh, Rose, she thought with an aching heart, you never had a chance to finish it. She closed her eyes, feeling Hesther's grief and madness well inside her, and understood why the knife was the easy option.

Did ghosts remain in their time? Or operate in a different time-scale, immune from past, present and future? Was the child in front of Matty suffering in an endless cycle of knowledge, seeking her mother, unable to free herself of the burden?

Matty's eyes flicked open. Rose was staring at her, one hand poised with the needle and thread, but Matty sensed that the child was looking through her and beyond. And as Rose stared into that long ago, the black irises in the blue eyes dwindled, the lips

442

drew back over the teeth and she flung up her hand in a gesture of terror.

'Rose, it's all right . . .' Matty tried to get up out of the chair, but her legs refused to obey her. 'Please, Rose.'

The cold intensified. Matty's confusion thickened. Panic followed, and with it a desperate feeling that she was trapped in something overwhelming. 'Why are you here, Rose?' she called out. 'What do you want from me? How can I help?'

A watery fog swirled in front of Matty's eyes, blanking out the room. She felt its wet spume crawl over her face, moisture trickle down the plane between nose and lip. 'What is it, Rose? Tell me.' She could hear her voice rising.

There was no answer, only the sound of running feet, stumbling away from the sight of flesh sucked into flesh below the dying lilies. Pounding over dry earth with the cracking of twig and leaf skeleton, and the sound of painfully drawn breath. There was darkness, the flash of the child running ahead, the feral smell of fox, hot night, and festering decay, the crack of the wooden jetty – and Matty was circling on the weed-filled river. Going down. Down. Drowning in anguish. Her black Dove dress billowing like a parachute, lungs filling. A pain flowered in her chest, sprouted through her body like a monstrous climbing rose, anchored with thorns fastened deep into her flesh.

It was you, Rose, she screamed. It was you who led me.

Down Matty went. And with her whirled the blue-frocked body of a child, whose thin, tender arms were thrown out for help – and for life.

Matty took a breath. Water flooded into her lungs. Petal by petal, the rose unfolded its bloom, filling her vision with shifting, smothering layers and the starbright, unfathomable stamen heart. No, she said into the weight pressing down on her body. No, into the blackness. I can't give in yet. Not yet.

Beside her, Rose whirled . . . and screamed her scream of pain and death.

Not yet. Matty began to fight her way back to the top.

*

443

When Matty woke up the fire had almost gone out and Mrs Dawes was coming through the door to clear away the tea. She peered at Matty.

'You look a bit pale, ma'am.'

Matty hid her hands under her tweed skirt and shook her head. 'I'm fine, thank you, Mrs Dawes. You'd better let Minerva out.'

Mrs Dawes closed the drawing-room door with a click that indicated she did not believe a word that Matty had said. Matty held out her hands over her lap. They were shaking badly. She felt cold, empty and nauseous.

Using the chair as a lever, she got up and crossed to the desk where she retrieved a bunch of keys from the right-hand drawer. She left the room.

The wind was louder up on the attic storey, savage yet more intimate with the house. Matty switched on the light and the passage flooded with a yellow glare. Picking her way through the boxes, now neatly labelled, and the stack of crutches that Matty was donating to Fleet hospital, she unlocked the smallest attic.

White Surrey was reared up on his iron cradle. The doll's house sat on the table, blind-windowed. The nursery clock on the wall was silent and the baize cloth thrown over the birdcage hid emptiness. Despite the clutter, it was barren, full of objects that had outlived their usefulness. There was no peace, no sense of tranquillity.

Still trembling, Matty pushed past the clutter from that other life – a tapestried firescreen, hunting prints, a boot jack, a large china jug – over to Hesther's trunk.

With the taste of the choking water in her mouth, Matty sank down on her knees. On her instructions, the lock on the trunk had been oiled, and the key slid home with a tiny click. She knelt with her hands poised on the lid and told herself that she owed Rose this much.

Then she lifted up the lid.

'Shocking, ma'am,' Mrs Dawes had said when she tackled the trunk on instructions from Matty. 'It's not right. I don't know who could have left it like this.' Mrs Dawes had smoothed

444

over the chaos, and brought tissue-papered tidiness to Hesther's things, tucking gloves into glove boxes and feathers into satin cases.

Matty lifted out the top tray and laid it on the floor. Then she sifted through the objects underneath. The journal was easy to find. 'Lovely, lovely', went the writing underneath the 'Général Kléber', the words of a woman enraptured by a rose and in love with her brother.

It wasn't Hesther's fault, Matty thought. You don't choose whom you love. No one can. You didn't choose to be loved either. Had Rupert suspected where Hesther's affections lay before he scrawled 'Bitch' across the letter, and went on to ignore his children? Was he innocent of complicity?

Probably not. From her own experience, Matty was increasingly surprised by the human capacity to ignore, to suffer, to tolerate the intolerable. Not to acknowledge the truth.

The past seemed to rise from the trunk. A woman's life – and death – was contained in it, and Matty was an intruder. She closed the journal and laid it aside. One day she might tell Kit, but she was not sure.

Under the place where the journal had rested was a package wrapped in tissue which Matty hadn't noticed before. The letter 'R' was written on a label in black ink faded to sepia, and tied on with string. Matty fumbled to open it. She smoothed the paper over her knee and revealed a lock of flaxen hair: shiny, baby soft and fine, with a hint of curl at its ends. There was a note with it. 'My darling's hair', it read.

Oh, God, said Matty to the painted blankness of White Surrey's face, and smelt the reedy water and felt it slap at her body. Rose's drowning face flashed across her vision, lashes fanned into points over the closed and dying eyes.

'Rose,' said Matty desperately into the dead air. 'Don't be angry or frightened.'

She folded the paper back over the hair and laid it beside the journal. There was a box beside it and this time the label read 'Things from the nursery'. Inside was a thimble made of cherrywood, a sewing kit wrapped up in felt, a marble full of wonderful whorls, a piece of string, at the end of which was a very old, dried conker. Matty stared down at the remains of Rose's life, so childish, so important, and cradled them in her hands.

At the bottom of the box was a folded piece of canvas. Without being told, Matty knew what it was. Splotched and discoloured, frayed at the edges, R O S stared up at her from Rose's sampler.

Had it been finished the sampler would have been pretty, with its design of roses climbing through the letters. Those of the roses which had been sewn were worked in different-coloured pink silks with a knot in their middle to represent the stamens. Some were buds, some in bloom, some about to fall. Whoever had drawn it possessed skill and taste. Matty imagined Hesther bending above her best-loved daughter as they worked at it together.

Below the unfinished letters on the canvas was a suggestion of a tracing in pencil. Matty got to her feet and carried the sampler to the light in the passage. As far as she could make out, the tracing was of a castle with a moat and high hedge.

'Once upon a time, there lived a king and a queen with a daughter named Briar Rose ...' she remembered the old story well. Matty fingered the silks, a child's story with an unchildish meaning locked into it. She went back into the attic, looking up at the suspended clock on the wall as she did so. No one would ever kiss Rose into life.

The paradox of the rose. A symbol of division during medieval wars, a symbol of unity for the Tudors. A flower associated with the heart, with supreme spiritual ecstasy, with beauty, with eroticism, with wounds and with healing, with sweetness, with danger – a paradox of innocence and corruption.

Rose's death, Hesther's suicide, the discovery of a pink rose growing in Hesther's garden, Kit's betrayal, his bringing home of a rose for Matty to plant. The secret locked into the garden.

Outside, the wind continued to shriek around the garden and the house. Matty listened for a minute or two and grew anxious. Carefully, she returned all the objects to the trunk where they belonged. 'Goodbye, Hesther,' she said. 'You have lost your power to disturb me. Goodbye, Rose. I understand now. I shall think of you, but you must go and leave me in peace.'

The lid slid out of her grasp and banged down displacing dust. Startled, Matty swung round, her shadow licking up the wall, and encountered the painted snarl of White Surrey. On impulse she put out a hand and pushed at him. With a creak, the rocking horse subsided, and White Surrey was no longer frightening, only a toy.

Matty swallowed. 'I lived, Rose. I wish . . . I wish that you had too.'

She left the attic, and the dust settled after her.

By dusk, Hurricane Betsy had thrown herself at the west coast of England, and was tearing her way through a swathe of felled trees, wrecked buildings and flattened vegetation. A man died as he walked from his farmhouse to the cattlesheds when a tile struck him on the head. Another was hurled against a stone wall and fractured his skull.

Trees toppled like a child's ninepins: they lay across roads, brought down electricity lines and telephone wires.

As it passed over the Bristol Channel, Hurricane Betsy drew up more energy and gathered force.

Matty called a conference with Tyson, Robbie and Mrs Dawes. Each of them, she said, was responsible for securing various parts of the house: doors, windows, shutters. Also, she asked Tyson, would it be a good idea to get Ned in for the night to help with the horses? Tell him not to worry about Ellen, she said. We can put her up for the night in Mrs Dawes's wing.

Half an hour later, Tyson rang through on the house telephone from the stables to say that he had Ned, and Ellen was settled. He also said that Ivy Prosser had insisted on coming up to the house for the night, in case 'madam needs me'.

'How nice of Ivy,' said Matty, and wondered with a bitter

little *moue* if Ivy would show Daisy the same loyalty. She hoped not.

She lay in bed in a new lace-trimmed nightdress, getting used to its filminess, and listened to the orchestra of sound made by the wind. The creak of wood, the snap of twigs and the rustle of old leaves. The house withstood the force – after all, it had been through it before.

Matty dozed and then slipped into a deep sleep.

She awoke with an unfamiliar light filtering through the curtains, its quality acrid, fluid and ominous. A yellow, flaring light. Matty threw back the covers, and half hopped, half ran to the window.

In the garden the wind was beating the trees into witch-like shapes, and sent a stream of cloud across the black sky. Matty looked over towards the stables, and her hand flew to her mouth in shock. Fire.

She whirled, ripping off her nightdress as she did so. Her hand hovered by the light switch on the wall, and then she remembered in time: don't touch electricity. She pulled open the wardrobe, fought frantically with the clothes on the hangers, found and dragged on her breeches. Please, God, she breathed as she rammed a navy wool jersey over her bare breasts. Please, God.

CHAPTER ELEVEN

S UMMER WAS sliding over Antibes, and the evening was warm and restless. A wind had sprung up – scion of the gale that was battering Grande Bretagne, they said in the bars. Gouts of dust swirled in from the *maquis* countryside lapping the town, bringing with them the scent of herbs and pine. Windows rattled, shutters banged and the debris in the gutters lifted.

The Dion slid to a halt in front of the convent. Kit got out and went round to the passenger door.

'*Je ne vous fais pas attendre très longtemps,*' he said to the nursemaid sitting in the passenger seat. Young, and more than a little nervous in a wilting starched collar, old-fashioned hat and linen coat designed expressly to conceal the female form, the girl nodded and fiddled with the buttons on her gloves.

This time when Kit knocked at the wooden door it swung open at once to reveal the hushed corridor beyond.

'Monsieur Dysart. If you would step inside.'

Ushered firmly, but politely, into the portress's room, and no further, where there was a table and a chair, Kit understood he had sinned too greatly to be shown into the Mother Superior's cell. On the table, papers had been arranged in front of an inkstand. A nun, face sculpted by time and prayer, was waiting under the window. As Kit entered, she stepped forward.

'Monsieur Dysart. I am deputed by the Mother Superior to act for her in this matter. If you would read the papers before signing them, please. They are to witness that you consent to take the child, that the mother also consents . . .' The nun paused, and Kit imagined that she was forcing the words over her tongue. 'That you do so in the capacity of the father of the child.' She spoke good, fluent English.

Kit smiled his uneven smile at the face which had retreated so

449

far into holiness that it did not belong in the living world. 'I'm sorry, Sister. You must find this difficult.' For a second the nun's expression almost yielded to Kit's charm and to his entreaty, and then it hardened.

'You are wrong, Monsieur. I do not find it difficult, only sad for the child.'

'I understand, Sister,' he said gently. 'This must be distasteful for you, but could I ask you to do something for me?' He waited until the nun gave an infinitesimal nod. 'This concerns Miss Chudleigh's future plans. She will be staying in France for a little while and I have bought a small villa at the Cap for her use. The papers are being finalized at the moment in her name. Would you please tell her that the *notaires* will call on her as soon as it is considered wise, and that she may move in at the first opportunity. Tell her also that I have contacted Miss Annabel Morely who is travelling over with Mrs Chudleigh, her mother. I thought she would like to know. Miss Morely is a very close friend.'

'I will do so, Monsieur.'

Kit hesitated. 'Could you tell Miss Chudleigh one more thing, please, Sister? It's important. Could you say that the house comes from the American shares, and from *nothing* else. She will understand.'

He held out his hand for the pen. Careful to avoid physical contact, the nun gave it to him.

It has been agreed between Sir Christopher Dysart and
Miss Marguerite Chudleigh that the former should take
possession of his son at the request of the latter. The child
has been handed over willingly . . . the father undertakes
to convey the child to a safe and suitable home . . . etc.
Dated 21 May 1932.

There were three copies written in small, neat script, and Daisy's signature was appended at the bottom of each. The unfamiliar version of her name startled Kit.

Without wasting any more time, he dipped the pen into the inkwell and signed beside Daisy.

'Thank you, Monsieur.' The nun blotted the paper. 'I am sure you will understand, Monsieur, that we needed to be quite sure that we are permitting the right thing.' She looked down at the papers on the table. 'The child is the most important consideration.'

'Yes, of course.' Kit picked up his hat.

'We will give one copy to Mademoiselle Chudleigh. The other will be placed in our archives. This is your copy. And here . . . here is the birth certificate.' She regarded Kit without a trace of sympathy. This is an extraordinary, distasteful business, she seemed to want to say. Instead, she clasped her hands into her sleeves and turned towards the door. 'If you will have the goodness to wait for a few minutes, Monsieur, the baby will be brought to you.'

Kit toyed with the idea of making a second dash to Daisy's room and rejected it. They had said goodbye, and that part was over. But for Kit, the prison gates of his childhood had been pushed open.

It was – had been – more painful and prolonged than he ever could have imagined, this sloughing of the passion first acknowledged at the Villa Lafayette. He had read once that to master pain required room: the space of a desert dune or mountain sweep, rather than a portress's tiny cell.

He thought of Daisy lying in the white bed, and traced every breath, every murmur, every heartbeat. He smoothed his finger over the wide mouth, the forehead, the full breasts. Each ache of her shrinking, still bleeding womb, each flicker of discomfort as her body returned to normal, the heavy weight of fatigue on her eyelids, all were his. Her tears were his. As he waited for their son, Kit possessed Daisy and said goodbye.

The baby could be heard wailing long before he was brought into the room. A thin, reedy howl, accompanied by a pair of feet moving down the corridor.

Please take him, Daisy had said, turning her tired, drained face to his. I owe it to him. The world, you know, is not a kind place. I trust you, Kit. You will know what to do. Don't worry, I won't ask for him back. Not ever.

451

The ward sister was all smiles under her coif. 'Here is the little man,' she said, relinquishing a parcel wrapped in a shawl. She peered at Kit. 'Apprehensive, Monsieur? The responsibility . . . Do not worry, there is milk made up in the basket. There is spare clothing and I have written out a timetable with instructions for the feeding. Your nurse will be able to deal with it.'

Kit hefted his son from one arm to another and wished he had had the sense to bring in Mademoiselle Motte. 'Thank you, Sister. You are kindness itself.'

Her head dipped and swooped like a white swallow. 'The baby is in good health,' she said.

'And his mother?'

The white swallow came to an abrupt standstill. 'She is as well as can be expected, Monsieur. Now, if you will excuse me.'

And that begrudged piece of information was all Kit had left of Daisy.

Mademoiselle Motte fussed over settling the baby into the back of the car. According to the registry in Nice, she was both competent and experienced and Kit was more than happy to leave the details to her. Eventually, the baby fell asleep in the cumbersome travelling box (bought at some expense), and Kit and Mademoiselle Motte climbed into the car. The Dion eased its way out of Antibes.

From time to time, Kit was conscious that Mademoiselle Motte sent him a furtive glance from under her hat. Was she, it asked, expected to make conversation during the long night ahead? No, said Kit to himself. Definitely not.

He negotiated a corner and said, 'You must try and get as much sleep as possible, Mademoiselle. I don't know how often you will need to feed the baby.'

She shrugged and looked straight ahead so he could see only her profile. She had a pretty, delicate nose. 'Perhaps twice. I don't know him yet.' He could tell that she considered the arrangement odd but, in receipt of a substantial payment, was prepared to go along with it.

'We will stop for dinner in about an hour.'

She shrugged a second time. 'Of course, Monsieur.'

They ate at an unprepossessing looking hotel at the side of the road. Mademoiselle Motte ate her way silently through *moules farcies, boeuf provençale,* some excellent local cheese and a *tarte aux pruneaux.* She also drank a respectable amount of wine.

The sun set in a swirl of red light, and a black cloth was thrown over the landscape. They motored through scrub and pine, dotted with stone villages whose oil lamps sent cornets of light into the blackness. At Avignon the road turned and they headed north, leaving the scent of the south behind.

Near Montelimar, Mademoiselle Motte became restless. 'Monsieur,' she said finally, 'I think . . . I think I must ask you to stop. I do not feel well.'

Kit brought the car to a halt. Mademoiselle Motte wrenched open the door and stumbled out into the night. Sounds that should have been kept private floated back to him: obviously she was being copiously sick. Kit sighed and swivelled in the seat to check the baby. He, at any rate, was asleep.

Mademoiselle Motte did not reappear for fifteen minutes or so and Kit was leaning against the car, smoking, when she lurched back into sight, the linen coat now creased and stained.

'I apologize, Monsieur. Perhaps it was the motion of the car.'

Near Valence, they were forced to stop again. This time she spent considerably longer in the darkness and when she dragged herself back, she was moaning.

'My God,' said Kit, taking one look at her. 'I'd better get help.'

Smelling of vomit which she had tried to disguise with cologne, Mademoiselle Motte hunched into the seat and pressed a handkerchief to her mouth. Behind them, the baby stirred and woke, and she said faintly, 'I am afraid, Monsieur, I don't feel well enough to give him his bottle.'

Kit swore and got out to retrieve the basket stored on the ledge at the back of the car. Inside it, he found a curved bottle wedged against the side wrapped in a napkin. He extracted the baby from the box in the back, clamped the now screaming little body against his and applied the teat to the open mouth.

The baby ignored it, and continued to wail. Kit looked up at the sky dotted with stars. He had survived desert treks, inadequate food and little water. He had been fever-ridden in filthy rooms and in danger from angry natives. Surely to God he could manage to give his son a bottle?

Once again he tried to insert the teat. The baby opened his mouth, drew back his lips, caught the smell of milk and roared even harder. Then, unexpectedly, the lips swooped down on the teat. There was silence and Kit realized he was sweating.

'Mademoiselle Motte,' he called softly, 'is he supposed to finish the bottle?'

She stirred and groaned and did not answer. Kit peered at the bottle in the dark: the milk level was descending. Five minutes later, a bubbling noise indicated that the bottle was empty. The baby let go the teat, turned his head and gave a fretful whinge. Kit stared at the shape in his arms. He couldn't still be hungry? Now awkward to hold, the baby tensed and gave a sharp cry. Kit threw the bottle onto the driver's seat and hauled the baby upright. The small form was now rigid and screaming in earnest, a different calibre of scream from previously. Frightened that he had given him too much milk, Kit did the only thing he could think of and held him up against his shoulder. Then he began to pace up and down along the gritty road.

'Shush,' he said into the darkness. 'Shush.'

The dark outlines of the trees lining the road did not seem friendly.

The little head on Kit's shoulder reared up, and then sagged like a stuffed cotton doll. Instinctively, Kit put up a hand to support it and felt the warm, downy skull fit into his palm. Again the baby screamed, and Kit began to feel panic edge into his stomach.

Suddenly, the baby belched explosively, and the crying faltered, drained away and stopped. The peace that followed was invested with a miraculous quality, despite a damp stain spreading over Kit's shoulder.

454

Delighted by his triumph of baby management, he grinned up at the sky. 'Good boy,' he said.

'*Fire!*' screamed Matty, knowing her voice would not carry very far, and flung herself down the main staircase at Hinton Dysart. 'Fire in the stable! Get up, everyone! *Please! Please get up!*'

She skidded to a halt on the rug in the hall and looked up at the landings. No one answered her. Nothing stirred in the blackness. She cupped her hands and screamed through them, '*Fire!*' Then, in desperation, she seized the hammer and beat the gong on the telephone table. '*Get up! Get up!*'

She jettisoned the hammer and flew down the passage towards the back door. The door to the Exchequer was open and the fierce, unnatural light flickered through its window. Matty stopped only to dart into the laundry room and scoop up a handful of sheets that had been airing before tackling the bolts on the back door.

Tyson was in the stableyard filling buckets from the tap. He had not had time to put his boots on and his stockinged feet slipped over the cobbles. Already the game larder was ablaze and the flames were leaping towards the gun room.

'Will it reach the house?' Matty shrieked at him above the roar. 'Which way is it blowing?'

'From the west. I've telephoned for the fire engine. The house should be all right if it gets here quickly.' Tyson's face was a lurid black and orange. Behind them the horses drummed their hoofs against the stalls and whinnied in fear. Matty thrust the sheets at Tyson.

'Help me wet them.'

Holding boxes of ammunition, Ned emerged from the gun room, ran across the yard and placed them on the lawn. Then he dived back into the gun room.

'*Quickly!*' said Matty. 'The horses! How long will the fire engine take?'

'I don't know, ma'am.' Tyson filled the next bucket. 'I must douse that wall to try and stop the flames getting a hold on the house.' He pointed.

Matty's fear rose. She made herself say, 'Where are the halters?'

'In the stalls.'

'I'll see to the horses.'

Oh, God. Not horses, not horses, not horses. Matty felt her skin turn icy in the heat of the fire. Then she thought, You damn well do it, Matty Dysart.

Choking in the smoke and debris, the horses were almost demented with fright. Matty fought with the bolt fastening the door of the pony's stall and wrenched it open. With a shudder and a shriek, the pony pressed back against the wall, gathered itself up and flung forward, hoofs scrabbling on the flagstones, sending Matty reeling.

'Hey ...' Matty pulled herself upright and ran after the terrified pony. It swirled in a crazy circle, mane and tail skirling and drifting, and disappeared up the path towards the walled garden.

Matty stumbled out of the stall.

Behind her, flames slid up the central block towards the cupola and roared as they torched the roof. Shaking with terror, Matty hesitated, then hurled herself at Guinevere's box, where the horse sidled and sweated and rolled her eyes. Catching up a sheet, Matty slid back the bolt and let herself in.

'Easy,' she said, her hands, clumsy with fear, and tried to remember what Tyson or Flora did with horses. Guinevere tossed her head and backed away. In desperation, Matty grasped her mane with one hand, edging the other towards the halter hanging on the peg.

'Come on,' she whispered, grabbing the halter. Her fingers scraped over the velvet nose and Guinevere jerked. Matty had a vision of being trampled under the huge hoofs.

For Christ's sake, Emma Goldman, she thought, don't desert me now.

'Your mistress wouldn't want you to be difficult, would she?' she whispered to the horse. 'I know you're frightened, so am I, we're both frightened, but just do as ... you ... are ... told.'

For a fraction of a second, Guinevere listened, not sure whether to trust this voice or not. Matty seized that second, and thrust the band over the terrifying head and pulled the horse's ears through. With a scream, Guinevere threw up her head, almost wrenching Matty's arm from its socket, and swung her haunches against the wall. Matty was pulled forward and smashed into the wood. Her hands bleeding from the rope she grabbed the sheet and some-how, she never knew how, wrapped it around Guinevere's head.

'Come on,' she said, low and soft, as the animal quietened. 'Come on.'

If she doesn't come . . . Matty said to herself. *If she doesn't come* . . .

She pulled at the halter rope with one hand while with the other, she eased open the stall door. The glare was brighter and the heat hit her. The horse stiffened and, for a second, Matty thought she was going to refuse to move, but the wet sheet cut off the stimulus, and Guinevere allowed Matty to lead her out of the stall.

Talking to her in the soft, gentle voice, Matty pulled Guinevere up the path towards the walled garden where iron tethering rings were set into the wall. Then she collapsed panting and shaking with shock against it.

Holding the baby in one arm, Kit banged at the front door of the Hôtel des Voyageurs which looked neither prosperous nor wel-coming. Wild poppies and flax wove through the slats in the wooden fence and the iron bell-pull was rusty.

Anxious for Mademoiselle Motte, who no longer responded when spoken to, Kit knocked harder. In the crook of his arm, the baby made snuffling noises.

'*Qui est là?*'

A head poked out of an upstairs window and Kit stepped back and launched into his explanation as to why a lone man, holding a baby, had arrived on the hotel doorstep at one o'clock in the morning.

Madame Regne proved to be one of those women to whom emergencies were the breath of life. Within minutes, Kit was ushered inside, the baby had been commandeered and tucked into a cradle, which just happened to be spare, and Mademoiselle Motte had been conveyed to bed. The doctor was summoned.

'It could be serious,' he said, after he had made his examination. 'Acute seafood poisoning. She ate *moules*, you say? She must stay where she is.'

At first, Madame Regne was horrified when Kit explained that he would continue the journey alone with the baby. 'You cannot, Monsieur, it would be highly unwise.'

But Kit, nagged by unease and by the need to settle things with Matty, was not prepared to take Madame Regne's advice. He left a large sum to pay for Mademoiselle's medical expenses and promised Madame faithfully that he would let her know when he arrived in England.

Eyes pricking with fatigue, Kit drove on through the night towards Paris, pulled home by connections more numerous than he had imagined – some so tenuous that a jolt would sever them, others that were pulsing with life.

He glanced at his watch. According to the wonderful Madame Regne the baby would want his milk in twenty minutes or so. Kit picked up the map lying on the passenger seat and squinted at it; providentially he would reach Auxerre in twenty minutes or so where he would give his son and himself their breakfast . . .

When, at last, he drove into Paris, back aching, head throbbing, seat damp with sweat, Kit congratulated himself on managing the journey so well. At Auxerre the baby had taken his milk without a murmur and fallen asleep, leaving Kit free to observe the snub nose with its funny sunburnt look, and eyelids so transparent that he could see a suggestion of the pupils underneath. He was getting the hang of it, Kit concluded.

He was getting the hang of having a son.

Negotiating the Place de la Concorde, a thought struck Kit. It was neither a philosophical thought, nor one that was to have huge ramifications in his life, but it was important all the same.

He had forgotten to change the baby's nappy.

*

458

Grabbing another sheet, Matty scraped hair which felt like red-hot wire out of her eyes and looked up at the flames. They were inching closer to the house. Tyson and Ned were heaving buckets and throwing the water feverishly into the flames.

Matty hovered in front of the stalls, willed herself to go back in, and with a little cry, pushed herself at Vindictive's stall. At her entry, the horse reared – a black, quivering mass. Matty froze, cast a look over her shoulder – at the rolling flames and burning debris – and almost ran for it.

This is Kit's horse, said a voice in her head. It's his, you are not going to leave him to burn. Or his house.

It's your house.

Matty flung the damp sheet over the horse's head. 'Come on, Vindictive, boy, don't let me down.' Slowly, far too slowly for comfort, she coaxed the sweating, trembling beast through the doorway. 'Come on, boy, come on . . .'

'Get out, ma'am.' Tyson appeared in the doorway. 'You must get out. It's too dangerous to stay.'

'Help me, then,' she panted, dragging the terrified horse at the end of the halter. With a slither and high whinny of distress, Vindictive ejected himself from the stall and bucked over the hot stones, with Tyson clinging to his mane.

'Here,' Matty thrust the rope at Ned, 'tether him by the walled garden.' She did not wait for Ned's reply. 'Tyson!' she shouted. 'The house. We must do something.'

Out of the corner of her eye, Matty saw that Robbie and Ivy had appeared, drenched ghosts in cotton nightdresses. They were taking turns to fill the buckets. Ivy's nightdress hampered her and, with a deft movement, she knotted the hem around her thighs, revealing a pair of slender white legs. Robbie's nightdress was even more of a hindrance, its soaked lace and flounces flapping under her dressing gown.

'We must try to save the house!' Matty shouted.

Matty fetched, carried, threw and ran because she was not going to let it happen. It was as if the fire had penetrated to some secret, molten source in her, a lava-flow of energy which burst to the surface. A spark scorched a hole in her jersey and, at one point, she was too near the flames and felt the ends of her hair frizzle and split. The heat burnt through her slippers and her hands were raw. But she pushed on.

'They're here,' shouted Robbie, stumbling across the yard. 'It's here.'

Clanging the bell, the village fire engine drove up the drive with ten or so men hanging off it and skidded to a halt.

Ned caught Matty as she staggered away from the flames and pulled her out of the yard into the garden, where they stood, huddled together, and watched.

Like an offering from the Spanish Inquisition, the cupola, now a blazing cross of fire, collapsed with a hiss into a whirlwind of ash.

I saved three horses, she thought, in bewilderment.

Nether Hinton's fire engine might have taken its time to arrive, but it was efficient when it did. Amid the roar and the crackle, the men set to and directed the hoses onto the west side of the house and fanned out ready to tackle any new blaze.

'Go on,' prayed Matty through gritted teeth, thinking of Kit's face if he came back to a burnt-out shell, and how she would do anything to prevent it. Hardly conscious of what she was doing, she clung to Ned's arm and he steadied her. They watched the sparks rain over the garden, and spill softly onto the roof of the house.

A figure staggered out of the trees and over the lawn.

'I've come to help,' shouted Danny.

'Right,' said the chief fireman. 'Over there.'

The wind was dropping and Matty, Ned, Robbie and Ivy watched in silence for the next few minutes. 'How do you think it happened?' she asked Ned at last.

'Tyson thinks a lamp went over. Maybe Jem left it. He isn't sure. Either that or the wind blew the electricity cables together and they shorted.'

But Matty was not listening. 'What am I doing standing here?' she said. 'We ought to be getting the paintings and the furniture out of the house.'

'Easy.' Ned restrained the small figure with both hands. 'Look, they've got it under control, Lady Dysart. See?'

With a hiss, the water hit the roof and pooled in the gutters, sending eddies of steam into the dark. Men ran in all directions, shouting orders, their boots ringing on the stones. Gradually, the glare dimmed into yellow, then red and eventually extinguished. The air was thick with the smell of burnt hay and wood.

Matty tasted scorch on her own lips and salt from where she had sweated and cried. Clinging to Ned, she shuddered with shock and anti-climax — and, because it was a strange and unrepeatable situation, Ned put out his arm and drew her to his corduroyed chest as he would have done to Betty.

'There,' he said. 'Don't take on.'

'I must tell the men what to do,' Matty said, through chattering teeth. Ned let her go. Stumbling, aching, eyes and skin smarting, bones made of water, Matty walked forward to organize the aftermath of a disaster in her house.

'Ivy,' she called. 'Could you and Ellen organize hot water and some tea?'

Teeth amazingly white in her black face, Ivy nodded, untied her nightdress which was causing some merriment among the men, and disappeared.

'Robbie.'

Matty looked round for Robbie, and a virtual stranger stepped forward. 'Oh, Lady Dysart,' she said.

Matty looked at Robbie. Someone must have driven a hat pin into her: the large figure had shrivelled. 'It's all right, Robbie,' she said gently. 'Would you like to go down to the cellar and bring up a couple of whisky bottles? The best malt. I think we all need some.'

Robbie fingered the torn, blackened lace on the sleeve of her nightdress. 'If you wish.'

'What to do next, ma'am?' said Tyson, materializing out of the dark.

They were all expecting something from Matty — the men from the village and the people who lived in her household:

461

courage and direction, perhaps, and Matty had never imagined she possessed much of either. But perhaps – perhaps, after all, she did.

After the storm, a mist came down over Calais and hung over the huddle of buildings at the port. Seagulls swooped, screaming, up to the sun which shone above. The air was chilly: Kit turned up his coat collar and tried to light a cigarette. The thought of his home warmed him, and he pictured it in the spring sunlight, surrounded by brown and green fields.

The loading was due to begin any minute. He scrutinized the ferry boat, then the rough, crested sea outside the soothing influence of the port, still unsettled from Hurricane Betsy. Almost three years ago, Matty had proposed to him on a ferry and set in train a series of events, of causes and effects. Hurt, unsure, hung-over, Kit had gone with her.

On such half measures, he thought, as embarkation began, are lives made.

The hotel in Paris had telephoned through his reservation for a private cabin, and instead of settling himself in the first-class lounge with a brandy as was his habit on crossings, he remained in the cabin with the baby. The baby fussed and grizzled. Remembering his previous transgressions, Kit sighed and picked him up.

'Nappy, is it? You're testing me again.'

He wrestled with the pins. The little bottom was red from insufficient changes and Kit dabbed at it with a dampened towel. That produced a real shriek. To quieten him, Kit laid his hand on the round, froggy little belly.

'I'll get you some of my famous ointment,' he told his son.

The baby opened light blue eyes and focused on his father. With its huge head and spindly limbs, there is a curious imbalance about a baby's body, and Kit, who had never studied one before, found himself stroking the diminutive pelvis and ribcage, and offering his finger to be grasped.

Apparently enjoying the air on his bottom, the baby made a

462

feeble kick and Kit caught his foot. Like tiny molluscs, the toes were almost transparent, traced with hairline veins and studded with pearly nails. All this had come from Daisy. For a moment, Kit stared at the foot, hating the baby for what he had done to Daisy. For her suffering. Then the baby kicked again, and the blood pulsed under the tender skin. Deep inside Kit a new emotion stirred, powerful, adhesive, fiercely novel, and he surrendered to it. This was his son and he loved him.

With it came fear for the preservation of a small life, and then a second, more profound, terror — that he might have to give up his son. The idea made him shake inside.

Matty was in her garden when Kit arrived, and did not hear the car spin over the gravel and stop with a jerk in front of the burnt-out stables. Nor did she hear his shout of anguish at the sight.

Kneeling in front of the main bed under the wall, partly because her feet hurt, partly because she needed to feel the earth on her fingers again, she snipped, pruned and pulled up straggles of couchgrass and bindweed. The earth smelt of spring and crumbled between her fingers into a satisfying loam.

Compost and manure, she thought.

The tail-end of Hurricane Betsy blew over the garden from the Harroway and whipped up over Jonathan's Kilns but, protected by the wall, her garden was secure and still. A curlew dipped above Matty's head and sent out its cry. Soon, the swallows would be coming in from Africa. Matty thought that in future she might keep a record of them, when they came and when they departed.

A clump of infant cat-mint gave off a spicy smell: Matty had chosen the giant kind to sprawl in the bed beside the path. Behind that rose the spikes of a white bearded iris and the buds of a 'Sarah Bernhardt' peony. Matty sat back on her knees and contemplated her creation. Perhaps the effect needed a little more greenery? Perhaps a grey-green senecio?

Did it need more compost? She rubbed her hands together and got to her feet.

Where was Kit? The wind sent a chill through her contentment. Except for yet another brief telephone call from Paris saying he was on his way back, there had been nothing.

The 'Perle d'Azur' clematis was in need of more pruning – she should have cut it right to the ground last winter but had been too tentative – and she stopped to tidy it up. She was so busy clipping and tying it in that she did not hear Kit.

'Matty . . . Matty? Are you there?'

She shaded her eyes. Kit was hurrying down the path through the birch trees. The secateurs dropped by her feet, and she made a gesture as if to run to him, to tell him she was so glad, so very glad, that he had returned.

'Matty, I'm home.' He stopped a little way from her and, suddenly, her elation vanished. Out of habit, she fumbled for her handkerchief, no longer sure about her capacity to continue suffering for love. Kit moved towards her.

'Are you all right?' he asked, in the voice she now knew so well and had longed to hear. 'I've just heard the news. You're not hurt.'

After so long, he was almost a stranger. 'Yes,' she said. 'Perfectly, apart from my hair . . . and my hands.' She held them out.

'Thank God for that and thank God no one else was hurt.'

'No. Everyone is fine.'

He came closer. 'I'm back now, Matty, and I want to talk to you. Please.'

'Yes.'

Matty's heart thudded, and dived. The terror of new anguish made her sound cold and distant. Riven with doubt now that he was here, and with the enormity of what he was going to ask, Kit faltered. He took off his hat.

'Daisy is over, Matty.' He took a step closer to his wife and she saw his hands were trembling and that helped to steady her. 'I have to ask you something.'

To give herself time, Matty picked up the secateurs and dropped them into the trowel. Despite the scorched hair, she looked well, thought Kit. He had forgotten how small and

464

exquisite she was, and how the brown eyes suggested comfort. Unfamiliar tenderness took him by surprise, and he wanted to snatch up her damaged hands and cherish them between his own.

Matty rubbed her forehead with her forearm and pushed back the frizz from her face – just as she had so long ago on the ferry and as Kit had seen dozens of times since. She was wearing an expression with which he was also familiar, a still, frozen expression which now he understood: the look of a woman who was frightened to be happy in case it was taken away. With a flash of guilt, he also knew he had helped to keep it there.

'What is it, Kit?'

Kit shoved his tell-tale hands inside his pockets, for he knew he was going to push Matty to the limit – and he had pushed her so often, and so far. Daisy's tear-streaked face hovered in his mind, and he closed his eyes for a second. Then he opened them and looked at his wife.

'I would go down on my knees,' he said, with a hint of his uneven smile, 'if it would help.'

'No,' she said.

He smiled properly at her vehemence, moved towards her, put out his arms and pulled Matty to him. She did not resist and he said, 'Daisy is finished, Matty. For ever. I've come back home to ask, not only for forgiveness, but for *you* back and our marriage back. But before you make up your mind, I have something else to ask you.'

Matty gave a shuddering sigh and disengaged herself, almost, he thought, as if she could not bring herself to trust him. He searched her face for clues.

'What I am going to ask you is so big, and will require such enormous love—'

'What is it?' she interrupted. 'What more do you want from me?'

He winced at that. 'A very big thing,' he said. 'Which I could only ask of you.'

She did not dare to reply.

'Will you wait a minute while I fetch something?' he asked.

She swallowed and fluttered a hand. 'If you wish.'

'Stay there, then.'

Matty watched as he disappeared up the path and, because she could not think of anything else to do, turned back to the clematis and chopped at it with frantic, jerky cuts.

Her back was towards him when he returned, carrying the white bundle. 'Matty. Will you still allow me to ask you?'

He sounded so strange that she swivelled sharply, took in the shawl and the baby and understood the mystery of Daisy's telegram. She swayed in shock and disbelief.

'What *are* you asking me, Kit?'

Kit held out the sleeping baby. 'Matty, you do not have to accept him. I will stand by whatever you decide. Believe me, that is my punishment. If you do not want him, can't accept what I ask, then I will take him away for adoption and, whatever happens to us, I will never reproach you.'

Matty's chest rose and fell.

'Do you understand, Matty?'

Bitter anger clenched the muscles under her sternum. Agony. Jealousy. Pain that it was not she, never would be, whose body brought forth Kit's son. Humiliation that she had been brought to a position where her husband offered her another woman's baby. Daisy's baby. Truly, oh, truly, she had come to the end.

Kit, she cried silently. Where have you taken me? Down a valley paved with ashes. Blindly, she turned as if to run away.

'Matty!' Kit cried out, despairing. 'Matty. Forgive me.'

A note sang out from the field below Hook Meadow. Thin and uneven. Another followed. Then a third.

Matty stopped. The bugle band of the Odiham–Nether Hinton Scouts was practising, and someone – one of the boys? – was playing the Last Post.

It rose into the air, playing for the Hamps, the Wilts, the miners, sappers, messengers and bombers. For Danny and Rupert, Edwin and Hesther, Robbie and her Sergeant Naylor who never came back, for Rose, for Bert Stain's missing lung, and Hal Bister's missing mind. For all who had lost.

And with it rose a shadowy multitude, limping on rotting feet and gas-filled lungs through the crushed poppies and dog roses into the mist and smoke and roar of battle. An army – no, ten thousand, thousand armies, of crowding shades.

They had gone. They had all gone.

'Oh, no,' said Matty. She took a step back into the flowerbed and the earth sank beneath her feet. The sun slid a beam across the garden, lit up the plump rosebuds and threw a shadow from the statue – if you looked quickly it could almost be said to resemble the outline of a small girl.

The pulses in Matty's neck, wrists and deep in her groin beat in painful time to her heart.

'Your son?' she said, a thaw more agonizing than her anger rushing in her chest. Slowly, infinitely slowly, she stretched out her blistered hands and accepted the weight of the baby as Kit placed him between them. 'A son?'

The bugle stopped as abruptly as it had started, and in the silence that followed Matty looked up from the baby to Kit. Their eyes caught and held, each questioning the other.

Love was an act of will. You had to keep on living it. Each day, each moment, each second. It had to exist without conditions. It had to be carried, nurtured and suffered for. You loved, and that was it. Again, she stared down at the small human in her arms, who could confirm that truth. He stirred, and she shifted him so that his head rested more comfortably, and, then, propelled by an urge she could not control, drew him into her breast.

'Kit?' she said, painfully, tentatively. 'I think . . . I think it's all right.'

Kit picked up the fork lying by the 'Queen of Denmark' and drove it deep into the earth. He was crying – with relief, with gratitude, with aching loss, with the knowledge that he had been vouchsafed more than he deserved. He put up a hand to wipe the tears away, then he turned and drew Matty and the baby into his arms.

The shadow under the statue lifted and all resemblance to a child vanished.

With all its blood-lettings, its sudden passions and silences, with its longueurs, its ententes, its peaces, a marriage had begun.

HARRY

Linked by old happenings and mistakes, families wax and wane. Like the flowering year, they are doomed to repeat the cycle — the omissions, the shortfalls, the lack of love and forgiveness.

I know because it happened in my family — and the wounds inflicted by one member are repeated in the next generation, until a chain is linked together.

Mine is a very English story which could only have happened at a particular time, and yet, I think, has universal application. I have written it to show you where it went wrong and where it went right, how the seeds set by one generation flower again and again. How, despite our quirks (Thomas) and disappointments (the loss of the house), in the end love can grant us a future, and serenity. The grace of a long, contented life, like mine.

Above all, there is the garden. An Eden of stone and brick, of brown and green, of forks and spades, of seed trays and compost heaps, conjured by rain and sun into beauty from which we draw nourishment. Life-giving, ever changing, always there, an indestructible source for the spirit. The garden triumphant, in which are found the lily and the rose locked into their spiral of fecundity, death — and resurrection. So, you see, it came right.